# Body Swap

## Books 1 – 4

**Katrina Kahler**
Copyright © KC Global Enterprises Pty Ltd

# Table of Contents

# Dedication

*This book is dedicated to Richard Axtell…a very funny and extremely talented young man who knows exactly how to piece together a hilarious story.*

Book 1

# Catastrophe!

# Hiding

`Jack, R U alrite?`

That was the first text I got from Tom, my best friend. I peeked out from under the comforter to read it, then wrapped the blanket around my head again without replying. I wasn't in the mood to deal with him right now. I wasn't in the mood to deal with *anyone*. I just wanted to lie in the dark and pretend I didn't exist.

The cell phone buzzed again. I sighed.

I made a little hole, just large enough for my eye, and stared angrily at the phone. I wanted it to realize what it was doing was wrong. That I wanted to be *left alone*. The phone stared back at me, a small notification light flashing on the top of the device. I picked it up and looked again.

`R U there? I heard U askd Jasmine 2 the dance! R U crazy??? D: )-:<`

I *wished* I was crazy. That would have made everything so much simpler. When I retreated back into my cave this time, I tried putting my pillow on my head too, hoping that it would stop the sound of the phone from cutting into my solitude. I closed my eyes as tightly as I could and tried to wish everything back to normal. That works sometimes in the movies, right?

**BUZZ BUZZ.**

"Agh!" I jumped slightly as the phone somehow buzzed even louder this time (how did it *do* that?) and the pillow flew off my head. Sunlight shone in through the window, blinding me. I squinted and waited for my room to blur into focus. The white walls, my posters of awesome superheroes, my laptop, my guitar… I grumbled as I leaned over and looked at my phone screen again.

`Wat abt HOLLY? UR GRLFRND? Ppl are sayn she is v. upset!`

I threw the phone down on my bed. It bounced twice and ended up balancing on the edge of the mattress. I didn't blame Holly. I was also v. upset. A few weeks ago, my life had been pretty much *perfect*. I had the hottest girl in school as my girlfriend, I was a star player on the football team, I had a band that was definitely going to be famous someday soon, and it was *all* going my way.

Now it was all gone, swirling towards disaster. Actually, disaster was a while back. Now things were definitely swirling towards complete chaos.

My life was destroyed and I was hiding in my bed. That *doesn't* happen in the movies.

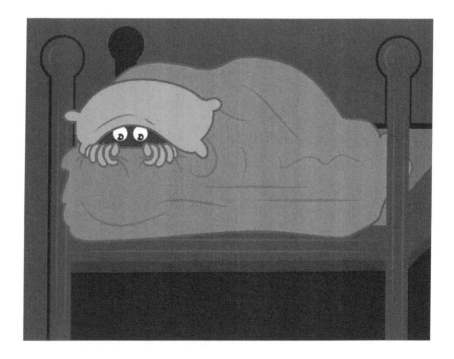

My phone buzzed again.

This is a jk, rite?

A joke. That's a good way of describing it. My life was a complete joke. I had no idea what to do.

What happened? Let me explain.

# The Unbeatable Plan

It all started a few weeks earlier. You know when you are having the *worst* day ever? Where everything goes wrong, no matter how hard you try? You trip over the smallest thing, you spill drinks all over your clothes, you seem to have somehow forgotten how to act like a normal human being? Well, it was one of those days, only times a *million*. No, actually *ten million*. *A million hundred million!* (Is that even a number?) Never mind, I'm just trying to say it was *really* bad.

It started off like any other day. Another *boring* day at *boring* school. It was a particularly *boring* day because I had the lesson I am worst at: Math. As usual, it was a disaster. Mr Thomas, my grumpy, goblin-like Math teacher, yelled at Tom and me for '*talking when we should be learning*'! I tried to tell him that we were 'discussing the problem' (we were actually talking about our favorite candy, but how could *he* know?) and that 'learning was very important to us' (I stole *that* line from my Dad), but he wasn't having any of it and made us stay late afterwards to do *more* Math work.

When Tom and I left, I had to hurry. After all, today was the day I was going to put my **plan** into action.

"You sure you're ready to do this?" Tom asked as we rushed away from the classroom, ducking and dodging past anyone who got in our way. If you saw us both, you'd think Tom was the bravest: after all, he was as tall as most teachers and looked a bit like a tank with a flash of blonde hair on top. But really it was little ol' me who dared to push the boundaries of awesome.

"Oh yeah," I grinned. "The **plan** is foolproof."

What was my **plan**?

Well, you see, today was the day I was planning to ask Holly Lawson to go to the dance with me. It is well known that you don't ask a girl to the dance without a serious **plan** to make sure she says yes.

Who's Holly Lawson? Only the most *beautiful* girl in our school. She is tall, slim, and has long blond hair that somehow manages to stay perfectly smooth and silky no matter what she is doing, or what the weather's like. I think it might be magic. *Girl* magic. My hair springs around on my head, making me look like a mad professor if I even breathe in the wrong direction.

It's not just me who thinks she is beautiful. Someone wrote: 'Who is the most beautiful girl in school?' in permanent marker in the boy's bathrooms outside the geography classes and within a few days, 'Holly Lawson' was written around it in a bunch of other pens by hundreds of different people! (Someone also wrote 'Jennifer Hunds' in small, neat handwriting near the bottom, but everyone knows that was written by Kyle Williams who has had a crush on her since Kindergarten, so that doesn't count.)

Everyone who was *anyone* wanted to ask Holly to the dance. Luckily, no one could because she is *my* girlfriend. Still, I wanted to be extra sure she would say yes, so I came up with the **plan**. I even wrote it down on a piece of paper so I wouldn't forget. This is what it said:

     1.     *Wait until Holly was putting stuff in her locker. It's on the ground floor right on the end.*

     2.     *Put on 'cool guy' shades and jacket (which never fail with the ladies because I look so awesome in them).*

     3.     *Lean against the wall, smile, put on my cool guy voice and say: "Hey Holly, you're my girlfriend and you're really pretty and stuff. We should totally go to the dance and stuff. For real."*

Tom helped me come up with what to say. He just *knows* how to talk to girls. It's like a sixth sense or something. Needless to say, the plan was pretty much perfect. Tom suggested I bring flowers or something as well, but I was saving up for a new game so I couldn't afford it. Anyway, no girl (even one as hot as Holly) could resist the

**plan**!

There was one slight hitc͟    ͟rning I was running late and I left m͟y    ͟ my bed at home. Tom said that it didͻ    ͟ecause Holly was already my girlfri͟e    ͟wesome I was.

That's why Tom is my    ͟s his stuff.

By the time we reached    ͟e breathing heavily and had to lean against ᴛʜᴇ ... ͟    ͟uld see Holly sorting out her stuff. We still had time.

"Go... get 'em... tiger..." Tom said between breaths.

I put a hand on his shoulder, leaning against him and said: "Thanks... buddy..."

By the time I walked over to Holly, I had caught my breath. I leaned against the locker next to her, and cleared my throat.

Holly tucked her perfect hair behind her ear. "Hey Jack," she smiled. "What's up?"

I prepared myself mentally and put the **plan** into action:

"Hey Holly, you're my - Dad!"

Her locker door slowly closed and she looked at me with confused, brown eyes. "Excuse me?" she asked.

As I said. Disaster.

I should explain.

Just as I was about to say the smoothest line in the history of dance invitations, who should walk down the corridor in the opposite direction? My dad.

If you're wondering why my dad would casually be strolling around the halls of my school, it's because he works here. Yeah, I know. I'm the child of a teacher. He actually teaches the other 7th grade class. Not the one I am in, thankfully.

Having your dad work at your school is bad and good. It's bad because it's your *dad* at *school*. He learns about EVERYTHING. Every mistake, every time I am told off, every breath I take, he learns about. It's horrible.

"Did you just call me your *dad?*" Holly asked, frowning.

"No, no," I began. "I just… you see… a **plan** and… well…" I didn't do a very good job at explaining myself.

"Jack Stevenson," my dad's voice boomed down the corridor. "What aren't you at *football practice?*"

Everyone in the corridor turned to look at me. My face felt like it was on fire. I tried to rapidly back away, but Dad managed to close the distance between us in record time. "I was just going!" I squeaked in a tiny voice, hoping the floor would swallow me up there and then.

Holly let out a small giggle. That's when I noticed I had been *leaning on some gum*! It had stuck itself to my t-shirt and now clung to me like an unbreakable spider web!

I felt sick. It was *disgusting!* The **plan** had failed and it was *all Dad's fault!*

# Football Practice

Dad escorted me to the changing rooms. It was a walk of shame and everyone knew it. Holly offered a small wave as I walked past and I hung my head. I couldn't look anyone in the eye.

Tom had very smartly disappeared off to football practice as soon as he saw Dad coming. He was lucky.

Dad, on the other hand, didn't notice that he was ruining my life. He gave me the same old speech:

"You need to take *responsibility* for your actions, Jack."

"You're almost an adult, Jack. You need to take charge of your life."

"You're letting the *team down*, Jack."

Blah, blah, blah. Seriously, I could recite it in my sleep. Every time I tried to say something to try and explain what I was doing, he would raise his finger to his lips and shake his head until I stopped talking. He wouldn't listen to anything I was saying!

He left me in the changing room. I was glad to finally be rid of him as I put on my football kit and headed out onto the field, only to find out it got *worse*.

Who was there, waiting with the coach and the rest of my team? You guessed it. My dad. He was deep in conversation with Coach as I slowly walked towards them. I managed to glance over at Tom, who shook his head with wide eyes, as if to say *Run. They're talking about you!*

I was about to do just that when Coach saw me and gave me **THE LOOK**. Coach is a chubby man, with no hair and a baseball cap permanently attached to his head. Tom once joked that he looked like a big baby. He is anything but that! When he uses **THE LOOK** you know you are in trouble. His forehead creases down into a tight 'V' shape and his lips are pressed so tight together they turn white and almost disappear.

"Stevenson!" He barked in a voice which made me

flinch. "You're late!"

"I am, but..." I began to defend myself.

"No excuses," Dad said, shaking his head. "Coach and I have decided that the best thing for you to do now is to apologize to your team."

"Exactly!" Coach shouted. "Get apologizing Stevenson! Show me you *mean* it, and then 20 laps of the field!"

It was awful. I had to stand in front of my team as they sniggered and laughed at me, and say:

"I am very sorry for being late. I have let the team down and it will never happen again."

I might as well have committed social suicide right

there. Even Tom was giggling by the end of it. He tried to fight it, but I saw his cheeks tighten as he fought not to smile. My dad, however, nodded slowly as I did it, pointing towards the team whenever I looked angrily at him.

When you are running around the football field, somehow it seems a *lot* larger than before. As I began my punishment and my friends went back to playing football, I was *furious*. If my dad hadn't been here, everything would have been fine. The **plan** would have been a success, I would have been playing football with them, and I wouldn't have to explain to Holly why I called her my dad. Instead, I was getting all hot and sweaty; my legs burned from running around the rectangular field with the cheerleaders laughing and jeering every time I went passed them. With every step, the same thoughts looped through my mind:

Why couldn't my dad see that he was *ruining* my life? He doesn't understand that what he does is the *worst*. I wished somehow he could see it from *my perspective*. Maybe then he wouldn't be so smug.

Little did I know, I'd later regret I had even thought that.

# After Practice

When practice had finished, I was still angry. I had missed half of it running around the field, and by the time I managed to get back in, my head was all over the place and I played terribly. Coach yelled at me for 'not giving it my all' and it just made things worse.

"Huddle up!" Coach called us all together in a group once he had finished yelling at me. "Now kids, I've got a little announcement."

Tom glanced at me to see if I knew anything. I shrugged. I didn't have a clue.

"I've heard that some of you have a little Math exam tomorrow," Coach said, looking directly at me. "And I've decided that if you *don't* pass the exam, you aren't going to be playing the first match in a few weeks."

The team broke out into protests and shouts, mine being the loudest, but Coach raised his hands, silencing us all. "Don't think being good at sport means you can slack off in class. That's all, let's get changed." He blew his whistle and waved us back to the changing room.

Tom moved next to me as we ran. "I bet Mr. Thomas spoke to your dad about today and your dad spoke to *Coach.* This is their doing."

My jaw tightened. Tom was right. This had my dad's and Mr. Thomas's evil smeared all over it. They were actively trying to make my life *hell.*

I tried not to think about it as I got changed, but failed. My dad had ruined my chance with Holly, and now he wanted to ruin my chances to get on the team as well? What was wrong with him? Why did he want me to be unhappy?

To make things worse, I still had to wait for him to finish work at school. After I said goodbye to Tom, I decided to head back to the field and kick field goals until Dad was done. I had managed to catch a glimpse of a new technique taught by Coach during the practice, every time I passed them when running laps, so I decided to have a go at that while I waited.

I dropped the ball, and kicked it as hard as I could. It flew off, a bit off target from where it was supposed to go, but it felt good. The thump of my foot against the ball was great. I imagined it was my dad's head the next time I kicked it, and laughed as the imaginary head went screaming into the air in front of me.

Sure, I probably looked a bit *crazy*, but it was worth it.

Soon, I was really getting the hang of the new technique. I was sure that if I kept it up, I would go pro in no time. Not only would that be amazing, but it would also mean I wouldn't have to do any more Math lessons, or stupid Math exams.

After a few more kicks, I was sure that I was doing the *best* I had ever done (no one was there to see…typical). I put on my 'Football Jam mix' on my phone and listened to my favorite band: The Spiky Monkeys. Every kick was perfect and with the band rocking out in my headphones I was beginning to feel a lot better.

Then, of course, it started to rain.

As I looked up at the sky, now dark and grey, I remembered that it was incredibly sunny when we had started practice. But now, the sun had disappeared and thick, dark clouds had appeared in its place. It was the perfect end to the perfect day. Typical.

"Jack!" A hand placed on my shoulder made me jump. I turned to find Dad standing next to me and pulled out my headphones. "Come on, time to go home."

Something inside me clenched in anger and I refused to move. "I'm going to do one more kick," I said, picking up the ball again and walking back up the field.

"Excuse me?" Dad said, following me. "I said we have to go, come on."

"I'm going to do one more kick!" I snapped back, all the anger of the day coming back. "I missed most of practice after all!"

Dad stopped, stunned for a second, his mouth opening and closing like a fish. "Don't kick that ball, Jack," he said quietly. "I'm warning you."

*He's warning me,* a little voice in my head taunted. I looked him dead in the eye and raised my foot.

"Don't do it, Jack," he said again.

I dropped the ball and kicked it with all my strength. *That'll show him,* I thought. The ball flew off down the field.

Dad's face went all red, like he was about to yell at me, but it was at that exact moment that the rain *really* started to pour down. There was even a loud crack of thunder across the sky.

We both looked upward. The sky was black now, apart from the occasional flash of lightning. The wind whipped around us in a howling gale and I could barely hear my dad as he shouted, "Jack! We need to get to the car!" I wanted to kick the ball again, but with the weather as it was, I knew it wasn't going to happen. I shook my head and walked towards him.

"Don't think I've forgotten about that kick," Dad yelled at me through the rain.

"Don't think *I've* forgotten about how you're *ruining my life!*" I screamed back. The thunder even crashed right after I said it (it was pretty awesome).

We were both running now towards the parking lot where Dad had left his car. Dad pointed at the gate on the other side of the field. "If we can just…"

CRASH.

Whatever Dad was *going* to say was lost as lightning struck the end zone of the field in front of us! On the ground was a little scorch mark where it had struck. Dad and I both stopped and stared at it.

"Run!" Dad shouted. "Over the fence!"

He pointed towards a short cut. The parking lot was just over a small metallic fence. We could climb over it in no time and cut the distance in half. I didn't argue. That could be done later. We both set off at a sprint in that direction.

CRASH.

Lightning struck again, right where my Dad had been standing previously. It was like it was *trying* to strike us!

That persuaded me to run a little faster.

We both reached the fence at the same time. All we had to do was hop over it. We both grabbed it to leap over it and-

CRASH.

That's when the world went black.

# After the Storm

When I opened my eyes, I was staring at the gray sky above me. The inside of my mouth tasted like Dad's 'Chicken Surprise' (the surprise is that it tastes like old fish wrapped in foil and that he *still* tries to make it every few weeks) and my head was spinning. The lightning, however, seemed to have stopped. The weather had gone back to a light rain.

I sat up and saw that I was on the other side of the fence. Had I been struck by *lightning?* Whatever had happened, I had made it to the other side successfully. I decided to get to the car as quickly as possible, in case the weather decided to change again. Slowly, I pushed myself to my feet. My legs wobbled and shook with each step, but I managed to convince my feet to work together long enough to get to Dad's green Rust Bucket (that's what I call his car. It's a piece of junk). I opened the passenger door and went to sit down.

CLONK.

My head struck the door frame. Pain spiked through my skull and shook my teeth.

*Ow* I thought, rubbing my head. I *really* didn't need that right now. I stared angrily at the Rust Bucket, blaming it for my pain. Something was wrong though. The Rust Bucket was *smaller* than I remembered. I frowned and got inside, still rubbing my head.

The other door to the car opened and closed as Dad got in. We both sat in silence for a while.

"What happened?" Dad asked.

Except… it *wasn't* my dad's voice. His voice was high and strange, like he had been sucking on helium balloons. I turned, shocked and not at all prepared for what I saw. Sitting in the driver seat of the car was a young boy, with a straggly mess of hair on his head, wearing my school's football kit. It wasn't my dad. It was *me!*

"What…" I began, my hands shaking, when I realized something else horrifying. *My voice was low.* It was like my voice was a truck's engine. I looked in the rearview mirror to see what was wrong and what stared back at me was horrifying. I was *old*. My hair was neatly combed into place. I was wearing a strange shirt that had all the buttons done up tightly. I was in *my dad's body!*

Unsurprisingly, I freaked out. I tried to back out of the car quickly, wanting to get some fresh air, but only managed to hit my head on the roof again as I pushed away.

CLONK.

"Ow!" I hissed again in my very *very* deep voice.

Dad, wearing my face, looked at me with horror and I stared at him.

Now, in situations like this, you should probably stay calm. That's what they tell you to do at school when it's an emergency, and this was definitely an emergency.

So I decided to say: "Oh dear, we seem to have swapped bodies, whatever shall we do, Dad?"

The only problem is it sounded like this:

"ARRRRRRGGGGHHHHHHHHHH!"

When he recalls the story later, he says that *he* said: "Keep calm, Jack, everything will be alright." However, to me, it sounded a lot like:

"ARRRRRRRGGGGHHHHHHHHHHHHH!"

We continued to scream and look at each other and scream and look at ourselves and scream for a while. Right until our throats pretty much gave up on screaming and we had to sit in the car in a dull silence.

When we had both finally calmed down, I turned to my dad again.

"How...but...why...?" Words were hard. My brain felt like porridge and I still felt uncomfortable speaking in my dad's voice.

Dad rested his hands on the steering wheel of the car, slowly turned to me with wide eyes, and said in a very quiet voice: "You need to drive us home."

We both looked down. Dad wiggled his new legs in the direction of the car pedals. They were too short.

"Oh," I said. *Oh no*, I thought.

# A Driving Lesson

I had always hoped that my first time driving a car would be when I was sixteen, and I would be a master at it right away. After all, whenever I played racing games against Tom, he *always* lost because I was so good. So driving a car in real life shouldn't be so different, right? Just push the buttons (or pedals) and it goes forward.

Wrong.

After we had swapped seats, Dad spent what felt like an hour explaining to me the different mirrors, the pedals, how to break properly, how I needed to be *aware* at all times and lots of other things like that.

I just sat with my hands resting on the steering wheel in front of me and stared out at the parking lot, terrified to move.

"Are you ready?" he finally asked. "We are going to take it *slow* around the parking lot, OK?"

My mouth was dry. Really, really dry. I nodded.

Slowly, I turned the key in the ignition. The engine of the car rumbled to life. I felt it vibrate the seat beneath me. Had it *always* been like this? The car suddenly felt like a large, hulking, uncontrollable monster.

"Nice and slow now," Dad repeated.

I took a deep breath. "It's OK, Dad," I said. "I think I understand the-"

I put my foot on the accelerator and the Rust Bucket jolted forward, A LOT faster than I expected.

"SLOW SLOW SLOW!" My dad shouted and I slammed my foot onto the brake pedal. We were thrown forward in our seats as the Rust Bucket came to an abrupt halt.

I turned to Dad. He scowled at me. I grinned back. "Easy as pie," I said weakly. Dad didn't seem to agree. I wasn't sure I did either. My heart was pounding loudly in my ears.

I had always dreamed of turning up to school in a red Ferrari and making all my friends jealous, (ultimately, of course, they would all want to hang out and go on road trips with me). Now I could see that dream melting away in front of my eyes, slowly being replaced by one single emotion: terror. Why did they make it look so easy on TV?

We started again slowly. I gently pressed my foot onto the pedal and the Rust Bucket rumbled to life, slowly creeping forward. After doing a few laps around the parking lot, Dad took a deep breath and said: "OK, let's guide her out onto the road. Slowly."

I nodded. *I can do this* I thought to myself. *I am Jack Stevenson and I can-*

HONK.

I slammed my foot onto the break again.

A red car accelerated past us. I tried not to focus too hard on how I had nearly gotten us both killed. Dad gripped onto the door with white knuckles. "It's OK," he said, over and over again. "It's all a dream. I'm going to wake up in a second. Everything will be fine."

"Dad?" I asked, ignoring him. "Should I go now?"

He slowly opened one eye and looked at the traffic around us. "OK," he said. "Slowly now."

'Slowly' became the word of the trip. Every time I started to go slightly faster than a snail's pace, my dad would scream at me and I would slam my foot onto the brake, throwing us forward.

I always used to wonder why my dad got angry at other drivers when he was in the car, but after five minutes on the road, I began to realize why.

HONK. HONK. HOOOOOOOOOOOOOONK.

Every other driver honked their horns. Red, angry faces glared at us through windows as they sped past or crept behind us.

Everyone seemed to be in an extreme hurry to get somewhere and they were very angry at me for not going fast enough. When I finally turned off the main road into our quieter street, I felt the pressure in the car go down as we both let out a long breath.

"Well done," Dad said.

"Thanks," I grinned.

"I was talking to myself," Dad replied, wiping sweat off his brow. "From now on, we are *walking* everywhere!"

I would have argued, but I was too tired. I pulled the car slooooooowly into our drive and turned off the engine. "It wasn't that bad…" I mumbled as Dad got out of the car.

I sat silent and alone in the car and closed my eyes, hoping and praying for everything to return to normal.

I wasn't that lucky.

# The Next Day

When I woke up the next morning, my prayers hadn't been answered. The only thing that was different was that I had a pain in my neck from sleeping in my bed, which was suddenly far too small for me, and ice cold feet because they had been sticking out from under my comforter.

I sat up in bed and groaned a loud, deep groan. Is this what it was like to be an adult all the time? I never wanted to grow up. It was so tiring. I looked down at my new legs, and saw how they were so big and lanky, covered in dark, black hairs. They felt all itchy and strange and on closer inspection in a mirror, my face was sprouting hairs as well. Everything felt *wrong*. No wonder Dad was so weird.

With a grimace, I stepped over my clothes on the floor and opened my bedroom door.

"Agh!" I shouted. Stood right outside was Dad, a sleepy look in his eyes, or *my* eyes. He yawned loudly and held up the bottom half of his blue pajamas with his free hand. They were *way* too big for him in my body and were constantly trying to fall down.

"We haven't changed back," he said. "This isn't good."

"You're telling me. How do you live like this?" I asked, scratching my new head.

Dad stared at me for a while, blinking the tiredness out his eyes. He had never been a morning person. I could see his brain slowly working through all possible ideas to help us out of the situation. His brain finally gave up and he simply said:

"Breakfast."

I nodded. At least we could agree on that.

It turned out that even simple things like breakfast were now difficult. Dad kept dropping things, unsure how to use his smaller hands properly. I had to reach into the higher cupboards to help him get the bowls out and when he tried to pour the milk on the cereal, he fumbled and dropped it, spilling it everywhere.

As we both stared at the milky mess on the floor, he sighed loudly. "Great," he mumbled. "This isn't going work." He then decided two things:

1.	I couldn't go into his work today. After all, I didn't know how to teach a class.

2.	If this body swap hadn't sorted itself out by the end of the day, we were going to the doctors to see if they could help.

As much as I *hated* the doctors, the thought of being stuck in my dad's body for much longer was worse, so I agreed. It was the smell that I really hated, so I decided I could just hold my nose for the time I was there.

"I could probably teach a class," I said, stirring my bowl of cereal with my spoon. "How hard could it be?"

Dad didn't stop mopping up the milk on the floor. "No," he said without looking up.

"Just a little class, don't know if I don't try, right?" I grinned.

Dad stopped and looked me dead in the eye. "No, Jack," he said (it would have sounded a lot more serious in his voice, I'm sure). "I can't have you acting unprofessional in front of my students."

"I *won't* be unprofessional!"

Dad looked at me as if to say: *Really?*

Yes, OK, I probably would have been a *little* unprofessional, but I had a reason! There's a boy in his class, Tommy Wilkins, who is a *super* nerd. He thinks he is smarter than everyone, even some of the teachers, and likes to rub your nose in it. Honestly, he's just really annoying.

I just wanted to see how he would cope with a trip to the Principal's office to ruin his 'perfect student' rep....

"You're not going in, end of story."

I shrugged. I wasn't going to complain about a day off. "Wait," I said. "What are *you* doing?"

Dad dropped the sponge he was using in the sink. "I'm

staying off too."

I wasn't going to say anything, when something clicked in my head. The Math exam! If I didn't manage to pass it, I wouldn't be allowed to play in the first match and then we wouldn't win and…a master plan suddenly formed in my head. A masterfully crafted master plan.

Dad was about to leave the room when I squeaked: "But what about my *grades*?"

Dad paused. I had him like a fish on a line. "I mean," I continued, "I have a test today. An *important* one. We shouldn't let a little thing like swapping bodies affect my studies, should we? Not if I want me to go to a good college." I let that one dangle in the air for a while. "I mean, you could leave right after you've done it, pick up my homework and make sure I don't miss anything."

He turned back to me with an odd smile on his face. "I'm proud of you, Jack, for being so mature and thinking about your studies. You're right." He nodded to himself.

"I'll go in and pretend to be you. Shouldn't be too hard."
And with that, he turned and left the room.

"*Shouldn't be too hard!*" I shouted after him. "What does that mean?"

It was a few minutes later when he emerged from my room that I found out what he meant. Maybe my masterfully crafted plan wasn't as great as I thought it was.

He was wearing the worst outfit I had ever been forced to wear for my aunt's fortieth birthday last year: a tight white shirt with an itchy, dark blue sweater vest over the top, a bow tie (where did he even *find* that?) and black, smart trousers. He stood in my doorway, smoothing down the vest and smiling to himself. "Very nice," he said. "Smart and respectful."

"No!" I shouted. "You aren't wearing that!"

He looked offended. "Why not? I think I look pretty snazzy."

"Snazzy? *Snazzy?*" I felt like my head was about to explode. "You can't wear that to *school*! I'll be the laughing stock of the whole city!"

Dad shrugged. "I think it's alright. When I was at school...."

"Dinosaurs ruled the earth and didn't have any fashion sense," I interrupted him. "Look, let me sort out what you're going to wear." I pushed past him into the room and started rummaging through my wardrobe.

"You need to tidy your room," he mumbled, standing behind me.

I snapped my head around. "Not now," I snarled. Dad just chuckled.

As I sorted through my wardrobe for a decent pair of jeans and a clean t-shirt, Dad disappeared from the room. By the time he came back, I had an outfit laying down on the bed ready for him.

"That's what you're wearing today," I announced.

"Maybe," he said and then held out a small piece of

paper. "If you do this."

I took the paper. "What is it?"

"A script. I need you to call in sick for me. With *my* voice," Dad grinned. I recognized the grin on his face. On *my* face. I thought for the whole time I was playing him, but he had played *me* as well. I sighed and looked at the script in my hand. This is what it said:

Call Mrs. Jade the receptionist 'Beverly' because that is her name.

READ THIS WHEN SHE ANSWERS THE PHONE:

Hello, Beverly. It's David Stevenson here. I'm afraid that I am not going to make it in today as I am very sick. I am very sorry for the inconvenience I have caused. I hope you can find an adequate supply teacher. Thank you very much. Goodbye.

If she tries to say anything more <u>say you are too ill and hang up!</u>

The last line was underlined. He obviously didn't want me speaking too much. I glanced at Dad. "You want me to read this?"

"Word for word." He handed me his mobile, the number of the school already typed into it. "Just do it now and quickly."

I rolled my eyes as he waved the bowtie at me again. I made a secret promise to *burn* the bowtie when this was all over and pressed the call button on the phone. It began to ring. Nerves shot down my body with each ring. I had to sound convincing.

"Hello?" Mrs. Jade's soft voice spoke on the other end of the line.

"Hello, Mrs., ah, Beverly… It's Ja- er David Stevenson here." I could feel my palms getting incredibly sweaty. Dad shook his head slowly as he watched me. I decided to get it done as soon as possible.

"I'mafraidthatIamnotgoingtomakeitinasIamsick." The words spilled out of me as nerves gripped my throat.

"Pardon?" Mrs. Jade said. I silently kicked myself and tried to get some oxygen into my lungs.

I started again: "Hello, *Beverly*. It. Is. David. Stevenson. Here. I'm. Afraid. That. I am. Not. Going. To. Make. It. In. Today. As. I am. Very. Sick."

"Oh David!" Mrs Jade replied. "I'm very sorry to hear that. What's wrong?"

I blinked. There wasn't an answer to that on the script. Dad stared at me hopefully. I decided to plow onward. "I'm very sorry for the in… incon… in…" I stared at my Dad's handwriting. What was the word? Dad started waving his hands and mouthing: HANG UP! HANG UP!

I gave up. "Sorry, I'm too ill. Going to vomit! Byeeeeee! *bllleeeeuuuugh*" I hung up while making sick noises just to add to the effect and then smiled sweetly at my dad.

"Better than nothing," he sighed, snatching the clothes off the bed.

I felt like I had won that round.

# The Day Off

Dad stood by the open door and watched the school bus drive slowly down the street. He looked like he had just eaten a rotten egg as he watched the ancient metal beast chug slowly towards us, yellow paint scratched off after years of use.

"I have to go in that…deathtrap with all those kids?" he groaned.

I nodded, not trying to hide my smile at all. "Don't sit too near the front, or people will throw stuff at you. Oh, and don't sit too near the back either. The *weird* kids sit there." Dad blinked at me, his brain clearly not processing the information I was giving him. "They will probably try to bite you," I added, stirring him up further, just for good measure.

I handed him a letter he had typed out so he could hand it in at the office, allowing him to leave early. "You can sign this, I'm sure."

He took it reluctantly and shook his head. "I can't believe I'm doing this."

"Oh and don't forget, you have to *walk* home this afternoon."

"Walk?" His eyes widened. "But its *miles* away!"

I remembered the first time I had to walk home from school. It was a very long way and my legs were killing me by the end of it. My smile widened even further. "Welcome to my world!" I winked and then closed the door before he could protest. I was home alone and I could do what I wanted!

What followed was, in short, the best day *ever*. Sure, I was stuck in my dad's body and sure, I had to wear his boring clothes (all of which smelled like that odd 'man perfume' that Dad is so fond of wearing. It smells like something you would use to clean a toilet), but I got to do whatever I wanted. I decided to make the most of my free time and wrote out a list:

*Awesome things to do for my awesome day:*
1. *Eat Candy*
2. *Play Minecraft*
3. *Play Skylanders*
4. *Eat MORE Candy*
5. *Listen to SUPER LOUD MUSIC*
6. *Minecraft it up again. (Or Call of Duty, or both)*
7. *Junk Food/Candy*
8. *Maybe a nap?*
9. *Play guitar and drums REALLY LOUDLY*
10. *Junk food again. Or Candy. Maybe both.*

I'm not going to lie: I made it through most of my list. It was a really productive day! Although, by the time I reached number seven, I had eaten so many bars of chocolate (Dad stored them in the cupboard I couldn't reach, but now I *could*!) that I was starting to feel a little sick and decided to maybe give eating a little bit of a break. I managed to build so much on Minecraft, it was insane. At first, Dad's big floppy fingers made holding the controller weird and I kept dropping it. However, after a few hours I got the hang of them. I would even go as far as saying that I was *better that before!* I also managed to set up a little fort on the couch made from pillows and blankets (so I could defend the house in case anyone decided to try and get in).

The only person who tried was the postman, but he just pushed letters through the door and walked away again. If he *had* tried to get in, though, I was ready for him!

I even started to think that maybe this body swapping thing wasn't the end of the world. I decided I could probably cope with it for a little while.

I didn't notice Dad coming home in the afternoon. I was too busy fighting zombies. I only realized he was back when he slumped down on the sofa beside me, dropping my school bag to the floor. He sighed loudly and closed his eyes. I didn't bother to pause the game or even look his way. I just grinned and said: "Fun day?"

I could feel his scowl burning into the side of my face as I continued to shoot zombies.

"The school bus was… stressful," he said. "I see you've gotten comfy while I've been away."

I smiled even wider. "Well you know, I kept myself busy," I joked. "Didn't want to get bored."

"Yes, that would be terrible," he replied sarcastically, picking up a handful of candy bar wrappers from the floor. He stood up and turned on the computer in the corner of the room, the screen glowing as it sprang to life.

"What are you doing?" I asked, spraying the handful of chips I had just shoved in my mouth everywhere and finally prizing my attention away from my own screen.

"I'm seeing if the Internet has any answers to our little… *problem.*" He waved his hands between us. "It is a powerful tool, after all."

Wow, leave it to my dad to make even the Internet sound boring. 'A powerful tool'. *Really?* It wasn't a terrible idea. My character screamed as zombies began to eat him alive. I threw my controller on the floor and wandered over to my Dad, to see if his search was going to produce any results.

Dad typed (incredibly slowly, with one finger) the words "Body Swapping" into the search engine. He scrolled down the screen and we examined the results.

Here are a few:

WOMAN CLAIMS TO HAVE SWAPPED BODIES WITH CAT – SAYS SHE COUGHED UP HAIRBALLS FOR A WEEK.

SALLY'S FASHION BLOG – 15 FASHION TIPS TO SWAP YOUR BODY WITH THE BODY OF YOUR FAVORITE CELEB

SWAP YOUR FAT BODY WITH A FIT BODY IN THREE DAYS WITH THIS SIMPLE TRICK!

Dad hovered over the last one for slightly too long. I placed a hand on his shoulder and shook my head.

"It's a scam, Dad," I said. "Just let it go."

Dad rolled his eyes. "Obviously. I am well aware of that." Slowly he moved the mouse upward and bookmarked the page. He never listens to me. "Just in case," he mumbled as I shook my head disapprovingly. He clicked on the next page and shook his head. "This page just had a bunch of links about an actress called Lindsey Lohan. What's she got to do with this?"

I shrugged. "Not a clue. Have you tried 'Lightning strike'? Or 'Mind swap'? Or maybe a search which involves…."

Dad stood up. "I can't stand technology. You do it." He walked to the door of the room. "I'm going to start making dinner."

My stomach ached at the thought of more food after the amount I had stuffed myself with, but I didn't want Dad to know that, so I replied: "Good plan. I'll stay here."

What followed was an Internet search which went on

for *hours*. OK, it was closer to twenty minutes, but by the end I was horrifically bored and no more enlightened. I did however find out that the chances of being struck by lightning were 300,000 to 1 which meant that Dad and I were... lucky? I guess? I informed him of what I had found when he came back into the room with plates of sandwiches.

"Oh," he said. "That's interesting. But what if-" he was interrupted by the house phone starting to ring. He looked at me and I looked at him. We both looked at the phone. "Answer it!" he whispered to me, pointing at the phone.

My eyes widened. "You answer it!" I whispered back. I wasn't going to answer the phone. What if it was one of Dad's friends? How was I supposed to talk to them?

"What if it's someone from work?" Dad said frantically.

"Tell them I am ill... or you're ill... or... just answer it!"

Dad slowly edged towards the phone like it was an atom bomb and picked up the receiver. "Hello?" he said quietly. There was a pause. A long pause. It felt like forever before he finally said. "Oh, hello Tom!" I breathed a sigh of relief. "I suppose you want to talk to Jack..." I stopped breathing again.

*No Dad, you're Jack now! Remember?!*

Dad suddenly realized what he had said and backtracked poorly. "I mean *I'm* Jack! Of course I am! You want to talk to me. Your best friend. Jack. Who is me."

He looked at me apologetically as Tom probably called him crazy on the other end of the line. My hands clenched tightly on the arms of the seat. Not being part of the conversation was torture. What was Tom saying? By the way Dad frowned, it wasn't something good. "OH," Dad suddenly said very loudly, as if I couldn't hear, "TONIGHT. THE DINNER PLANS WE MADE. OF COURSE. AT YOUR HOUSE."

Fear clamped down on my stomach, threatening to bring back the day's worth of junk food. In all the excitement of body swapping we had completely forgotten about the dinner plans we had made for this evening!

It may sound a bit weird, but my dad and Tom's mom, Sarah, had been sort of thinking about dating for a while. Dad had sat down and asked me if it was OK and at first I was horrified by the idea. Dad had suggested that maybe if we all sat down to dinner one evening, then maybe I would have a change of heart. I wasn't *completely* convinced, but when Dad said that I could spend the evening gaming with Tom while he and Sarah talked, I didn't say no. I mean, what was the worst that could happen?

Obviously I never expected to be stuck in my dad's body! The thought of having to date Tom's mom made those candy bars start to rise into my throat again.

"No, no, sorry, we can't do tonight," Dad said. I let out a sigh of relief. "Why? Oh, Dad's far too ill. Yeah, he's been vomiting all day, it's been really super gross...er...dude."

*Dude?* I shook my head. No one says 'dude' anymore! My dad was stuck in the past.

Dad laughed uncomfortably. "Yeah I do sound like my dad, don't I? He is such a...dork. I mean...yeah, you know."

It was painful watching him pretend to be me. I started gesturing to him to put the phone down. He nodded.

"Alright, byeeeeeeee." Dad put the phone down and shook his head. "That was awful."

"You're telling me," I sighed. "We need to get back into our own bodies as soon as possible." Dad nodded in agreement.

"I'm booking a doctor's appointment for tonight," he said.

# Back on the Road

"I really didn't want to have to do this again for another few years," I groaned as I sat in the driver's seat of the car.

Dad nodded, doing up his seatbelt and testing it a few times. "Don't think that I *want* you to do it, but we need to get to the doctor's appointment and we will be late if we don't drive." He took a deep breath. "Don't worry, this time, we are going to take it nice and slow, no panicking, just a calm and easy drive."

I looked at him. He was an awful liar.

"Just remember," he said sternly. "Listen to what I say!"

"Do you mean when you say things like: 'Oh God, I'm too young to die?'"

"Yes, well…no," Dad mumbled, getting flustered. "Just take it slow. Slooooow." He spoke to me as if I was a kindergartener.

I shook my head and turned the key. The Rust Bucket rumbled to life. "Ugh, not again," I whispered and gently put my foot down on the accelerator.

Every time we went over ten miles per hour, Dad let out a small squeak and told me to slow down. We crept along the road, people honking their horns and overtaking us whenever possible. I tried to hide my face whenever they passed, but it would just make Dad scream more if I 'wasn't paying attention to the road'. It was so *embarrassing*.

"Careful!" Dad shouted again for what felt like the 100th time.

"Why? Worried we are going to lose control of the car?" I moaned back wiggling the steering wheel back and forth, making the car shake and wiggle.

"No, I mean that…."

The siren from behind us interrupted Dad before he could finish his sentence.

"The police are right behind us," Dad sighed. He closed his eyes and leaned back in his chair. "This is going to end badly. I can tell."

"Thanks for the vote of confidence," I mumbled. Although, to be honest, I didn't have confidence in me either! My hands were shaking as I pulled onto the side of the road. I was far too young to go to jail, even if I didn't look it. I briefly considered driving away, but Dad shook his head.

"It'll be fine," he whispered, handing me his license from the front of the car. I didn't believe it. He didn't believe it.

We both sat and waited for the police officer to pull up behind us and get out of his car. He seemed to do everything in slow motion, getting out of his car, standing and staring for a few seconds and then walking towards us at a snail's pace.

"Why is he taking so long?" I squeaked.

"To make you panic. You need to *stay calm*, Jack. Just do what he says and everything will be alright." The way Dad spoke to me, his voice wobbling like mine, made me realize that he was as freaked out as I was. I had no idea what to expect.

TAP. TAP. TAP. The cop finally reached the window beside me and tapped his knuckle against my window. That's when I noticed how much my hands were sweating. "Open the window!" Dad said, poking me in the arm.

"Oh, right." I fumbled around with the window control until finally the glass pane slid downward with a quiet buzz. The cop watched from behind big, round sunglasses. He didn't look anything like the fat, donut loving cops I was used to seeing on TV. This cop was built like a brick wall, with puffed out cheeks, square jaw and a mouth that looked like it had never learned how to smile.

"Hello," I croaked. "How can I help you?" I was already failing to stay calm. I just hoped it wasn't *too* obvious.

"License and registration please, sir," the officer said in a stern monotone voice that suggested he could break me in half like a twig and then chew up the remains. I glanced over at Dad, who just pointed frantically at the police officer again. I handed him the license that Dad had given to me, hoping that my hand sweat wouldn't be all over the card. The officer took it and stood for a while writing something down in a tiny notepad he produced from his pocket.

He wrote.

He wrote some more.

He glanced at the card.

He wrote something more.

I glanced at the clock in the car. This was worse than Math.

OK, maybe that was going a bit far.

Finally, he handed the card back and said: "Do you realize how fast you were going, sir?"

I thought about it. Was he joking? He didn't *seem* to be joking. I wasn't sure he could do any emotions other than terrifying or angry. "I definitely wasn't going over the speed limit!" I said with a (hopefully) cheerful smile. I mean, that's what people are arrested for right? Going too fast?

The police officer started at me for a second. I could hear the cogs whirring in his head. "No sir, you most certainly were not."

*Good*, I thought to myself. *I guess he'll just let us go then. Maybe he just wanted a chat.*

We weren't that lucky. Instead, the officer lowered his sunglasses, revealing terrifying light blue eyes, and asked: "Have you been drinking sir?"

Before I could respond, Dad pushed forward and leaned over me. "Of *course* he hasn't!" he said in an irritable voice. "He is *far* too young to be doing anything like that!"

The officer opened his mouth and then closed it again. He looked incredibly confused. I wasn't surprised. I dragged Dad backwards and tried to smile again.

"He means…er…" I racked my brains to come up with something that didn't sound completely insane. "That the night is young! It's too early to drink now, so I'm not drinking yet. Not that I plan to drink later. Of course not. Don't drink and drive." I smiled with too many teeth as the officer tried to get through the absolute madness that had just spewed out of my mouth.

"Right," he said. "Please step out of the car sir; I believe you are driving under the influence of alcohol."

"But I'm not!" I tried to argue.

"Do I have to *remove* you from your vehicle, sir?" He took an aggressive step forward.

"No, no, no," I squeaked. "I'm getting out." I imagined being removed from the car would involve the cop squeezing the vehicle like a tube of toothpaste until I popped out. I opened the car door. My legs began to wobble like jelly and I tried to look confident and, more importantly, innocent.

As I did, the officer said: "No one drives *that* slow if they're not trying to hide something!"

I had to admit, the cop wasn't too far off. We were trying to hide something, just not what he thought.

"Er, *Dad*," Dad popped his head out of the car window. "Is everything alright?"

"Yes, this very nice police officer just thinks we were driving too slow, *son*." I shot Dad a look to suggest it was all his fault. He looked ashamed.

"Please return to your seat," the police officer said to Dad and then turned back to me. He produced a small device which looked like a box with a straw on the end. "This is a breathalyzer," he said. "I want you to breath into here," he pointed at the straw, "and *then* we'll see if the night is too young for drinking or not!"

I took the box and examined the straw, trying not to think how many other people had breathed into it. It looked like someone had even tried to chew on it as well. Closing my eyes, I put the straw in my mouth and blew into it. It tasted like soap. I kept blowing until the device beeped and the cop signaled I could take it out of my mouth. I spat on the ground as he took the device back and tried to wipe the taste away.

"That tasted awful!" I moaned, spitting again and again. "Do you ever clean that?"

The officer didn't bother to look up at me. "That is the

taste of *justice*," he said, pressing a button on the device. It beeped again.

"Well, justice tastes *gross*," I said, grimacing. "What does the breathy thing say?"

After what felt like another horrifically long pause, the device beeped again. The officer didn't do a very good job at hiding his surprise. "Oh," he said. "Er... it seemed that you aren't as drunk as I thought you were."

"That *is* a surprise," I said, rolling my eyes. "I thought I was incredibly drunk."

The police officer raised his eyebrows. "Excuse me?"

"I was joking!" I squeaked.

"The police department does NOT have a sense of humor! If you are drunk and my device is malfunctioning, you are required to tell me RIGHT NOW!" He moved right up into my face until I could smell his sour, old coffee breath.

"No, no, no, no, no!" I stammered. "I'm not drunk! Not at all!"

He stared...and then moved away. "OK then," he said. "I'll let you off this time. But I'll be watching you."

"T...thank you!" I squeaked and hopped back into the car. I let out a long breath as I sat and stared out in front of us. "Is he gone?" I asked.

"Nope," Dad said. "He is just staring at us."

"Right," I said, deciding that getting as far away as possible from the police officer was a good idea. "I might drive a little faster this time, if you don't mind."

Dad agreed. "But only a little bit," he added as I pulled away from the curb. I shook my head. When would he learn?

# 300,000 to 1

Even though we drove a little faster from that point, we were still *very* late for our doctor's appointment.

The doctor's office was located in a small building just on the edge of the city. We entered the small waiting room, both sweating and breathing heavily. Dad was the first to go up to the desk. "Sorry, we're late. We have an appointment under the name Stevenson."

The nurse behind the desk looked at Dad and then over to me. She took a long, slow breath and then pulled out some forms from a drawer under her desk. She handed them to Dad. "Have your dad fill out these forms, kid," she said, before turning back to her computer and clicking down the keys. Dad looked down at the forms and then waved me over; the only pen available in the office was on a small chain next to the nurse.

"You have to fill out these forms *Dad*," he said with a roll of the eyes. I went over and, with Dad telling me what to do, I filled out each box slowly, trying to keep my handwriting as 'adulty' and neat as possible, occasionally adding little flicks for effect. The nurse glanced over with a raised eyebrow as a young son told his dad what to do, but didn't seem too bothered by it overall. When we were finally done, I handed her the form and she shoved it back into her drawer without even bothering to read it.

She just thrust a finger at the waiting room chairs and said: "The doctor will call you when she's ready."

We sat down in the chairs and began to wait. An old man on the far side of the room coughed and wheezed and choked. A baby cried and exploded snot out of its nose with every scream, spraying anything that was too close. I shuffled closer to Dad. *This* is why I hate going to the doctors. We watched the old man disappear into a room when called. We watched the mother drag her crying baby into another room. We continued to wait.

"I could have driven even slower and been pulled over *again* at this rate," I joked to Dad. He didn't reply. He looked like a dark cloud had settled over his head.

"I can't believe they're making us wait this long."

"Well, I mean we were-" I was interrupted by a doctor appearing in the doorway. He looked a little like one of the teachers at school, with spiky brown hair that stuck out the sides and a large bald patch on top of his head. He glanced down at a clipboard in his hand and said:

"Stevenson?"

We looked around the waiting room. It was empty except for us and the *germs*.

"I guess that's you!" he said with a grin. "I'm Doctor Edwards. Follow me."

He led us down a tight corridor to a small room at the end. The further we went into the building, the more it smelled like disinfectant and illness. I tried not to breathe too deeply, in case something decided to leap into my mouth and infect me.

His office was surprisingly large. Certificates of different degrees covered the wall and he sat on the other side of the desk. Typing something into his computer, he turned back to us with the same smile as before.

"So, how can I help you?"

I was about to speak when Dad said: "We were struck by lightning."

Doctor Edwards blinked. He turned back to his computer, as if to type something in, but his fingers hovered over the keyboard. He turned back to us. "Struck by lightning? Both of you?" he said, as if unsure of the words coming out of his mouth.

"Apparently there is a 300,000 to 1 chance of it happening," I chirped in. Dad gave me a look. I shrugged. "What? It's true. I read it on the Internet."

"Ok…er… *Where* did you get struck by lightning?" he asked

"On a football field," I answered.

"No, I meant on your body," he said again.

"Oh," I paused. Where did I get struck? That was a good question. I didn't hurt anywhere and I didn't want to examine my dad's body too closely for marks. Ew. "Er, well I don't really remember, do you, Dad?"

Dad looked at me and shook his head.

"What?" I said.

"You just called your son *Dad*, Mr. Stevenson," the doctor said quietly.

"My son?" I mentally kicked myself. Here I was

complaining about Dad forgetting all the time that we'd swapped bodies, and I had gone and forgotten myself! *Still* I thought to myself, *if anyone should know, it would be Doctor Edwards.*

I looked at Dad. He seemed to understand what I was thinking. He shook his head slowly, obviously not wanting me to reveal what had happened. But then what was the point in coming to the doctor?

"Are you OK, Mr. Stevenson?" Doctor Edwards asked, a concerned look on his face. I glanced at Dad one more time. I clenched my fists and spoke.

"I'm not Mr. Stevenson!" I said, much louder than I had expected. Nothing happened. No explosions, no police cars, nothing. Maybe it wasn't so bad to tell him after all. He glanced at his computer again.

"My computer says you are, unless you gave a false name? Because that's against the…"

"No, no, that's not what I mean," I began.

"It doesn't matter. He's crazy," Dad said. "We are here about being struck by lightning."

"Yes," I said. "*Exactly*. And when we were struck by lightning…."

"It hurt," Dad interrupted again, trying to stop me.

"We," I started.

"No we didn't," Dad said.

"Swapped."

"Didn't happen," Dad interrupted again.

I sat and folded my arms. "You're being a pain, you know that?" I said to Dad.

"Welcome to *my life!*" Dad shouted back.

The doctor blinked as we stared daggers at each other. Slowly, he said, "Is there something you would like to share, Mr. Stevenson?"

"Yes," I said, sitting up in my chair. "There is."

Dad shook his head, "This isn't going to end well."

I didn't bother listening to my dad anymore. Here we

were in front of a *trained professional*, someone who would know how to help us, and Dad *didn't* want to say anything because he might look a bit silly? No, I wasn't having it. I shifted myself to a comfortable position in my chair, looked the Doctor straight in the eyes and said, "I am not David Stevenson. I am his son, Jack Stevenson. David Stevenson is over there," I pointed at Dad. "We have *swapped bodies*. Can you help us? We don't know what to do."

Doctor Edwards suddenly looked incredibly interested in his computer screen again. He opened and closed his mouth a few times, scratched his head, rubbed his eyes and then turned back to us. "You've… swapped bodies…" he said.

"Yes," I nodded. "When the lightning struck us, we woke up in different bodies."

"You've…" he pointed at each of us in turn.

"This is going about as well as expected," Dad mumbled.

Doctor Edwards typed something into his computer. "Interesting," he mumbled to himself. "So you're, Jack?"

"Yes!" I said. We were finally getting somewhere!

"And you're…David?"

My dad shrugged. It didn't matter, the doc got the idea.

"Yes," I said. "Is there anything we can do? Like a pill? Or a cream? I mean, I don't *really* like taking pills, but if it means I can get out of this mess, I'm fine with it! Or is it an injection? Dad gets a little woozy around needles, so we might have to let him lie down first." My mouth was on overdrive at the possibility of finally getting this solved.

The doctor typed something into his computer and pressed print. Dad and I watched a small piece of paper come out of the device next to us. "What's this?" I asked.

"That," the doctor paused, "is the phone number of a Doctor James Turner. He's a specialist in…er… *these* sorts of cases. If you've really been struck by lightning."

"Oh really?" I said, grabbing the piece of paper. "So

people have body swapped before?"

The doctor glanced at Dad. "Sort of."

I looked between Dad and the doctor. They weren't telling me something. "What's up?"

"It's a psychiatrist, Jack. He thinks we are crazy." Dad stood up, putting on his coat. "This was a waste of time."

"But... but..." I frowned. "You said you were going to help us." I looked down at the piece of paper in my hand, betrayed.

"No, no, you aren't *crazy*," Doctor Edwards assured us. "You could be suffering from some kind of shock. I just think a specialist who knows how to deal with these issues...."

"Issues? We don't have issues! We just need help!" I felt myself begin to get angry. I threw the piece of paper on the floor. "Thanks for *nothing!*" I was furious as I stormed out of the room, the door crashing loudly against the wall as I flung it open. I didn't even turn when I heard the doctor calling after me. I just wanted to be out of there. Away from the liars.

I marched past the nurse, who asked me to stop as well, and kept going until I was sitting in the front seat of the car again, listening to the sound of my own breathing. What were we going to do? How were we going to solve this? I looked out the windscreen of the car, up at the sky. Night had fallen and I could see the stars against the inky black above me. I felt the fist clenching rage inside me subside and I let out a breath. There was only one thing we could do now. Go back home.

# Skate Park Disaster

Once I had gotten home and calmed down, the doctor's office called us back. I now had an appointment with Dr. Turner in a couple of weeks' time at his office. I got to tell them I was *really excited* and then slammed the phone down without saying goodbye. It might have not been an *adult* thing to do, but it felt great. Even Dad didn't complain.

Luckily, the next day was Saturday, so we didn't have to worry about work or school. I lay in bed for a long time thinking about the future. What if this was *permanent*? What if I *was* crazy? I twisted and turned until I couldn't stay there any longer. I looked at the clock beside my bed. It was 8:30am. *Great,* I thought to myself. *I can't even enjoy a lie-in in this body.*

Slumping out of bed, I wandered downstairs to find Dad already stood in the kitchen, cradling a cup of coffee in his hands. He looked up at me and then back down at his coffee before taking a sip. "Bleugh!" he spat it back out. "Ugh, something must have happened to the coffee, because this tastes *awful.*" He tipped the rest of it down the sink.

"Just one more thing to go wrong in our lives," I said, wandering into the living room and slumping down on the couch. I didn't know what to do, so I decided to do what I did best: video games.

The TV glowed in front of me as it powered up. I glanced up again at Dad who yawned at me from the doorway. "I'm going to make bacon and eggs. Want some?"

"Uh huh." I lay down on the couch with my feet dangling over the edge of the arm rest, my favorite gaming position.

A few hours and one plate of bacon and eggs later, the front door opened and a cold wind blew into the room. I frowned, peering over the top of the couch to see Tom stood in the doorway, looking confusedly between the lounge and the kitchen.

Dad was still doing the washing up.

"Jack, are you doing the washing up?" Tom asked, wandering into the kitchen. I shook my head into gear, slapping myself on the face to wake up. I leapt over the couch, landing with all the gracefulness of an elephant on the other side.

"Oof!" I saw stars for a second, before leaping again to my feet and following Tom into the kitchen.

"Er...yes," Dad said, looking at his foamy hands. "I've got to do my chores and stuff."

"Ah," Tom said. "That sucks."

"And I was just *testing out* Jack's games console because we thought it was broken," I added loudly before Tom thought anything was off.

Tom nodded with an uncomfortable smile, "That's great."

He turned back to Dad. "Did you forget that we were going to the Skate Park today Jack? Everyone's down there already and we wondered where you were."

The *Skate Park!* All the plans I had made (and then completely forgotten about) came flooding back like the world's worst headache.

"Yes! He remembered!" I said, jumping next to Dad and ruffling his hair in what I assumed was a Dad-like way. "I'm just being a normal, boring, very strict Dad and making him do his chores before he leaves. Aren't I the *worst?*" I grinned. Tom looked visibly worried.

Dad moved out from under my hand, trying to re-adjust his hair.

"I mean, you're just doing what any *loving* father would *do, Dad,*" he said back to me through gritted teeth.

"Nope," I said back to him. "I'm the worst! So, so awful."

"Yeah," Tom frowned. "Are you both OK?"

"One hundred percent!" I shouted. "In fact, I'm doing *so* well, I'll even take you to the Skate Park. Just let me get dressed!

"No, really, Mr. Stevenson, it's OK,"Tom began to protest, but I had already left the room and was scampering upstairs. Sure, the Skate Park was within walking distance of our house, but I wasn't going to let Dad go off on his own with my friends. That would absolutely end in disaster!

What I didn't realize is that getting dressed would be a problem in itself. I looked in Dad's wardrobe at the different suits, shirts and *adult* clothes, all folded neatly or hanging from a hanger. I didn't know how he managed to keep it all in order, but it didn't work for me. I began to take things out and throw them onto the floor, like a *normal* person would.

"No," I said, removing a blue shirt. "Nope," I threw some black pants over my shoulder. I looked at a Hawaiian shirt that Dad loved. "Nooooooo!" *That* deserved to be burned and nothing more. Finally, deep at the back of his wardrobe, underneath spider webs and a thick smell of dust, I found an old t-shirt and a worn pair of jeans. I *knew* I would find some eventually.

With a sigh of relief, I chucked them on and headed back downstairs where Tom and Dad waited uncomfortably by the door. "Let's rock and roll!" I said. In my new deeper voice, it sounded *awful*. I made a mental note never to say it again. Dad and Tom walked silently behind me.

The Skate Park was just around the corner from our house. It was a small relief, because the drive there was *uncomfortable* and silent. Tom stared out the window and Dad was desperately clinging onto the door handle until his knuckles went white. I couldn't even brag to Tom about how *awesome* my driving skills were now (they were *super* awesome).

As I pulled into the parking lot next to the Skate Park, Tom couldn't get out of the car fast enough. I came to a stop and he leaped out, closing the door behind him. I decided to use this time to talk to Dad.

"Dad," I began.

"Listen, I know a few skating tricks from my youth, so this won't be terrible," he interrupted me. "Might even go well."

I snorted out a laugh. Yeah right.

"Just keep it short," I hissed back. "Make up an excuse and we'll go back home, as long as…oh, no." My eyes caught a flash of perfect blond hair floating towards us.

Dad turned to see what I was looking at. At the edge of the park, roller skating through the entrance, was the one person I didn't want Dad to bump into. It was *Holly*. She did that cute little smile she is so good at and waved at Dad. He waved back uncomfortably.

"So is Holly your *girlfriend?*" Dad asked.

The question came out of nowhere. I started mumbling and stuttering. "W-w-what?" I said, feeling the heat rise to my face. "I mean, girlfriend is a strong word, we talk a lot and stuff, I mean if you want you *could* say that."

Dad nodded, "Uh huh. Girlfriend then. I'll try not to embarrass you." He then did the kind of smile that said: *I am absolutely going to embarrass you, but without meaning to.* That was, after all, Dad's specialty.

*Too late,* I thought as Dad got out of the car. I knew that I couldn't go anywhere while Holly was here. I sat in the car and watched Dad awkwardly greet her with a wave even though she was expecting a hug. It was painful. Tom and Holly offered a polite wave at me too and I waved back. They then turned and headed into the Skate Park.

I looked down at the car keys in my hands. At this point, Dad would drive away and then come back in an hour or so. That's what I needed to do so they wouldn't suspect anything was up. Just start the engine and drive away. Easy.

I glanced at my friends again. Start the engine...Tom made a joke and Holly laughed. ...and drive away...Dad just scratched his head uncomfortably. He didn't get it and was probably confused. *Ugh,* I thought to myself. *He's barely been here two minutes and he's already messing it up!*

I shoved the keys into my jean's pocket. I had no choice. I was going to follow them in.

# No Adults Allowed

I had been coming to this Skate Park since I was six. I had got a skateboard for my birthday (a tiny one made of plastic) and really wanted to test it out. Since then, this place had become like a second home to me.

I knew the steps where I had fallen down, cut my knee, and everyone had thought I was really brave because I didn't cry. I knew the corner where Tom first attempted to climb the 'unclimbable' wall.

He didn't succeed, but he still holds the record for getting up the highest. I knew the small hut in the corner which people say is haunted by the skaters who have died here and no one will go close to when it gets dark.

As I entered through the front gate this time, it felt *different*. I felt like Neil Armstrong stepping onto the moon for the first time. To begin with, everything was smaller. Once epic-looking half pipes and grinding rails now looked alright, if a little sad. The high, concrete walls that surrounded the park now looked like I could easily climb them. There was no sense of awesomeness or comfort. It felt unnatural, like someone had taken my favorite place, shrunk it down and covered it in *boring* paint.

I stood out like a sore thumb. Teenagers roamed in packs around here. Tall, thin, and dressed in dark clothing with piercings that looked more uncomfortable than practical. Some of them had even started *shaving* and liked to flaunt their new chin hairs. They stood in little groups in different parts of the Skate Park, usually corners where they could huddle together and laugh at everyone else. But now they weren't laughing. They were *watching* me as I went past. I felt like a gazelle on one of those nature programs my Dad loves so much. They were the lions.

As if to prove my point even more, spray painted on a nearby wall, surrounded by a clump of teens were the words:

## DEFF TOO ADULTS!

and

## NO ADULTS ALOUD

I think what they meant was 'Death to Adults' and 'No adults allowed,' but I wasn't going to go up and ask them. Normally, I would have looked at the spray paint and smiled, but today I was an *adult*. I was trespassing on their land. It wasn't my land anymore. I started walking a bit faster. Better to get this over with quickly, I decided.

I found my friends and Dad right at the back of the park (as far away from me as they could possibly get, obviously). But I couldn't have prepared myself for what I saw.

Dad wasn't a *complete* loser when he was younger. Just like me, he really enjoyed skating. It turned out, even though it had been years since he had been on a board, he still had some skills! Crowds of kids gathered around the half pipe as he dropped into it. He swung down and then flew up the other side, using the momentum to launch into the air and... He flipped, grabbed the edge of his board and twisted in the air, a move I had never seen before!

"OOOOOOOOOOOHHHHhhhhh," said the crowd watching him.

He came up the other side and did another trick, this time saluting the crowd *while in the air.*

"AAAAAAAAAAaaaahhhh!" the crowd said again, bursting out into applause. I even found myself pausing to watch what was going on. I didn't want to admit, it but my Dad was actually being pretty... cool. I would never tell him I thought that, of course.

He kept going for a few more minutes and then he finally stopped, stamping on the edge of the skate board, making it flip into his hand. The crowd let out one final cheer and Dad waved at them before turning to my friends with a wild grin on his face. My face.

Something twisted inside of me when I saw that Dad was actually having *fun* with my friends. I'd expected him to have the worst day of his life, just like me. Holly ran down into the half pipe to my Dad and wrapped her arms around him.

"That was awesome!" I heard her shout and my Dad, after recovering from the shock of the hug, grinned even wider and hugged her back. The thing inside me twisted again. A small voice in my head whispered: She never hugged *you* like that.

That's when I realized I was jealous of my *Dad*! It was crazy. I tried to shake it off. *In a few days, everything will be back to normal,* I told myself. *I will be hanging out here with my friends like usual. Everything will be fine. FINE.*

But as I watched Holly continue to hug him, I knew I was lying to myself. How did I know that anything would be normal again? What if I was stuck like this *forever?*

The thing inside me popped an evil thought into my mind. If Dad was acting like me, I decided I was going to act like *Dad*.

"Jack!" I shouted, making my way towards the half pipe.

Dad and Holly both turned to look at me. Holly stepped away from Dad, her cheeks going red. I saw her whisper to him: "What is your Dad doing here, Jack?" I didn't give him a chance to respond.

When I reached him, I put a hand on his shoulder and said: "I'm proud of you, son. That skating was really *rad*."

It worked like a charm. An *uncool* bomb was set off at his feet and spread around the Skate Park. Any cool points he had just achieved were instantly destroyed by a parent getting involved. Parents are the opposite of anything cool. The reaction was most visible in Tom's face as he stood at the edge of the half pipe. He flinched like he had just bitten into a lemon. Holly stepped further away, trying to escape from the damage I had caused.

Dad, however, seemed oblivious to the whole thing. He looked up at me with a big, wide grin, like he had just received the best compliment of his life! What was *wrong* with him? He was such a *weirdo*.

"Thanks," he said. "That's really kind."

*No,* I thought. *Not a weirdo. An uncool adult.*

Then, to make things worse for himself, he hugged *me!* I couldn't believe it! It couldn't have worked out better!

And yet for some reason, I felt...bad. Not because I had just ruined my own reputation (that little fact wouldn't occur to me until much later). No, it was the fact that Dad was happy, I was proud of him. It was actually something that he wanted, not something he thought was uncool.

"Er," I said, stepping back. "We've got to go, something has come up."

Dad looked at Holly and Tom, who were whispering to each other. "I'm sorry guys, I've gotta go!"

"Ok," Holly said. "See you later."

"That you will," Dad replied, and then he *winked* at her. Holly bit back a laugh. I cringed inside. Dad was trying to *help* again. I hate it when he does that.

The car journey home was quiet. I kept running the events at the Skate Park though my head. I still felt like I had done something *wrong*. It was so weird.

"You alright?" Dad broke the silence as we pulled into our drive.

I shrugged. "Alright as I can be."

"Well, why did we leave early? I thought I was doing a pretty decent job."

*Yeah,* I thought to myself sadly, *of stealing my friends.* But I said something else: "I realized there was something else we need to prepare for. Probably your biggest test yet."

Dad looked at me like a lost puppy. "What do I have to do now?" he whined. "Being a kid wasn't *this* confusing when I was your age."

"Well, tomorrow," I said solemnly, "is band practice."

# Band Practice

Dad stood near the drum kit in our garage holding a drum stick in each hand. He looked at the different-sized drums and cymbals in front of him.

"What do you think?" I asked.

"How hard can it be?" He grinned and raised the sticks into the air like some kind of nerdy rock star. "Let's rock!" Then he started to play.

When I played the drums, I was a well-oiled machine. I could feel the beat of the music running through me and the drums were my heartbeat. In fact, that's why I formed my band. Me on drums, Holly with the singing voice of an angel, and Tom who could strum a few chords on his guitar. Together we sounded awesome.

I could tell that this next band practice wasn't going to be the same. Dad on the drums was like a confused octopus who couldn't tell left from right.

"No!" I said, forcing him to stop. I pointed at the round

snare drum directly in front of him. "You hit that one twice and *that* one," I pointed at large bass drum below him, "four times. Not the other way around."

Dad shrugged. "Does it *really* matter?"

I wanted to pull out my hair. He was so *frustrating*. "Of course it matters!"

Dad sighed. "Alright, let's have a go again."

It continued like this for the rest of the day. It took me a few hours to get a basic rock beat into his mind before he gave up because he was "tired". He wandered off back into the house, despite my encouraging him to continue. "Do you *want* me to look stupid?" I shouted after him. He ignored me.

It was like he was actively trying to fail. At this rate, he would *never* convince my friends that we weren't body swapped.

The next morning, I was pacing around the house, nervously. Dad calmly sat in front of the TV watching the news.

"This is a terrible idea," I said. "We should call them and...."

The doorbell rang. I almost jumped out of my skin.

Dad rolled his eyes and went to open the door, but I grabbed his shoulder stopping him. "What if we pretend we're not here?"

Dad leaned close to me. "They can see us through the window, Jack."

I looked up. On the other side of the door, Holly and Tom stood chatting to each other. I let go of Dad and forced a fake smile onto my face.

"Oh," I whispered. I opened the door, silently reminding myself that we needed to appear *normal*. Like nothing was different. Sunday was band practice. It always had been.

"Hello, Jack's friends," I said. *That sounded natural right?* I thought to myself. "Welcome again to this house that you have been to before." The nerves were affecting my brain. It was like I was in the kindergarten nativity all over again. I was a star then and forgot my one line: "The child is born!" and instead said: "I'm tired and bored." My acting career went down the drain before I knew it.

"Oh," Holly said uncomfortably. "Hello, Mr. Stevenson, is Jack in?"

I sighed quietly. "Yeah, he's here. Are you planning on doing band practice?"

"Yes, Mr. Stevenson. I hope that's OK," Tom said. Every time he called me 'Mr. Stevenson,' it was like being poked with a pin. It felt wrong on so many levels. Dad joined me by the door.

"Head into the garage guys, I'll see you there," Dad said. Holly and Tom set off. He turned to me. "Don't worry, it'll all be fine. I'll pretend to hurt my hand or something."

I nodded. Everything was fine. We had a **plan**.

Five minutes later, I could tell everything *wasn't* fine. I was listening to my band through the door, and it sounded like Dad had somehow gotten *even worse* even though I had told him what to do. At the end of the first song ("Why must you steal my video games?" by the Spiky Monkeys, a classic) Tom was already annoyed by Dad.

"What was *that*?" Tom said. "Has your brain stopped working?"

"I just need to…er…warm up." Dad said, pathetically. "My hands are cramping."

"Warm up?" Holly asked. "You don't usually need to."

That was it. It was time for damage control. I stepped into the room with my best Dad grin, making everyone jump. "How's it going guys? Sounds like you're *rockin out hard!*" I tried not to look too disgusted at what I had just said, maintaining the grin on my face.

"Are you OK, Mr. Stevenson?" Holly said. "You look a bit… strange." She glanced at Dad. I knew that look. It meant PLEASE GET YOUR DAD OUT OF HERE AS SOON AS

*POSSIBLE.* Unfortunately, I wasn't planning on moving. Instead, I found the nearest clear space and sat down on it.

"Why don't you play me a song?" I asked. "I've always been interested to hear you guys play."

"Really?" Dad asked. "You've never come in before. You've given us. Our. Space." As he said the last few words, Dad pointed his head towards the door. He wanted me to leave. I didn't move.

"I guess I was a bad parent up until now, because I'm super interested!" I grinned. "Go on, I won't mind."

"We're still practicing," Holly said quietly. I felt a little bad at putting her on the spot, especially as she didn't really like performing, but there was *no way* I was leaving my Dad in here alone with them.

"That's OK, I understand," I said, still not moving. Tom glanced at Dad, who shrugged.

"Let's...*sigh*...rock then," Dad said with a roll of the eyes. "1,2,3,4."

He didn't even count them in right. Holly and Tom started together, but Dad came in too fast. I had told him again and again to start after 4, but he always began playing too soon.

"My games are all I need," Holly sang in her perfect voice.

*Twang twangalang,* Tom rocked out on guitar.

**Thump CRASH bang**. Dad stumbled across the drum kit.

"But you took them away..." Holly cringed as she tried to keep going.

*Twangle twang twang.* Tom looked like the sound actually hurt him.

**Thummmmmmmmmmmp.** Dad was grinning and having a good time. Of *course* he was.

"Now they are gone, I don't know what to say,"Holly began the rise towards the chorus when....

"LOOK OUT!" Dad shouted. One of his drumsticks

flew right out of his hand as he hit the drum too hard. Time seemed to slow and everyone could only look on in horror as it flew through the air and- CLONK.

It smacked Holly right between the eyes!

She stumbled away from the microphone, stunned for a moment before finally raising her hand to her forehead. "Ow!" she said. "What's *wrong* with you today, Jack?"

My dad got up, eyes wide with embarrassment. "I'm sorry!" he said over and over. "I'm so, so sorry!"

I stood up as well, walking over to her. "Are you OK Holly? Do you need anything? A plaster? A hug?" I held my arms out. Holly looked at me like I was Frankenstein's Monster.

"I think I just want to go home," she said, tears forming in her eyes and she ran out of the room.

"Holly, wait!" I shouted after her.

Tom was quick to follow. "I'll make sure she gets home OK, Mr. Stevenson," he said too quickly. "Jack, you've got to get your head in the game!" he added quietly, before leaving the garage and going back into the house.

"Jack," Dad began. "I'm sorry I thought I...."

"Just save it," I snapped. I didn't want to hear his excuses. Once again, he had ruined everything. I stormed out of the room after my friends, leaving Dad sitting behind the drum kit, staring at the remaining drumstick in his hand.

I tried to catch up with Holly, to tell her that I was really sorry and that Dad had, I didn't know. I was running out of excuses. Luckily (I suppose), Holly and Tom were long gone by the time I reached the front door. The house was empty and quiet. I sighed and went upstairs. I'd had enough of today. I'd had enough of everything.

# Mr. Stevenson, teacher, expert

Mondays. No one likes Mondays, and for good reasons. The weekend is over and you have to start a *boring* week all over again. Of course, I didn't expect my week to start quite like this.

I sat behind Dad's desk at school and stared at his empty classroom, listening to the sounds of students yelling and playing outside. His classroom suddenly looked a lot bigger and scarier than I was used to. I looked towards the door. His class would be coming in shortly. The *other* 7<sup>th</sup> grade class. The door looked a million miles away. I had no chance to escape.

"It'll be fine," Dad said, placing a stack of papers on the desk next to me. "We can't afford to miss any more days."

"I definitely can," I said, trying to ignore my shaking hands. Suddenly, the thought of being a teacher didn't seem so hilarious or fun.

"Just follow the **plan** and everything will be fine," Dad said, tapping the paper on the desk in front of me.

That's right. We had a **plan**. Considering how well the last **plan** went, I didn't have high hopes for this one either. At least Dad couldn't walk in and mess it up. I looked down at my scribbled handwriting again, to double check I knew what was happening:

*Morning – **Math** (ugh) - Get students to do the <u>worksheet</u> (the one Dad printed out). I just need to sit at the front and watch them work.*

*Break – You are on duty! Go outside and stand around. Look like a teacher who knows what he is doing. (Find students who are having too much fun and tell them to stop. <u>Teachers do not like fun!</u>)*

*Before Lunch – **Geography** – Students have a 'map project' to finish. Get them to do it. (They should know what 'map project' means)*

*Lunch – Eat lunch. Chicken sandwich and a candy bar for*

*energy.*

*After lunch* – **History** *– Get them to write an essay on the Fall of the Roman Empire! (No talking, no laughing, no enjoying. No happiness. School and happiness do not mix)*

My phone buzzed in my pocket and I looked at the message. "Tom is looking for me...you...you as me, at the front of the school."

Dad nodded, "Don't worry, I'll stay quiet all day, say I have a sore throat."

I nodded. It was for the best. If Dad couldn't speak, he couldn't say anything *stupid.*

"I won't forget to pick up your homework either," Dad grinned, punching me playfully in the arm.

Yay. Homework! Uggh!

As he left the room, I let out a breath. I could do this. Teaching would be *easy.*

Teaching, it turned out, wasn't that easy. After the students came in and settled in for the morning, they wouldn't sit down and just do the worksheet! Nooooo! They kept coming up to me and asking me questions.

First it was Sally Bride: "Mr. Stevenson, what's thirty-five divided by seven?"

I didn't know. I had to use a calculator and then Sally asked why *she* couldn't use a calculator. "Because you're not old enough!" I said, sending her back to her chair.

Ken Matthews then came up to me *barely a second later* saying, "Mr. Stevenson, I accidentally dropped my worksheet out of the window, can I have another one?" In the course of the lesson, I had to get him ten new sheets, until I realized it would just be easier to close the window he sat next to.

Every five minutes there was also: "Mr. Stevenson, why do I have to stand and face the corner? What have I done wrong?"

Just stand and face the corner, Tommy Wilkins!" I said for the hundredth time, secretly grinning. "I'm your *teacher*. You have to do *as I say*." I sat back in the chair behind the desk and let out a sigh. Who knew teaching was so *tiring*?

When the bell finally rang for break, I let out a long sigh of relief. So did the class. I waved them off to break without saying a word and slumped my head down onto the desk, scattering hastily collected worksheets everywhere. Teaching was *lame*. I opened one eye, and looked back into the classroom.

"Oh," I said. "You can go to break too, Tommy."

The boy turned from the corner, let out a whoop of joy and ran out of the room. I'd always thought being in control would be fun, but it was like trying to balance plates on sticks but the plates and sticks keep asking you *why* you are balancing them and *how long* you plan to balance them and a thousand other questions. I glanced down at the **plan** again and groaned.

I was on yard duty. Would this day *never end?* I got up, picking up my coat, and slowly trudged outside after the class.

## Break time

The sky was gray and the wind was blowing. Unlike all the students who got to run around and keep warm, I had to stand still and hug myself, hoping my Dad's thin coat would protect me from hypothermia. I stared longingly at a colorful poster which hung on a nearby wall and read it.

The poster was covered in glitter, sparkles, and had pictures of stickmen dancing on it. The dance committee, run by some tenth graders and the drama teacher, Miss White, had really gone all out this year. Glitter pens don't grow on trees after all.

The dance…it was only a few weeks away. It was when the cool kids got to be their coolest. Naturally, I would have been one of the stars of the dance. I looked down at the body

I was in. I looked at the tight, uncomfortable shirt and tie that Dad had made me wear and the black shoes that pinched my feet. How did *anyone* wear stuff like this?

"Mr. Stevenson," Samantha, a small girl from eighth grade, ran up to me.

Go away!" I snapped.

She stared up at me with big brown eyes that slowly filled with tears and then she ran away. *Oops.*

I considered going after her and making sure she was alright, when I caught sight of Holly and Tom hanging out on a bench nearby. I started to head towards them and then remembered who I was, so I hung back. They didn't look happy. I frowned. Where was Dad? Holly looked up across the yard and I followed her gaze.

"Oh, no!" I said out loud.

If there was one person I *didn't* want my Dad hanging out with in the entire school, it was *Jasmine Walder.* So guess who he was currently standing next to on the far side of the yard and actually *talking* to? You got it. *Jasmine Walder.* She was part of the nerdy gang who thought they were better than everyone else because they had such *good grades.*

Why did I want to avoid her specifically? Well, that's another story.

This had taken place a few years earlier, when Matthew Lane brought in a GAMEKID 3D™. Nowadays, the GAMEKID 3D™ is an old console. Since then, they have released the GAMEKID MINI 3D™, the GAMEKID- PRO 3D™ and even more recently the GAMEKID 3D VIRTUAL PLUS™ (which is super awesome, I've been trying to get my dad to buy me one for weeks). But when this happened, the GAMEKID 3D™ had only just come out and I *really* wanted a go. Matthew even had the ADVENTURES OF KRON, which was (and still is) the *best game ever made ever!*

I begged Matthew to let me have a go. I said I would do *anything*. I would buy him candy, I would give him my toys, *anything*.

Matthew was one of those kids who liked to make mischief, so he said that he would let me go if I completed his dare. Naturally I said yes!

He said, "I DARE YOU TO KISS JASMINE WALDER!"

I was reluctant at first, but Tom told me if I didn't do the dare, not only would I not be able to play the GAMEKID 3D™, but I would also be labeled as Jack, King of the Wimps, for all of eternity.

So I did it. I walked over to Jasmine on that same break with all my friends watching, smiled sweetly at her and said: "Hey Jasmine, you're looking great and stuff," (I was a smooth talker, even then) and when Jasmine blushed and said thank you, I closed my eyes, held my breath, puckered up and *kissed her on the cheek.*

(If you're wondering, the GAMEKID 3D™ was absolutely worth it. But that's not the point.)

I would take it back if I could, because since then Jasmine Walder has been *obsessed* with me. She always tries to talk to me, she tries to be my partner in *everything,* and I've been told that her books are covered in doodles saying JACK & JASMINE 4EVA in little pink hearts.

It sends a shiver down my spine just thinking about it.

As I considered how to deal with the situation (could I just lock Jasmine in a cupboard? Are teachers allowed to do that?), I side-stepped closer to Holly and Tom to eavesdrop on their conversation. I was careful to stare in the other direction so they wouldn't know I was listening.

"I don't *get* it," Tom said. "Why is he acting like that?"

"I don't know," Holly said. "He acted as if I didn't exist today."

"But he's your boyfriend!"

"Yeah, I mean, I *thought* he was..."

"Has he asked you to the dance yet?"

"No," Holly said quietly.

My heart sank in my chest. Holly was having second thoughts about us and it was *all because of Dad*. I knew we should have stayed home again today, but no, Dad really wanted to go in. I bit my tongue, trying to stop myself from screaming in frustration.

"Maybe he's ill?" Tom tried to talk Holly back from where she was going.

"Or maybe he just sucks. I'm going back inside." As Holly ran past me, I could see tears in her eyes.

It was too much. I had to take action and I had to do it now. I set off towards Dad.

Jasmine's laugh echoed across the yard. It was a nasal, screechy laugh which made my ears sting the closer I got. Her brown pig-tails bobbed as she and Dad continued their conversation and she stared intensely at him. Could Dad not see what he was doing? Was he really this blind?

"Jack Stevenson!" I shouted in a voice that had been used so many times against me. It felt weird to command it myself. "Come over here, please." I felt *weird* using my voice like that, but it got Dad's attention. He walked over to me, frowning.

"What?" he asked.

"What? *What?*" I almost squeaked. "What are you

*doing?* Why aren't you with Tom and Holly?"

Dad glanced over at Tom on the bench. "Jasmine sat down next to me in class and, well, I think she's a really nice girl. You could use more friends like her, Jack."

"I don't *need* 'more friends like her'," I hissed at him. "I already have friends. You know, Tom and Holly? Not Jasmine and her crew. This isn't how it works here."

Dad frowned, glancing back at Jasmine. She waved.

"I think that Jasmine and her "crew," as you put it, are wonderful students," Dad said stubbornly.

"But they're not cool and I am. I can't be *seen* with them or I'll be bullied."

"Maybe if you hang out with them more, they will get more "cool" and won't be bullied as much," Dad said, folding his arms.

He wasn't listening to me, again. It felt like a one-sided conversation. But this time, he didn't have all the power. *I did!*

"Jasmine," I said in my best teacher voice, side stepping Dad. "Mr. Thomas was looking for you inside."

Jasmine's eyes snapped up to me. She looked panicked, unprepared to be talked to by a teacher. "Yes, Mr. Stevenson!" she squeaked before dashing off to see what her precious Mr. Thomas wanted.

Dad sighed behind me. "That was very rude of you, Jack," he said, shaking his head. "We are going to talk about this later.

I looked him dead in the eye and scowled at him.

"No," I said, "we aren't." And with that, I turned and stormed off.

# Lessons are Boring

I was still angry after lunch, and it was time to 'teach' history now. I looked down at Dad's **plan**. The students were meant to write an essay on the fall of the Roman Empire. I clenched my fists and, in a moment of anger, I crumpled the piece of paper into a little ball and threw it in the nearby waste bin. School was boring enough without *essays*.

It felt strangely freeing, throwing away the **plan**. I suddenly realized I could to *anything I wanted* now. There was nothing Dad could do, there was nothing *anyone* could do because, after all, I was the teacher. A small grin burst out on my face as the students began to drag themselves in from lunch. I could see on their faces the fear of a long, boring afternoon, but I had other plans.

I was living the life every kid at school had dreamed about during a hot sunny day of pop-quizzes and surprise tests. I was the *teacher*. I held the power. I was king.

Raising my feet, I put them up on the desk and leaned back on my hands. "Ahhh," I let out a long, comfortable sigh. I could already see a few of the students looking around, wondering what was wrong. What had happened to their *normal, boring* Mr. Stevenson?

He was long gone.

I yawned loudly and checked my fingernails for dirt. "Everyone have fun at lunch?"

There was a bored murmur from the class saying yes.

"Want to keep having fun?"

The students said, "Yes!" but were unsure. I knew what was going through their heads. What did their teacher have planned? A pop quiz? Another exam?

I smiled at them. "Go on then. Do what you want."

The students stared back at me. They didn't know what to say. Not even smarty pants Tommy Wilkins, who usually had an answer for everything.

"I'm going to take a nap," I said. "Don't make *too* much of a mess." With that, I placed a history book over my eyes and leaned back into my chair.

Nobody moved in the classroom. They still thought it was too good to be true. I started making snoring noises. ZZZZZZZZZZzzzzzz *snort* zzzZZZZZZZZzzzzz.

Still, nobody moved.

I took the book off my face. The students all stared at me like a herd of deer caught in front of headlights. I rolled my eyes. "Come on guys, don't just sit there. You can do *whatever you want*. I don't care. You won't get in trouble."

Realization slowly spread across the class that I wasn't joking. As if to test out the theory, Johnny Jacobs slowly stood up at the back of the class and then, via his chair, climbed on top of the desk, standing taller than everyone else in the room. Tommy gasped in horror.

I nodded. "Johnny's got the right idea. Good on you, Johnny."

Johnny grinned like it was Christmas. When Dad had been teaching, I don't think he ever praised Johnny like that. But I was in charge now!

Other students slowly began to catch on. There was a murmur of a conversation starting in one corner. Another student pulled out his phone and started playing games on it, and then *finally* everyone started to do what they wanted. Windows were opened and Ken started dumping worksheets out of them. Sally put on some music and began to dance, people laughed and joked.

Fat Gary in the corner (his name wasn't *actually* fat Gary, but everyone called him that - even his Mom) was surrounded by an increasing mountain of candy wrappers, as if he was trying to eat twice his weight in them.

I sat back in my chair and watched it all. I was definitely the coolest teacher around.

Everything was going great.

It was around the point when the students formed a conga line and started knocking books off shelves and stationary onto the floor that it happened.

KNOCK, KNOCK, KNOCK.

I didn't hear it at first. I was too busy listening to a Spiky Monkey album on my phone. But the second time it was louder and more insistent.

**KNOCK, KNOCK, KNOCK.**

The room fell silent.

Everyone looked at me.

I pushed myself out of my chair and crossed the room, opening the door slightly and peering around to see who it was.

It was the last person I wanted to see.

The frowning, angry face of the principal, Mrs. Kent, stared back at me. "Mr. Stevenson! What is the meaning of all this racket?"

I paused, holding the door slightly closed so she couldn't see inside. "Er... history?" I said with a smile.

Mrs. Kent didn't seem impressed. "It sounds like you're trying to destroy the school!" she said, her eyebrows twitching. "What *are* you doing in there?"

She tried to enter the room, but I held the door closed. Her face turned red and she looked at me as if she was about to explode.

"Ee, just, give me a second," I smiled sweetly, closing the door in her face.

Panic flooded through my body. How was I going to explain all this to the principal? Could I pretend to pass out?

Maybe climb out of the window? I searched Dad's desk for anything that could help me. There was nothing except Dad's stupid history books. How were they going to...

BING. A light bulb lit up in my mind.

"Annnnnnnd stop." I shouted at the class. They all looked at me, perplexed. "Well done guys, that was a good demonstration of the *barbarians* who destroyed the Roman Empire. Out of control. Disaster. Very, very good."

The students looked at each other and at the mess of the room they had made around them.

I clapped my hands together. "Now, let's pretend we're the Roman Empire. Tidy up! Last person with a tidy table gets detention!"

Panic fluttered throughout the room as the students started to swarm around, tidying up everything.

My heart was beating fast too, because at that same time, Mrs. Kent flung open the door and strode into the room.

"What's going on in here!" she shouted.

The class, now sitting at tidy tables, stared back at her.

"History, Mrs. Kent," Tommy Wilkins smiled sweetly.

I smiled at the principal. "Yes! Well done, Tommy." Maybe having a nerd in the class wasn't *too* awful.

Mrs. Kent narrowed her eyes and looked around the room for anything suspicious. She turned to me. "I see," she said quietly.

It was at this exact moment that Gary decided that he had eaten too much candy while pretending to be a barbarian, and threw up all over his desk in a large eruption of vomit!

The girls near him jumped up, screaming. Other students tried to take photos with their phones.

It was *gross*.

Mrs. Kent looked at me with a raised eyebrow.

"I don't suppose you want to clean that up?" I asked.

"I believe *that* duty falls to the teacher," she said with a sneer, raising her nose and walking out of the room.

"Of course," I sighed.

The rest of the day was filled with…you got it, worksheets. Gary was sent home and it took me hours of wiping and cleaning to get rid of the lumps he had sprayed everywhere. By the end of the day, I was more tired than I had ever been and couldn't get the smell of vomit out of my nose.

When the final bell rang, I said a silent prayer and told the class to leave. Teaching, I decided, was awful.

I gathered up my things as quickly as possible and left the classroom, heading towards Dad's (or my) classroom. As I went through the hallway, I heard something which sounded a lot like shouting.

"Admit it!" It sounded like Mr. Thomas. I would recognize that goblin-like tone anywhere.

"I won't because it's not true!" The other voice surprised me. It was Dad!

## In Trouble

By the time I reached the source of the shouting, I found Mr. Thomas pointing an accusing finger at Dad. His face was starting to turn red, clearly from all the yelling he had been doing. I had never seen him this angry before! What had Dad done?

Dad, however, was giving as good as he got. He was also red in the face and stood, arms folded, staring angrily at Mr. Thomas.

"You're lying and I know it!" Mr. Thomas shouted.

"I'm not!" Dad shouted back. "Why are you not *listening* to me?"

Mr. Thomas was going purple now. I was sure that he would explode if no one stepped in. I was quite happy to stand back and watch it happen, but sadly he saw me.

"Mr. Stevenson! Mr. Stevenson!" he said, plodding over to me and grabbing me quite tightly by the arm. "Your son is answering back to a teacher! He is *questioning my authority*!"

I tried not to laugh. "So?"

Mr. Thomas's eyes bulged. "Well…well, he cheated on the math exam! He got an A+!" Mr. Thomas wiggled a piece of paper in front of my eyes. "He had *never* got higher than a D, and that was on a *really* good day!"

Oh *no*! The Math exam? The exam that would let me play in the first match of the season? I realized I had to do some serious damage control here.

Dad folded his arms and looked at Mr. Thomas stubbornly. "If he can find *evidence* that I cheated, then I will gladly accept the punishment."

"Now, Jack," I quickly stepped in. "You don't *usually* get A+ on an exam, do you? You can see why Mr. Thomas might be a bit *confused*." I tried to give him a look that said: YOU WEREN'T MEANT TO DO SO WELL. YOU WERE SUPPOSED TO JUST DO IT AGAIN AND GET A LOWER MARK. I'll admit, it was a tough one to pull off. There was a lot of eyebrow wiggling.

Mr Thomas spun back around to Dad. "I don't need evidence! I am your teacher, I *know* it is true. You will be in detention for the rest of the week so you can realize that we do not allow *cheaters* in my classroom."

I was about to speak up in Dad's defense, but then I had a thought. If Dad was in detention, then he couldn't mess anything else up with Holly or Jasmine. Dad looked at me pleadingly. It was a look I had given to Dad so many times during my life. One he had ignored. I knew exactly how Dad would have responded. And besides, I talked to him before the test about the grade I should get. Even though he wanted me to get top marks, I knew it wouldn't look right. He only had himself to blame!

I nodded politely and said to him: "I think this is for the best, son. You need to take responsibility for your actions."

Dad's mouth dropped open. I tried not to burst out laughing there and then. It was *priceless*. I nodded to Mr. Thomas, who seemed very pleased with the situation and disappeared back into his room. Dad fought for words but none would come out. Now he would *definitely* understand what it was like to be me.

"Come on," I said cheerfully. "You've got to get to football practice!"

Dad didn't say anything until much later, when we stood outside the changing rooms. He turned to me, eyes filled with fury, and demanded to know, "Why didn't you stand up to Mr. Thomas?"

I blinked at him. Wasn't it obvious? "You wouldn't have, if it was me."

"But you *knew* I wasn't cheating."

"Isn't knowing all the answers already kind of cheating?"

Dad opened his mouth and closed it again. I had got him with that one. "I see," he said quietly and went inside the changing room. I knew what he was feeling. Betrayed, hurt, completely alone. I knew because I had felt like that so many times before, like the adults just *didn't understand me*.

Except I did understand. Did that make me worse? I shook my head and decided not to think about it as I headed towards the field.

# Date Night

Football practice was *awful*. Dad had no skill whatsoever. He kept dropping the ball, he ran in the wrong direction, and that field goal technique I had perfected last week? Dad just dropped the ball and managed to kick *himself* instead. All I could do was watch and cringe and try not to scream. To make things worse, Holly and Jasmine were both watching! I thought maybe I could get close to Holly, make up some kind of excuse as to why 'Jack' had been acting so weird. I ran through a few in my mind. Jack wasn't getting enough sleep? Jack was actually a superhero by night? Jack was abducted by aliens?

It didn't matter, by the time I was close to her, a noise on the field made me turn. Dad had fallen over again. I rolled my eyes. He deserved to….

That was when I saw it. Jasmine was *running onto the field*. She ran over to my dad and hugged him, trying to help him up. Dad smiled and nodded as she talked to him, probably telling him how great he was. It was *terrible*!

Then I remembered that Holly was watching as well! I turned, quickly, to say something, anything, to make things right, but it was too late. She was gone.

After the game, I waited for Dad to get changed. When he finally emerged from the changing room I shook my head.

"That was…" I couldn't even find the word I was looking for. Dad didn't say anything, he just looked up at me and then moved on.

As we got in the car, there was a *tap tap tap*, on the window. Outside stood a woman with brown hair tied neatly into a pony tail at the side of her head. She wore a flowery dress. It was Sarah, Tom's mom. I lowered the window.

"Hi Sarah!" I said. "What's up?"

"I see you're feeling better, David. That's good to see!

How would you like come around to my place tonight? Make up for missing that date last week?"

"Er…well…I mean…." I wasn't sure how to say *NO* in a polite way. Unfortunately, Sarah took my hesitation to mean, *Oh yes, absolutely!*

"Brilliant! Just drive on over to our house and we'll see you there!" She smiled and walked away from the car.

I glanced back at Dad who was sitting, wide-eyed, watching her go.

"I guess we're going to Tom's!" I said cheerfully. Dad sank down in his chair.

"This is going to be terrible," he whispered.

"A bit like you today then," I said back, starting the engine. Dad didn't reply.

I was getting the hang of driving now. It only took us twenty minutes to get to Tom's house because I managed to drive at a sustained 20 miles per hour. Dad had taken to covering his eyes so he couldn't see what was going on, which helped.

Tom's house was large and old. It looked a bit like one of those haunted houses you see in films, with pointed roofs and three floors. It even had a basement (where Tom refused to go because he was *sure* there was something down there). We rang the doorbell and a series of loud, ominous DING DONGs echoed around the house. I glanced at Dad, who shrugged.

"Let's just keep this quick and simple," Dad whispered. "No stress, nice and…."

The door opened. Sarah and Tom stood on the other side. "Hello," Sarah smiled. "Took you a while to get here!"

"Er... car issues," I said. "What's for dinner?" I suddenly realized that I was *starving*. The day had really taken its toll on my stomach! It growled quietly. I hoped she had prepared something big.

"I don't know!" Sarah said. "I bought all the items you told me to buy. What are you planning to make?"

My stomach growled again, in anger. Dad had a weird habit. He *enjoyed* cooking. He is such a weirdo. But that meant I now had to cook dinner at Sarah's house. She pointed towards the kitchen and I felt myself go pale. "Right," I said quietly. "I'll go and cook...."

"I'll go with you!" Dad said quickly.

I frowned and then slowly nodded. "Yes, son. Come and learn from your old dad!"

"You're not *that* old, Dad!" he said with a big, forced laugh.

"I'm *pretty old,* son. I might even have to buy a walking stick soon!"

Dad shot me a look telling me to be quiet. I grinned

back at him.

Sarah clapped her hands. "Oh, fantastic! Both of the Stevenson chefs working together!"

Dad followed me into the kitchen. It was way bigger than ours, and cleaner too. I stared at the ingredients neatly left on the side.

"Shall I open some wine?" Sarah asked, waving a bottle at me.

"Well," I began.

"No!" Dad shouted, "No wine!"

Sarah jumped in shock. I laughed. "Don't listen to him, he's just excited. I would *love* a glass of wine." After all, it looked like grape juice. It probably tasted the same too.

"I'll go get some glasses," Sarah jogged out of the room.

"What are you *doing?*" Dad snapped. "Are you trying to ruin everything?"

"You mean like you have been doing with my life so far?" I snapped back. "It's like everything I *tell* you to do, you go and do the complete opposite."

"Well, maybe my way is *better!*" Dad argued.

"Well, maybe *my* way of living *your* life is better!" I said as Sarah came back into the room.

"Is everything OK?" she asked.

"Perfecto!" I said with a grin. "I'm just giving Jack here some safety tips."

"Like always wash your hands before cooking!" Dad said, turning on the taps in the sink.

"Exactly!" I said, joining him.

My phone buzzed in my pocket. I glanced at the message.

WAT R U DOING? U R MAKING ME LOOK BAD.

It was from Tom. I was supposed to be gaming with him right now. I sighed and put the phone back in my pocket.

"So what are you making?" Sarah asked popping back

into the room and leaning in close to me. I took a tiny step away, glancing at the ingredients. Beef mince, onions, sweetcorn...

"Er, we are making meaty-onion-corn!" I said with a grin. I heard Dad cough behind me like he had something stuck in his throat. Sarah frowned.

"Meaty," she began.

"Lasagna," Dad said. "We're making lasagna."

"Or 'Meaty-onion-corn' as my family like to call it, eh Jack?" I ruffled his hair with my hand just because I knew he hated it.

"Great!" Sarah said. "I'll leave you to it!" She winked at me and left the room. Dad sighed.

"This was a terrible idea," he said.

## Tasty meaty-onion-corn

My stomach was doing flips inside me when we sat down to eat in Tom's dining room. Dad had done a great job of cooking and the steaming plates of food looked *amazing*. I was sat on one side of the table with Dad, and opposite us sat Sarah and Tom. I glanced over at Tom who looked like he was in a *bad* mood. He was staring daggers at Dad, who was too busy helping lay the table, to notice.

"Wow, this looks *amazing*, David," Sarah said.

"Thanks," Dad replied. "I worked pretty hard on it."

Sarah laughed, filling up my glass with wine. I glanced at Dad, who shook his head.

"Jack, I'm sure you made it *even better* by helping out," Sarah said. "See, Tom? If you help out more like Jack, who *knows* what you could achieve."

Tom folded his arms. "Yeah, great."

It was going terribly, so I took steps to distract everyone. I lifted up my glass of grape juice liquid. "To awesome food!" I said. "Let's eat!"

Sarah raised her glass too, tapping it on mine, as did Dad. Tom, however, just started to eat, ignoring us all. I took a sip of the wine and instantly learned that it TASTED NOTHING LIKE GRAPE JUICE.

It was *revolting*. No wonder adults were so grumpy all the time if *this* was what they had to drink. I wanted to spit it back out, but I couldn't make a scene in front of Sarah.

"Are you alright?" she asked.

I nodded, forcing the mouthful of wine down my throat. "Nice stuff," I croaked. It felt warm and strange in my stomach.

Sarah smiled again, taking a sip of her own.

As the meal went on, Sarah talked about her life and stuff and I ate the delicious lasagna. It was quite easy actually, as Sarah did most of the talking. I even drank some more wine. It didn't taste so bad the second time. Or the third time. After a while, I really began to enjoy myself. I might even say I was having a good time. I decided I would *help* Dad. After all, he wanted to date Sarah, right?

I swallowed a mouthful of lasagna and said: "You have a LOVELY smile, have I ever told you that?" I said to Sarah. It was strange. I wasn't moving, but the room seemed to be swaying from side to side.

"Oh," Sarah blushed. "Thank you."

Dad finished his meal, placing his knife and fork down. "Dad," he said quietly. "Would you like a glass. Of. Water." He said the last bit through gritted teeth.

"NO!" I said, a bit louder than I had planned. "Would YOU like a gas of WATer?

Sarah laughed. "I had no idea you were such a lightweight, David."

I drank the last bit of my wine. "A white date?" I frowned. "What'sssss that?

The room spun a little. Dad started to gather up the plates. "Dad," he said, more insistently. "Why don't we go *wash up?*"

"Hmm?" I stared at the plates in his hand and back up at him and then back down at the plates. "OK then."

I waddled after Dad into the kitchen, the room spinning around me. My phone buzzed again. I looked at the screen.

Wht is up with ur Dad???

Another text from Tom. I giggled.

Dad shook his head. "We need to go, right now. You're making a fool of yourself!"

I folded my arms. "You're making a fool of yourself!" I said back to him in a high pitched voice. "That's how you sound, you know? Squeaky and weird."

"This is *your* voice!" Dad snapped.

"Well, you're using it wrong," I said. "And we're going when I say we're going."

I left the room before Dad could stop me going back to

the dining room. If Dad wanted me to make a fool of myself, I would do *exactly* that.

Sarah was standing up now, wiping down the table with a cloth. Tom still sat in his chair, typing another text into his phone. I heard Dad following me. I walked over to Sarah and put my arms around her shoulders. She jumped slightly, before looking me in the eyes.

"Oh… hello David," she smiled. "Finished already?"

"I just wanted to say…" I hiccupped slightly. "You're really pretty and stuff. Also your hair is really nice and I like how you speak and stuff."

Tom's eyes widened.

Dad stared at me in horror. I'd used those exact words when I asked Holly out for the first time. They *guaranteed* that the girl would want to go on another date.

"Er, thanks David, that's really…nice," Sarah slowly stepped back from my arms and smiled. "Maybe you've drank a bit too much, eh?"

"But," I began.

"I DON'T FEEL VERY WELL," Dad suddenly shouted. "I WOULD LIKE TO GO HOME."

I looked at him, frowning, about to tell him what a bad idea it was.

But then Sarah said, "Maybe that's for the best."

We took the bus home. I was in no state to drive, and Dad couldn't. We both sat in silence as the bus rumbled along its route.

"I don't know what to do," Dad whispered. "Everything is going wrong."

I didn't reply, but I felt exactly the same way.

## No chance at the Spring Dance

This is a jk, rite?

A joke. That's what it felt like right now. I could have laughed if I was feeling so down in the dumps. I forced myself out of bed, out of my room and into Dad's. I pushed open the door, fury raging in my gut.

"You asked *JASMINE* to the dance?!" I shouted.

Dad, it turned out, was also lying on his bed underneath his comforter. He groaned as I entered.

"I didn't ask her, she asked me," he said. "What was I supposed to say?"

"You say no! You say go away! You say..." I flopped onto the end of his bed. "I don't know."

We sat in silence for a moment. "She asked you? Really?"

Dad sat up. "I know, weird right?"

I shook my head. It was too late to do anything about it now. After all, it was Friday. The day of the Spring Dance. We had lied and bounced our way through the week, going from one disaster to another, trying to avoid everyone and everything. The only satisfaction we had was that tomorrow was Saturday.

"I have an idea," Dad suddenly said.

"Not another **plan**," I groaned. "They never work."

"No, an idea," Dad said, pushing back his bed covers. "This is it. We can fix a lot of the damage of the last week *tonight*." He looked at me, a grin spreading across his face. I frowned, then realized what he was suggesting.

"No." I shook my head. "No, no, no, no, no."

"Yes, yes, yes, *yes*!" Dad said, grabbing my shoulders. "This is *it*, Jack. If we go to the dance, I can make things right with Holly, and you can make things right with Sarah!"

"This is an awful idea," I said.

"We just need to apologize, say that we had an off week. They'll understand."

I didn't even reply, Dad was off in a world of his own. "If we can make things right with them, then we'll go on holiday or something. Really focus on getting this body swap thing sorted. It'll work, Jack. I know it!"

I shook my head. "You're crazy."

"Crazy AWESOME!" Dad shouted. "Come on! Let's get ready!"

When Dad came downstairs later, he was wearing the tux we had rented together for the dance. It had a cool red bowtie and when I tried it on, it made me feel like James Bond.

"How do I look?" he asked.

I looked at him sadly, remembering how excited I had been when I tried the tux on, thinking about dancing with Holly on the dance floor, imagining that it would be the night of our first kiss.

"You look great," I said quietly. I looked at what I was wearing. Dad's school clothes. Another day as the supervising teacher. "Shall we go?"

When we arrived at the school, Jasmine was waiting outside already. I'll admit, it took me a few times to realize it was her. She wore a frilly blue dress and her hair was no longer tied in braids. It flowed down in waves around her head.

I was surprised at her appearance - until she opened her mouth.

She broke into a wild grin when she saw my dad and said "Jacky!" in a high-pitched squeal.

"Jacky?" I asked Dad. "Really?"

"She came up with that one," Dad frowned. "I couldn't get her to stop."

"Yeah, that's a common thing with her. Remember the idea?"

Dad nodded. "We just need to get inside fir-URST," Dad couldn't finish his sentence because Jasmine had thrown her arms around his neck and squeezed. I will admit, it was a little funny.

"Shall we go?" I grinned.

The school looked completely different to normal. The normal beige walls had been covered in large signs reading: SPRING DANCE and lots of sparkly tinsel. We could already hear the thumping music from the sports hall as we got closer.

"I'm so EXCITED!" Jasmine squealed, still clinging onto Dad's arm.

"Yeah…" Dad said, looking at me with fear in his eyes.

It was the perfect time to say, "You two have fun! I'm going in round the back!" I left Dad to fend off Jasmine in the queue of students waiting outside while I dashed around the building.

The teachers and parents who were supervising went into the sports hall through a different entrance. We didn't need tickets, after all. When I entered, the hall looked completely different to normal. It was dark, and a DJ had set up a large booth at one end. He was pumping loud music out of the speaker. Different colored lights spun around in circles, flooding the room with a cloud of color. I stood and took it all in.

"Yeah," I said to myself quietly. "This would have been awesome."

I had hoped to get to Sarah, who was also one of the parent supervisors, before they let the students in, but I was too slow. Before I had even crossed the hall to the other teachers to ask where she was, students ran into the hall, screaming with excitement. I had to step around, dodging and twisting to make sure they didn't run into me.

"Woah!" I said. "Slow down! I'm- wait- careful!" Even crossing the hall was dangerous with these students running around everywhere. I stood still and tried to see what I could do. Near the entrance to the hall, I caught sight of Dad being dragged by Jasmine onto the dance floor. I shook my head. *He should be looking for Holly!* I felt frustration rising again, but I focused my search. I had to trust that Dad would do what he was supposed to.

That was when I saw the flash of Sarah, by the DJ Booth. Sarah was smiling and dancing by herself. I pushed my way through the sea of students, the music slowly getting louder and louder, until I stood next to her.

"HI!" I shouted.

"I can't hear anything you're saying!" She said back.

"WHAT?" I shouted back.

"We should go over there," she pointed to the other side of the room. I nodded, pretending I understood what she meant.

We both made our way through the dancing kids, Sarah pointing at some occasionally and saying something I couldn't hear.

Finally, we reached the back.

"Hey Sarah," I said.

"David," she replied.

I took a deep breath, Dad and I had been rehearsing what we were going to say all the way here. Mine was relatively simple.

"I'm sorry," I began.

"Yes?" Sarah asked.

***

That was when Holly decided to enter the hall. She was wearing a beautiful pink dress that sparkled like a rainbow with all the lights in the hall. Her hair curled and bounced around her shoulders and I thought she looked like a princess. She was everything I had ever dreamed about and more.

She was alone. She hadn't come with anyone. She had been waiting for me to ask her.

"David? Are you OK?" Sarah asked again. I ignored her. I was looking for Dad. Where was he?

My eyes scanned the dark room. I couldn't make anything out. That was when I saw him, leaving the dance floor to walk towards her! Yes!

Followed by Jasmine! No!

He began to talk to her, but Jasmine pushed between them. She looked angry; she was shouting something at Holly who was shouting back. My breath froze in my throat. I turned back to Sarah.

"I've got to go!" I said, pushing back into the horde of students.

"Mr. Stevenson!" Tommy Wilkins shouted, waving at me.

"Not now, Tommy!" I shouted back, continuing to push through.

Holly was trying to leave, but Jasmine grabbed her by

the arm. Holly tried to shake her off and Dad stepped in between them. He waved a finger at Jasmine, trying the 'I'm very disappointed in you' face, but it failed. Holly turned and ran out of the hall.

I managed to get through just in time to see Jasmine lean in to try and kiss my dad!

Dad stepped back, horrified. "No!" he said. "That isn't what I wanted at all!"

Jasmine burst into tears. Dad looked up to see me rushing past. "Jack!" he said, but I ignored him. The idea had failed. I was on damage control now.

I burst out the front of the building and walked down the path. "Holly?" I shouted. "Holly? Where are you?" I couldn't see her anywhere. I followed the path back round the building to the yard where we had our lunch breaks. "Holly? Where..." I stopped when I saw her.

Her hair had been ruined in her attempt to escape from Jasmine. She was sitting on the bench we always sat on at breaks, staring off into the distance.

"Holly!" I said. "I found you!"

"Mr. Stevenson?" she asked, clearly confused.

I made a decision. I wanted to be *me* again. I had had enough of this.

"No," I said. "I'm not Mr. Stevenson. I'm Jack! It's me, Jack, Holly!"

Holly shifted on the bench, clearly trying to put some distance between us. "What are you saying?"

"I'm saying that...Ok, this may sound weird and crazy, and I know, because it is. Right," I took a breath. "A week ago, Dad and me, we were struck by lightning on the football field, something happened and we swapped bodies! I'm Jack! In my dad's body! You've got to believe me!"

Holly frowned. "You're...Jack?"

"Yes! Not Mr. Stevenson, not my dad, I'm me! Me!" I laughed. It felt so good to say it out loud. "I'm your boyfriend!"

"I don't understand!" Holly said, moving away even further. "You're a teacher!"

"What?" I said. "Not at all. Holly, listen."

"Jack? Where are you?" Another voice came from behind me. It was Tom! I could tell him too! He'd believe me!

"Mr. Stevenson, you're acting really creepy!" Holly stood up.

"Wait, Holly!" I tried to grab her arm, but she was too fast. She ran away.

Tom came around the corner and looked at me, confused, as Holly ran past.

"Mr. Stevenson?" he asked. "Have you seen Jack?"

I dropped to my knees, all energy leaving me. I was tired. Tired of everything.

"No," I said quietly. "No, I haven't."

In the distance, thunder rumbled quietly.

Book 2

# I'm a Kid!
# Get Me Out of Here!!!

## How Does This Make You Feel
## KA-THOOM!!!

...Thunder crashed and I was transported back to the football field, running for my life. My heart was pounding as bright bolts of lightning spiked downwards from the sky, striking the grass around me and leaving patches of scorched earth. I needed to run faster. I looked over at Dad. He had the same panicked look in his eyes as I had. We weren't going to make it to the parking lot in time. We needed to take a short-cut.

"Run!" Dad shouted. "Over the fence!"

Between us and the parking lot was a small metallic fence. We both ran for it.

The lightning struck the ground again. It was like it wanted to hit us!

We both reached the fence at the same time, we grabbed it and...

The world went a maze of colors. And then it turned black.

"Mr. Stevenson, you can open your eyes now." The

doctor's soft voice pulled me out of my waking dream and back to his office. I didn't want to open my eyes, just in case I got struck by lightning again, so I only opened one, looking at my surroundings.

A pale yellow ceiling with a fan and odd looking stains had replaced the dark gray skies. The walls were covered by bookshelves, filled to the brim with hundreds of heavy looking books that were probably really *really* boring. One wall, however, was a window. A deep orange light shone through, indicating that the sun was setting for the evening. There was no sign of a storm. Everything was fine. I finally opened both eyes.

The couch I was lying on was comfy, even if it did smell like old coffee and sweat. Across from me, perched on a wooden chair, was the psychiatrist Doctor James Turner. He was yet another name on the growing list of people who thought there was something wrong in my head.

"And how did being struck by lightning make you *feel?*" he asked, peering over down his long, pointed nose which reminded me a little bit of a crow. Doctor Turner, it turned out, asked a lot of questions like that. He liked to know how things made you feel.

"Well," I frowned. "I guess it *hurt*, although I passed out so I can't really remember."

"Interesting. Interesting." Dr. Turner started scribbling notes down on the notepad he had on his lap and scratched the white, wispy beard which stuck out of his chin. I tried to glance at the notes he was taking, looking for the words 'Loony' and 'should be locked up in a padded cell,' but his handwriting was even worse than mine! The words seemed to gather together in one endless collection of letters.

Patientseemstobeundertheimpressionthatheistrappedi nsidehisfather'sbody.Isthissomekindofschizophrenia?

I gave up and listened to the sound of his pen scratching the paper while I studied one of the brown stains on the ceiling. The stain looked a bit like a puppy which had bat wings. A bat dog. Maybe it could fight crime.

Dr. Turner finally cleared his throat, looking up. "How does that make you feel?" he asked.

"How does *what* make me feel?" I asked.

He shook his head. "Oh right, sorry. Force of habit." He glanced down at his notes again. "And after this you..." he wiggled his pen in my direction, as if he was too scared to say the words. I glanced toward the corner of the room. My dad was sitting on another wooden chair, staring at me and shaking his head. At least, *I* knew it was my dad. He didn't want me to say anything, but I'd had enough of hiding it.

I nodded. "Yes, *that's* when me and Dad *swapped bodies.*"

If anyone else had looked at the corner of the room, they would have seen a twelve-year-old boy dressed in jeans and a white t-shirt with his black hair neatly combed (Dad had an annoying habit of combing it when I wasn't looking). They would have seen *me*.

And if they had looked at me, they would have seen a man in his late thirties, wearing an untucked shirt which probably needed ironing, and trousers covered in food stains. They would have seen David Stevenson, my dad. But as a really smart guy once said, *you can't judge a book by its cover* (which is very true, I generally google them first).

. "I am Jack Stevenson, *his* son." I thrust a finger at my dad, pointing accusingly at him. "That is my dad."

Dr. Turner frowned and turned to the corner of the room.

"And you are..." he paused, almost as if he had to force himself to say the words. "David Stevenson?"

Dad looked from me to the doctor, almost as if he hadn't expected to be involved in this conversation. He looked me dead in the eye and I knew what he was going to say. We had driven all the way here (not easy to do when you've only driven four times and you're a twelve-year-old stuck in a thirty-five-year-old's body!), talked with this doctor for what felt like weeks, spilled the beans on everything to him, and Dad was going to reply with one word that would ruin it all.

"No," Dad said quietly. "I'm Jack."

The doctor nodded and started to write in his notepad again.

I sat up, furious. "But he's *lying,* can't you see? He doesn't *want* me to tell you the truth because…."

The doctor looked up at me. "Could you lie back down on the couch, please?"

I looked at the brown leather couch. "Sorry," I mumbled, lying back down and staring at the ceiling. "He's lying."

Dr. Turner stopped writing. "How does that make you *feel?*"

He made me tell him the story over and over for what felt like a thousand times. We were only meant to see him for an hour, but he made it feel like a lifetime. Finally, after telling him the story once more, and watching him jot down even *more* notes, I heard him sigh.

We sat in silence for what felt like a long time. I stared angrily at Dad, but it didn't work because he was busy examining his shoes. Sorry, MY *shoes*. He even had the shoe laces tied up. Who *does* that?

"Right, Mr. Stevenson, our hour is almost up and I think I can help you," Dr. Turner finally said.

There was a surge of excitement through my body. Could he help me? Did he know what to do to get me back into my own body? I sat up on the sofa. "Yes?" I asked. "What do you want me to do?"

Dr. Turner scratched his nose before answering. "I think you need a *holiday,* Mr. Stevenson. Maybe it's the stress, maybe it's some side effect of thinking you were struck by lightning…"

"I *was* struck by lightning!" I shouted. "So was Dad!"

"You may think you were, but there is no *evidence,*"

Dr. Turner said. "I think what's best for you now is a holiday, maybe for a month or...."

"I *can't!*" Dad suddenly chirped up. "I mean... *he* can't! He's a teacher and the school fair is only two weeks away and..."

I gave Dad a death-stare and he quieted down.

Dr. Turner frowned. "I see, being a teacher is a lot of responsibility." He glanced down at his notes. "Alright then. Two weeks. You can work for another two weeks until after your school fair, then you will come back here and we will assess whether you need a holiday or not. But you need to try to keep calm and avoid stressful situations, okay?"

Dr. Turner looked at me. I looked at Dad. Dad looked at the floor.

Two weeks. Two weeks to figure out this body swapping mess and get everything back to normal.

"Okay, sounds good." I swallowed.

Two weeks. How hard could it be?

# Band (needs) Practice

*Stay calm. Avoid stressful situations.* The words echoed in my head as I pressed my ear to the cold wooden door to my garage and tried to resist the urge to burst through it. It was Sunday, and that meant one thing: band practice. Every week, my best friend, Tom, and my girlfriend, Holly, came round my house and we rocked out in my garage to songs from our favorite band: the Spiky Monkeys. We were even starting to develop some of our own songs. At least, that was what it *used* to be like.

I knew that this week would be different when I received a text from Tom which said:

Holly sez she is 2 ill. She's not coming 2 band 2moz.

Something was definitely off. Holly had *never* missed a practice. She was our lead singer after all. But I hadn't seen Holly since the dance a few weeks earlier, when I had tried to tell her about Dad and me swapping bodies. I had begged her to listen, but she had just gotten confused and run off.

Since then, she'd been avoiding both me and Dad.

To make things worse, we were playing at the school fair in two weeks and we needed the practice.

To make things *even* worse, I have never seen anyone play the drums *worse* that my dad, who was currently in the garage pretending to be me.

Tom, who played guitar for the band, was trying to keep it together, but I could hear he was failing. Dad couldn't hold a beat, not matter how hard he tried, and Tom was getting very frustrated.

"No!" he snapped, stopping them again for what felt like the fiftieth time in the last few minutes. "You're doing it again. Why do you keep hitting the cymbal so hard?"

There was a pause as Dad thought of an answer. "I thought it sounded awesome. Like Pa-**CHOW**." Dad smashed the cymbal again with his drumstick. What followed was the sound of the cymbal crashing onto the stone floor of the garage.

Tom sighed. "No."

I heard Dad fumbling around the side of the drum kit, trying to pick up the fallen cymbal. "Alright," he said. "Maybe if we go from the top again we can...."

Tom interrupted him. "Nah, I think we're good. Let's have a break."

It must have been just as bad as I thought it was. They had only been going for ten minutes.

"Plus," Tom said in a hushed voice. "I think your dad is hanging around outside again. It's a bit creepy."

"What?" Dad said in a loud voice. "That doesn't sound like my dad. He is a *great* and *respectful* parent. I WISH I WAS AS WONDERFUL AS HIM. I'LL GO CHECK OUTSIDE THE DOOR WHERE HE WILL NOT BE HIDING."

Dad got up and I looked around frantically for a place to hide. I was standing in the cramped utility room and there was only one place I could really stand apart from where I was now. I clambered into the bucket which was behind the door and held the mop in from of my face, praying that somehow my ninja skills were better than I thought. Slowly, the door creaked open.

Dad's head peeked out, and he cast a look around the room. He was about to say something when he turned and looked *right at me*. He shook his head. I grinned uncomfortably back at him.

"Nope," he said to Tom without taking his eyes off me. "Nothing out here except a *stupid looking mop*."

I opened my mouth to tell him that *he* was a stupid looking mop, but thought better of it. I would get him back later.

He rolled his eyes and went back into the garage.

"Huh," Tom said. "I thought I could hear him breathing."

"Probably just the house," Dad said too quickly.

"Yeah," Tom lied. "Probably."

There was another pause as I heard Tom putting his guitar away. "So," Tom said. "You know Ana?"

*Uh oh.* Tom had that excited '*I'm about to reveal big news*' voice. It was going to be the kind of news that needed to be shared with a best friend first. The kind of news that required the best friend to be supportive, excited and ready to celebrate its awesomeness. I knew it. I just hoped Dad did too.

"Ana Willet?" Dad said. "She's in your... *our* class. Of *course* I know her."

Tom had had a thing for Ana for a while, although he would never admit. I'd seen him staring at her in class, and whenever she tried to talk to him, it was like his tongue got twisted in a knot and he had fallen on his head. He talked completely nonsense. I'd been pressuring him to ask her out for a while, but Tom was reluctant to do something about it.

"Well, I danced with her at the dance," Tom said, the latches of his guitar case snapping shut.

My eyes opened wide. This *was* big news! If he had danced with her at the dance then... did he ask her out? Were they *dating* now? I wanted to run into the room, grab him by the shoulders and demand he told me everything! Excitement bubbled up inside me, only to quickly be replaced by dread. Dad didn't know any of this. He wouldn't know how to respond. Everything depended on how Dad answered right now. I silently prayed. Surely he couldn't mess it up, could he?

"Well done." Dad said. My prayers went unanswered. ASK HIM ABOUT HER! ASK HIM! I silently screamed at the door. He was so frustrating!

"Yeah, so we danced," Tom continued. "And theeeeeen..." he paused for dramatic effect. "I *asked her out.* She said yes!"

I did a little dance in the utility. *You go Tom!* I thought

107

to myself. Finally you've managed to-

"Are you sure that it is appropriate to be dating someone at school?" Dad said. My dance came to a sudden halt. WHAT DID HE SAY?! "I mean, you've got to focus on your studies and...."

I had to stop him. I had to end this conversation **now**. I grabbed onto the door handle and was about to burst into the room, but my feet got tangled in the bucket that I was still stood in. The floor suddenly got very close, very fast.

WHAM!

"Ow..." I whispered.

BOP!

The mop followed, the wooden handle smacking me on the back of the head. Stupid mop.

I lay on the floor and groaned.

"What was that?" Tom asked.

Slowly, the door opened and Tom peeked around the door. His eyes widened as he saw me on the floor, feet still in the bucket with the mop on my head.

"Mr. Stevenson!" he said. "Are you okay?"

I moved the strands of mop away from my face and looked up at him, ignoring the throbbing pain in the back of my head. "Oh hi, Tom, I didn't realize you were here," I said in my most normal sounding voice possible. "I was just doing some cleaning."

Dad's head poked around the door too. He raised his hand to his face and shook his head.

"I don't think that's how you use a mop..." Tom said quietly, as if hesitant to say such a thing to a teacher.

I looked down at my feet, then back up to him. I blew another strand of mop away from my mouth.

"You know, Tom," I said. "I think you're right."

# The Letter

Normally, I wouldn't be too worried about Dad being the *worst drummer in the universe*. We'd had bad practices before and, hopefully when this was over, we would have bad practices again. But the problem was that earlier in the year, we had auditioned to be the main headline band at the school fair and we had won! In the next two weeks, Dad and I needed to figure out how to swap back – otherwise the school fair would be ruined, and so would be my, and the band's, reputation. I mean, who was going to play if Dad couldn't figure out how to use the drums like a normal person and not an octopus being electrocuted?

Unfortunately, Tom had left shortly after that. There was a brief goodbye, which could only be described as 'painful,' between Tom and Dad, and then Tom had walked out of the house without another word. I offered him a lift home, hoping to pry some more information out of him about Holly, but he simply shook his head, waving a bus timetable at me before closing the door.

I sighed. *Stay calm*, I thought to myself. *It will all be fine*. Even as I thought it, I knew it was a lie. I was not any closer to figuring out how to turn back to normal, and my life as I knew it was crumbling. *What would go wrong next?*

My question was quickly answered by Dad clearing his throat. I turned to see him holding a white envelope in his hands. "I guess, as we've got a few more hours on our hands, now is the best time to mention this." He held the letter out to me.

It had already been opened, that was clear enough. In the center of the envelope was our address, above it the words:

TO THE PARENTS/GUARDIANS OF JACK STEVENSON

I took it from Dad and stared at it. "Looks official," I mumbled. Dad didn't respond. I instantly knew that it wasn't going to be a fun letter telling us we had won the lottery.

I pulled out the single white sheet of paper inside. When I saw the insignia on the top of the letter, my heart instantly sank. In big, black letters underneath were the words:

RIVERSIDE MIDDLE SCHOOL

It was a letter from my school! I glanced up at Dad, eyebrow raised. He avoided my gaze, in a similar way as I used to do when I was in trouble. I kept reading.

Dear Mr. Stevenson,

I am writing to you today on behalf of Mr. Thomas, teacher to your son, Jack Stevenson. Mr. Thomas has requested your presence for a parent-teacher meeting next Monday at 5pm. The subject of the meeting will be your son's failure to attend multiple detentions, despite being previously warned of the consequences.

Jack has apparently continued to resist Mr. Thomas's attempts to discipline him, although those attempts have followed school policy to the letter.

A meeting is therefore deemed necessary to discuss the future of Jack Stevenson at Riverside Middle School, in the hope of reaching an agreement that will satisfy both teacher and parent, whilst keeping Jack's, and the school's, best interests in mind.

We look forward to seeing you,

Mrs. Jade

School Receptionist

I looked down at the letter in my hands, reading it through again and again. I finally looked up at Dad.

"They sent a LETTER?!" I was surprised by how loud I shouted. Dad even flinched slightly. "You *missed* detentions? What were you even doing when I thought you were at them?!"

Dad spoke slowly and quietly. "I was catching up on the work I have been missing. Marking and so on."

I opened and closed my mouth. So *that* was how the marking was getting done. I assumed someone *else* did it and left it on the desk in the classroom every morning. I frowned. Then there was another surge of anger. "But what about the DETENTIONS? YOU AREN'T A TEACHER ANYMORE DAD!" *Stay calm,* a voice urged in my mind and I took a deep breath.

"You're not a teacher *either,*" Dad snapped back. "You're not an adult! You're just a twelve-year-old boy who is way out of his league."

*Out of his league.* Something about the way Dad said that stung. I looked down at the letter again, blinking the tears out of my eyes. I was trying as hard as I could, but everything I did seemed to end up creating more disaster.

Dad sighed. "I'm sorry, Jack. I went too far."

I took time to reply. "You're grounded," I said.

Dad frowned. "What?"

I took another deep breath, wiped my nose and looked him dead in the eye. "You're grounded. If *I* got a letter from school for misbehaving, you'd have grounded me. So I'm grounding you."

"You can't...but...." Dad spluttered and shook his head. "I'm *your father*! You can't ground me!"

"Yes, I can," I folded my arms and tried look as 'Dad-like' as possible. "You say I'm not an adult, well fine. I'll *act* more like an adult. And you need to *act* more like me, so go to your room!" I pointed upstairs.

Dad looked at me, then looked towards the stairs. He looked at me again. "You can't be serious."

I narrowed my eyes. "As serious as I'll ever be."

Dad was about to say something back but then his eyes softened. "Alright, Jack," he said. "I understand."

And with that, he turned and walked upstairs to his room!

I stood beside the front door, shaking a little. Did I just *ground* my dad? What did that mean? What was going to happen? I looked down at my hands. They were shaking. I decided to go and lie down on the couch for a while and wandered into the lounge.

As I lay down on the couch, I was instantly reminded of the visit to the doctor's and the fact that the clock was still ticking. I had less than two weeks to figure out what had made us change and somehow get us to change back. Sitting up, I stared at the television. Something had happened, something that had made us swap bodies, and I was going to figure it out.

# Parent-Teacher Teacher-Parent

It was after school on Monday, and we were sat outside Mr. Thomas's classroom, waiting to go in for the meeting. Dad had come down from his bedroom on Sunday and we had discussed how we would handle it. Dad had said that I should try *everything humanly possible* to get him out of detention. After all, he was innocent and didn't deserve the punishment! I remembered that I'd tried that line on Dad a few times, and he had totally ignored it. So I came up with a little plan of my own.

As we sat, I pulled out the letter again and read it for what felt like the hundredth time. I grinned as I did. I was starting to see the funny side of it. "I think we should get this framed and hang it up," I joked. "It would look good above the TV! I still can't believe you got a *letter sent home*."

Dad groaned and shook his head. "I don't want to talk about it."

I looked over at the door to Mr. Thomas's room. I could hear him moving around inside.

"I don't think you've got much of a choice," I grinned.

"Yes, well..." Dad began.

*Click.* The door slowly opened. Inside the classroom stood Mr. Thomas with a solemn, goblin-like face. He looked first at me and then at Dad. "Come in," he said. "We need to talk."

Dad glanced at me as Mr Thomas turned his back to us. I mimicked pointing a gun at my head and shooting.

Dad shook his head, but I could see he was trying not to smile. We both stood up and walked into the classroom.

It was strange, being back in my old classroom. Everything looked the same but... *different*. And that wasn't just because everything was smaller. I could see the boring posters put up on the far wall which had all the multiplication tables we needed to remember (in black and white of course, Mr. Thomas didn't like color), I could see the graphs and school work which had been hung on the other walls and doodled on by bored students. I could also see the famous 'motivational' poster that Mr. Thomas had hung over his desk. It was black and white (naturally) and simply read: I LOVE MATH.

Seriously, what kind of weirdo has *that* in their classroom?

It all felt familiar, but like it was part of some kind of past life, drifting away from me. A strange uncomfortable feeling passed over me, although I couldn't pin-point if it was due to the thought, or the fact that Mr. Thomas had two or three pictures of *himself* on his desk.

Dad and I were instructed to sit on two smaller chairs, while Mr. Thomas took up a higher position behind his desk. He reminded me of the judges I saw on those boring law shows that my dad liked to watch. I suddenly felt like Dad and I were on trial and if we didn't say the right things, we would end up in jail.

"David," Mr. Thomas said to me in a calm voice. "I have invited you here today to talk about Jack's behavior at school."

So far, so good. Everyone was calm, no one was overreacting, all was-

"Don't forget to mention how you accused me of cheating *without evidence*," Dad chirped up.

I saw Mr. Thomas twitch slightly. He seemed to swallow whatever he was about to say, and closed his eyes for a second. "As you can see," he continued, "Jack has…*trouble* when it comes to respecting authority. Now, this is nothing new, I've seen it for a while, but recently…."

"Hang on." It was my turn to interrupt. "You've seen this for a *while*?"

"Oh, yes," Mr. Thomas nodded. "He has been quite the thorn in my side for a while, but you see, David, over the last few weeks he has become *increasingly insolent*."

I looked at Dad, my eyebrows raised in mock surprise. "Really? I'm very disappointed to hear this, Jack." Something bubbled inside my stomach. I had to really focus to stop myself from giggling.

Dad took a deep breath. "I just think...."

Mr. Thomas interrupted him. "I have *tried* various methods of discipline. I have made him write lines, I have kept him in at break, I have even tried detention for a week but he had *resisted* all attempts to...."

"No!" shouted Dad. "You have no *right* to punish me because you have no *proof* that I cheated!"

We had decided to try and keep things *calm* and *easy*, but it looked like that idea had just flown out of the window.

"Proof?" screeched Mr. Thomas, standing up from the desk. "You want proof?" He stormed across the classroom, sat down at his desk, opened up a drawer and pulled out a piece of paper waving it in front of Dad's face. "Here is your proof!"

I looked at the paper. It was an old test I did *before* Dad and I had our swap. The test had a big F in red pen scribbled onto the top. I shuffled uncomfortably on my feet. During that particular test, I had tried texting Tom under the table for the answers, as I had been too busy gaming to prepare for it. It turns out, he hadn't prepared for it either as he had been playing exactly the same game.

"No one goes from an F to an A+ in a week! No one!" Mr. Thomas slammed the sheet down on the table in front of Dad. Dad stood up, ready to match Mr. Thomas blow for blow.

I could see Dad was *furious*. It was a very strange scenario, because it was one I had been in so many times before, but I was where my dad was sitting now. I could almost exactly pinpoint his feelings right now. Betrayal. Anger. Embarrassment. It was all there on his face.

He stood his ground. "Maybe I just *prepared* for the exam. Where is your faith? You pick on me during class. You don't listen to what I have to say. You are a *bad teacher*."

Mr. Thomas's eyes widened. There was a moment of silence as his brain processed what had just been said to him.

I looked between Dad and Mr. Thomas as they stood, facing each other, their faces red and twitching. I could tell this wasn't going to end well, but I couldn't deny that it wasn't *awesome*. It was better than any TV show I had ever watched. Even better, Dad now knew exactly how it felt to be me. How Mr. Thomas had made every moment in his math class a living hell for me ever since I started at this school. Dad *knew* what it was like to be me.

But instead of shouting and screaming, Mr. Thomas suddenly backed off. He turned towards me and said in a completely calm voice: "You see,, *David*, *this* is the kind of behavior I have been referring to. It happens here before your very eyes."

I glanced towards Dad. I think he had managed to

*break* Mr. Thomas.

I snorted out a laugh. Both Mr Thomas and Dad turned to me with shocked looks on their faces. I covered my mouth, trying to pretend I was coughing.

"Sorry," I said quickly. I put my *serious adult face* on. "Please continue, Mr. Thomas. Er...*Rodney*."

His name was Rodney Thomas. I tried not to burst out in a fit of giggles again just saying it.

Mr Thomas didn't seem to notice. He just nodded and continued, "I think the best course of action right now would be to continue the discipline at *home* as well as at school. Clearly, Jack has some control issues that he needs to overcome. Both you and I need to stand strong on this together. I suggest he does more work at home, to make up for the time he is wasting at school. *Triple homework*."

The words *triple homework* felt like a dagger to the gut. I didn't think anyone could be that cruel.

Dad almost exploded. "*Triple!* Are you *insane*? You only need to take that course of action for *really* misbehaving students! All I have done is do really well on a test and challenge you when you accused me of cheating without evidence! I think this is highly inappropriate don't you, Ja... Dad?"

He managed to hold it together enough to stop himself from calling me Jack, but *barely*. Dad stared at me pleadingly and I looked between Mr Thomas and him. A small devil on my shoulder whispered into my ear.

I adjusted myself in my seat and cleared my throat. "Well," I began. "I can see what Mr. Thomas is saying, Jack. I mean, maybe you just need something to help you *focus* more at home."

A small smile spread across my face. I was repeating words Dad had said to me a few weeks earlier, when we had attended a *different* parent-teacher meeting with my art teacher, Miss Pomp. She believed more focus at home would help me 'become a better artist'. I didn't agree.

Dad opened his mouth to protest but, as realization spread across his eyes, he sagged a little and said quietly: "I see."

But I wasn't done. It was pushing it, I could tell, but if Dad wanted to be able to act like me, he had to *understand* what it was like to be me. "Also, I feel an *apology* is required to really set everything straight here, between teacher and student."

Dad looked up at me with eyes I recognized too well. He was shocked and horrified. Mr Thomas, however, thought it was a *wonderful* idea and sat behind his desk, nodding enthusiastically.

"Oh yes, that would be *greatly* appreciated," Mr Thomas said. A wide grin spread across his face, like that of an alligator having just found the hunter who made his mother into a handbag.

Dad took a deep breath. It seemed to take every single muscle in his body to force the words out of his mouth. "I'm... *sorry*, Mr Thomas. It won't happen again. I was out of line."

He stared at me the entire time he said it.

I was definitely in trouble now.

# Betrayal

We were halfway out of school when Dad finally burst into an angry shout: "You made me *apologize!*"

I couldn't help the smile that popped back onto my face. "Yeah," I said. "Being forced to do something you don't want to do must be *horrible*. I wonder what *that* is like." I let the words hang in the air between us. He knew exactly what I meant. After all, he'd made me apologize to the football team for being late and embarrassed me beyond belief just a few weeks ago!

Dad stood in my way, bringing me to a halt. "You and I need to *talk*, mister. I think you're letting this *adult* thing go to your head!"

I nodded. "Uh huh, uh huh."

I wasn't really listening. I was distracted by the two figures coming out of the sports hall in front of us. I frowned. Why was anyone still in the school at this hour? Did *more* people have parent-teacher meetings? Then I remembered. Today was the day of the *school fair meeting*! I grabbed Dad by the collar and dragged him behind a nearby tree. Dad was still ranting about the apology as I did.

"We need to-Ow!" Dad snapped. "What are you doing?"

"Shhhhh!" I put my finger to my lips and pointed at the door to the hall. We both turned to look.

Standing by the exit was Tom, and following closely was...Holly! I couldn't help but smile when I saw her again, her blonde hair shining in the sunset; I realized how long it had been since I'd last seen her. I mean, we had spent almost *every day* together since we started dating. Now, after a few days, it felt like I hadn't seen her in years.

My smile faded as I remembered what had happened at the dance. I had managed to mess things up completely. Did she even want to talk to me anymore?

I wanted to jump out from behind the tree and try to explain everything to her again. Explain that Dad was me and that was why he was acting so crazy. But I held my tongue and stayed hidden. Trying that had gone *so* well last time.

Both Tom and Holly were helpers for the fair. Holly was on the decorating team because she was so good at art. She was in charge of painting the large, colorful banners that were hung all around the school and said, COME TO THE SCHOOL FAIR. They looked pretty impressive: most of them were bigger than Dad and I combined!

Tom, who could usually compete with me for the laziness prize, had *somehow* gotten involved, too. He was on the music team, which I suspected was due to the fact that his mom was friends with Mr. Gibbins, the music teacher. I couldn't complain, though, because Mr. Gibbins had also got our band an audition to play at the fair, and now, because we were so awesome, we were headlining the whole thing. It was going to be our big break. A cold sadness flowed through me as I thought about the band. I focused on what was in front of me.

Tom and Holly walked together, coming towards the tree that Dad and I were hiding behind. We both shrank back into the bushes, trying to stay invisible, but also to hear what they were saying.

"So," Tom said. He scratched the back of his neck, which is something I know he does when he's about to begin a conversation he is uncomfortable with. "Have you talked to Jack recently?"

My smile was back. My buddy Tom! He was trying to get her to think about me. That's why Tom was my best friend. He was always sticking up for me.

Holly shook her head. "I don't want to talk about it."

Tom nodded and then stopped in his tracks, speaking quickly, as if the words were flying uncontrollably out of his mouth.

"Don't you think he's been acting a bit strange?"

"What?" said Holly, stopping as well.

Tom took a breath. "Do you think Jack has been acting...you know...*strange*?"

And the smile was gone again. I knew that Holly was upset with me, but now Tom was as well? They were beginning to notice how strange "I" was acting. It was Dad's fault. Sometimes I did wonder: had Dad *never* been a kid before? Maybe it was just so long ago, he had forgotten all about it.

Even now, as we crouched behind the bushes, he pulled the bottom of his pants (*my pants*) up so they wouldn't get muddy on the floor. He also crouched straight-backed so he wouldn't touch the tree or mess up the other clothes he was wearing. Dad shook his head as he listened, but also took the time to pick up some rubbish on the floor. I stared him in horror as he took little, quiet steps over to the nearby trash can and dropped the rubbish in.

*Crunch.*

We both flinched as the trash rattled at the bottom, but luckily neither Tom nor Holly seemed to notice. I glared at him and he shrugged.

Holly spoke again. "So, it *isn't* just me who's been noticing."

"No," said Tom. "I mean, first it was just little things like the skate park and band practice, but then the whole thing with Jasmine." Tom's voice trailed off.

I bit back the anger which bubbled in my throat. *Jasmine.* That was another of Dad's attempts to 'help out'. He had thought it a good idea to ask Jasmine Walder, one of the nerdiest and most annoying girls at school, to the dance, instead of my *girlfriend* Holly.

At least, I *hoped* Holly was still my girlfriend.

Holly's jaw tightened at the mention of Jasmine's name. She turned towards the tree, making both Dad and I duck down even further behind the bushes. A leaf on the bush tickled the end of my nose. It began to itch. I ignored it.

"Yes, well, Jack can make his own decisions. He clearly isn't interested in *me* anymore," Holly said, folding her arms.

The urge to leap out from behind the bush and tell her that she was wrong and I *was* still interested suddenly grew very strong inside me.

Dad must have seen on it on my face because he grabbed my arm and shook his head. I looked at him. It was his turn to raise his finger to his lips.

I looked back at my friends. The leaf wiggled a bit more. My nose twitched in response.

Tom shifted uncomfortably. "Yeah, I don't think he is *interested* in anything we want to do anymore. He seems to have given up on the drums, and now he's too busy *working* to even acknowledge me during lessons."

I turned to Dad and frowned at him. Who *works* at school?

"And what about Mr. Stevenson?" Holly suddenly said. "What do you think about him?"

Tom blinked. "Well... I mean, he's alright, I guess."

"He's acting strange as well. You know he came up to me after the dance and said all kinds of weird things like...."

"Like what?" Tom asked. Tension gripped my gut. Was she going to tell him? After the dance, I had run after Holly and tried to tell her everything. That I was Jack, her boyfriend, and that I hadn't forgotten about her like it seemed.

The only thing I had managed to do was freak her out (which I guess makes sense when a *teacher* tries to convince you that he is your boyfriend...ew) and I hadn't seen her since. Well, not until now, but I guess hiding behind a tree didn't really count.

Holly thought about it and changed her mind. "I don't know. It was just *weird*."

Tom nodded. "You know, Mr. Stevenson keeps listening to our band practices now? Last time I saw him hiding in a bucket behind a mop, and Jack pretended to not even see him! I just played along with it, but I'm not sure why."

Dad glanced at me with a raised eyebrow. I clenched my fists and felt the heat rise to my face. I was *sure* he didn't see anything, but I guess I was wrong.

"Isn't he dating your mom?" Holly asked.

Tom swallowed. "Yeah."

"Maybe he shouldn't," Holly said, shrugging.

There was a long pause as what Holly had said hung in the air around us like a cloud of noxious gas. Nobody said anything. Nobody moved. Dad's frown deepened. He looked as worried as I felt.

Now, I'll admit, dating my best friend's mom while pretending to be my dad had been... weird. There were some strange moments that I would rather not think about, but as I looked at the way Tom thought about what Holly had just said, I was *offended*. I mean, sure, I hadn't been the *best* date, but it had been all right.

Then Tom spoke: "Yeah, I think you're right."

I went cold. The itch in my nose became irresistible and I began to twitch uncontrollably.

I was going to....

I was.... A... a.....

Dad leaned over and clamped a hand over my mouth. I twitched a little bit, but managed to stop myself from sneezing. We both stared at each other in horror.

Here we were, listening to my friends, or at least people who I *thought* were my friends, as they plotted against us. As they walked past, I sank down completely to the floor. Dad sat next to me and we listened in silence to their footsteps disappearing into the distance.

Dad spoke first. "Wow," he said. "We are doing a *terrible job*."

He was right. I had spent all this time blaming *Dad* for doing a terrible job at being me, but I hadn't thought about how much I was messing up *his* life. I suddenly felt lost and unsure about what to do next. My head rested against the rough bark of the tree.

"I thought friends were supposed to have your back," I mumbled.

Then, to complete my feeling of total misery and rejection, a drip of rain fell onto my forehead. I glanced up. The sky was turning a dark gray color.

"Come on," said Dad, standing up. "Not much more we can do sitting around here. Let's get to the bus stop before the storm gets here."

*Before the storm gets here.* The words rang inside my head, sparking an idea into life. I suddenly pushed myself to my feet. I knew what we had to do!

"Follow me!" I said to Dad, breaking into a run down

124

the path.

"Wait!" he called after me, but I was already gone.

# The Storm: Round 2

My mind was so focused on my destination that I didn't hear Dad calling for me to stop. I pushed on through the school grounds, ignoring everything else as I put one foot in front of the other, my mind having one thought running through it: *The storm. There's a storm coming.* I didn't even notice the rain getting harder, slamming into my face like small, cold daggers, running down my chin and flattening my hair against my head.

By the time I reached my destination, I looked and felt like a drowned rat. Dad was breathing heavily, having to jog to keep up with me.

"Why?" He took another breath. "Why have we come back here Jack?"

We both looked at the football field in front of us. It was getting late now, and there was no one around, not even a janitor.

Dad shouted at me again through the rain. "We should be inside!"

"I'm waiting," I replied, looking up at the black sky.

The wall of rain closed in, making it hard to see much apart from what was right in front of us. The clouds twisted and turned like black eels in a bucket, all fighting to be at the top. We stood in the middle of the football field. The same place where it had all began. Where the storm had swapped us around. I stood and waited. Then, it happened.

## RUMBLE RUMBLE

The sound that came from the sky reminded me of my stomach when I woke up in the morning with a serious craving for breakfast. The storm was getting closer. I was going to fix this once and for all. At least, that was my plan, but then Dad caught on with what I was trying to do.

"You *can't* do this, Jack! It isn't going to work."

I turned to him, brushing the rain out of my eyes.

"You don't know that!" I said. I walked over to the small metallic fence between us and the parking lot and place my hand on it, looking at Dad. "If lightning strikes us again, we'll swap back!" I grinned. "We need to get this sorted. What better way to do it?"

"*Any* idea is better than getting struck by lightning *again!*" Dad shouted back over the howling wind.

Alright, I admit, maybe I wasn't thinking straight. I mean, I had just seen my two best friends discussing how they were going to betray me. But if it *did* work, then none of that would matter because everything would go back to normal. I could apologize to Holly, maybe pretend I was working *undercover* as a spy! That meant I had to go to the dance with Jasmine because *the fate of the entire planet rested on my shoulders!* She'd believe that. Right?

"Well, it's the best idea I can come up with at the moment!" I said, putting my other hand on the fence as well. "So let's do this. Grab this fence!"

Dad shook his head. "We don't know what will happen, Jack. We could be seriously injured."

"At this point, does it really matter?" I shouted into the sky. "My friends have abandoned me, I'm failing at being an adult, why don't we just take the risk?"

Dad's shoulder's sagged and he shook his head. He mumbled something to himself that was lost on the wind and then placed a hand on my shoulder.

"No," said Dad, "this isn't the way to do it."

"But," I began.

"I know you're feeling let down. By your friends, by *me*, by everyone. I've got my share of responsibility, and I'm *sorry.*"

"What's that got to do with it?" I started again, my eyes burning slightly (it was probably the rain, not tears. Absolutely).

"I know it seems like there is no other way out, but a solution that could leave you or both of us seriously injured, isn't a solution at all. We've just got to figure out another way."

"But we don't know how to figure it out!" I shouted back. "I mean, what if this solves it once and for all? I don't want to be stuck like this forever!"

"It won't," Dad said.

I sighed. "But how can you be certain?"

Dad pointed up at the sky. "Look." I looked up. The clouds had begun to pass us by. The dark gray sky was getting clearer by the second. The rain had gone from a torrent to a light shower. I hit the fence in annoyance. "Ugh, we were so *close*," I snapped. "I could feel it!" That was when the pain kicked in on the palm of my hand. Ow! Hitting metallic objects *hurts*.

Dad shrugged. "Maybe next time." He put a hand on my shoulder (he probably would have put his arm around me, but I was *much* taller than him) and we started to walk back across the field.

"Do you ever feel like no matter what we do, it all goes wrong?" I sighed.

Dad nodded. "Yes, a little." He paused. "What we really need," he said, looking up at the sky, "is some sort of **plan**."

I stopped in my tracks. I turned towards Dad, a slow grin spreading across my face. Now he was speaking my language! If we could work *together*, we could show my friends that everything was fine. We could show them that all their worries were for nothing.

"A **plan**, you say?" My smile grew even wider as ideas began to sprout in my head.

Dad frowned. "I'm going to regret this, aren't I?"

# A (New) Master Plan

We missed the bus and had to walk home. By the time we arrived, we were wet, cold and tired, so Dad decided that the best idea would be to sit on the lounge floor, wrapped in blankets, with a cup of warm coco. I decided that maybe this working together thing wouldn't be so bad after all! It was very unlike us. I don't even let Dad sit near me when I'm playing games, never mind having him on my team!

When we both finally stopped shivering, Dad got up and retrieved a notepad from his desk, along with two pens. He tore out a page and placed it on the floor in front of me.

I looked down at it. "What's that for?"

"Homework," he said.

"Bleugh!" I stuck out my tongue. "I don't want to do any *homework*!"

Dad rolled his eyes. "Believe me, I am painfully aware of that. But if I'm going to be a good *you* and you're going to be a good *me*, we need to write down what the other person needs to do. Just a short list to begin with."

I grimaced at the thought of having to *write* something down, but I couldn't argue with him. Reluctantly, I picked up the pen and began to write. This is what my list looked like:

### *HOW TO BE JACK (AKA THE COOLEST KID IN THE UNIVERSE)*

1. *Show Tom ur still cool!*
2. *Make sure you don't act <u>uncool</u> in front of Holly.*
3. *<u>Figure out how to play the drums</u> (Scool fair. V. important)*
4. *Stop brushing my hair! It looks weerd!*
5. *Play games. Minecraft, Skylanders, etc.*
6. *Buy me a new games console.*
7. *Do the triple homework (so u don't get in trubble)*
8. *<u>STOP HANGING OUT WITH JASMINE</u>*

I underlined the last one twice just so Dad would get the idea. For effect, I then drew a little picture of me wearing sunglasses and wrote KEWL GUY underneath it so he *really* got it (diagrams always help). Once I finished, I sat and waited for Dad to finish his, and then we swapped our lists. Here is the list that Dad gave me:

### HOW TO BE DAD

- *Make sure Sarah is OK. She is a kind-hearted woman.*
- *Be a good and respectful teacher – Help the pupils out (if you don't know the answer, try to get them to figure it out)*
- *DO NOT DRIVE THE CAR YOU ARE TOO YOUNG AND GO TOO FAST*
- *Wear neat clothes (tuck in your shirts!)*
- *Be polite*
- *Don't forget to wash your face and brush your hair before you leave!*
- *Do your homework. I'm not going to do it for you. (So you don't get in trouble)*

Dad frowned as he read my list. "This is filled with spelling mistakes. You even spelled school wrong."

I shrugged. "Blame my teachers," I said with a grin.

Dad frowned even more (I didn't think it was possible!) "Why have you put 'Buy me a new games console' on here?" he asked.

"I thought it would be a good idea. You could invite Tom around and play it and he would forgive me in a flash!"

Dad shook his head. "What's wrong with the one you have?" He pointed towards the old console, gathering dust underneath our television. I looked at it sadly. I hadn't been giving it the time it needed recently, with everything that was going on.

"It's not *next gen*," I said plainly. "They have better graphics, better games...."

Dad had already picked up his pen again and was

about to cross it off my list. "Nope," he said.

I quickly grabbed my pen as well. "I guess you won't mind if I…go for a drive in the car then," and prepared to cross out one of *his* list. The 'working together' thing was already going really well.

Dad sighed, lowering the pen. "I'll *think* about it."

I grinned. Excitement rose inside me as I imagined playing a next-gen console on a big widescreen TV that took up the entire wall. I could just lie down on the couch and, no matter where I looked, I would see the game. It would be heaven.

"Also, I think you're wrong about Jasmine. She's a lovely girl."

I shook my head. "No, she isn't."

"You just need to give her a chance. I know you think she's *nerdy*, but if you were her friend…."

"I'd lose all my other friends, my reputation, and could pretty much kiss any chance of a happy life goodbye!"

Dad didn't say anything. He knew I was right, I could tell.

He stared down at my list and clicked his tongue against the top of his mouth. "I guess we have a basic idea of what we need to do now," he said. "But there's one more thing I want to try."

Five minutes later, Dad had torn all the pages out of the note book, written something on all of them and had made two little piles between us. I drank my coco, which was rapidly getting cooler, until he looked up at me with a smile.

"I've made a little game," he said.

*If he's made it, it's probably boring*, I thought to myself, but didn't let it show on my face. "Oh yes?"

He pointed at the left pile. "Pick one up."

I did as he asked and read what was written. The card said:

*You bump into Mr. Gibbins who is drinking tea in the staff room at the end of the day.*
*He sees you and begins to strike up a conversation about music.*
*You don't know what he is talking about.*
*What do you do?*

"Ahh," I said. "I see. What would *you* do? I have to pretend I am you."

Dad nodded. "Well?"

I thought about it. "Ugh, tell him he is *lame*," I joked. Dad frowned. "Okay, okay," I sighed. "I would, tell him that I have a meeting and don't have time to chat. Laugh at the incredibly boring music joke he will definitely make and think is *hilarious*, and then leave the room."

The problem with Mr. Gibbins was that he thought he was the funniest guy on the planet. The other problem was that no one else on the planet actually thought that.

Dad nodded. "Very good."

"Also, tell him he is lame," I added quickly.

Dad rolled his eyes, picked up a note from the right hand pile and handed it to me. "Read it," he said.

"Ahem," I cleared my throat. "So, Tom has suggested that we go to the skate park after school. We can hang out and do awesome things, what do you say?"

Dad scrunched up his face, thinking of a response. He nodded. "Ok, I have this. I would say to him *That's awesome* and we would *begin* to go and then," he paused. "I would say that I couldn't because I am grounded and it *sucks*. Then I would leave."

I nodded. "Yeah, that seems like a good plan."

The game went on for an hour or so. We tested each other on different scenarios, tried to make things hard, mix it up more. By the time our eyes began to close and night had fallen outside, I felt more… confident.

I allowed myself to think that maybe we would be able to turn this around for a little while, and then we could focus on getting ourselves back to normal.

"Two weeks," I said to myself as I curled up into my bed. "We'll have this down in two weeks." I yawned and prepared to sleep better than I had in a while.

After all, we had the start of a **plan**. What could possibly go wrong?

# Date Night

The **plan**, I decided, would be codenamed:
**SUPERMASTERAWESOME.** After all, any plan needs a
decent name, right? And nothing screamed "THIS IS A
PLAN WHICH IS DEFINITELY GOING TO WORK OUT!"
more than a plan named: **SUPERMASTERAWESOME.**

The first step in the plan was to kill two birds with
one stone, which basically meant that we were going to take
the first thing on my list – "Show Tom u r still cool" – and
the first thing on Dad's list – "Make sure Sarah is okay, blah
blah" – and work on them both at the same time.

How were we going to do this? Well, Dad decided
that if he was going to have to game with Tom, I was going
to have to do something with Sarah, which meant another
date.

Yay?

Our plan went into action after school on Wednesday.
I managed to invite Sarah out to the movies (despite Tom's
many attempts to distract her while we were talking), and
persuaded her that our car had broken down, so she needed
to pick us up from school (that was Dad's idea. He was
really pushing the 'no driving' rule! You get trouble with the
police *once*…).

When Sarah's car pulled up beside the road and Dad
and I got in, I knew that **SUPERMASTERAWESOME** was
in effect.

It was a foolproof plan.

As she drove us home, to drop off Tom and my dad
so they could game together, she turned to me and asked:
"So what's wrong with your car?"

"Well…er…" I glanced back at Dad. I didn't know
anything about cars! Dad, it turns out, didn't really know
either. He just stared at me blankly and shrugged.

"Er…" I tried again. What do cars have? Wheels?
Mirrors? Er… Windows? "One of the… rear flow tubes

is...er... snapped."

Was a flow tube a thing? I had no idea. I hoped Sarah had no idea either.

"Oh no!" she said. "You know, I have a cousin who's a mechanic. I could give him a call and...."

"I'm sure it will be fine," I said slightly too quickly. "I mean, those crazy flow tubes right? Always breaking. Not so hard to replace."

I could feel Dad cringing behind me as the lie grew and grew.

"Yeah..." said Sarah as we pulled up outside our house.

I got out to let Dad and Tom inside. Dad chose that moment to walk up to me and hiss: "Are you *sure* that you know what you're doing?"

I waved a hand at him. "Of course I do. We played the game with the cards, didn't we?" I turned the key in the door.

"Yes, but cards are very different from...."

"Have fun!" I said in a loud voice, letting Tom inside. He smiled at me, but I could tell he wasn't looking forward to gaming. I silently prayed that *Dad* knew what *he* was doing. I turned back to the car and clambered back into it. Sarah's smiling face greeted me. She tucked a strand of brown hair behind her ear.

"It was nice of you to call. I didn't think we would be doing this again, after the dance and..." She trailed off. "Well, it doesn't matter now."

A few weeks earlier, I had abandoned her during the school dance to talk to Holly (remember that disaster?). After that, Dad had assumed the worst (that Sarah would never talk to him again) but the fact the she was here said differently.

"I guess I missed you," I said with a smile.

Sarah nodded, smiling herself, and started the car.

The drive to the movie theater wasn't too

136

uncomfortable. Sarah talked about her work (something about 'insurance'- I have no idea what that is, but it sounds *really* boring) and I managed to get away with nodding and saying 'Uh huh' occasionally. She asked me a question once (she was asking about the *government* and what it was *doing*. I hadn't got a clue!), and after a terrifying pause, I just shrugged. That seemed to be enough of an answer for her, luckily.

The theater was in the center of town. I'd only been there a few times since I was a kid, and it always looked the same. A large CINEMA sign on the front with a missing letter, a red carpet with odd stains leading to the ticket office. Everything smelled of popcorn.

"What do you want to see?" Sarah asked, glancing at the board. These were the choices we had:

**LOVE: A LOVE STORY OF LOVE** (It sounded awful. Plus Dad told me not to go for anything romantic, so I crossed this one off the list.)

**ROBOTSMASHER: HE SMASHES BECAUSE HE'S**

**A ROBOT** (I liked the idea, but when we walked in Sarah had looked at the poster of an awesome robot smashing things and rolled her eyes, so that one was off the list)

**TINY TIM'S TINY LAND OF MAGIC** (This one was for three-year-olds. NOPE)

**CROCO-VILE: THE RAMPAGE OF THE CROCODILE WHO IS REALLY VILE!** (I've already seen this one. It was EPIC.)

**SNATCHED 5: SHE GOT SNATCHED AGAIN** (They should have stopped making *these* movies a long time ago. I didn't need to see another one.)

The choice was limited. In fact Dad had given me a whole list of rules about movies I wasn't allowed to see, that it pretty much stopped me from seeing any.

"How about that one?" I asked.

The board said:

**THE LONELY HOUSE ON DEATH STREET Rated: MA 15+**

Sarah frowned. "Isn't that a horror film?"

I shrugged. "Not a clue." I was lying, of course. Tom had shown me the trailer. It was about a man who goes crazy and then goes on a killer chainsaw rampage of death! Tom and I both agreed that it looked AWESOME. There was no way my dad would ever let me see it, but a small part of me wanted to try it out, just to see if I could take advantage of the situation.

She grinned. "Alright then."

I paused for a second. I couldn't believe my luck. I still couldn't believe my luck when we went up to the ticket booth and bought two tickets without the ticket seller even blinking an eye! He just smiled at us and said, "Enjoy the show."

I grinned back and said: "Thanks!"

Sarah laughed at we went into the darkened cinema, choosing two seats close to the back so we would get the best view.

"I've never seen a horror film before," Sarah whispered in my ear as the lights went down. "I hope it's not too scary."

I grinned. "How scary can it be? I mean, it probably looks really fake and cheesy."

Sarah nodded. "Yeah, probably." She didn't sound too confident.

What followed was *not* what I had expected. It started off alright, a story about a man living in a house by himself. But when he found the chainsaw and the INCREDIBLY REALISTIC BLOOD started to spray everywhere, I started to feel a bit sick.

Every time the crazed chainsaw guy ran onto the screen, he gave a creepy laugh which sounded like HA *ha* HA *ha!* I knew I would be hearing it in my nightmares for weeks. To make things even worse, Sarah would scream loudly at the slightest jump and then cling onto my arm, burying her head into my shoulder. At one point, she even grabbed my hand too, squeezing it so hard I was sure it was going to explode! I tried to comfort her by lightly tapping her on the head a few times, but soon I found myself watching through my fingers as well.

No matter how hard I tried, she would *not* let go of my hand. Even when it got super sweaty. It was really weird.

The screams of the unfortunate teenagers still rang in my ears when the lights finally came up. Sarah and I sat in silence.

"That was..." she began.

"...horrifying?" I finished.

To my surprise, Sarah laughed. "Oh thank goodness," she said. "I thought you were going to love it and make us watch another one!"

I laughed. "Of course not! Let's get out of here before that chainsaw guy gets back!" (I secretly made a note in my mind to watch the movie with Tom, though. He would

LOVE it.)

Sarah nodded and continued to hold my hand as we walked out of the cinema. I wasn't sure how to get her to let go, so I just flexed my fingers and tugged gently on her arm. Unfortunately, she took it as a sign to come closer and leaned her head on my shoulder as we walked along. Ugh. Why don't girls ever understand what I'm trying to get them to do? It was very uncomfortable.

"I'm glad we saw it, even if it was terrifying," she said, finally releasing my hand as we stepped out of the cinema. "I had fun."

*HA ha HA ha!* The laugh ran through my head.

"Yeah," I said quietly. "I had... fun too."

"Want to go for coffee?" she pointed at the coffee shop "Coffee Co," next door to the theater.

I made a face. "I don't like coffee."

She laughed. "Well you don't have to drink coffee, silly!"

Soon we were sat on tiny, high up chairs in the cramped coffee shop. Sarah had ordered a black, foul smelling coffee and was cradling the paper cup in her hands.

I, however, had gone for the best thing on the menu: the SUPER DELUXE HOT CHOCOLATE. In front of me, in a similar sized cup, was a hot chocolate topped with whipped cream, marshmallows, chocolate sauce, sprinkles and a chocolate flake as well. I grinned as I bit into the foamy cream and Sarah laughed.

"You know," she said, swirling her coffee in small circles, "you're pretty good with Tom."

"'ank 'oo," I said through a mouthful of cream. Dad's words echoed in my mind: *be polite.* I forgot, I was supposed to be Dad, so I wiped my face and swallowed. "Thank you, Sarah," I said. "That is very kind of you to say."

She smiled for a moment, but then her face turned serious.

"I have something I want to talk about," she said.

140

I frowned. "What is it?"

"I just..." she sighed. "I worry about Tom."

Tom? Something was wrong with Tom? I sat up in my seat. "Something's wrong with Tom?"

"No, no." She looked out of the coffee shop window. "I just worry because he doesn't have a strong *male* role model in his life."

I blinked. A *what* now? I wasn't sure what she meant, but I was sure that Dad *would* know, so I just nodded and said: "I see."

Sarah took a sip of her coffee. I tried to look relaxed. "I just think... You could be that role model, you know? You've done so well with Jack, he's so polite and good mannered."

"Jack is pretty amazing in every possible way," I nodded. I was about to try and steer the conversation away from where it was going, when Sarah suddenly spoke.

"Listen, I have something I need to ask you, but it's a bit embarrassing."

I frowned. "OK?" What was she going to ask *now*?

"Someone needs to have..." she paused. "...the *talk* with Tom. I think it would be better coming from you than from his mom. Do you understand?"

A thousand answers flew through my mind at once ranging from WHAT? to NO! NO! NO! Did she mean the *TALK?* As in THE *talk?* She wanted me to have THE *talk* with Tom? I couldn't have the *talk* with Tom! I hadn't had the *talk* myself, how was I supposed to-

I think Sarah saw the fear on my face, because she smiled. "Don't worry," she said. "It doesn't have to be right away."

She placed her hand on mine and I glanced down at it. "Yeah," I looked at the clock. "Oh, look at the time!" I said quickly. "We should be getting back." I stood up, taking my hand back and moving towards the car.

"I guess so," Sarah nodded as well, glancing at the

clock. I only noticed then that the clock was broken and read: 2pm.

The drive home was silent. I kept thinking about Tom. What if *he* knew what was going on here? I shuddered. Thank goodness Dad was busy playing games with him. Tom would have every right to punch me in the face. Or maybe he'd go crazy and hate me forever.

*HA **ha** HA **ha**!* I imagined Tom laughing as he chased after me with a chainsaw. Did his mom own a chainsaw? I made a mental note to check next time I was around at their house.

As we pulled up outside my house, Sarah turned to me and said: "You're a great dad."

"Well," I grinned. "That's because I have a great son. Jack is pretty awesome. Probably the best kid in the universe. I am very lucky to have him." I was too busy complimenting myself to realize that Sarah had shifted forward in her seat. Her face was suddenly very, *very* close to mine. I blinked. I could feel her breath on my face.

Wait... where was this conversation going? I thought back to all the cheesy television shows where dating was involved and it occurred to me that this was the moment where the kissing probably happened.

*NOPE,* I thought to myself. *NOT HAPPENING.* I placed my hand on the door release slowly and looked at her. "I...er... like to think that he kind of looks after himself, you know?" I said, ready to bolt at any moment.

Sarah nodded, her eyes wide. "I think you're too harsh on yourself. You've done an amazing job." She looked me in the eyes.

Panic mode activated in my head. I was sure now that she wanted me to kiss her on the *lips*. I had never done it before, and I sure didn't want my first kiss ever was to be with Tom's mom! That would be *weird*! I felt a little ill just thinking about it. I leaned backwards slightly.

"Well, I...." The door release clunked open behind me

as I tugged on it desperately, but I didn't realize how much weight I had leaning on the car door. "WOAH!" I fell backwards, out of the car and onto the floor, my head smacking against the stone driveway.

"Oh my god!" Sarah cried. "David, are you ok?"

My legs stuck up in the air and I stared at the stars in the sky, which seemed to be circling around my head. "Huh?" I managed as I tried to sit back up. It was then that the front door opened and Dad came running out.

"Oh, hi guys! Having fun?" he said.

Sarah helped me to my feet, brushing me down. "Yes we did, thank you."

Thank goodness for Dad. That could have gotten *awkward*.

After that, there wasn't much more to do except say goodbye and find an ice pack for my head. As I sat on the couch and groaned, Dad paced excitedly around the living room.

"It *worked*," Dad said. "Plan **AwesomeMasterParty** worked!"

"It's **SUPERMASTERAWESOME**." I flinched as I tried to stand up, changed my mind and stayed put.

"Whatever," Dad grinned. "Tom beat me at every game we played and he *loved* it! I think we're going to figure this out, Jack!"

I tried to ignore the fact Dad had broken my proud tradition of being the best gamer out of all of my friends in one sitting. I lay down on the couch again and stared up at the ceiling.

"What's next on the list?" I asked.

Dad's smile grew wider.

# To the Museum

"It will be easy," Dad said as we rode the bus into school. "Plus, I will be there beside you the entire time, so you don't need to worry." But even though he said that, I didn't believe him. Why? Because the things that Dad finds 'easy' include Math, swallowing pills and getting all my homework done on time. When he says something is easy, you should prepare for a task that is going to be incredibly difficult.

Today, plan **SUPERMASTERAWESOME** meant that I had to cope with a school trip to the museum. Normally, going on a trip would have been an awesome break from lessons, and I could have chilled and not had to worry about doing too much work. Being a 'good teacher' and sticking to the plan, though, meant that I had to prepare *so much boring paperwork* before we even left the house in the morning!

When I rolled out of bed, I felt like a shovel had repeatedly hit my face. With a groan, I looked at the clock. It said *6am*! *Uuuugh.* I didn't even want to move right then, never mind getting dressed into Dad's uncomfortable clothes, but there was nothing I could do. I had to keep up appearances after all, and Dad's appearance was boring and uncomfortable.

As I sat stirring my cereal in a bowl, Dad slumped across the room and pulled a big box out from inside a cupboard. He then began drawing out sheet of paper after sheet of paper, while yawning loudly. I knew exactly how he felt. I hadn't slept well last night because every time I closed my eyes I heard *HA **ha** HA **ha**!* and dreamed that I was being chased by Dr. Turner holding a chainsaw over his head. It made me shiver just to think about it, so I decided to focus on something else.

"What's that?" I asked Dad as he started making a fourth pile of paper on the table in front of me. He yawned again, then placed his hand on the first pile.

"Permission slips for the students." He moved his hand to the next pile. "List of names for roll call." His hand moved to the next pile again. "Dietary requirements for the students' lunches." And to the last pile: "This one is a health and safety plan to make sure that everyone stays safe on the trip."

He then brought *more* papers out of the cupboard. "This one...."

I stopped listening, feeling sorry I had asked. Surely, all I had to do was make sure that the students didn't wander off and get in trouble? Why was there so much *paper* involved?

When he had finally finished putting the piles of paper in order, each one was topped with a sticky note telling me where to take it. Why couldn't I have swapped bodies with a rock star? Everything would have been so much more *awesome* then.

By the time we reached school, the sun had barely come up. I stood next to the bus in the parking lot, my eyes half closed, with my dad's class lined up in front of me, and a pile of paper in my hands. Standing at the other end of the bus was Mr. Thomas, with my class. I noticed that Tom and Dad were standing at the back, but they weren't talking to each other.

Mr. Thomas walked over to me and grinned his goblin grin, clearly more awake than anyone else. He looked at the papers in my hands. "Have you got the roll call sheets in that mountain of paper somewhere, Mr. Stevenson?" Each word was spoken in a mocking voice, as if he knew that I would have to look through the pile to find the sheet.

I looked down sleepily at the paper in my hand and handed it to him without a second thought. His eyes widened as suddenly the mountain became *his* problem, and he fought to keep it balanced.

"What are you..." he began.

145

I reached about halfway down the pile and pulled out a sheet with a yellow sticker on it, the one I knew was the roll call sheet. I held it up in front of me. "Got it," I grinned.

Mr. Thomas was about to reply when a gust of wind suddenly swept the paper pile off his hands and spread various sheets all over the parking lot! Mr. Thomas let out a strangled, screeching sound as he desperately made a grab for the first few sheets and, in the process, *dropped the rest of the pile.*

The wind, not being very kind, swept off the rest of the sheets, twirling and whirling them into the air in a very small paper tornado.

I watched Mr. Thomas run around, picking up sheets of paper, and yelling at any nearby students to "HELP ME OR YOU'LL BE IN DETENTION FOR THE REST OF YOUR LIFE!"

Soon, students were running everywhere, trying to grab paper out of the sky. I just stood yawning next to the bus. Sometimes being a teacher was a lot easier. I couldn't be put in detention, after all.

Ten minutes later, we were all aboard the bus. Mr. Thomas took roll call of his class as we pulled out of the parking lot. "Holly Lawson?" The name cut through the air and made my sleepy brain snap to attention. I glanced over at Mr. Thomas, waiting for her to answer.

No answer came.

"Holly Lawson?" Mr. Thomas shouted again, irritably.

"She's not here," Tom shouted from the back of the bus.

Mr. Thomas shook his head and marked her as away on his roll call sheet. My heart sank. I had been secretly hoping that I would be able to solve my issues with Holly today, while at the museum. I would have at least been happy to see her, but out of everyone in both classes, she was the only one missing. I turned back to look out of the window and watched the busy streets pass by.

All of seventh grade were going to the Science and Wonder Museum, so we could later do a project on it at school. Tom and I had renamed the museum 'Boring and Boringer,' since no matter what it claimed to have, and no matter how amazing it tried to make it out to be, it was always boring. A few years ago, we had been taken to see an exhibit on dinosaurs. I was so excited, I couldn't wait to see T-Rex's and Brontosauruses – but instead, we spent the whole time looking at a picture of a rat. A fluffy prehistoric rat, but a rat nonetheless. Instead of giant monster lizards, we got... rats. Typical of our school, taking the fun out of everything.

When Mr. Thomas finally sat down, he began to grumble and moan.

"I don't even know why we are going to the museum," he said with a sneer. "Keep children in the classroom, that's what I say. Why do they need to go outside? It's not like they spend time outside at home. Just stay inside and play Mindcraft all day."

"Minecraft," I corrected him.

"Eh?" He turned to me.

"Never mind," I sighed, thinking it was better not to argue.

"Kids," he said, grimly. "Who needs 'em?"

It felt like it took forever, but we finally arrived. The museum looked like it had been taken straight out of ancient Greece and dumped in the middle of town. It was a building made from mucky white stone, and the front door was surrounded by large columns. Luckily, I managed to give Mr. Thomas the lead and only had to follow behind everyone, yawning occasionally. Mr. Thomas did the whole 'everyone stay together' speech, warning the kids not to get lost. I used that time to side step up to Fat Gary.

"Hey, Gary," I whispered.

Gary glanced up from his packet of chocolate candy, eyes wide, like he had done something wrong.

"Give me one," I said.

He looked down at the packet and then back up at me. Slowly, he handed one over, placing the small, bright green candy in the center of my hand like he was giving away his first born child.

"Good boy." I threw it into my mouth and patted him on the head, slightly revolted when my hand came back sticky. I wiped it on my pants. The sugar burst was good. I needed it to stay awake.

As the group wandered forward, a perky museum steward in a bright orange t-shirt leaped out from behind the front desk. She was tall, thin, and had round glasses on her nose that nearly took up her entire face. With a wild grin and a fake sounding voice she squeaked: "Hello! Welcome to the Museum of SCIENCE AND WONDER!" She shouted the last few words and I could see some of my classmates flinch away from her. "Are you ready to learn?"

The classes looked at each other. A few glanced at me. I rolled my eyes and nodded.

"Yes," mumbled a few of them.

"I can't hear you!" the museum steward said louder, trying to get everyone to shout.

"You should listen better then," Mr. Thomas snapped. "Start the tour."

The steward blinked a few times, pushed her glasses up her nose and then nodded. "Right," she said. "Right! Let's go learn some stuff!"

As she led the group through the museum, my eyes lit up. We were heading towards a sign which read:

The words were surrounded by stars, rocket ships and little green aliens. My mind sparkled with the possibilities. Space craft, burning suns, colorful nebulas. Maybe this trip wasn't going to be as bad as I thought.

I was wrong, obviously. Instead of turning *into* the exhibit, we walked *away* from it and headed towards another room. This one had an old looking sign that bore the words:

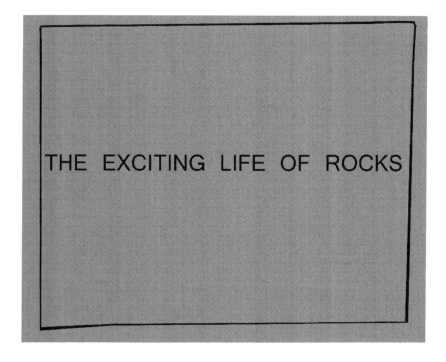

THE EXCITING LIFE OF ROCKS

The sign didn't have *anything* exciting on it, no pictures, no colors, no fancy font. It was dull and gray. I nodded to myself. *Yep, this is more like it.*

The tour began with a selection of gray rocks. Then, there were a few brown ones, and then a few more gray ones. The tour was boring coated boring with a boring filling. Somehow, the steward managed to remain perky and excited, even though what she was talking about was as exciting as watching dry paint age.

Luckily, as a teacher, I could stand at the back and lean against the wall with my eyes closed. Maybe catch a few seconds of shut eye without anyone noticing. There were a few perks to this job.

"Who can tell me what this is?" The steward held up a hunk of orange colored rock. I opened one eye and snorted quietly to myself. *No one is going to get that,* I thought.

To my surprise, a hand rose up in the crowd of students. Someone knew what it was? I stood up a little bit to see who the super nerd was… and then my body went cold.

"That's sandstone!" chirped Dad with a big grin on his face. On MY face.

The steward's eyes almost popped out of her head in excitement. "Exactly! Can you tell me anything else about sandstone?"

Dad thought for a second. I silently pleaded that he didn't know anything more about an orange rock. I mean, how much *can* you know about rocks? "I know that it's a sedimentary rock which means it isn't igneous or metamorphic," he said.

My mouth dropped open. I didn't even know what half those words *meant*! What was he doing? I could see other students whispering to each other and pointing at Dad. I needed to stop him.

The steward did a little dance and clapped her hands. "Fantastic! You're great at this. Maybe you should come up here and be my assistant for the rest of the presentation."

I was about to open my mouth to say something, but it was too late. Dad, with a big grin on his face, wandered up to the front of the class and stood next to the steward. Once again, he had managed to win the 'most embarrassing person' award. I could already see people giggling as he stood next to her. Tom was trying to hide his face, and Tommy Wilkins looked incredibly angry that *he* hadn't been chosen as the assistant to the steward.

For once, I *wanted* Tommy Wilkins to be a super nerd. Didn't he know anything about rocks?

By the end of the tour, I'd had enough. I managed to drag Dad to one side and tell him to stop, but he shrugged. "I knew the answers, I wasn't going to hide it."

"Yes, but that's because you're *you*. You need to start thinking like *me*," I snapped.

Dad shook his head and walked away.

As we guided everyone back to the bus, Mr. Thomas stood next to me. "I see your home discipline is working," he grinned. "Your son did very well today."

"Yeah," I said. "He's great." I made a silent promise to myself to lock Dad in a closet and never let him see the light of day ever again.

# Football Practice

"WHAT ARE YOU DOING, STEVENSON?" Coach yelled at Dad as he dropped the ball *again* for the tenth time.

*Yeah Dad, what are you doing?* I thought to myself. I was sitting on the bleachers with my head in my hands, sulking. My football skills, just like my drumming skills, had clearly not been inherited from Dad. It didn't surprise me, as Dad had always been a soccer fan, and often complained that for a game called 'football,' it seemed to have the players carrying the ball in their hands more often than not.

Dad scrambled to pick up the ball again, only to be surrounded by the opposing team's players, who knocked him down and took the ball. The sound of Coach's whistle was a piercing screech across the playing field. Coach, by far the widest and scariest looking of all the teachers at my school, towered over Dad and yelled at him at the top of his voice.

"YOU THINK I'M GOING TO LET YOU PLAY FOR THE TEAM IF YOU KEEP GIVING ME *THAT* PERFORMANCE? GO SIT ON THE BENCH!"

Coach thrust out a finger and pointed at the small wooden bench at the side of the pitch. It may not have looked like much, but to be benched was the *worst* thing that could happen to a player on the team. It meant that they might not be on the team for long.

I watched through my hands as Dad slowly walked towards the bench, hanging his head in shame, his fellow players shaking their head in disapproval. I was about to get up from the bleachers and tell Dad what I thought of him when there was a movement to my right. I turned to see a flash of brown hair floating through the breeze, rushing to Dad's side and sitting next to him on the bench. The brown hair belonged to the person I least wanted to see.

*Jasmine.*

She shifted up the bench until there was barely any room between them and put an arm around him, whispering in his ear, no doubt to make him feel better. I could see that she was distracting Tom from the game: he kept looking over to Dad and frowning, which meant he didn't see the other players in front of him and accidentally ran straight into them.

"TOM!" Coach shouted. "PAY ATTENTION!"

Tom pushed himself to his feet with a frown.

I stood up. It was time to take action. Dad was *clearly* ignoring the list *again*. I was about to give him a piece of my mind when Holly came striding across the field, her face red with anger. She grabbed Dad by the arm and dragged him to his feet, making Jasmine, who was leaning on him, fall backwards off the bench!

I smothered a laugh with my hand. It was rude to laugh. I snorted.

Holly poked Dad in the chest as she spoke. I didn't even need to get any closer to hear what she was saying.

"What is *wrong* with you?" she snapped. "I thought we were *dating* and here you are talking to Jasmine. I'm your girlfriend, remember?"

Dad began to fumble with his words, shrugging and gesturing toward Jasmine who was now pushing herself back to her feet. Jasmine grinned and took a step towards Holly. "Well," she said, maybe "I'm just better than you. Maybe Jack has finally realized that he needs a girl who can think for herself, a girl whose brain hasn't been fried by all the bleach she puts in her hair-"

Holly's face flushed red. "How *dare* you! This is my *natural* color!" She took a step forward, and now the two girls were within fighting distance. Dad took action at last. He glanced up at me, clenched his jaw and stepped in between the two girls.

"Jasmine!" Dad shouted. "You can't just say things

like that!"

Jasmine stepped back, shocked. Her arms were draped helplessly by her sides and it was obvious that she was not expecting to be yelled at.

Holly's mouth dropped open. A smile broke out on my face.

"Well... I... I mean..." Jasmine mumbled and spluttered, before breaking out into tears and running away from the pitch, back towards the school.

The smile on my face disappeared as guilt rose up inside me. I didn't want to make her cry, did I? I suddenly felt like a cruel person. I had never thought much about Jasmine, but since Dad and I had swapped bodies, I had never once stopped to consider her feelings. She might be a nerdy, awkward girl, but after all, she was also a human being.

Dad turned towards Holly, clearly intending to patch things up, but Holly was still angry from her confrontation with Jasmine.

"Don't think this makes everything right, Jack!" she said, before turning around and storming off in the opposite direction. Dad was left alone in the center of the field. He looked like he had been struck by lightning again, his face confused and dazed. I decided to climb down from the bleachers and approach him.

"Wow," I said. "That was *intense.*"

"Do you feel better now?" Dad said, an angry look on his face. "I just made Jasmine cry because I stuck to your list. Do you feel 'cooler' now? Have I been a 'good Jack'?"

A lump formed in my throat as Dad turned and sat back down on the bench, frustrated. He was right. Perhaps I had forced him to be too harsh on Jasmine. I mean, I was trying to get him to act like me, but he *wasn't* me. I stared out at the football pitch, watching the game unfold in front of me.

"I'm sorry about the football. I never was any good at it," Dad said quietly. "And the museum. I just wanted you to realize that being smart *isn't a bad thing.*"

I nodded. "I'm sorry that I went to see an M15+-rated movie with Sarah."

"You *what?*" Dad turned to me.

I flinched, realizing my mistake. "I thought we were getting everything out in the open!"

"But I told you…" Dad's voice caught as a look of realization covered his face. "Huh, maybe that's our problem. We just don't listen to each other."

"Sorry, what did you say? I wasn't listening," I joked. Dad grinned at me, punching me in the arm playfully.

Coach wandered over to us. "Mr. Stevenson," he nodded at me. "I hope you're having a serious talk with your son! The rate he is going, he will be cut from the team!"

*Cut from the team.* I shuddered inwardly. The thought was too horrible to comprehend, but I couldn't take it out on Dad, not this time. It wasn't his fault, after all, he hadn't been to practices every week like I had.

Dad looked at me, worried.

"It's my fault," I said to Coach. "Jack isn't feeling very well and I forced him to come to practice today."

Coach frowned. "Oh, right. That's why he's been playing poorly?"

Dad flinched. I pretended not to see. "Yeah. I think he just needs to go home."

Coach nodded. "Alright, Jack, go get changed. You get better and I'll see you at practice next week!"

Relief spread over Dad's face. "Thanks," he said, looking at me.

"Let's go home, son," I grinned.

# Math Attack

I used to think teachers had it all. They could just sit back and relax at the front of the classroom while all the students did the *real* work. I was sure that teachers had a super-secret evil agenda in which they simply set out to make their students' lives as boring as possible. But that time feels like *centuries* ago now. I have to *be* a teacher, and I am beginning to think there might be an even greater evil force controlling the teachers as well – because sitting at the front of a classroom is just as boring, *if not more*!

A few days after the football practice, as I was standing in front of Dad's class and looked down at the notes he had given me, I realized I had no idea what I was doing. The night before, Dad and I had stayed up well past bedtime, trying to get me to understand the new math technique that he wanted me to teach his students. Dad wrote it down in as simple a language as possible, but every time I looked over his shoulder at his notes, it just seemed like someone had written a page of Ancient Egyptian Hieroglyphics, then messed *them* up, and expected me to read them out in front of a room full of students.

"Okay," Dad said. "It will be easy." (I really wish he would stop saying that.) "All you have to do is take the two numbers, draw a grid like this, put them in these boxes, divide them by two and if you see right here you can...." He started making even more furious notes on the piece of paper in front of him, drawing numbers in little boxes which apparently made absolute sense to *him*. He multiplied, divided, added and subtracted like it was as simple as picking your nose.

I watched him. None of the information went into my head. All I could think of was Holly storming off in a rage that day on the football field. How she had said, "Don't think this makes everything right!" How *could* I make everything right? I mean, Dad had rejected Jasmine *right in front of her*. What else did she want? Girls are so confusing.

I was chewing the end of my pencil and thinking about it when I realized Dad was no long talking. I looked up to find him staring at me with a teacher-y look in his eyes. It didn't suit my face at all. "Your turn!" he said, pushing the paper towards me. "It's simple enough, isn't it?"

I looked down at the piece of paper on the table in front of me. I reluctantly dragged it towards myself and tried to figure out what exactly he wanted me to do. "Ok, the two numbers you can use are 18 and 12 and a half. So write them down there on the paper... that's it... and away you go!" Dad grinned.

It went about as well as trying to use a submarine made of toilet paper (which is to say, it didn't go well at all). I had barely even started when Dad frowned and said: "What are you doing?"

I looked up. "I'm adding them."

Dad shook his head, looking almost offended that I would dare treat his precious numbers this way. "Why? No, no, that's not right at all. Weren't you listening?"

I leaned back in my chair, spinning the pencil between my fingers as if it was a drumstick. "One hundred percent. I *love* Math."

That, it turned out, was the *wrong* thing to say. Dad got angry, shouting at me, telling me that I needed to 'pay attention' more and that if I didn't, the **MASTERCHICKENPARTYPLAN** would not work (he didn't even give me a chance to correct him). He told me that I would be a 'terrible example' to the students.

I was going to tell him that *he* was a terrible example to every kid in the universe, but I didn't have the energy. I just dropped the pencil and stormed upstairs to my room. He didn't control me after all, as much as he would like to.

Now, standing in front of the class, the students staring at me with blank eyes, I kind of wished I had listened just a *little* bit. If I had, the next hour wouldn't have been as painful as I suspected it was going to be. The shirt collar felt tight around my throat as I picked up a red marker and turned to write on the white board behind me. Slowly, I began to draw out the grid, just like Dad had done, and silently prayed that everything would be alright. It was just math, right? How hard could it be?

Ten minutes later, I turned back to the class at the end of the explanation and smiled my most teacher-like smile (which meant I just let the corners of my mouth twitch a bit). "So, do you all understand?"

The classroom was silent. For the briefest of seconds, I was sure that I had actually done it correctly and that I was acing this 'teacher' thing. Nope. That was wrong. Surprise, surprise, my entire fantasy world crashed down around me when Tommy 'King of the Nerds' Wilkins slowly raised his hand.

I sighed. This wasn't going to be good. "Yes, Tommy?"

Tommy's eyebrows were raised high on his forehead in confusion. "I see what you are trying to do...kind of..." he began. "But I don't quite understand what the point of drawing a picture of a duck was? Maybe it's just me, but I don't think art really helps in a Math formula."

I glanced back at the board. There was a small duck in one of the grid's empty spaces (I couldn't remember what was supposed to go in it). I had secretly hoped no one would ask, but of course Tommy Wilkins wouldn't let me get away with anything. I let out a long, drawn out sigh, trying to waste time and think of an appropriate answer. I decided just to wing it.

"Well," I said to Tommy, "Math is as much an *art* as it is a *science*." I stole *that* line from my dad, actually, one time when he had tried to convince me that Math was 'fun' (he failed). "So, naturally, if you ever find a blank space or a part of an equation which is too hard, or something like that, a small drawing might actually help us significantly. It might even help you find the answer."

The class were looking at each other now, probably thinking I had gone mad. Tommy looked visibly disturbed. The only person who seemed to agree with me was Johnny Jacobs at the back of the class. Johnny, usually one of the slowest people in the class, who was only good at being the Quarterback on the football team, was nodding enthusiastically. He really seemed to like the idea of drawing little ducks on his Math work, and I didn't want to tell him that it was probably all wrong.

"So," I clapped my hands together. "Let's do some Math! Worksheets are on the front table. First one to finish gets... I don't know... a prize or something."

I didn't actually *have* any prizes planned, but the thought of winning something seemed to excite the class enough that they got up and picked up worksheets and didn't bother to ask any more questions. I slumped down at my dad's desk and tried to look busy so no one would bother me. I glanced at the clock. Only one more hour until lunch.

## Another Plan

It was almost exactly an hour later that Johnny walked up to the front of the class and proudly presented me with a worksheet covered in little doodles of ducks. Some had little hats on, others sunglasses, one was holding a sword and at the bottom of the worksheet, there seemed to be two whole teams of ducks engaged in what looked like a very intense game of football.

Jake pointed at a duck at the top of the page that had spiky hair very similar to his own. "That one's me," he said with a grin.

I had to admit, I was impressed. Sure, he had done it all completely wrong, but he had *listened* to me. Also, the drawings of the ducks were surprisingly realistic. He had clearly put some effort into them.

"I'm first! Do I get a prize?"

I nodded and reached into the top drawer of Dad's desk, unsure what I would find. The first thing I grabbed and dragged out was Dad's wallet. He couldn't carry it around all day in my body, so he stored it there for safe keeping. I looked at it and shrugged. Why not? I pulled out ten dollars and handed the note to Johnny. His eyes widened.

"Woah," he said, holding the money out in front of him like it was the Holy Grail.

The rest of the class gasped in amazement and disappointment at what they had missed.

"You're the King of Math, Johnny, don't you ever think otherwise," I grinned. Sure, he wasn't *really* the 'King of Math', but why ruin his day? What really surprised me, however, was that small tears began to form in Johnny's eyes.

"T...t...t...hank you Mr...St...sstevenson!" he said, wiping his nose on his sleeve. "I'll never forget this."

I shifted my chair away slightly. "No problem," I said, feeling a little awkward.

I needed to get out of this situation, quick. Luckily, the bell did that for me.

*BRRRRRRRRRRRRRRRING!*

"Alright everybody! Lunch time! Out you go!" I waved the class out of the room and slumped back in my chair. That was a *tough* one.

I was admiring my sandwich, just about to bite into it, when the next challenge of the day wandered in. Its name was Dad.

"Er... Jack?" he whispered, poking his head around the door. I frowned at him.

"Shouldn't you be outside, random student?" I said in

a booming teacher voice. "You're on the right way for a detention, young man!"

Dad rolled his eyes. "Ha ha, very funny, Jack. Listen, we have a situation. I need to tell you..."

My phone buzzed on the table next to me. "Hold that thought," I said, grabbing my phone and looking at the screen. It was a text from Tom.

HOLLY IS ON THE WAR PATH. WAT DID U DO?!?

I looked at my phone with a frown. What had upset Holly so much? I glanced up at Dad. He stood, shifting uncomfortably in the doorway to his own classroom. I knew I had my answer. "Oh, no..." I said. "What have you done?"

Dad scratched his head, a move I recognized that he did whenever he was feeling guilty. The last time he did it, he had just stepped on (and broken) my GameKid™.

"What did you *do?*" I asked again, standing up from my chair.

"Right," said Dad. "You know how you told me not to talk to Jasmine, and that I should focus on Holly..."

"You mean the *specific instructions* I gave you and told you to *follow exactly and to not do anything else under any circumstances or chaos and disaster would happen?!*" I felt my voice getting louder.

Dad nodded. "Yes, that sounds about right. Well... I didn't follow them... exactly."

I almost exploded. "You WHAT?"

Dad backed out of the doorway slightly. I took a deep breath and tried to calm down. "I know, it seems bad..." he began. My phone buzzed again on the table. I didn't look at it. "But I thought after the episode on the football field, Holly needed some space..." I realized that Dad might have done something that was beyond fixing. "And... well... I *tried* to avoid Jasmine, I really did, whenever she came over, I made an excuse and went in the opposite direction, and I didn't sit next to her in class or anything."

"But?"

"Buuuuut," Dad closed the door to the classroom, shutting us inside so that no one else could hear. "Jasmine was upset, she was *crying*, and I didn't know what to do. I mean, we were *responsible* for that, Jack! We have to take responsibility for our actions!"

I pinched the bridge of my nose with my fingers and closed my eyes. I really didn't want to know what had had gone on.

"What happened?" I asked quietly.

Dad shuffled on his feet again and scratched his head. "Well," he said. "I went over to her, and told her I was sorry."

"Okay..." I said. Maybe it wasn't that bad then.

"Then I hugged her."

Okay, *that* was bad.

"Also... Holly may have seen the whole thing."

I sat down in the chair again, staring out across the classroom at nothing. I blinked a few times and listened to the sound of myself breathing.

"Jack?" Dad asked. "Jack? Are you okay? You've gone really pale."

I knew that this was *bad*. Super bad. We needed to figure out a way to solve this, but I couldn't think of anything except locking Jasmine in a crate and mailing her to Mexico.

"That is bad." I said.

"I know, Jack, but..."

I raised a finger to silence him. "Don't speak. We need a **plan**."

Dad waited silently as I sat and thought about what to do. He opened his mouth a few times, but I silenced him with a glare. He had done enough damage. Now it was *my* turn to do some damage control. At first, nothing came to my mind. All I could think about was how my life was ruined and I would be stuck as Dad forever. I glanced at the wallet on the desk in front of me. Maybe I could just get a plane ticket with Dad's money and fly somewhere with sun and sand and just – start a whole new life. He probably had enough money to do that, right? I mean-

An idea sprang to life. I stood up with a grin.

"Alright, Dad. Here's what we are going to do," I said.

Dad leaned forward expectantly.

"It's lunchtime now, but Holly will be at dance practice for the first half hour. That means we have time to get to her locker and meet her there. When she arrives, we will get *you* to tell her how sorry you are, and how it was a complete misunderstanding and you are never going to see Jasmine again, and that *I*, meaning you, forced *you,* meaning me, to hug Jasmine or you would get grounded. okay?"

Dad's face twisted in a similar way to mine when I was trying to figure out what he meant with the math grid. Slowly, he nodded. "So we are blaming me... I mean... you... I mean... Mr. Stevenson?"

I nodded. "Yes. I think." I frowned. "Wait... what?"

We didn't have long. It was a strange feeling walking through the school with the students all there. I could see them stopping their conversations when I got closer, glancing at me as I walked past, as if I was some kind of threat. I felt a bit more *powerful* than usual. I found myself walking faster, and more upright because of it. *This* was what it was like to be a teacher. I could see why some might want to take advantage of it.

Holly's locker was right at the end of one of the corridors. As we approached it, I recalled the day we got struck by lightning, when Dad dragged me from here to football practice. Now I was the one dragging him *to* here. Weird.

I positioned Dad by the locker and told him to wait. I could stand just around the corner, out of sight, and still be able to hear the entire conversation. As I took my position, I pretended to inspect one of the boards on the wall. It was a poorly made display of some math work done by eighth grade students. There were a lot of graphs and things that I didn't understand, but I pretended to be very interested in it. I walked up to the board, tracing my finger across the pencil lines of a graph drawn by a boy called 'Tony Lindon'. He seemed to be very nerdy. Even his handwriting was super neat and *joined up*.

I glanced around the corner, pretending to do up my shoelace. I could see Tom walking down the corridor towards Dad. There was no sign of Holly, but I decided to listen to their conversation, so I wouldn't miss anything and could leap in if necessary.

"Hi, Jack," Tom said as he approached.

"Yo, dude," said Dad (Yeah, this was his attempt to talk 'like a kid'. The only problem was that people stopped talking like this when the dinosaurs disappeared). "How you doing, man?"

"Yeah... about that..." Tom said, uncomfortably. "Are you waiting for Holly?"

"Totally," said Dad. "Bro," he added.

"Well, I hate to break the news to you, but she isn't coming. She thought you would try and meet her here so she gave me this note to give to you." Tom handed Dad a note. He glanced my way and I hid back beside the wall, examining the graph again. What was on the note? What was going on? I was trying to listen to their conversation when *another* voice distracted me.

"Ahh, math. Beautiful, isn't it?" It was Mr. Thomas. I really wanted this guy to go and fall down a hole somewhere.

I glanced at him. He stood next to me, looking at the work on the board as well. "Er, yeah, it's great," I said quickly, hoping he would go away so I could go back to listening. Of course, he didn't.

"Yes, Tony Lindon is quite the math whiz kid. Doesn't draw *any* ducks on his work at all. Or bribe them with money." Mr. Thomas let that last statement hang in the air. There was a pause as he looked at me.

I didn't make eye contact, but felt my back break out into a nervous sweat. "What did you say?"

"It's interesting," Mr. Thomas continued, as if I hadn't said anything. "What the children say at lunchtime. Especially one Johnny Jacobs, waving a ten-dollar note around saying Mr. Stevenson is the *best teacher ever*. Claiming to be 'King of Math' because all it required was drawing ducks on the paper! Even though we *both* know he couldn't add his way out of a paper bag."

I was about to reply, but he continued. "I'll admit, the duck comment confused me, until I popped into your classroom and looked at the worksheets on your desk."

I went cold. What was he trying to say? Should I deny everything? But he had gone into my dad's classroom. Wasn't there a law against that or something? "I...er..." I began.

"Don't say anything, David." Mr. Thomas's voice went down into a hissing whisper.

"I respected you as a colleague and even put up with your..." the words spluttered out, "*bratty* kid who is the *worst* at Math. But now it is all clear. I can see that *you* are just as bad as him."

I was surprised by Mr. Thomas's honesty. I mean, I knew he didn't like me, but this was a bit much. I didn't realize he *hated* me. I was flustered, unsure what to do with this new information.

"You're a cheater and a liar, and I'm going to expose you, Mr. Stevenson. You just wait. You'll be out of this school before summer!" Mr. Thomas didn't give me a chance to reply. He spun on his heels and stormed down the hallway, leaving me blinking and feeling like a fool. At least no students were around to hear that.

I was shaking. I didn't know what to do, and my brain was on melt down. Dad's voice broke through my thoughts.

"Jack? Jack?"

I turned around to face him.

"I'm so sorry, Jack, I didn't realize he would do that! We'll find a way to solve it, I promise!"

I blinked again. "Mr. Thomas?" I asked.

Dad frowned. "No, Tom. Didn't you hear what he said?"

I frowned. "No, I was... distracted. What did he say?"

Dad looked down at his feet sadly. "You're out, Jack. Tom fired you from the band."

## Detention

"I'm WHAT?"

Instantly, all of my worries about Mr. Thomas disappeared in the face of newer, more pressing concerns. I was *out* of the band? How could Tom fire me? We were playing *next week!* He couldn't fire me! Not unless Holly agreed as well, and then...

My train of thought stopped. He needed Holly to agree with him. This was probably Holly's idea, I realized sadly. All because of Dad trying to make Jasmine feel better. I wanted to be angry with him, I really did, but I couldn't hold it against him for trying to help. Dad looked embarrassed, and unsure of what to do.

I let out a loud sigh and collapsed against the wall. Once again it felt like I was back at square one. Actually, it felt like I was at the square *before* square one.

*BRRRRRRRRRRRRRRRING!*

The bell began to ring again. It was the end of lunch. *I didn't even manage to eat my sandwich*, I thought sadly. I slowly pushed myself to my feet.

"At least today can't get any worse," I said, watching the flow of students begin to walk down the hall.

Dad cringed. "Well..." he said.

"Oh, what now?" I groaned.

Dad looked incredibly apologetic. "I forgot to tell you something..." he said quietly. "I...er... I have to run detention at least once per month. Usually you're at football practice while I do it, so I guess I never told you."

"*Run* detention? I have to go to *detention*?" I blinked. Here I was, sure that a teacher would never get detention. It never occurred to me that I would have to *run* it. "How do I do that?"

"It's easy," Dad said, not looking me in the eye. "I've

170

got to run to class, I'll text you the details! Have fun!"

I was left standing in the middle of the corridor, all alone, trying to figure out what I had gotten myself into.

The rest of the day drifted by in a gray haze of sadness as the reality of it all slowly clamped down around me like a vice and squeezed. First it was Holly, now it was Tom. Was there anything else I could lose? Probably not. I sighed. What else could go wrong?

I found out after school, as I stood in front of the classroom filled with students in detention. This classroom wasn't as colourful or as nice as Dad's or mine. This one had gray walls, windows that were far too small to let any light in, and the whole place felt suspiciously like a prison. I hadn't been here many times, but the few times I had, I had kept my head down and stayed out of the way of everyone else.

The worst of the worst were here. Billy Krugs from eighth grade, with his wonky nose, who liked to get in fights. Suzy Watts from ninth grade, who liked to smoke *during class,* and who (people said) carried a knife in her socks at all times. Even Chad Vanderhauser. Chad had been held back a grade so many times he must be at least thirty by now. He sat at the back of the class, towering over everyone else, with a grimace on his face suggesting he might want to set everything on fire.

I decided to remain firmly at the front of the classroom. No need to get anywhere within biting distance. Chad liked to bite people, especially teachers.

Dad's instructions were simple: all I had to do was sit at the front of the class while the students did work that they were given by their teachers. *Easy,* I told myself. It was only an hour. It would be over before I knew it. I sat down behind the desk and pretended to do work. I wasn't actually going to do any; I had just planned to play games on my phone until the hour was up. Still, I balanced a math book in front of me to make it look like I was reading.

**THUNK.**

Something hit me in the head! I reached up to see what it was and instantly regretted it. Stuck in my hair was a ball of chewed up paper, soaked in someone's spit! "Ugh!" I said, flicking it down to the floor and looked up at the class. No one seemed to be looking at me. Everyone was too busy, heads down doing their work. I looked up at the ceiling. Maybe it had fallen down from there?

**THUNK.**

This one hit the board behind me. I snapped my head back around and looked at the class again. No one was looking.

*Someone's playing a game with me,* I realized. They wanted to see how much they could get away with. *Well,* I decided. *Two can play at this game!*

I stared at the class. Everyone was working hard, heads down. I narrowed my eyes. Yeah, as long as I stared, the class couldn't do any...

**BUZZ.** I received a message on my phone. I glanced away for a millisecond and-

**THUNK.**

I looked up again.

"Who is doing that?" I shouted angrily.

"Doin' *wot?*" Chad smirked at me from the back of the room. His teeth reminded me of a shark. It was like he *wanted* me to go down there. He was taunting me.

"If anyone does it again..." I said, looking at Chad.

**THUNK.**

This time it hit the side of my head! I reached up, wiping the spit ball away in horror, and turned. No one was doing anything. How was this possible?

I stood up, wiping the sticky ball from my cheek. "Right!" I shouted. "Pens down!"

The students all looked up at me. "But we *gotta* do our homework!" Chad smirked even wider. "You want us to *stop*?"

"I..." I thought about it. "No, I just..."

"Because if we ain't allowed to do work, *you'll* get in trouble!" Chad said, standing up. "I'm gonna go home."

"You can't go home!" I said. "Sit back down! Pick up your pens, everyone!"

"Make me," hissed Chad, squinting his eyes at me. They flashed with a terrifying hunger. I noticed that even though my dad's body was tall, Chad was even taller. This was rapidly getting out of control.

"Alright," I said, backing away. "Let's not go crazy." I tried to think of a way to right the situation. What would I do if the biggest bully in school wanted to fight a teacher? "One second," I said, stepping out of the room.

As I closed the door behind me, the room erupted in a big cheer and I knew I had lost. The students started talking and messing around. I heard glass smash. Who *knew* what was going on in there! I sighed. I didn't think I was cut out for this teacher thing. I decided to use the time to check my phone. Maybe something was interesting on it.

It was a text. From my dad.

It simply read: DON'T LEAVE THE ROOM. YOU WILL LOSE CONTROL.

*Huh.* I thought to myself. *I guess I should have checked that one earlier.*

That was when I heard the sound. The sound of

tapping footsteps on the floor. The sound of someone who was very prim and proper and wanted a school to be run like clockwork, without a hint of trouble in any corner. I heard a voice, too. A voice I didn't want to hear.

"Oh yes, it's David's turn on the roster, Mrs. Kent. But I've been worried about him recently. He's been starting to show signs that he can't handle the stress of the job," said Mr. Thomas. "Did you know he got his class to draw *ducks* on their math work?"

Why was Mr. Thomas bringing the principal to the detention room? Panic kicked in instantly. What was he doing here? How had he managed to bring Mrs. Kent here so quickly? It didn't make any...

Oh, but it did. Mr. Thomas *knew* that the students would act up in detention.

This had been Mr. Thomas's plan all along. Sabotaging my detention class. He had probably bribed Chad to mess it all up. I didn't stand a chance.

In a weird way, that made me feel better.

Now I needed to make a decision. Did I go back inside the room, risk my life, but save Dad's job? Or did I wait out here, looking like a failure of a teacher, but then use the fearsome Mrs. Kent and her piercing gaze to help me calm the students down?

It was a tough one. The angry faces of the principal and Chad danced around in my mind. Which one was the lesser of the two evils? I didn't know. They were both pretty evil, at the end of the day. Maybe I should just run away? I thought to myself. No, I couldn't do that. Or could I? I mean, I was meant to be on holiday anyway. Dr. Turner thought it was a good idea. Maybe I should start my holiday now?

Then a third choice presented itself to me. I looked at the wall on the opposite side of the corridor. A red box was attached to it, and written on it in white letters were the words:

FIRE ALARM

I stared at the box. If I pulled the small lever inside it, the fire alarm would go off and everyone would have to evacuate the building, but I could get in a lot of trouble. The footsteps were getting closer. I was in a lot of trouble either way. At least this way, Dad got to keep his job.

I pulled the alarm.

BRRRRRRRRRRRRRRRRRRRRRRR...

The sound began instantly, wailing through the corridors with a piercing ring. I opened the door to the detention room and yelled into it:

"Come on out, guys and gals! Fire alarm's going off!"

It worked like magic. The students stopped messing around and all stood up, happy to have a reason to leave the room. They all ran past me, laughing and cheering, heading towards the fire exit. Only Chad stopped, looked me dead in the eye with a chilling gaze, and then broke out into another shark-like grin.

"Well played, Mr. S," he said, nodding towards the fire alarm on the far wall. Then he walked towards the fire exit like nothing had happened. Something told me I would have to look out for him in the future.

At that same moment, Mrs. Kent and Mr. Thomas came around the corner and saw me escorting the detention students out of the building. I smiled at them as they saw me, and Mr. Thomas looked back with an angry glare.

"Mr. Stevenson! Are all the children safe? Do we know where the fire has started? I need to go check on my office!" Mrs. Kent was obviously very surprised by the sound of the alarm.

She turned on her heels and swept back along the corridor.

"Student safety is *very* important. Isn't that right, Mr. Thomas?" I looked directly at him. He nodded slowly, but didn't stop glaring. With a final grin, I left the building, hoping no one would realize just how terrified I actually was.

When I finally managed to leave the school, I met Dad by the bus stop. He was soaked in sweat from football training and when I asked him how it went, he just shook his head. I wouldn't be on the team for much longer at this rate. I was about to sit down next to him when I heard the sound of a car speeding up at the end of the road. I frowned, and turned just in time to see Mr. Thomas driving past!

He made sure his car hit a large puddle on the side of the road. I tried to move out of the way, but was too slow. Cold, muddy water soaked me from head to toe!

Dad sniggered. "What was all *that* about?"

I groaned. "I'll tell you later."

# The Note

For once, *Dad* had a plan. By the time we got home, he decided that he *could* learn the drums and so set about playing them all evening. He disappeared into the garage as soon as I opened the front door, only appearing later to eat some of the takeaway pizza I had ordered, and then disappearing again to continue the crashing and banging that he called 'drumming'.

I didn't bother telling him that it was far too late to do anything. I was out of the band, so there was nothing we could do about it – except accept it and move on. I slumped down on the sofa with my pizza in my hand, preparing to drown my sorrows in a long gaming session. There was nothing more therapeutic than killing a few zombies.

That was when I saw it resting on the edge of the coffee table, in the middle of the living room. It was a small, square, crumpled up piece of paper that Tom had given Dad when he was talking to him: a note from Holly.

I didn't want to read it. I knew whatever she had written was not going to improve my mood, so I turned over and ignored it. It wasn't going to help me at all.

I rolled back. I had to read it. No matter how bad it made me feel, I needed to know what she wanted to say. I picked it up from the table.

Slowly, I unfolded the note and looked at the familiar handwriting that I knew was Holly's. The note even smelled like her, like flowers on a sunny day. I took a deep breath and began to read:

*Jack,*

*Over the last few weeks you have been acting strange. You are no longer the fun, happy Jack that I used to know and because of that, I don't think we should be boyfriend and girlfriend anymore. Recently, you have become far too serious, making me feel bad and even telling me off for doing things that you would have once thought fun.*

*I see now that you were just trying to tell me that you liked Jasmine more than me. It hurts to find out this way, seeing you hugging her instead of me hurt me more than you could know. You are a cruel person, Jack. I don't want you to talk to me or try and get in contact with me. If we see each other at school, please don't approach me because it would hurt me too much to talk to you. Please delete my phone number too.*

*We are over.*

*Holly.*


*We are over. The* words played over and over in my mind. It was official. Me and Holly were over. I couldn't understand how we had gotten to this, so I read the words again. I was a 'cruel person'. I sighed. She just didn't understand that it was Dad. Sure, he had tried, but he tried to be a teacher, not a boyfriend, or even a friend for that matter.

The thumping and banging of the drums in the garage continued. I slowly folded up the letter and placed it back on the table. I had been right. I didn't feel any better. I picked up a slice of pizza and was preparing to shove it into my mouth when the doorbell rang.

Who would come around at this time of night?

I made my way to the front door and slowly opened it, peeking outside to see who it was. On the front door step, with an angry scowl on her face, was our neighbour Mrs. Justine, in a frilly grey and white nightgown and pink slippers. She carried a matching pink bag under her arm. I often saw her with that bag. I think she took it everywhere.

Mrs Justine was an older woman whose face was a mix of wrinkles and anger. She stared at me with cold, light

179

blue eyes.

"It's after ten!" she snapped. "Do you not have any decency?"

At least, I think that's what she said. All I could really hear was the crashing and smashing of Dad in the garage, playing the drums. "What?" I shouted back.

Mrs. Justine opened and closed her mouth and probably said something very rude (she didn't like to hold back on the insults). I thought about closing the door on her, but then I saw that she had wedged her foot between the door and the frame. I frowned and leaned closer to her. "What?" I shouted at her. "You'll have to speak louder."

"I SAID," she shouted in a voice so unexpectedly loud that I had to take a step back. "GET YOUR SON TO STOP PLAYING THE DRUMS. I'M TRYING TO SLEEP! THE LITTLE ROTTER IS KEEPING ME AWAKE!" She stared at me with a fire in her eyes that suggested that if I didn't do anything, she would kick down the door to the garage and sort it out herself. I wouldn't have been surprised if she had, either. She was that kind of lady. It wouldn't have been pretty. I nodded.

"OK!" I shouted back. "I'LL DO THAT!"

She scowled at me and pulled back her foot, finally allowing me to close the door. Had she called me a little rotter? Did *everyone* not like me now? Was that going to become a thing? I walked towards the garage door, the sounds of pounding drums getting louder with every step. I opened the door and shouted as loud as I could: "DAD!" Nothing happened. Dad didn't hear me and continued to pound the life out of the drums. "DAAAAAAAAAAAAAAAAD!" I shouted, taking off one of his slippers and throwing it at him.

Dad stopped playing and turned to me, clearly shocked at being hit by a flying shoe.

"Stop playing you little rotter!" I put on the best Mrs. Justine voice I could. "People are trying to sleep."

Dad looked up at the dusty old clock that hung off the wall in the garage. His eyes widened. "Oh, I didn't realize it was so late."

"Yep, off to bed. It's a school night." I turned to go back into the house and stopped in my tracks. What was I *saying*? *Uuuuugh*, I sounded just like Dad when he was talking to me! I felt like I needed a bath or something, to wash off the smell of adulthood that hung over me as if I had just stepped in something messy.

I turned back to Dad. "Actually, do what you want." With that, I went upstairs. I'd had enough of the day.

181

# The School Fair

I was woken up every day for the rest of the week to the sound of Dad drumming. He got up especially early, as if he *was* trying to remind me that I was no longer part of the band, and to make sure I didn't get enough sleep at night.

## Crash! Boom! Thump! Ting!

He drummed late into the night (much to the annoyance of Mrs. Justine, who began to make regular visits – sometimes accompanied by her walking stick – to bang at the front door) and started again early in the morning. I couldn't really tell if he was actually getting any better, or if he was getting *worse*.

## Crash! Thump! Ting! Splat! Bong!

Then one day, I woke up to silence. I frowned. Maybe Dad had finally broken the drums, or maybe, *maybe* he had finally given up.

I lurched out of bed and yawned, wandering towards the door of my bedroom, only to find Dad standing outside, already dressed. "Why aren't you up yet?" he asked with a frown. I looked at the calendar that hung limply from the wall of my bedroom.

"It's a Saturday," I said. "Why do I need to get up?"

Dad shook his head. "Did you forget? It's the school fair today! We need to get moving."

Something inside my body went cold with the reminder. The school fair. I could see Dr. Turner's face in my mind's eye, giving me two weeks to 'sort it all out'. Now look where I was. In exactly the same position, if not slightly worse off, and the two weeks were up. What was going to happen now?

I got dressed, but I didn't hurry. I mean, what was waiting for me at the school fair? I wasn't playing in the band anymore. Sarah would be there, probably with questions about our last date, and why I hadn't contacted her since.

Also, Tom and Holly would be there. My *maybe* best friend and my now ex-girlfriend. It made me sad just to think those words. Ex-girlfriend. No longer my girlfriend. Just Holly now. *We are over.* I didn't know what would happen when I saw her face, but I knew it wouldn't be good. How could it have all ended up so bad?

Dad must have seen how sad I looked, because he patted me sympathetically on the shoulder. "Let's just get this done," he said. "Then we are home and free. It's nearly the summer break after all."

I nodded, although the thought of a whole summer break as Dad, without any friends to spend it with, didn't sound very appealing. *Well,* thought a small voice in my head. *You could always hang out with Jasmine.* Another shudder went down my spine. *That* wasn't going to happen. No way. I just needed to figure out a plan to sort this all out.

Somehow those words seemed very hollow as I thought them.

When we arrived at the school, it was buzzing with activity despite it being the weekend. Teachers, parents and students all scurried around putting up signs, laying out tables and doing everything to prepare for the fair. Dad was usually in charge of the 'lucky dip' stall. It had a big bucket on it and, when people paid two dollars, they could reach into the bucket and pull out a prize, which could be anything ranging from candy to a small toy frog which said 'Good day!' in a strange voice when you squeezed it (I got that one last year. It sits on my shelf in my room. I haven't touched it since).

It wasn't long before I saw someone I wasn't particularly looking forward to see. Tom was standing on the main stage that had been set up in the sports hall. This was where we were going to do our big performance. I still had the list of songs we were going to perform in my head.

1. Minecraft Is Finecraft
2. Why Won't You Buy Me More Games?
3. Ate Candy, Feel Sick
4. I Can't Tie My Shoelaces
5. Rocking Gamers
6. A Song Without A Title Yet But It's Still Really Good So We Are Going To Play It.
7. Rocking Drum Guitar Singing Song

I stopped listing the material when I realized Tom was frowning and seemed to be arguing with Holly. I was about to get a bit closer when Dad spoke up from beside me.

"Huh, Jasmine can't make it."

I turned to him. "What?"

Dad was looking at his phone (he had Jasmine's number, *really?*). "Jasmine just sent me a text. Apparently she's got some kind of stomach bug and is too ill to come." He frowned, holding the phone closer to his face. "What does 'Less than symbol and then a three mean?"

Dad showed me his phone. In the middle of the screen was this:

# <3

I rolled my eyes. "It's a heart, Dad. Just ignore it."

"Oh," he grimaced.

"I see you're working hard," Sarah said to me,

making me jump. I spun round to see her standing on the other side of my stall.

"Oh...h... hi... Sarah," I grinned, scratching the back of my head. "I didn't realize you would be here." I didn't mention that I had already seen her three times, but had deliberately ducked behind tables and chairs just to avoid her seeing me.

Sarah took me to one side, glancing at Dad. "How is Jack doing? With the whole 'band' thing?"

I glanced at Dad, but I thought about myself. "He isn't doing good. He's really upset. It was very important to him."

Sarah nodded. "I hope Tom and Jack can work it out. Especially as the band probably won't be playing now."

My eyes widened. "Oh really? Why not?"

Sarah shook her head. "Their replacement drummer, a boy called Tommy Wilkins, apparently has a stomach bug and can't make it. They can't play without a drummer." Sarah looked again at Dad and back at me. "If only there was someone here who could play drums." She winked at me. "I've got to go back to my stall now." With a quick squeeze of my hand, she turned and walked away.

Excitement built up in my chest as a thousand thoughts buzzed through my head at once. The first thought was: *TOMMY WILKINS? THEY REPLACED ME WITH TOMMY WILKINS? HOW COULD THEY DO THAT?!*

But then it changed to: *They don't have a drummer. They can't play.*

But *then* I thought that *I could drum!* I could save the day. Sure, it would be weird to have a teacher drumming but...

"What are you thinking about?" Dad asked, poking me in the back with a finger. I explained the situation to him as fast as I could, how we could possibly use the situation to our advantage.

"Ifwecangetthebandtoplayitwouldbereallyawesomea ndHollywouldloveitand..." I wasn't taking a breath between words. Dad frowned and seemed to be keeping up. He nodded.

"I've got an idea," Dad said and began to walk from behind my stall towards the main stage.

"Wait!" I shouted after him. What was he trying to do?

**"Jack?"**

Everyone looked up at the main stage. Standing on stage, next to the microphone, was Holly. She had said my name by accident and it had been amplified VERY LOUDLY across the entire fair. Now she covered up her mouth in shock. Dad looked back at me, poked out his tongue in a crazy way and winked. It was not like him at all.
He grinned at me and then walked over to the stage. What was he planning?

## The show must go on

I decided the best idea was to panic. Somehow, I needed to get up onto the stage and stop Dad. He was sitting behind the drums, grinning at Tom, who was talking excitedly to him. Holly stood by the microphone, frowning at both of them. It was going to be the biggest disaster in school history, and it would have my name all over it. I could imagine the headlines of the school newspaper already:

JACK STEVENSON DESTROYS SCHOOL FAIR WITH HIS AWFUL DRUMMING!
WHO LET THAT GUY PLAY?!?

I was moving from behind my stall when Mr. Thomas came to stand in front of me. "Trying to get out of your duty as a teacher, *David*?" he asked. "There's no fire alarm for you to pull this time."

"Rodney, I really don't want..." I began.

Mr. Thomas took another step forward, blocking my way. "I'm going to watch you, David," he said. "For this whole fair. If you do *one thing* wrong, I'm going straight to Mrs. Kent. She's on the Candy stall, David. You know how she *hates* to be interrupted when she is selling candy."

I clenched my teeth and took a step back. Mr. Thomas grinned evilly at me and walked over to his stall, right next to mine. All I could do was sell lucky dip tickets, and watch helplessly as Dad prepared to play with my band. My dad with my band. My dad who had no idea how to play the drums, playing in front of the entire school.

"Your son plays drums. That's pretty cool."

I looked up. Chad stood on the other side of the stall with his shark-like grin. I groaned.

"What has Mr. Thomas bribed you to do this time?" I groaned.

Chad looked at the bucket on my table. "For ten

dollars, I'm supposed to mess up your bucket and spill it everywhere." He grabbed the edge of the red bucket on my stall and I tensed. "Thing 'bout bribes though," Chad grinned, "is that if someone pays me *more*, I'll stop doing this and might do something else." Chad looked over at Mr. Thomas's stall. He was selling tickets to guess how many pieces of candy were in a tower balanced on the stall in front of him. The person whose guess was the closest won a large amount of money.

Would I do that? Would I sink down to Mr. Thomas's level, and bribe Chad to sabotage his stall? I pulled Dad's wallet out of my pocket. "You got change for a fifty?" I grinned.

A few moments later, the beautifully stacked, colourful tower of candy on Mr. Thomas's stall collapsed onto the teacher's head. Chad stood in front of it, holding a key piece of candy between his fingers and grinning at me. Mr. Thomas's screeches, followed by Mrs. Kent shouting: "CHAD VANDERHAUSER! WHAT HAVE YOU DONE?" from her stall were music to my ears. I left my stall and began to make my way to the main stage. A large crowd was gathering around the stage, and I had to push my way through, trying to get as close as possible.

"Excuse me, sorry," I said, shoving parents out of the way. They shot me angry glares but I didn't care. I needed to get there soon. I was so close. I pushed through to the front and...

BOOM!

The band sprang to life with the intro of the song *Minecraft is Finecraft*. I cried out, realizing I was too late, and waited for the impending doom.

Tom finished his guitar intro and nodded to Dad. Dad began to play.

It was...

It was...

It was good! My mouth dropped open as I stared at

Dad. It was like he had been playing the drums all his life! He kept the beat, grinned along with them and even sang the harmonies at the right time. He caught my eye at the front of the crowd and winked at me as if to say: *This is for you, son.*

I smiled back. Dad, to my surprise, was *awesome.*

An arm hooked around mine. I turned to see Sarah standing next to me, smiling. "They managed to solve all their problems then?"

I smiled. "Yeah," I said. "I guess they did."

The show was a success. The fair was a success (apart from Mr. Thomas ruining his stall! What a shame).

I didn't stop smiling, even while I was helping pack away. Everything had worked out surprisingly well. I walked towards the main stage to congratulate my dad, and my smile dropped slightly.

"Thank you, Jack, you were *amazing!*" Holly beamed at Dad.

Then she wrapped her arms tightly around him. Dad hugged her back just as tightly. "I didn't think we would be able to perform, but you fixed *everything*."

I waited for Dad to stop hugging Holly, but he didn't. Instead, he said: "I did it for *you*, Holly. I want us to get back together."

Holly hugged him even tighter and then let go. She looked at him with a smile and stroked his cheek lightly with her hand. "Maybe," she grinned. "If you keep doing things like this." Then she hugged him again.

A pang of jealousy bit through my chest. Dad was hugging *my* girlfriend. Why wouldn't he stop? I felt my fists clench and I coughed loudly.

Holly and Dad separated, both flushed red with embarrassment.

"Jack," I smiled sweetly. "Can I talk to you for a second?"

Dad nodded and, with a final glance back at Holly, jumped off the stage. I took him around the corner, out of Holly's sight, and hissed: "What are you doing? That's *my* girlfriend you're hugging there!"

"I know, Jack, I know, I just..."

"Just," I sighed. "Keep the hugging of *my* girlfriend to a minimum until we figure out how to get back into our own bodies. OK, Dad?"

Dad nodded. "Yeah OK. I guess."

I rolled my eyes and was about to say something else when I noticed that Tom was standing right behind Dad! He had been packing away his guitar and we hadn't even noticed him.

His eyes were wide as he looked between us.

Finally his eyes settled on me, his face twisted with confusion.

"Jack?!" he said.

*Uh oh.*

# Book 3

# I Want My Body Back!!!

# The Skate Park

Skate Park. 8pm. Come alone.

That's what the text from Tom said. The first text I had received from him in days. At first, I just stared at my phone in shock. Was it broken? Was this some kind of fluke? I texted him back after running around my bedroom a few times in excitement.

R U sure?

I waited, kneeling on my bed and clutching the phone in front of me, staring at the screen. Slow minutes passed. It could have been hours. It *might* have been hours. I refused to take my eyes from the screen.

**BUZZ BUZZ.**

"Agh!" I dropped the phone on my bed when the next text came through. It bounced harmlessly off my pillow. I scrambled to pick it back up and opened the message. One word flashed on the screen in front of me:

Yeah.

I let out a loud laugh, waving the phone in the air in triumph. Bursting out of my room, I rushed downstairs, taking the steps two at a time, the wind rushing past my face as I sped to the bottom. I burst into the living room, the door swinging open and banging against the wall. Dad turned from the sofa, his face a deep frown.

"Jack, you can't just run around the house-"

I didn't let him finish.

"It's happening!" I grinned at him, shaking the phone in his direction.

"What's happening?" he asked.

I smiled wider. "I'm getting my best friend back!"

OK, so maybe I was a *little* over-excited. I realized this when I arrived at the skate park and checked my phone. It was 7:30pm. I was early. *Really* early. To make things worse, the sky had turned a blotchy dark gray above me and the first pitter-patter of drops fell onto my head. It was going to rain. Typical.

By 7:45pm, I was glad that my dad's selection of coats were all practical and waterproof (even if they did look *ridiculous*). I had picked a black one that had a weird red fish on the front. It was the least offensive of all of them. I now did the zip right up to my chin and pulled the hood over my head as the sky opened and released as much rain as it could. It was like standing under a waterfall. I blinked raindrops off my eyelashes, but all I could see were streams of horizontal rain. Everyone in the skate park ran for shelter. I was left alone.

By 8:05pm, I felt certain that I was being set up and that this was an elaborate ploy by ninjas to assassinate me (I don't overreact! What are you talking about?). Every movement catching my eye seemed more evidence of something dark and dangerous prowling the skate park, waiting to catch me. As I stood shivering in the entrance to the park, I seriously considered going back home.

"Why are you standing in the rain?"

I jumped a mile into the sky when Tom appeared behind me. "Don't *do* that!" I shouted over the rattle of the rain on the ground around us. "You scared the life out of me!"

When I had recovered my senses, Tom beckoned me over to a nearby bike shed where we sheltered from the rain.

"Jack?" he finally said after a pause.

"The one and only," I grinned back at him. He had been confused ever since the school fair last week, when he had found out about the *incident*. I had tried explaining it to him, over and over: my dad and I had been struck by lightning and swapped bodies. It wasn't *that* hard to understand, right? Still, it had taken him a while to... recover from what he had learned. I mean, if anyone had looked at this bike shed, they would have seen Tom, a 12-year-old boy wearing a t-shirt with our favorite band's logo on it, and Mr.

David Stevenson – teacher in his late thirties, in an old waterproof coat. An old waterproof coat that I was now learning had *holes* in it. Great.

"So you're Jack," he said again.

"Still yes. And my dad is me. Not Jack. I am Jack." I frowned. I was beginning to confuse myself.

"No," Tom said, leaning against an abandoned BMX. "This is crazy."

"Believe me, I know," I nodded. To Tom, I probably looked like a crazy old man who had lost his mind. But my dad had confirmed my story. Didn't that count for something?

"Prove it," Tom said. "Prove that I'm not going crazy right now."

"What about all the weird things I have been doing at school?" I asked. "I've been *enjoying* Math, haven't I? Would I ever do that?"

Tom nodded. "That's true, but maybe you just... maybe you just caught a virus or something that made you *like* Math!"

I shivered. What a horrible thought: *liking* Math.

"Tell me something only Jack and I would know!" he said.

A slow grin spread across my face. This was going to be easy. The skate park was where Tom and I had spent a *lot* of our childhood. If there was anywhere I could prove myself, it was here. I stuck out a finger into the rain and pointed at some nearby stairs. "That is where I nearly broke my leg trying to impress Holly by standing on the stair rail. When my dad asked what had happened, you told him I hurt it helping a cat out of a tree."

The corner of Tom's mouth twitched as he remembered the story. "Yeah, I guess."

I kept going, pointing at a half pipe on the other side of the park. "That was where we almost had a fight once because we thought a hot girl liked both of us, until it turned

194

out she was just trying to get us to give her money for ice cream. Her name was..." I blinked. What *was* her name? I frowned.

"Tabby, short for Tabatha," Tom grinned openly now. "I would have won that fight."

"If you say so," I grinned back.

Tom stared out into the park. "This is *so* weird. I mean, you're an *adult*."

"I know, right?"

"You tried to drive yet?"

"I did. Almost got arrested."

"Wow."

"I know."

Even though it was raining, I felt like the sun was shining and this was a beautiful day. I hadn't been able to speak to anyone like this (apart from my *dad*) for weeks, and talking to an adult was like talking to a boring brick wall sometimes.

I sighed. "You have no idea how great it is to talk to someone about this. Things are going to be so much *easier* now."

Tom turned to me and frowned. "How long have you been in your dad's body?"

"Since before the school dance," I told him.

"Woah," Tom said. "So everything that has happened since then... Playing the drums in band, that whole thing with Jasmine, the weird way that you actually did school work and did it so well that you actually got everything right..."

"Yep," I nodded. "All Dad in my body."

Tom looked like his whole world had been thrown into a washing machine, spun around a hundred times and then left hanging upside down to dry. "Huh," he said. "That answers a *lot* of questions."

"I know, right?" I agreed.

Tom's eyes narrowed. "Wait..." he took a step

forward and poked me in the chest. "Who has been *dating my mom then?!?"*

*Uh oh.*

I backed away into the rain. "Well, listen, it's not that simple... I mean we went to the movies once, but..."

"YOU WENT TO THE MOVIES WITH MY MOM?" Tom shouted.

It wasn't going as planned. I backed away a bit more and glanced at my wrist. "Oh, look at the time, I've got to get back home. Curfew and stuff."

Tom stalked after me. "You aren't wearing a watch, Jack! Get back here!"

"Gottagobye!" I said quickly, turning and running to the entrance of the skate park.

I heard Tom shouting my name, demanding I return,

and I couldn't help but smile. It was great to have my best friend back.

# Time for a Holiday

I was *soaked* when I got back, but I was still grinning. Tom would get over it, I was sure. He was talking to me now and that was all that mattered. Triumphantly, I entered the living room. My dad was still sitting where I had left him, staring at the TV (that was off) with a strange expression that I had never seen on his (well... my) face before. It looked like he was lost in a deep thought, and that thought wasn't a happy one. I decided to snap him out of it by throwing the coat over his head.

"I'm baaack!" I said cheerfully as he fought to get the soaking wet coat off himself.

When he finally yanked it away, his hair wet and stuck to his head, he scowled at me and threw it back. "Hang that up, Jack," he scolded me. "You're making the sofa wet!"

For once, it didn't suck to be scolded by Dad. I just smiled and picked up the coat and hung it on the hook in the hallway.

"Did you have fun while I was out?" I joked. "Life must be *boring* for you when I'm not around."

Dad rolled his eyes. "How do I cope without you?" He stood up and punched me playfully on the shoulder. "Listen, Jack," he said, his tone serious. "I've been thinking..." he paused, avoiding my gaze.

What was up with him? He looked like he was about to reveal the biggest secret of his life. I secretly hoped that I was an alien from another planet and had awesome super powers, but instead he just seemed to snap out of it and said, "How about we go on a holiday?"

I was stunned for a second. Dad didn't *do* holidays. Unless you counted a short road trip to the nearest museum. He always likes to say that *learning is fun*, but it isn't. It really, really isn't.

"You don't want to go to the Paper Museum again, do you?" I groaned. "Paper is *not as interesting as you say it is.*"

Dad laughed. "No, no, not there. Although – just because you *don't listen* doesn't mean it *isn't interesting.*" It was an old argument that Dad and I had often. It went a bit like this:

Me: It's boring!
Dad: You just need to listen and take it all in.
Me: If it wasn't boring maybe I would listen more!
Dad: But you don't listen enough.
Me: Because it's boring!
Dad: Because you don't listen!
Etc. etc.

The argument usually goes on for a while until we both give up and go for ice cream.

"Anyway," Dad said, pulling a piece of paper from his pocket. "Remember this?" As he handed it to me, I realized it wasn't a piece of paper, but a photo. It was old and crinkled, probably from years of being stuffed in a drawer.

"Wow," I joked. "Super retro."

The photo was a picture of me and him. I must have been about two years old, and I was sitting on his shoulders. We were both in t-shirts and shorts, and it was a bright sunny day. Behind us was a wooden cabin of some sort and beyond that, I could just make out what looked like a lake. On our faces were the biggest, happiest grins. We looked like we had just won the lottery.

I was surprised. I couldn't remember the last time I had seen Dad grin like that. He almost looked like a completely different person.

"Where was this taken?" I frowned. "I don't remember this at all."

"That's our cabin. We got it when we lived in Minnesota. Haven't been there since you were... oh... two and a half? It's been quite a few years."

"We have a *cabin*?" I said, surprised. "This is awesome, why didn't you tell me?"

Dad shrugged. "We haven't had the time to go back since. I didn't want you to be disappointed. But with Dr. Turner and his forced holiday time, I thought maybe we could check it out again. See how the old cabin has handled the years without us."

Dr. Turner was the psychiatrist we were sent to by *another* doctor whom we had tried to get to help us out with the whole body swap incident. He had decided (without listening to me) that I had clearly gone crazy, and had given us two weeks to sort it out or he would force us to take a break from work.

Two weeks had gone by. Nothing had changed. Dad was now on 'forced vacation,' which wasn't too bad since the summer break was only a couple of weeks away, but he was clearly anxious about being away from his job. In fact, recently he'd been acting weirder than ever. Maybe a break from all of this *would* do both of us some good. I definitely felt like I could use a little time away.

Dad gave me a smile that seemed forced and was almost creepy. It was like he was *desperate* for me to say yes.

"Alright," I smiled in return. "Let's go rock out at the cabin!"

"Great!" Dad looked relieved.

But then he continued, "Oh...and there's one more thing."

I raised an eyebrow. He was acting really strangely and I wasn't sure what to expect. The odd look on his face was making me nervous. I started to worry, thinking that something was definitely wrong. And then he finally spoke.

"We should take Tom and Sarah with us."

## Tom's House

The next day, I stood in front of Tom's large house but I was struggling to climb the steps to his front door. If you've ever seen an old haunted house in a scary movie that is kind of what Tom's house looked like.

It wasn't that I didn't want to go on vacation with Tom. No, the thought of going on holiday with Tom was *awesome*. We would have a great time. It was Sarah that would be the issue. *Yes*, I had been pretending to date her for the last few weeks, and yes, it had been *super weird*, but I was pretending to be Dad then. I had been trying not to wreck Dad's life, just as he had been (poorly) trying not to wreck mine. Tom hadn't known it was me then, but now...

"Maybe they aren't home?" I said.

"You have to *press the doorbell* to find out, Jack. That is the point of doorbells," Dad replied. "Plus, look," he pointed at Sarah's car in their driveway, "why would they be here and leave their car?"

"But..." I said.

"Push it," said Dad.

"Fine," I groaned.

A tinkling of musical DING DONGs ran through the house. Dad patted me on the shoulder as if he was congratulating a kindergartener. I growled at him and he smirked back at me.

We waited. The urge to run away grew and grew inside me, and I tried to ignore it. I wondered what would happen if I ran away now, right down the street, and never came back. "I think-" I began, but I was interrupted by the door opening and Tom greeting us with a confused look on his face.

"Jack?" he said to me. "Mr. Stevenson?" he said to my dad.

"Hi, Tom," said Dad.

I grimaced. "Run, Tom," I whispered. "Run for your life."

Tom's eyes widened.

"Ha. Ha." Dad said. "Ignore him, Tom. Is your mom in?"

Tom's eyes narrowed. "Why?" he asked suspiciously.

"No reason, let's go!" I spun on my heels, but Dad hooked an arm around my waist and stopped me from moving.

"Tom?" Sarah's voice came from upstairs. "Who is it?"

Tom rolled his eyes. There was no way he was going to be able to keep us out of the house now. "It's Jack and..." he looked at me. "David. They wanna talk to us about something."

"Well, let them in!" she shouted. "I'll be downstairs in a second."

Tom shook his head and sighed. "Come in, I guess."

Dad walked in in front of me, and Tom pointed him towards the living room. As I was about to enter, he spun around and stood in my way. "No funny stuff," he said. "That's my mom, remember."

"Cross my heart, hope to die," I said, drawing a cross on my heart. "No funny stuff." Tom held me for a second longer... and then nodded, letting me pass. I sighed and walked into his house.

Tom's living room was very different from ours. Dad liked things simple. One color on the walls, a few pictures, but not much else. We once tried to put a plant in the corner, but I think it died of boredom. Tom and Sarah's house, though, was like walking into a rainbow. Their lounge was covered in different pieces of art, pictures of Tom and Sarah doing different things together, other pictures of Sarah with people I didn't recognize, paintings, thousands of paintings covering every inch of available space.

It suddenly made sense why Tom complained so much about his house smelling of paint all the time. Sarah was a painter. I had never really thought much about her beyond 'Tom's mom' or 'Dad's kind of girlfriend but he has trouble admitting it'. She was a full on person beyond that simple label. The idea was bewildering.

When she entered the room, she was wearing a long white shirt covered in paint splotches of different colors. Her brown hair was tied back into a hasty ponytail, and she smiled as soon as she saw me.

"Hi, David, hi, Jack," she grinned. "I'd hug you but I'm in the middle of a project at the moment."

Tom looked at me. "I'm sure they'll survive," he said, narrowing his eyes.

"Can I get you a cup of coffee? Tea?" Sarah said.

"No, thank you," Dad said. "Me and Ja.... Dad are just

popping over to ask you a question."

Sarah raised an eyebrow. "Oh really?"

Tom said, "Oh *reaaaallly?*" and looked at me accusingly. I flashed him an innocent grin.

Dad looked at me.

"Yeah, I mean, whatever, it doesn't really matter, I mean..." I looked around the room. "Nice paintings." Dad, seeing that I was avoiding the question, stepped *politely* on my foot. *Get on with it*, his eyes seemed to say.

"Hmmm." I clenched my teeth to avoid wincing at the pain. "We would like the two of you to...er... come on holiday with us," I said. "To a cabin we have in Memphis."

"Minnesota," Dad coughed into his hand.

"Minnesota," I corrected myself.

"Oh wow, a cabin?" Sarah said, her eyes wide. "What's it like?"

I glanced at Dad who shrugged. "It's next to a lake," I said, as that was the only other piece of information I had about the holiday.

"Yes!" Sarah said excitedly and far too fast. She glanced at Tom guiltily. "I mean if you want to, Tom."

"Yeah, Tom, what do you think?" I asked.

Tom looked between both of us as if he had just been asked the million-dollar question on a TV quiz show.

"Er... yeah?" he said. "Sure? Why not?"

"Brilliant!" Sarah grinned and moved across the room to hug me, but at the last second, she pulled back. "Right, sorry, paint. Paint is bad."

"What are you painting now?" Dad asked, clearly annoyed that she hadn't gone to hug *him*.

"Wanna come upstairs and have a look?" she grinned, before jogging excitedly out of the room.

"I guess we're going upstairs," I said to Dad.

"I'll pass. Painting is *boring*." Tom said, turning on the games console under the TV. "Wanna game when you come back down?"

"Yeah," I grinned hopefully. "If I can manage it without your mom thinking it's weird!" I hadn't had a proper gaming session with Tom in weeks and I was willing to risk the fact that Sarah would probably think it strange to see me sitting on the couch gaming with her son.

Upstairs, Sarah stood proudly by her work, a large canvas that took up the entire wall of one room. On it were patches of bright colors and some black lines that formed a kind of colourful pattern...but I didn't quite know what it was meant to be.

"What do you think? I call it: Rainbow on canvas."

I nodded, turning my head slightly, thinking that it didn't look like a rainbow at all.

"Yeah!" I said. "Well named!"

"Brilliant!" Dad said with a smile.

Sarah punched me in the arm. "You guys are terrible liars," she laughed.

# Packing

The next day, Dad waved a piece of paper in front of my face and said, "This is important."

I tried to look around his hand at the TV, as I was deep in a game. "Is this 'homework' important or 'brand new game released' important?" My character in the game let out a scream as he fell down a dark pit. I groaned.

"Homework," said Dad, then his eyebrows lowered. "No, wait... it's a new game. Wait... which is more important, homework or a new game?"

I glanced up at him. "I don't know. What's the game?"

Dad sighed. "This is *very* important, Jack. It's a list of clothes you need to pack for me before we go on holiday in a few days. I know you won't want me to choose the clothes, so you need to do it."

I paused the game after my character tottered over the edge again, letting out yet another scream. Dad was so *distracting*.

I finally took the list from him and scanned it.
*JACK'S PACKING LIST*
1. *10 pairs of underwear*
2. *10 pairs of socks*
3. *5 pairs of pants (NO JEANS PLEASE)*
4. *2 waterproof coats*
5. *5 pairs of shoes for walking, wet weather, muddy weather and anything else.*
6. *A hat for sunny days*
7. *Two towels*
8. *Swimming trunks*
9. *Toothbrush*

I frowned at the list. "Do I even own ten pairs of socks? And five pairs of pants that *aren't* jeans? I don't know if that is possible."

Dad shrugged. "Maybe we should go shopping then."

I stuck out my tongue. "Ew, no." I picked up a pen from the table, turned his list around and began to write.

"What are you doing?"

"I'm writing *my* list," I said. "You think you can have a list and I can't have a list?"

Dad didn't say anything. He just looked at me with that disapproving look he is so good at (even with my face!). After a few seconds, I handed him back my list. It said:

CLOTHES PLEASE.

I looked up at him and grinned. He rolled his eyes. "Oh, ha, ha."

The next few days were a blur of activity. As I tried to get further and further into my game (that hole was *really* hard to cross! I must have fallen down it at least one thousand times!) Dad rushed around the house, washing clothes, drying them and then folding them up neatly and packing them into his suitcase. Occasionally, his head would pop around the door and he would say, "Have you packed yet?" And I would reply, "Pretty much! Just a little bit more!" and he would be happy and go back to whatever he was doing.

The day before we were due to leave, Tom texted me.

Tom: Wat R we gonna do there?

Me: Dunno. Sumthin awesome.

Tom: Cool

I hadn't seen him this excited in a long time! I decided that maybe it was time to start packing, so I went into my room and started grabbing clothes from my cupboard then shoving them in the suitcase Dad had left on my bed.

They didn't need to be folded because they were going to get creased in the suitcase anyway, right?

The next morning, Dad woke me up by prodding my face.

"Jack," he said. "Get up."

I opened my eyes. It was still dark. I flopped around on the bed like a jellyfish, my arms and legs not quite awake enough to do what I wanted them to.

"Glurb?" My tongue flopped around in my mouth.

"Huh?" said Dad.

"What... what time is it? Is the house on fire?" I mumbled.

"No, we just need to get up now. We have to get to the airport."

The world 'airport' meant something important, but my brain couldn't figure out what it was. I yawned loudly as Dad walked back across the room, stepping over old clothes and tutting at the mess (as he always does when he is in my room). I tried to sit up. Gravity felt very strong this morning, pulling me back down... down to my pillow... my comfy pillow and my warm comforter that wrapped around me like a cloud... and... and...

"WAKE UP," Dad shouted.

My eyes shot open. It was still very dark. Adrenaline kicked my brain into action. "Airport?" I said. "Why do we need to go to the airport?"

"We have to get to Minnesota, remember?" Dad said. "What do you want to do, walk?"

I opened my mouth and closed it again. How far away *was* Minnesota?

"Now, get up!" Dad said. "We are meeting Sarah and Tom at their house in half an hour!"

I rolled out of bed and hit the floor with a *smack*.

"*Uuuuuurgh,*" I groaned.

Forty-seven minutes later, all four of us were standing at the bus stop, staring at the empty road in the darkness. The sun hadn't even risen yet. I yawned loudly. Tom yawned loudly. Sarah and Dad didn't yawn. I suspected them to be robots in disguise. Who *wasn't* tired at this hour?

Sarah and Tom's bags looked a lot newer and nicer than the one I had given to Dad. And they certainly had a lot more stuff.

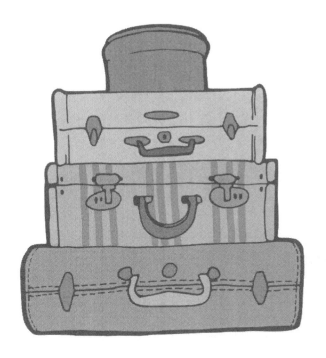

Sarah made it worse by asking Dad: "Is that all you're taking, Jack?"

He looked at me with a frown. "Apparently so."

"Those crazy kids," I joked. "Never packing enough. You'll regret that when we get there, won't you?" I ruffled his hair with my hand in a way that I knew was *very* annoying. He looked at me with eyes that said: *Not as much as you'll regret it!*

I grinned at him. This was my revenge for forcing me to get up so early.

When we were all seated on the bus and it was heading down the road, Sarah moved closer to me. She wrapped her arm around mine and leaned her head on my shoulder. "Are you ready for an adventure?"

Tom shot me a look very similar to the one Dad had

just given me.

I gulped. This was going to be a very long vacation!

# At the Airport

As the bus pulled up outside the airport, my mouth dropped open. The airport was like a city in the middle of the city! The sun had risen now, just in time to make the glass building sparkle and shine like no other building I had seen before. Excitement bubbled inside of me. Suddenly, our vacation felt like a proper adventure! I was somewhere new and exciting and I hadn't even left the state yet.

Sarah laughed at me as I pressed my nose against the glass of the building. "You're like a little kid," she grinned. "Come on, let's go inside."

I blushed as she turned away. Was it *that* obvious? I needed to act like an adult around her. An adult who had already seen and done all these things. It was going to be very difficult.

I straightened my back and walked towards the entrance, passing Tom and Dad as I did so.

"Come on, boys," I said in my most adulty voice. "Let's go. Chop chop."

Tom frowned. "Why are you speaking like that?"

"Because I'm an *adult!*" I said, marching around him in a circle.

"Ahh, trying to fool security," he nodded knowingly. "Got it."

As he passed me and entered the building, I tried not to show how terrifying his last few words sounded. Security? It hadn't even occurred to me. Now a big wave of terror came crashing down on me.

Airport security. I had to pretend to be my dad in front of people who were *trained* to spot liars.

As we crossed the airport, dodging travellers from all over the world, coming and going, all dragging suitcases of different shapes and sizes, I felt the nervousness growing inside me. My eyes darted around at the large security men and women who seemed to patrol every corner. They were tall, and looked like they meant business. Their bodies were covered in protective armor, like they expected lions to fall from the sky and attack them at any moment. They could probably have taken me down with the blink of an eye. I was no lion.

I felt a shiver of fear run down my body. *Everything is cool,* I told myself. *Nothing to worry about.* I tried to control my breathing, slow it down and focus on just putting one foot in front of the other.

"Are you alright?" Sarah said, making me jump. "Your knuckles are really white."

I looked down at my hands. They were clamped so tightly around my suitcase handle that almost all the blood had drained from my hand. I took a breath and tried to loosen my fingers, smiling weakly at Sarah. "I just... well... I...."

"Dad's afraid of flying," Dad leaped in to save me. I glanced over at him. I was surprised at *how* quickly he reacted. I nodded.

"Yep. Terrified. Scary. Flying? A big no no."

Sarah smiled warmly. "Aww, don't worry, David. It's only a little flight. It'll be over before you know it." She hugged me and rubbed my back with her free hand. Tom stared at me from behind her with fire in his eyes.

*What are you doing?* He mouthed.

*It's not me, it's her!* I mouthed back.

"Did you say something?" Sarah said, pulling back.

"Me? Nope. Tom, did you say something?"

"No," Tom said darkly. "Not yet."

I didn't fail to notice the threat in Tom's eyes. *If you don't leave my mom alone, I'm going to tell her everything.*

I took a few steps away from Sarah, just in case. That was the *last* thing I needed right now.

*Everything will be fine,* I told myself.

It wasn't. For what felt like the next few hours, we stood in a queue, watching other people step up to a little desk where a woman in a strange orange uniform sat. She even had a small hat on the side of her head, but I couldn't figure out how it stayed on. She must have been using some kind of hat magic.

But even the mystery of the hat lost interest after a while. Both Tom and I started to get incredibly bored, tapping random beats on our legs, sighing loudly and just staring off into space as the queue crept along like a snail that didn't like to rush things.

"Uuuugh, will this never end?" Tom groaned.

"It feels like we have been here foreverrrrrr," I groaned as well.

Sarah gave me an odd look. Dad shook his head and turned away. I realized I was acting like a kid again.

"I mean…" I quickly stood up straight. "Waiting is good for you, Tom, helps you learn patience and…er… stuff." I nodded knowingly.

"You don't know anything," Tom mumbled, as frustrated as I was.

"Tom!" Sarah looked horrified. "Apologize to David! That was very rude!"

Tom quickly straightened up too. "I'm sorry, Mr. Stevenson," he said through gritted teeth. "I was very rude."

I couldn't help myself from grinning at him. "That's fine, Tom. I, Mr. David Stevenson, knows nothing at all. I am completely brainless."

Tom snorted out a laugh.

"I'm sure you know *some* things, *Dad*," Dad said, his eyes narrowed. "Maybe quite a lot of things. You are a *teacher* after all."

"Nope." I said. "I am like a stupid monkey, OOO OOO AHH AHH!" I started waving my hands around and doing a monkey impression. Tom joined in. Soon we were both pretending to be monkeys in the line at the airport.

"Er… David?" Sarah whispered. "People are looking."

"DAVID WANT BANANA!" I said. Tom laughed out

loud. Dad shook his head.

Sarah giggled. "You're a strange man, David Stevenson."

I laughed too, finally feeling calmer. For a second, I had convinced myself that this whole airport situation wasn't as bad as I thought it was.

By then we were next up at the desk, and the fear came back in a massive flood of panic. My palms started sweating. We moved up to the desk and the woman smiled at me.

"Hello Sir. Madam. Do you have your tickets?"

I produced a blue wallet that Dad had put into my backpack and told me was full of the documents we needed. I noticed my hand was visibly shaking. I placed the wallet on the desk in front of me and waited as she took the passports and tickets out of it, one by one. She looked at each ticket, each passport.

Tom's ticket. Tom's passport.

Sarah's ticket. Sarah's passport.

My fingers clenched in my palms.

Dad's ticket. Dad's passport.

I felt a bead of sweat run down my forehead. I wiped it off as quickly as possible.

My ticket.

She looked at it.

She glanced up at me.

She looked at it again.

She typed something into her computer.

I saw a security guard watching us from the side of the room. Was he going to come over and arrest me?

"And you are David Stevenson?" she asked.

"Yep. Yep. That's me. Absolutely me. No one else. That's me. I like Math and I am a teacher and I am very smart and things. I am David Stevenson, yes."

The woman smiled a confused smile at me.

"Very nice. All done," she said. "Place your luggage on

the conveyor belt next to me and have a nice flight."

I blinked. That was it? I lifted up my luggage, placed it on the moving belt next to her, and smiled. We all walked out of the queue.

"Well," I said with a big grin. "That was painless! I could do that all day." I felt like a great weight had been lifted off my chest.

"Well, the tough part comes next," Sarah grinned. "Security. Don't look too suspicious!" She laughed loudly and happily as the great weight landed back onto my chest with a thud. It wasn't over.

"Heh, yeah," I said quietly.

I laughed too, but inside I felt like I could dissolve at any second. My legs were jelly.

We joined yet another queue, but this one was shorter. At the end of this queue wasn't a friendly looking woman sitting at a desk, but a big, mean looking man who scowled at everyone who got too close. He stood on the other side of a big, metal machine that people had to walk through when he told them to step forward. It must have been the metal detectors I always heard about. All around us were big signs that said things like:

NO MORE THAN 100ML OF LIQUID

MAKE SURE YOU REMOVE ALL METAL ITEMS

DO WHAT YOU ARE TOLD BY SECURITY PERSONNEL

It was like school, only a thousand million times worse. Everything looked terrifying. I was terrified.

Slowly we inched forward and Sarah started sorting out Tom, making him take off his jacket and shoes. I frowned, and glanced at Dad who nodded in their direction and indicated that I should probably do the same. I removed my backpack, the old jacket and uncomfortable shoes that Dad had made me wear, and placed them into a box on the conveyor belt. I was last again, forced to watch Sarah, Tom and Dad walk through the machine one by one on a nod from the beastly looking security guard who stood on the other side.

I watched my backpack disappear into the machine. I tried to remember what I had put inside it. Was there anything dangerous? I didn't think so, but suddenly my mind was a blur.

"Step forward sir," the security guard said without a hint of a smile. He wore a white shirt and black trousers, but his muscles bulged with a ferocious anger underneath it. I imagined that if he wanted to, he could squash me with one hand. I closed my eyes and stepped through the machine and...

BEEP BEEP BEEP BEEP!

I panicked and looked around. What had I done? What was going on? Should I run? I didn't want to be squashed! I looked at Dad, who grinned at me. Why was he grinning?

The security guard stood close to me and grimaced. He started waving a small machine around my body. It hummed as it passed my face and went down my chest. As it hit my waist, it went, 'EEEEEEE'.

I looked down. *What* did I have on myself that would make it go EEEE?

"Lift up your shirt," the guard commanded.

I glanced at him, worried, and then lifted up my shirt.

The security guard shook his head. "Your belt, sir. It set off the machine."

I looked down at my trousers. I was wearing a belt with a metallic buckle. Of course! That was what had set off the machine. I grinned helplessly at the security guard.

"Sorry?" I said.

"Move on," the guard grunted.

# Flying out of Control

After that, it was smooth sailing. We sat in a restaurant and had lemonade until it was time to board the plane. After standing in yet another queue, we were pushed onto a small plane which smelled a bit like cheese. I was squeezed in the back, between an extraordinarily fat man and Tom. He had persuaded Sarah that he wanted to sit by me so we could 'bond'. She seemed to love that idea! Somewhere else on the plane, she sat with Dad. Getting tickets next to each other was apparently impossible.

Tom sniggered as he saw that the fat man had *already* fallen asleep and was using me as a pillow.

"This is going to be fun," I groaned. I could feel the blood seeping out of my arm.

The plane's engine started off as a rumble, and then grew to a roar as we sped up the runway. I grinned at Tom and he grinned back at me as we felt the wheels lift off from the ground. We were flying! I felt a rush of adrenaline as we pulled higher and higher into the sky, and my ears popped as the pressure changed. I really loved flying.

Truth be told, I felt a lot better being a fat man's pillow than being harassed by the security guards. Tom and I were settling down to a good gaming session on his Game Kid Ultra 3D when there was a commotion further up the plane. I tried to look over the seats to see who it was, but I could already tell. I rolled my eyes. Dad was causing trouble again.

I sat up straighter, nudging the fat man's head away, so it clonked against the plane window, and tried to listen as best I could.

"I just... I just need to breathe..."

"Madam, could you control your son? He is stepping on my dress! This is a Chanel dress! Do you *know how much this cost?*"

Three rows in front of us, I could see Dad climbing

between the seats trying to get out into the aisle. He seemed to be standing *on* the seats, climbing from his, next to the window and onto the unfortunate woman's seat next to him! The woman tried to bat him away with her hand, but failed. A hostess walked over, her orange uniform similar to that of the woman who had served us at the desk.

"Sir, could you please sit down? The seat belt signs have not yet been turned off..."

I groaned. Why could it not just be an easy flight?

"You don't understand," Dad said, breathlessly. "I can't breathe properly in this plane, I need to just walk around and..."

"Sir, we need you to sit down, or we are going to have to land the plane. Sir, sit down, please."

My eyes widened. Dad *was* afraid of flying! I thought that was just a joke he made up to stop me from looking stupid, but here he was panicking! He needed something to calm him down fast. I looked around the plane. Other people were watching, some were laughing. It was *so embarrassing*.

Sarah reached up from her seat. "Jack, Jack, calm down," she said. "It'll all be OK."

"No, you don't understand," Dad replied, trying to step forward again and making the woman between them squeak a bit more. "I'm not Jack, I don't..."

*Oh no! Dad is going to tell Sarah if I don't do something soon.* I looked frantically around me for something to help calm Dad down or make him stop. On the lap of the fat man next to me, there was an open packet of sweets. Tom leaned over me and looked at the sweets as well.

"That might get his attention," he grinned.

I snatched the packet of sweets off the fat man's legs with a little apology (he didn't hear anyway, he just continued snoring) and took the first, round red sweet in my hand, holding it between my first finger and my thumb.

I sighed. "Well, here goes nothing." How hard could

it be?

I aimed at Dad and threw it across the seats in front of me. It missed Dad and hit an old lady in the back of the head. Oops. Turns out throwing sweets is not as easy as throwing a football.

"Oh, heavens!" she said, turning around to see what had hit her.

I ducked and looked at Tom, who cringed and snorted a laugh. "You hit her really hard!" he hissed.

"Shh!" I snapped, standing up again. "That was a practice throw."

"Sir, you really need to..." The air hostess turned as something hit her on the shoulder. Something small and green. She frowned, but then turned back to Dad.

"You're rubbish at this," Tom chuckled.

"I don't see *you* helping!" I said.

Tom held out his hand. "Gimme some. I want a go."

I reluctantly held out the packet of sweets and Tom took a handful. He aimed and threw one.

It rattled off a nearby wall. I snorted with laughter. Tom growled and snatched another sweet, aiming again.

The passengers of the plane were starting to wonder where all the sweets came from when I finally struck Dad on the cheek. He was balanced between two armrests, his face squished against the air vent as he tried to climb over the seat.

He frowned and looked down the plane, right at me.

From deep inside me, I summoned the teacher voice that I had been using over the last few weeks. I didn't like it, but it was effective.

"SIT. DOWN," I said through gritted teeth. Even Tom shuddered when I used it.

Dad paused, thought about it and then climbed down, back into his chair again. He mumbled a "sorry" to the woman beside him, who was still ranting to Sarah about her dress.

A few people on the plane applauded. The air hostess looked at me with relief. I sat back down with a sigh.

Tom gave me a strange look.

"What?" I asked.

Tom shook his head. "How did you do that voice?" he asked.

I shrugged. "Don't know. I just call it the 'teacher voice'. I had to use it in school a few times, and Dad uses it all the time."

"That's creepy," Tom said. "Do you ever think that maybe you swapped *more* than just bodies?"

"What do you mean?" I asked.

"I'm just saying," he shrugged. "You seemed more like the parent there and Mr. Stevenson was more like... you know... us.... I don't know..." Tom thought about it. "Like a kid, I guess."

I opened my mouth to reply, but couldn't think of anything to say. *More* than just bodies?

## Lying on the Ground

When we finally got out of the plane, it felt like we were finally free of a prison that we had been trapped in for hours. No one looked more relieved to be off the plane than Dad, and as we passed the air hostess on the way out, she waved us off with a very fake smile. I think she was glad to see the back of us, too.

We all filled our lungs with the fresh(ish) air of the new airport, which was a *lot* smaller than the previous one, and headed towards the luggage collection point. As we watched the conveyor belt spin around and around with luggage of all different shapes and sizes, I took Dad to one side and whispered to him: "So, you're afraid of flying. Didn't think of mentioning that *before* we got on the plane?"

Dad sniffed. "I thought I would have gotten over it by now. It's been years since I last flew."

"You haven't," I pointed out.

"I haven't," Dad agreed.

"Anything else you're not telling me?" I closed my eyes. I think I had a headache coming on.

Dad picked up his suitcase as it tried to roll past him. "Well, about the next part of the journey..."

"All good?" Sarah interrupted us. "I managed to grab your suitcase too, David," she smiled and offered me the ancient brown thing from under Dad's bed.

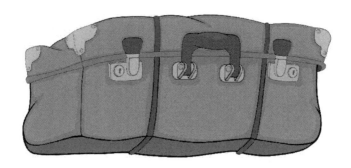

"Thanks," I said, taking it and praying it would disintegrate and we'd have to spend the next few hours picking Dad's underwear off the floor.

She looked at us both, suitcases in hand. "Brilliant! We can go and get the car then."

"Yes," I said. "The car." I glanced towards Dad. I had no idea what she was talking about. Sarah set off in a brisk stride, humming pleasantly to herself. The rest of us had to jog to keep up. Tom yawned loudly.

"How can she have so much energy after that flight?" he groaned.

It soon became clearer where we were going. We followed Sarah out of the main building, along a walking path crowded with people, and into another smaller building that had a bright green sign over the top. It said:
CAR RENTALS

As we were about to go inside, Dad grabbed me by the arm and hissed: "You can't drive, Jack. You've got to think of an excuse."

"Why did you *rent a car* if you didn't want me to drive?"

"Well technically, Sarah rented it," Dad said, as if that made it better. "There's no other way to get to the cabin. I thought we could get her to drive. You have to pretend you're feeling ill or something."

I scowled at him. I remembered the good old days when Dad told me that *lying was wrong* and that it *hurt people*. Now he just wanted me to lie all the time. I racked my brains but they were too tired to come up with something worthwhile. Sarah talked to the man at the desk and began to fill out some forms. I slumped next to Tom in a plastic chair by the window.

"I've got an idea," Tom said. "I know how to get you out of driving the car."

"Yeah?" I grinned.

"Yeah," he said. "It's fool proof. Just follow my lead."

I nodded. At least *Tom* was trying. Dad was just standing by the doorway nervously rubbing his hands together.

Finally, after another long wait, the man behind the desk handed Sarah some keys. "I hope you're ready to drive us," Sarah told me with a grin, then turned towards the parking lot. We gathered our belongings and followed her out. She was trying to find the car, looking for space H165, when Dad suddenly squeaked: "He can't drive!"

"Why not?" Sarah said with a frown.

"He's...er... well..." Dad tried to think of something.

"Drunk!" Tom chimed in. I turned towards him, wide-eyed, and he winked at me. "Completely drunk off his face. I saw him drink three of those little bottles on the plane. I told him to stop and that it wasn't good for him, Mom, but he wouldn't listen." Tom shook his head at me and I tried to resist the urge to strangle him right there.

*DRUNK? THAT WAS HIS BRILLIANT IDEA?* I realized that Tom was, again, trying to sabotage my relationship with his mom. By the way she was looking at me, almost shocked by the news, I wondered if he had actually managed to do it.

"Is this... true, David?" she said quietly.

I looked between grinning Tom and silently pleading Dad. They both wanted me to say yes for completely different reasons. After a long, loud sigh, I turned towards her. "It's true," I nodded, although the lie tasted like dirt in my mouth. "I am drunk. Completely. I am in no condition to drive. I didn't think, I'm sorry."

Sarah shook her head. "No, you didn't think." Her words stung. "Alright, I'll drive then."

With that, she stormed off towards the location of the car, leaving us all standing there.

"Oooooh," Tom whispered. "You're in trooouble."

"No thanks to you," I hissed back. "I'm drunk? Really?"

Tom shrugged. "You're not driving, are you?" He bounced off after Sarah with a spring in his step. I growled and followed him, leaving Dad to bring up the rear.

We found the car we had rented on the other side of the parking lot. Tom whistled. "That is a *big* car," he said. He wasn't lying either. The car was at least twice the size of the one we had at home, and three times the size of Sarah's. She looked at it worriedly. "Are you sure we have the right one?" she asked.

I looked down at the piece of paper in her hand. The name of the car on it was an
**UBER GRAND SUPER TRAVELLER DELUXE EXTREME.**

I looked at the car. Those same words shone on the door in a bright silver. I nodded. "Looks like it."

Sarah sighed. "Alright then." She turned towards me. "You can sit in the back, David, and sleep off the alcohol." She twisted on her heels and opened the front door of the car, getting in. She slammed the door closed.

Tom grimaced. "Ouch, that looked painful." I stood blushing in the parking lot.

"You're enjoying this too much," I said. Tom nodded with a big grin on his face.

I sat in the back of the car with Tom, and there was still enough room left for a whole party with dancing and a DJ booth. "Wow," I said, "This is amazing," stretching my legs out. It made a nice change from the cramped plane.

"Shouldn't you be asleep?" Sarah snapped and turned on the engine. It rumbled to life like a dragon waking from a deep sleep.

I decided to close my eyes, just to make her feel a bit happier. I secretly hoped that she would forgive me by the time we reached the cabin.

To my surprise, when I next opened my eyes, the scenery outside had changed dramatically. I must have fallen asleep without realizing it! We were far from the city, on a long winding road surrounded by tall pine trees. Even the air smelled fresher and cleaner. I stared out the window in astonishment, trying to take it all in. I listened to Sarah talking to Dad in the front of the car.

"Does your dad usually drink like this, Jack?" she asked.

Dad didn't answer right away. "No, he doesn't. Never, really."

"I'm just worried about him," she said. "I mean, do you think he is uncomfortable with me or..."

"No," Dad said. "Not at all. I think he is just nervous. He wants to make a good impression on you and got a bit carried away. Like at the dinner party."

A few weeks earlier, we had had a dinner party where I had drunk wine (by accident...! And then I had a bit more). The results weren't great, but it turns out Sarah was surprisingly forgiving, even when I stumbled about her house all night.

"Oh," she replied. It sounded like she was smiling.

## At the Cabin

When my eyes opened next, someone was shaking my shoulders. "Wake uuuup, lazy bones!" Tom shouted in my ear.

I mumbled and sniffed, wiping the drool off my cheek and tried to bat him away like he was an annoying fly. "Why are you so *loud*?" I grumbled.

Tom grinned. "Because we're *here*! We made it to the cabin."

I turned to look out the car door, and squinted as sunlight blinded me. Protecting my eyes with my hand, I could make out a muddy path, surrounded by tall pine trees which led up to the wooden cabin I remembered from the picture. It sat waiting for us, overgrown with shrubs that hadn't been trimmed in years.

I unclipped my seatbelt and stepped outside the car, stretching my legs and arms. Dad, by the front of the car, was doing something similar. "Ahhh," he said. "That's more like it. This place is exactly how I remember it."

Sarah frowned as she passed him to the trunk of the car. "How old were you when you last came here, Jack?"

"Twenty-ei..." Dad stopped mid-sentence. "Two and a half. I just have a really good memory," he added quickly.

"Apparently so," Sarah said.

I decided it was time to check out the cabin. I took a step forward and-

SQUELCH.

"Aww gross!" I said, looking down at Dad's sneakers on my feet. I had trodden right into a deep, muddy puddle. Cold water began to seep into my socks.

"Oh, yeah, look out for that," Tom laughed. I shot him a scowl and tried to recover as much of my foot as possible, but it was too late. I shivered as the mud dripped deeper into my shoe.

I attempted to pull myself free, but somehow I felt my feet sink further into the mud. I pulled on one of my feet and it came out with a *plop!* Then I gently placed it down on the dry ground in front of me. Then. I. struggled. to. pull. out. the. other. fooooooooooot. PLOP.

I almost fell forward when the mud finally let me go. Stumbling towards the cabin, I grabbed hold of Tom's shoulder to stabilize myself. His whole body shook as he laughed at me.

"Thanks, Tom," I said coldly.

Tom grinned at me, and I could hear Sarah and Dad chuckling too from the other side of the car.

"Can we just go *inside*?" I sighed. The steps of the cabin beckoned. As I got closer, I realized that the place had definitely seen better days. The steps alone were broken and cracked, a strange green moss was growing up the posts that held up the roof and the windows were covered in dust and spider webs. I walked up to the door, each piece of wood creaking as I did so, and tested the handle. It was locked.

"Do you have the key, D... er... Jack?" I asked.

Dad began searching in his backpack. "Yeah, I've got it here somewhere. Let me just..."

"Hellooooooooo!" A deep, booming voice made us all turn and look up. A large man in square framed glasses and a red shirt jogged down the dirt track towards us.

"Oh, yeah," Dad mumbled as if he was remembering something that was probably vitally important. I was right.

"David!" shouted the man with a big grin. "It's been *years*, buddy! How have you been?"

The big man crossed through the mud like it was nothing and held out his arms wide.

"Er.. Hi," I said just as the man wrapped his arms around me in a big bear hug.

"I never thought I'd see you again!" he chuckled loudly into my ear.

"Ack... ack... aaaack!" I said, desperately trying to breathe. He *finally* released me and looked at me with a smile. I took in a long, soothing breath. Ahhh oxygen!

"The old cabin's in rough shape, eh?" He patted a wooden post, looked at his hand and then wiped it on his pants. "She's seen better days, that's for sure, but you'll get her back up and running in no time, eh? I think the generator still works round back. I've tested it a few times over the years." The man talked and talked with a big smile but I still had no idea who he was.

"Er... thanks," I said. "It's good to see you too." I tapped him on the shoulder and smiled. "It has been too long."

The man smiled wider. "Come round the cabin tomorrow, Stacy would love to see you again. Especially since..." The man's voice trailed off. "Well, you know." I really had no idea, but I nodded anyway. The man turned and saw Sarah standing by the car. It set him off again. "And she would love to meet your new friends!" He marched over to Sarah and also gave her a hug.

"Welcome to Pine Valley!" he said. "You are?"

Sarah recovered her breath and wheezed. "Sarah... And that's Tom."

Tom waved and ducked behind the car, wisely hiding from the hugs.

"I'm Greg!" I made a mental note to remember the name. Greg. Crazy hugging man's name was Greg. "I hope you have a fantastic time here! And YOU!" Greg turned his sights onto Dad. "You must be JACK! Wow, you've grown so big."

Dad nodded. "I have, haven't I?"

Greg held out his arms and squeezed. Dad, somehow, was prepared and managed to squeeze right back.

"Wow!" Greg said. "This guy knows how to do a Pine Valley greeting! You've taught him well, David!"

I smiled weakly, hoping my lungs hadn't been

crushed beyond repair, and nodded.

"I'll see you all later! Have a great stay!" And like that, he was gone, marching off back up the road the way he came.

"Wow," I said. "That was..."

"That man sure knows how to hug," Sarah laughed, from her spot behind us.

Dad handed me the key to the cabin and whispered quietly, "Sorry about that, I forgot about Greg and his rather intense hugs. If you hug him back though, they aren't so bad." He rubbed his chest. Maybe he hadn't managed to avoid the worst of it after all.

I turned the key in the lock. There was a soft click. "Clearly you remembered enough to keep your lungs intact," I whispered back. "We just need to..." I stepped into the cabin and looked around. Something in the back of my mind sparked in recognition. Of old times, long ago. I recognized the now faded carpet on the floor that was red and had elephants on it. I recognized the mirror at the other end of the hall. In it, Dad's face stared back at me.

Aaaaa CHOO! I sneezed.

"Phew," I said. "This place needs airing out."

I took a few more steps inside.

"That's one bedroom," Dad pointed at a closed door next to us as he headed quickly through the house ahead of Sarah and Tom. "And the other bedroom is there."

"Cool," I said, stepping over to the nearest door. "Let's have a look at this room th-"

I stopped talking. My mouth dropped open as I stared into the room. "Dad," I hissed. "What is *that?*"

# The Picture

In the center of the room sat a double bed. The mattress looked like it had survived quite well over the years it had been abandoned, but that wasn't the point. The point was that it was a *double* bed. A double bed that I would have to share with *Sarah*. My throat tightened. This wasn't good. Apart from the fact that Tom would probably explode and try to murder me, I would have to *share* a bed with *Sarah*. That would be super weird!

"Ah, I'd forgotten about that!" Dad said. "Yes, that is a problem."

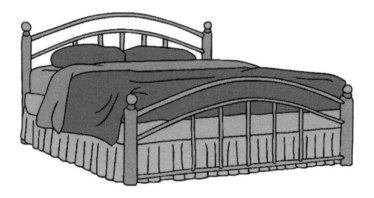

"What's a problem?" Sarah asked.

I slammed the door closed before she could look inside and then spun around. Sarah stood in the doorway, holding two suitcases in her hands.

"Nothing!" I said quickly. "Nothing at all. Everything is great. Greater than great. Super great. Your bedroom is down the hall." I smiled sweetly and Sarah frowned and nodded slowly. She pulled the cases behind her down the corridor. When she went into the other room, I turned back to Dad. "What are we going to *do*?" I hissed.

"I guess we're sharing a bed," Dad grimaced.

I sighed. I had to *share* with *Dad*? Ugh. This holiday

was getting worse and worse by the second. I just wanted to chill out for a week, but now I realized that it was going to be a lot more difficult than that.

"Are you *sure* this is my room?" Sarah shouted from the other end of the cabin.

"Yep, absolutely. Isn't it great?" I said quickly.

"Stop saying *great*," Dad whispered.

"But there's only one bed in here," Sarah's voice came again from the bedroom.

"Great," I groaned. "I mean... fantastic." I shot another angry glance at Dad, who looked guilty.

"There's a bed under the sofa," Dad chimed in quickly. He glanced at me. "That is where Tom is sleeping."

"Ahhh," Sarah said, emerging from the room.

Tom stood in the doorway. "I'm sleeping on the floor? How is *that* fair?" he said.

"Do you want me sharing a bed with your mom?" I hissed.

"The floor can actually be surprisingly comfy," Tom quickly agreed. He disappeared back into the living room.

Dad wandered into the bedroom and started rummaging through the cupboard. He told me to get our bags from the car. After all, my shoes were already caked in mud, so what would a little more do?

I grumbled and groaned and grumbled as I wandered over to the car and got our bags out of the trunk. I had to hold them up so they wouldn't drag along the ground and get muddy in the process. By the time I reached the cabin again, my arms were aching. I breathed out heavily as Sarah walked past me again.

"You need to work out more," she grinned. "Keep going, big guy."

I was breathing too heavily to reply. Maybe I *did* need to work out more. This old guy body was getting annoying.

With one final effort, I dragged the bags inside and opened the door to the bedroom. "You know," I said between breaths. "You could help me."

Dad was sitting on the bed holding a picture frame in his hands. He didn't seem to hear what I said, and just continued to stare at it.

"Dad?" I said. "Earth to Daaaaad?"

The door closed behind me and I sat on the bed next to him. "What are you looking at?"

I looked at the picture in Dad's hands. It showed my two year old self, wearing a ridiculous hat and sunglasses far too big for my toddler head. I was in a woman's arms, and she too was smiling, her face warm and happy as she stared at me lovingly. Her face was partially obscured by the sweeping brown hair that covered half of her face, but I could see enough to know that she was beautiful. I recognized that face, but I hadn't seen a picture of her in years.

Something caught in my throat.

"Is that Mom?" I whispered.

Dad swallowed and then put the picture on the bed, facing downward.

"I found it in the wardrobe," he said in a quiet voice. "I forgot about all of this."

"Why would you hide the pictures away?" I asked.

"It's..." Dad took another breath. "It's in the past. We need to move on."

In the past. It suddenly clicked in my brain why we hadn't come back to the cabin in so many years. The last time we had been here was with Mom, just before she died. I had been so young, it hadn't really affected me, but Dad – for Dad it was all there. Still fresh in his memory.

"We can't just *move on*, Dad," I said, my voice rising more than I expected. "That's Mom. You can't just pretend she never existed!"

Dad stood up. "You don't..." he began in a shout, but then lowered his voice. "You don't understand, Jack. You were too young. It was difficult."

234

"Well, tell me then!" I said. "I'm old enough now."

"No," Dad said. "I.... I can't." He walked towards the door and opened it, storming out of the room.

"Dad!" I called after him.

By the time I reached the doorway, and looked out of the cabin, Dad had already left. He was stalking down the road away from the cabin, and back towards where – I assumed – Greg lived. I was going to chase after him, but something made me turn back and look into the room.

He had taken the picture with him. A small part of me wondered if I would ever get to see it again. Anger suddenly rose up in me. *Let him go,* I thought to myself. *He just wants to hide everything from me, as always.*

"Are you OK?" Sarah stood at the door. "You look pale as a sheet. Was that Jack storming off out there?"

*No.* I thought. Wouldn't it be easier if we just told her everything? Yet something made me hold my tongue. "Yes, he is a bit upset. Let him walk it off."

Sarah nodded. "I understand. Do you know where the generator is? We should probably get some power on in here. It's getting dark."

I glanced at the window. "It's around the back," I said, remembering Greg's words. "I'll go have a look at it now."

"Thanks, David," she said.

*Yeah,* I grumbled to myself, *thanks a lot, David.*

# Finding the Generator

It was dark around the back of the cabin. I could hear the wind whistling through the trees, and those weird bugs that make that creaking sound at night. Compared to home, it was like a completely different world. I stood and looked across the lake for a while, lights sparkling in the distance. I tried to make out what they were, but it was too far. Probably some kind of building, maybe a house, I decided.

I got to what I assumed was the power generator. It was a hulking beast that smelled a lot like a gas station, only much, much worse. I held my phone up as a makeshift torch, and that was when I truly realized how terrible a torch my phone was.

The generator was a metal contraption with bits of plastic all over it. Tubes and wires were stuck in on every side in a way that made no sense. I quickly came to the conclusion that I had no idea what I was doing, and should probably wait for Dad to get back from his little walk.

But when *would* he be coming back?

No, I thought. I am the adult here now. I can figure this out.

A twig snapped under my foot and it made me jump. I laughed and rolled my eyes at the sky. This was stupid. How hard could it be?

I glanced at my phone. No signal. I doubted there was WI FI anywhere either. No chance of looking up the answers on the internet. I was going to have to figure this one out on my own. I studied the top of the generator. There was something that looked like somewhere to pour stuff in, and there were two buttons, too. A green one and a red one on the top. I shrugged. Green means go, I thought to myself. Surely I just had to press the button and everything would be fixed, right?

My brain agreed. Go brain power! I had a mental image of the generator blowing up in my face. I mentally made a note to stop watching so many action movies.

I closed my eyes and pushed the button.

There was a growl, a roar from the machine that made me step back a little. Then it settled into a soft 'chug-a-chug' before the lights in the cabin flickered on. There was a cheer from inside.

"Woo!" I threw my arms up in the air. "Jack One, Generator zero!"

As if in response to my celebration, the generator suddenly stopped making a noise with a quiet hisssssss and the lights flickered out in the cabin again.

I lowered my arms. "Fine," I groaned. "Jack one, generator, one. But this isn't over!"

I realized that I was talking to an inanimate object. That probably wasn't a good sign. I turned around and looked back at the lake. The lights on the other side taunted me with their ability to turn on.

I leaned on the generator and sighed. It was clear that I had no idea what I was doing. I was going to have to wait for Dad to get back.

My hand itched. I frowned and brushed it with my other hand. My hand continued to itch. It was very annoying. I stared down at it. I couldn't see anything in the darkness. Bringing up my phone, I looked at the offending hand to see what was wrong with it.

I quickly wished I hadn't.

My hand was covered in hundreds of little red spiders from the nest I had accidentally disturbed. They were crawling all over me!

"Argh!" I screamed, shaking my hand and trying to get them off me. Suddenly, my whole body was itchy beyond belief. They were all over me! "Argh! Get them off! Get them off!" I started dancing around in a little circle, trying to pat down my whole body. I couldn't see anything except little red spiders everywhere.

"David?" Sarah had come out to see what all the noise was about.

"Spiders!" I shouted. "All over my body!"

"Oh no! I hope they aren't the biting type!" Sarah said, holding a hand in front of her mouth and looking around at the floor. The *biting* type? I hadn't even considered that. A whole new level of fear swept through my body, and I launched myself towards the lake.

"David?" Sarah called after me.

I didn't hear her, I was deaf with fear and the itching was going crazy all over my body. I didn't think. I just acted on instinct. It wasn't long before I was running down a little wooden pier, the timber decking thumping under my feet. I ran and I ran until there was no more pier and that was when a little voice in my head said:

*Hmm. Maybe this wasn't the smartest plan.*

"Davi-!" Sarah screamed.

### SPLOOSH!!!

It was even darker in the water, and there was complete silence except for a quiet ringing in my ears. Then I realized how cold it was. Icy cold. I wanted to kick my legs and swim back to the surface, but they were too sluggish to respond. It was like getting out of bed in the morning, except I couldn't breathe and I was freezing cold. My hands tried to grab for something, anything to pull myself out, but all that surrounded me was darkness.

*At least you got rid of the spiders,* the little voice in my head taunted.

I kicked and kicked again, but I sank further and further into the lake. I realized that if I didn't do something soon, this was going to be the end of Jack Stevenson, most handsome boy in the world.

I was going to drown.

The little voice in my head perked up again with its last comment on the situation.

*Worst. Vacation. Ever.*

# Out of the Lake

The lake was deep and the lake was cold. The further down I sank, the darker the world became. I needed to think of a way out of this, and fast. I was pretty sure that I had seen this exact scene in a movie once. I closed my eyes and tried to think of how the hero of that tale got out of the water.

A *jetpack*. He had used a jetpack to blast himself out of the water.

I realized that maybe I watched too much TV. It wasn't going to help me this time.

My legs seemed to have given up completely now. They felt like lead weights, dragging me deeper and deeper into the water. My arms were definitely going the same way. The water wrapped around me like the world's coldest blanket and the last bubbles of air popped out of my mouth, floating to the surface.

"You're just going to give up?"

My eyes opened. Floating in front of me in the water was my girlfriend, Holly.

I frowned. *She* wasn't having any trouble moving

around in the water. She wasn't having any trouble speaking, either.

"Come on, Jack," she said. "You can't just sink down to the bottom of the lake. It is *gross* down here. I mean, look at that!" She pointed at some trash that floated by. "If you want to see me again, you're going to have to kick."

I pathetically attempted to kick my legs. They wobbled a bit.

"Harder!" she shouted. "Get moving!"

I kicked again, and again. Slowly, I began to rise.

"It's about time." She rolled her eyes.

*Wow,* I thought. *My underwater visions of Holly are really judgmental.*

Then it happened. Hands grabbed my arms and pulled. Holly was helping me out of the water.

When I finally reached the surface and felt myself dragged back onto the end of the dock, the world lurched back into life in an explosion of sound. The wind rushed through my hair, the trees creaked, birds sang and the world exploded in color. Everything was blurry and spun around me. I heard a distant voice, as if it was at the end of a tunnel. A long tunnel.

"Holly?" I mumbled.

Then she was over me. "It's OK, I've got you," she whispered to me, her damp blond hair dripping on me. "You're safe now."

"Holly," I tried to say, but all I could feel was water filling my mouth still. Holly leaned forward, our faces almost touching.

"It's OK," she said again. "I'll save you, buddy." I frowned. *Buddy?* But that was all washed away as she leaned in close, our lips almost touching as her beard tickled my chin...

*HOLD UP. Rough skin? Unshaved cheeks?*

My eyes opened, for real this time. Greg was leaning over me, his mouth pressing hard against mine. He breathed disgusting, hot air into my mouth. Horror took over. I wriggled and pushed him back off me, my lungs drawing in a long, desperate breath. My mouth tasted like garlic. I spat out onto the floor. I just *knew* that I would be tasting Greg for weeks. *Gross.*

Sarah stood behind him and clapped her hands. "You saved him!" she said with a big grin. "Oh thank goodness, I was so worried!"

"Those first aid classes sure came in handy!" Greg grinned. "I never thought I'd have to do the kiss of life on someone, but here you are, alive!"

"Did you *really* have to do the kiss off life?" I asked, scraping my tongue on the back of my hand. It tasted like lake water, so it wasn't much better.

"Well, you're alive, aren't you?" Greg patted me on the back.

"I am, I guess. Thanks."

"Not a problem, buddy!" Greg stood up. "I was just coming round to bring you this." He pointed at a steaming apple pie that lay on the dock next to us. "Stacy made it fresh this evening for you all. That's when I heard the splashing and commotion."

"Sorry, I'm a bit of a screamer," Sarah smiled with embarrassment. "Why did you jump in the lake, David?" she asked, the concern still on her face.

I shrugged. "I just wondered how deep it was. Turns out, it's pretty deep."

Both Greg and Sarah stared at me for a second, and then Greg burst out in a loud, hearty laugh.

"David, you crazy fool," he smiled. "Good to know you haven't lost that famous sense of humor!"

As Greg helped me to my feet, I tried to picture Dad as a 'crazy fool'. 'Boring teacher' was a much better description. Or maybe 'snore-inducing adult'. *Famous sense of humor?* Dad didn't have a sense of humor, never mind a *famous* one! I just nodded and smiled as if I had an idea what he was talking about. I wondered if he was confusing me with *another* David that he knew. It was possible.

Sarah wrapped her arms around me. *"Don't do that again,"* she said in a way that suggested she would do much worse things than try to drown me if I did.

"OK, I promise," I said, hugging her back. Don't get any ideas now, I didn't hug her in a weird 'I like to hug Sarah and I want her to be my girlfriend' kind of way. No, I hugged her because I suddenly realized how *cold* I was. My teeth were chattering as I shook in her warm embrace.

"David," she said, her eyes wide and worried. "You're shivering!"

Greg patted me on the back with a huge hand. "You get inside; I'll get this generator working. Last thing we want is you jumping in the lake again!" As he gave another barking laugh. I nodded and failed to stop my body from twitching. I wasn't planning on going back towards the lake for a while.

Sarah almost dragged me back into the cabin. The first thing she did when we were inside was throw a towel at me and give me strict instructions to get changed. I peeled the wet, smelly clothes off in my bedroom and changed into the comfiest pair of pajamas I could find. Making a mental note to buy myself a jetpack if I ever got the chance, I wrapped the comforter around me and walked into the living room like a big fluffy ghost. Tom was lying on the couch.

"You *jumped into the lake?!"* Tom said as I recounted what had happened. I decided to leave out the bit where Greg kissed me (I did brush my teeth about 200 times later though).

"Not my smartest move," I said. "It's pretty dark down there in the water, and cold. Very, very cold."

"Yeah, your lips are like purple," Tom said, poking my face.

I knocked his hand away.

"But, while you were swimming," he continued. "I found something weird here in the cabin."

I rolled my eyes. "*Please* don't tell me it's haunted. The last thing I need now is a pesky ghost chasing us around."

"*I ain't afraid of no ghost!*" Tom grinned. "But no, it isn't. Look at this!" Tom stood up and walked over to a cupboard in the corner. Opening the doors, he produced a guitar and a small black book. "I didn't know your dad played guitar."

I frowned. "He doesn't." Then it clicked. I swallowed. That was my *mom's* guitar.

"And look at this," Tom said, resting the guitar against the sofa. "It's a photo album filled with..."

The sound of the cabin door opening interrupted us.

"Anyone home?" Dad asked. Tom looked at me and a silent communication passed between us. Tom picked up the guitar, putting it back in the cupboard, and I slid the album under the sofa. We could look at it later.

Dad entered the room. "What's up?" he said. I didn't look at him and he didn't look at me. A silent agreement was made that we weren't going to talk about what had happened earlier. It was a Stevenson thing.

"You came back just in time!" Sarah said, emerging from the kitchen. "Greg brought pie!"

"Ooh, pie!" Dad said, smiling.

Tom glanced at me. This was going to be a *long* holiday.

# A long night

SNOOOOORRRREEEEE.

I stared at the wooden ceiling of the cabin, silently wishing that someone would tear my ears off.

SNNNNNNOOOOOOOOREEE. SNORT. SNNOOOOORRRE.

The snoring had begun about ten minutes after Dad had fallen asleep, and hadn't stopped since. I had been lying in the bed for about three hours now.

SNNOOOOREEEEE. SNOREY SNOOOOOORE.

I tried to distract myself by thinking about my mom's picture, about the guitar, and how little I knew about her. It occurred to me that Dad had held back a lot of information. I knew so little of her that she was almost a stranger, and yet there was still a small piece of my heart that *begged* to know more. What she was like, what she thought of me, what her favorite food was. Anything. I needed to find a way to get Dad to tell me more about her.

SNNNOOOOREE GLLABBLE SNOOOORE.

But that wasn't going to happen tonight. The only thing coming out of Dad's mouth tonight was a sound that reminded me of an angry chainsaw.

I tried turning away from him. I tried wrapping a pillow around my head. I even tried kicking him in the leg. Nothing seemed to end the violent roar of his throat. Soon I just lay there staring at him in disbelief. How could a noise like *that* come out of someone's throat? Come out of *my* throat?

SNNNNORRT. GRUMBLE.

It was the *worst*. I wasn't going to get any sleep at this rate. I lay back on the bed with the smell of unfamiliar bedclothes and unfamiliar cabin in my nose. Had this really been the awesome place in my childhood that the picture suggested? It was hard to imagine anything fun happening here.

*The most fun I've had here so far is nearly drowning,* I thought to myself. *Did I really have fun here when I was little?*

I strained to think back as far as I could in my life, but all I could come up with was remains of feelings, flashes of memories like perfume on the air when someone walks by.

Eventually, with a sigh of frustration, I kicked off the bedclothes and sat up.

SNNNNNORE SN.. SN... SNORE.

I couldn't stand to be in the bedroom anymore.

As quietly as I could, I slipped out of bed and, on my bare feet, I tiptoed out of the room and closed the door behind me. To my surprise, I wasn't the only one awake. A light from the living room shone a thin silvery crack under the door. Peeking around the door, I saw Tom lying on the couch, playing an intense game on his Game Kid through squinting eyes. He looked up, stunned for a second, but relaxed when he realized it was me.

"Sleeping here sucks," he whispered.

I nodded and stepped further into the room.

"Believe me," I replied. "It isn't any better out there." I sat down on the end of the sofa and pulled Tom's comforter over my legs. "I don't think we'll be getting much sleep this week."

Tom sighed. "And I really like sleep, too."

We sat and stared at the far wall for a while. The cabin didn't even have a television. What sort of evil place didn't have a television?!

We sat and listened to the creaking sounds of the cabin settling, and the croaking snores of Dad that even the walls couldn't stop.

"Well," Tom said, sitting up. "If we are here, we might as well look at the photo album." He reached under the sofa and pulled out the black covered book with the golden word ' Memories' on the cover. He brushed off a layer of dust and opened the book. It took all I had not to snatch the book from his hands and hold it protectively to my chest. Whatever was in there, they were *my* memories. I wanted to protect them.

As Tom turned to the first photo, I took a slow breath. We both leaned forward and looked at it.

Mom stood on a beach in a colorful dress, the sun setting on the horizon behind her. In both of her hands, she held wooden sticks and the tips of the sticks were on fire! She grinned at the camera.

"Woah," said Tom. "Is that your mom?" I nodded, the words sticking in the back of my throat. "She's really hardcore."

Tom turned to the next page and gasped.

My dad stood on the same beach, dressed in rainbow colored swimming shorts. He was holding the same sticks as Mom, except a third one was spinning through the air above him and he was looking up at it. He was juggling with fire!

"No, that can't be Mr. Stevenson..." Tom mumbled, leaning closer to the photo.

It was easy to understand his confusion. My dad did *not* do things like that. Nowadays, he would rant about safety and the dangers of fire and blah blah. Actually juggling with fire? No. That wasn't him at all. Tom turned the page again.

Dad was leaping off the side of a cliff into turquoise water far below. Nowadays Dad squirmed uncomfortably when I ran down the stairs.

Tom turned again.

Dad and Mom gave a thumbs up to the camera as they hung off the side of a sheer cliff by thin ropes, the ground out of sight below them.

"It's like he is a completely different person," I said with a frown. I turned the page this time.

Dad was underwater in scuba gear swimming amongst beautiful colored coral. It looked like a tropical paradise.

On the next page there was a photo of him inside a metal cage. Around him swam humongous sharks, and yet he looked completely calm, reaching out to the nearest one with his hand.

"Your dad is..." Tom struggled to get the words out. "...cool?"

I laughed. My dad wasn't cool! That was ridiculous.

"He *was* cool," I corrected him. "Now he's...well..." I gestured at myself and the boring body that I inhabited.

Tom nodded and continued to flick through the book. After a moment, he said: "What if it *was* him now?"

I looked up from the book. "What do you mean?"

Tom had *that* face on. By *that* face, I mean the one he uses when he is plotting and scheming. He usually reserves it for when we are gaming and up against a really tough challenge (or if I keep beating him – which happens a lot – and he is trying to think of a way to beat me). He stared at the far, television-less wall, and said, "What if we could make your boring dad of now go back to being the cool dad of then? That could make this holiday epic!"

A slow grin spread across my face as I considered the

possibilities. Not only would it make this painful holiday a lot more exciting, but he might also open up more about Mom. "You know what, Tom? That's a really good idea."

"What's a really good idea?" Sarah stepped into the room, rubbing her eyes.

Tom quickly hid the book behind himself and smiled sweetly.

"We were just talking about... stuff," he said.

Sarah yawned. "Stuff?"

"Yep," I said. "Talking. Doing talky stuff."

Sarah's eyes suddenly opened. "Ahhh," she said. "*That* talk. *The* talk."

A jolt of fear spread through my body. I had forgotten about that. Sarah had asked me a few weeks ago to have *the talk* with Tom about 'adult stuff'. I had agreed (because Dad would have agreed) even though I have never had 'the talk' myself. I heard it included stuff about birds and bees. It sounded really confusing.

I had hoped Sarah had forgotten and somehow, Tom and I had stumbled blindly right into it.

"So you feel... *better* now, Tom?" Sarah asked. "That you know... stuff?"

Tom's eyes widened as he turned to me, realizing what she was talking about.

"Er... yeah," Tom said quickly. "Now that I know about stuff and... things."

Sarah looked at me. "What have you talked about?"

My eyes darted between Sarah and Tom. They both looked at me expectantly. I had no idea what to say.

"We just covered the basics, you know? Important things that he needs to know for life and stuff."

Sarah raised an eyebrow. "Life and stuff?"

"So much life and stuff," Tom nodded in agreement.

There was a pause.

Sarah smiled. "Good," she said with relief. "I'm glad. You mind if I join you on the sofa?"

She sat down next to me after I scooted along.

"My room is *filled* with bugs," she said. "I don't think I'm going to get much sleep tonight."

"Join the club," I said.

Sarah rested her head on my shoulder and smiled. "OK!"

Tom scowled at me from the other end of the sofa.

Why is it never simple?

# Down Town

When I woke up, golden sunlight was streaming in through the cabin's windows and Tom's bare foot was pressed firmly against my left cheek. At first I didn't understand what was going on, tiredness clouding my mind. It felt like I was back in the lake, unable to make out anything around me. But then the cheesy smell of his toes entered my nose and I held my breath, gently pushing his leg away while he slept next to me. I tried not to gag.

The morning didn't get any better from there.

A scream from the bathroom woke everyone up, and we all left our rooms to find Sarah running out of the bathroom with a towel wrapped around her head.

"Sarah? What's wrong?" I asked as she ran around behind me and hid.

"A...a...rat!" she said. "In the bathroom! A furry evil little beast! And it's so *filthy* in there, David! Oooh, I need to sit down."

Tom guided her to the kitchen while I peeked my head around the bathroom door. Because the bathroom light didn't work none of us had used it the night before. No one was brave enough to go in there in the dark. Luckily, there was a separate toilet. But the first thing I noticed when I entered was that the room smelled *worse* that Tom's feet (I didn't think that was possible) and everything seemed to be covered in a brown layer of grime.

"Eww..." I whispered. Then I saw it. A brown flash of fur dashed across the floor towards me, almost as if it was out for my blood! I couldn't help but scream myself, and slammed the door closed just in time to hear a soft *thump* on the other side.

Tom looked at me from the kitchen.

"Don't go in there," I said.

Tom shook his head. "I never plan to."

So now we couldn't sleep *or* go to the bathroom on

this holiday. It was getting better by the second.

But the worst thing about the morning? It was Dad.

Dad was totally oblivious to everything. He was happy, he was relaxed, and most of all he kept saying, "Ahhh, what a *great* night's sleep I had," to everyone.

As we all gathered around the remains of Greg's pie for breakfast (we didn't have any other food left), Sarah broke the silence.

"I think we should head down to town today. There's a bus every half an hour and the thought of staying in this cabin *one second longer* is driving me insane."

Tom and I nodded in agreement. We also wanted to be as far away from the cabin as possible.

Dad frowned. "What's wrong with the cabin?"

Usually, when I think of vacations I think of sun, sand, relaxation, more ice cream than one human could possibly eat, swimming in the sea, stuff like that. For a brief moment, I pictured in my mind my dream island holiday destination.

But that image was quickly wiped away. So far, I had nearly drowned, had slept on a sofa, had seen a rat and generally was about as relaxed as a man sitting in an electric chair.

*A math exam would be better than this,* I thought to myself glumly as the small bus chugged its way around the small, winding roads towards the nearby town. Trees fluttered by outside as we tried to get comfortable on the strangely lumpy chairs. None of us talked. I stared out the window and tried to list the good things so far about the cabin. I hadn't even thought of one when my eyelids began to droop with the gentle rocking of the bus...

"Hey!" Dad shook me awake. "We're here."

I sat up. "Ergle bleh?" I mumbled, wiping a line of drool from my mouth. Following Dad off the bus, I squinted in the sunlight, blinking a few times. I had stepped into a completely different world.

The lake here was bustling with activity. People were on rowboats fishing, some people swam in the water, others sat on large, expensive boats drinking sparkling glasses of champagne to show off how fancy they were. And that was *just* the lake. The town behind me was filled with shops and people all walking and chatting, enjoying the sun. Suddenly, I felt like I was on holiday.

I grinned. "Yes," I said. "This is more like it."

Tom tugged on my sleeve. "Woah, look at *that!*"

Cutting through the water like a knife, a silver speedboat whizzed across the lake faster than I had thought possible. Four people in the back of the boat screamed with enjoyment, holding up their hands and laughing. It looked like great fun! "Wow," I said. "That looks really exciting!"

Dad nodded. "Ah, you saw it too. I'll admit, it is quite a thrill."

I turned to Dad, shocked that *he* would want to go on the speedboat. Was Fun Dad coming back already?

No. No, he wasn't.

He wasn't even *looking* at the boats. I followed his

gaze and couldn't help but grimace when I realized what he was staring at. Of course, the one place my dad would want to go to, even on a holiday.

The museum.

It had a big sign out front that read:

EDUCATION IS FUN!

I shuddered. *Nothing* could make me want to go in there.

"Oh, a museum," Sarah said. "You really want to do that, Jack?"

Dad turned to her. "Education is *fun*, Sarah, can't you see the sign?"

I had to resist the urge to strangle him right there. *EDUCATION IS NOT FUN!* I screamed at him in my mind. An idea popped into my head.

I laughed, loudly.

"Oh Jack, you joker," I patted him on the head for emphasis. "You don't have to pretend you want to go to a museum just to make your old dad happy!"

Dad turned. "But..." he began.

"No, no, no," I waggled a finger at him. "This is *your* holiday as well. I insist we do something *you* want to do. Like... oh, I don't know..." I pretended to look around the lake. "Hmm. Oh, I know, that speed boat! That looks like a lot of fun, doesn't it, Tom?"

"So much fun," agreed Tom.

Even Sarah smiled. "Yeah, that does look pretty awesome."

"I... but..." Dad looked back at the museum as if his favorite puppy had just been taken away. He sighed. "Yes, I suppose I would want to do that."

Tom whooped and began to run towards the docks.

"Yes, but *how* safe is it?" Dad asked for the hundredth

time as he checked the clippings on his life jacket.

"So safe, dude," the long-haired guy driving the boat grinned. "I only had one person fall out once and we were going so fast it was like *splat,* you know? They only broke, like, two of their arms."

Dad frowned. I could tell he was about to say something only a boring teacher would say, so I interrupted him. "That won't happen to you, Jack. Just chill."

"Yeah," the long-haired driver nodded. "Chill, dude. This guy gets it." The driver held out a fist and I fist bumped it.

Sarah laughed and shook her head. "You're a strange one, David Stevenson."

"I'm one of a kind," I grinned back.

Tom scowled at me again.

"The worst kind," I added quickly. "Just... so bad."

Sarah was about to reply when the driver kicked the boat into gear. It ROARED into life like an angry lion. "LET'S DO THIS!" he shouted.

"No, no, no, no, no!" Dad clenched the side of the boat and screwed his eyes closed.

WHOOOOOOOSH!

I was pinned back on my seat as the boat shot forward and a wild grin spread across my face. I could hear Sarah behind me doing a combination of a scream and a laugh. Tom cheered and threw his hands up in the air.

Water sprayed up from either side of the boat, splashing us as the driver turned a sharp corner to avoid a couple on a rowboat. We shot out into the open waters of the lake and I heard a deep roar of laughter burst out of my throat as adrenaline kicked in.

We twisted and turned and Dad continued to cover his eyes. He was missing out!

I held onto his arm and pulled it down then he stared, wide eyed at the boat.

"Arrrrrrrgh!" he let out a piercing scream, his face

white as a sheet.

Suddenly, the boat came to a stop. The driver turned around.

"Did someone get hurt?" he said. "I heard a woman screaming!"

We all looked at Dad, who folded his arms and stood up. "I want to leave this boat!" he snapped. "It is unsafe and I don't think it appropriate for a child of my age."

The driver's face twisted as his brain tried to figure out the words that had just been spoken.

"Dude," he said. "You sound like a teacher."

"I don't care," Dad said, sticking his nose up in the air. "This is not fun. Not at all. I want to leave."

Sarah stood up too. "Come on Jack, it isn't *that* bad," she said.

"Nope," he said. "I disagree. Get me off this boat now."

I stood up too. Dad wasn't being Fun Dad. If anything, he was being even *less* fun than usual. I felt defeated.

"Fine," I said, sadly. "You can get off the boat right now."

"Thank you," Dad sighed. Then he frowned. "Wait-"

SPLOOSH!

Dad didn't have time to react as I shoved him into the lake!

Tom burst out laughing. "Classic!" he said.

Dad spluttered and coughed, trying to stay afloat in the lake. "I'm going to drown!" he shouted. "Help me!"

I leaned over the edge of the boat. "Believe me," I whispered. "You aren't." I poked his life jacket and he stopped flailing. "Also, don't you know how to swim?"

"Oh," he said. "Yeah."

"David," a stern voice came from behind me. "That wasn't very nice."

I flushed with embarrassment and turned to face

Sarah. "Sarah, I..."

SPLOOSH!

Cold water wrapped around me as I ended up in the lake *again*. Sarah had pushed me in!

As I emerged on the surface, she was crying with laughter up on the speedboat.

After I spat the water out of my mouth, I started laughing, too.

# Greg and Stacy's Cabin

When we returned to the cabin, each laden with a heavy bag filled with provisions, we found a note stuck on the door. Putting my bag down on the floor, I pulled it off and read. It said:

**Howdy!**
**I hope you're all having a great time. Come round to mine and Stacy's cabin later tonight and we'll properly welcome you with a feast!**
**See you later!**
**Greg.**

Sarah read it over my shoulder and let out a little squeak of excitement. "Oh, maybe I can use their *shower!*" She clapped her hands together.

The rest of us turned to look at her.

"What?" she mumbled. "I like to be clean..."

We left for their cabin about half an hour later. As we rounded the corner into the grove where Greg's cabin was, we all stopped. I let out a little gasp. What stood in the clearing among the trees was not just any old cabin. It was a wooden *palace*.

Standing three stories high, this wooden gem made our cabin look like a worn-out cardboard box. I was convinced one of the rooms inside could have actually contained the whole of our cabin *and* the car *and* there would still be room to dance a tango.

Tom poked me in the side, "Why doesn't *your* cabin look like that?" He shook his head and gave me a smug grin.

Sarah poked him. "Don't be rude."

"Yeah," I said. "Don't be rude, Tom."

Tom stuck his tongue out at me. I stuck my tongue

out back at him.

Standing in the center of the front porch, by a large, intricately carved front door, was Greg, waving at us with a large grin. As we got closer, I leaned over to Sarah and whispered: "Do you think Greg is secretly a king in some country we don't know about?"

Sarah giggled. "It certainly looks like it. I bet his shower is *amazing.*"

"David and family!" Greg shouted happily. "I'm so glad you could make it!" He turned back towards his cabin and bellowed: "Stacy, they're here!" Turning to face us, he extended his arms. It was time.

On the walk over, Dad had reluctantly given me some pointers on how to cope with Greg's hugs (he still was trying not to talk to me because of the speedboat incident). I was up for the first hug. I tried not to cringe or flinch, I just extended my arms and took in a large breath. Greg's vice-like arms wrapped around me and he pulled me in. I hugged him back. This time it only hurt a little bit. Finally, after a few seconds, he released me and I took a long, deep breath.

I looked up at his front door and tried to smile, despite every bone in my body cringing at once. A wildly grinning woman appeared at the door of the cabin, her blond hair tied back into a braid on the back of her head. I did a double take. She looked almost exactly like Greg, only without the square glasses. She opened her really muscly arms and took me in for another embrace. I wasn't prepared for how strong she was.

Something crunched inside my body. I was sure of it.

"Welcome!" she said. "It's been years, David! I'm so glad you have come round."

I wheezed a response and she waved me into the cabin.

It wasn't hard to find out where the food was. I just followed the mouthwatering smell in the air, into a dining room. The table in the center was covered in food that would have been enough for ten people, never mind the six of us. I sat down on the nearest chair and felt my eyes slowly grow bigger than my stomach. Everything looked amazing and I wanted to put it all in my mouth.

When we were all sitting around their dining table, I noticed how large the dining room was. It felt like it was somehow *even bigger* on the inside of the cabin. Every inch of available space on the wall was filled with family pictures of Greg, Stacy, and what I assumed were their children, although they were close to Dad's age by now.

"We built the whole cabin ourselves," Greg said proudly, resting his hand on Stacy's.

I nodded along while piling food onto my plate. I noticed that, even though Sarah was talking to them, she was doing a similar thing. She glanced up at me and grinned. I grinned back, taking a bite out of the nearest slice of cheese on my plate.

"It was the first year we were staying in this place that we met David and Lana," Stacy said.

A hush fell across the room.

I stopped chewing on the cheese and glanced up at Dad.

*Lana.* It was Mom's name. Dad's face was as red as if he were choking. He took a long sip of his drink.

Greg glanced at Stacy like she had broken some unspeakable promise. No one seemed willing to say anything, and with each passing second it grew more uncomfortable. Dad stared into his plate and didn't move. Sarah avoided eye contact with everyone.

I decided to break the silence. "Yeah," I said. "That was a looooong time ago. Aren't we all so old now?"

There was an almost audible sigh of relief from the room and Greg broke out into a grin.

"Sure was, buddy," he said. "Oh, that reminds me!" He stood up and scurried out of the room like a giant beaver. Everyone left at the table glanced at each other uncomfortably until he finally came back holding a bottle of a brown liquid. He handed it to me and I looked at the label. It was old and faded, and clearly hadn't been used in a while.

"Stone Island Whisky," I said. Uh oh. Alcohol.

Dad's eyes widened as I said it and he dropped something onto his plate loudly. *How am I going to get out of this one?* I thought to myself.

"The very same," Greg said. "Remember it?"

I shook my head. "Nope." I offered the bottle back to him, silently praying that that would be the end of it.

Greg almost looked disappointed, but then he pulled out a glass from a nearby cupboard and poured some of the liquid into it. "Perhaps this will jog your memory."

"I don't think that-" I began

He handed the glass to me. I glanced at Dad who was shaking his head, his eyes open wide. He *really* didn't want me to drink this.

*Oh well.* I thought. *How bad could it be?*

"Bottoms up!" I smiled, raising the glass to him and flicked back the liquid.

For a moment, nothing happened. It tasted like I imagined licking the green stuff off the bathtub back at our cabin would.

"I don't see-" I began, then I stopped as my throat burst into flames! The heat spread all over my face and down into my stomach and I had to grip onto the table so I wouldn't try to pull my face off. "ARRRRRRRGH!" I shouted. "WATER!" I choked. "WATERRR!" I groped around on the table, until my hands wrapped around the jug of water and I began to chug it like there was no tomorrow. Greg and Stacy laughed.

"Ahh, yes," Greg said. "Whisky was always Lana's favorite drink more than yours."

The cool liquid calmed the fire in my throat, but I could still feel it warm inside me.

"But enough about the past. Who is *this* beautiful woman?" Greg smiled at Sarah, who blushed in response.

"You're too kind," she said through a mouthful of bread.

I was still coughing and choking when Stacy asked: "How did you two meet?"

Tom rolled his eyes.

Sarah grinned and looked at me. "Tell them the story, David. I'd like to hear your version of it."

"Er..." What was *the story* that she was referring to? I had no idea. I searched my memory for anything that could be considered a story that my dad liked to tell. All I could think of was how obsessed he was with telling me to clean my room. How *did* my dad and Sarah meet? I mean, I was hanging out with Tom a lot, but I didn't really know the details. "Oh well, Sarah and I... er..." I fumbled to find something to say. "Sarah's great," I smiled awkwardly. "You tell it Sarah, I'll let you."

Sarah frowned. "It's better when you tell it, David."

"I don't think so," I said back.

"Never mind then," Sarah said, eating some more.

The uncomfortable silence fell over us again.

Dad closed his eyes and sighed.

"Right," Greg said quietly. "OK."

Sarah looked at me and I could tell she was hurt by what I had said. I silently kicked myself. I was meant to be *dating* her and all I could say was 'Sarah's great'? What was *wrong* with me?

Sarah stood up. "Do you need help washing up?" she said to Stacy.

"No, dear, of course not," Stacy said.

"Please," Sarah said. "I insist." She glanced at me as she carried the plates out of the room.

I'd messed up again.

# The Dream

The next day Sarah was distant. Every question I asked she answered with a single word or less. She regularly found excuses not to be in the same room as me. Sometimes she would whisper something to Tom, he would sigh, walk over to me and ask me a question that she had clearly wanted to ask me, but wasn't happy enough to acknowledge my presence. I had really messed up. I had to figure some way to sort it out and fast.

For the most part, Tom was loving it. He clearly loved the distance between me and his mom, and he didn't even try to hide it. He bounced around, happy as a bumblebee in spring, and focused on trying to get 'cool, fun Dad' back. On the second morning, he placed a list of things to do down in front of me and Dad, and said: "I have the *rest of the vacation* planned out!"

Dad and I glanced at each other and looked down at the sheet of paper.

*TOM'S AWESOME LIST OF HOW TO MAKE THIS VACATION THE MOST AWESOME:*
1. *SKY DIVING*
2. *SCUBA DIVING IN THE LAKE*
3. *SKY DIVING INTO THE LAKE WHILE WEARING SCUBA DIVING EQUIPMENT*
4. *MOUNTAIN CLIMBING*
5. *SKY DIVING OFF A MOUNTAIN*
6. *SKY DIVING OFF A MOUNTAIN INTO THE LAKE? (WILL CHECK MAP)*
7. *SPA DAY.*

I looked up from the list, confused. "Spa Day?" I asked.

Tom shrugged. "I like massages. I'll check on my phone to see how close the nearest airfield is!" Then he bounced out of the room.

Dad picked up the list. "Sky diving? Is he serious?"

I nodded. "Deadly, I'm afraid."

It was on the third day that Dad took me to one side and said, "Jack, we *really* need to do something about this thing with Sarah. I think I heard her *crying* in her room last night. She was really hurt by what you said at Greg's cabin."

I felt like I had just taken a punch to the gut. Crying? I didn't realize it was *that* bad.

"What should I do?" I asked him.

"Well, you could...er..." Dad scratched his head. "Well..." He tapped his fingers against his lips and clicked his tongue. "I guess..."

Finally, he sighed. Neither of us had any idea what to do. It was a complete disaster.

We were in town later that day when Sarah walked off on her own because she needed 'time to think'. Now, I have enough experience with girls to know that when they need 'time to think,' you are in deep trouble. Something had to be done. I pulled out my phone and glanced at the signal. Luckily I had a few bars, so I called the only person in the world who knew something about girls and making them feel better.

I called my girlfriend Holly.

I mean, I'm pretty sure she's my girlfriend. Maybe. Kind of. It's complicated.

I felt my hands growing sweaty as the sound of the phone ringing echoed in my ear. What was I going to say? The last contact I had really had with Holly was watching her hug Dad after the school fair. She had seemed happy at that point. I didn't want to risk messing everything up with her as well.

But I didn't hang up in time.

"Hello?" The sound of her voice in my ear made something tingle in my heart. Or maybe it was the strange hot dog I had eaten earlier from a street vendor.

"Er... Hi," I said.

"Jack?" she replied. "Is that you? You sound really weird."

*Right.* I thought to myself. *I have Dad's voice.*

I quickly came up with an excuse. "Yeah, sorry, I have a throat infection. Really bad. Makes me sound like a gorilla. Also, the signal is bad. "

"I'm sorry," Holly said. "That sucks."

"You have no idea," I agreed.

"What's up?" she asked.

I took a breath. How was I going to explain this to Holly without giving everything away? I mean, the last time I had tried to confess everything to her, she ran away and thought that Dad was going insane. I'm still not one hundred percent certain I *haven't* gone insane. Although I tried pinching myself and it hurts, so at least I know it isn't a dream.

"I have a … friend," I began. "He needs help."

"Uh huh," she said. I could almost hear her eyes narrowing on the other end of the line. "How?"

"Well, I...er... he has a girlfriend but she is not happy with him at the moment. He messed up big time."

"I see."

It occurred to me then that she might think I was talking about her and me.

But I wasn't.

Was I?

Girls are so complicated.

"He needs to make things right, but he doesn't know what to do. He said some stupid things, which he regrets."

"Well, an apology would be a great place to start," Holly said.

*Of course! Why didn't I think of that?*

"To start?" I said.

"Yeah. She also needs him to make her feel *special*. You can apologize to anyone, but for her, he should go further. Make her feel wanted."

I frowned. How was I going to do *that*? "Uh huh... wanted."

"I think your friend can figure it out from there." she said. "If the relationship is destined to last, it will all work out."

"Destined to last... right," I said, trying not to think about what it would mean if we *weren't* destined to last. "Got it. Thanks Holly, you've been a big help."

"I'm amazing." Holly agreed. "Keep in touch more, yeah?"

"OK," I said. "I will. Bye, Holly."

"Bye, Jack."

Make her feel *wanted*. I assumed she didn't mean 'Wanted: Dead or Alive'. Or did she?

No, of course not.

I still had no idea what to do.

That night I lay in bed and stared at the ceiling again. Not because of Dad's snoring - I had cleverly bought some earplugs in town - but because I was still trying to work out what I needed to do in my head.

I tossed and I turned and I tossed and I turned. But eventually, I drifted off into a light sleep.

*"Hey, Jack."*

*Even though I hadn't heard it for years, the voice was instantly recognizable to me. I sat up in bed and realized I was back at home, silver moonlight shining through my bedroom window. Sitting on the end of my bed was Mom, looking exactly as she did the last time I had seen her, when she took me to school. She smiled warmly.*

*"Mom?" I asked. She leaned forward and hugged me. Even her smell was the same, a flowery, warm kind of smell that reminded me of home. She began to pull away, but I didn't want to let her go. Tears rolled down my cheeks and I hugged her tighter.*

"I didn't think I'd ever see you again."

She laughed. "I'm always around, Jack, you know that." For a while she was content to just let me hold her. She rubbed my back with her hand and hummed softly.

"Everything's so hard," I sniffed. "I'm trapped in Dad's body and being an adult is hard and... and..."

"Shhh, I know," Mom kissed my cheek. "But remember, it isn't easy for your dad either."

I frowned. "What do you mean?"

Mom pulled back slightly. "Did you ever stop to think why he isn't 'fun dad' anymore?"

I opened my mouth and closed it again.

She nodded. "He doesn't do crazy things anymore because of you. You're the reason."

"Me?" I asked.

"He wants to keep you safe, Jack. You're the most important thing to him."

I was so busy thinking about me this whole time, I didn't realize that Dad was thinking about me as well. Realization hit me like a train and tears were streaming down my cheeks all over again.

"I've been so stupid," I groaned.

"No, never," Mom said. "I'm proud of you, Jack, you're doing really well. I just need to you to do one thing for me."

"Anything," I said.

"Make your dad think about himself more, think about Sarah more. He needs to stop dwelling on the past, to stop thinking about me and how good it was. You need to show him what he has now. Can you do that?"

"That sounds difficult," I said. "How will I know what to do?"

She looked at me, her blue eyes filled with love. "You're a smart boy. You'll figure it out."

*"OK, Mom. I promise."*
   *"I love you, Jack." she said.*
   *"I love you too, Mom."*
   *She smiled.*

My eyes opened. I was awake, my face pressed firmly into my pillow. As I pulled away, I realized it was wet with tears. I smiled a little. Something that I thought had been missing from my heart for so long suddenly seemed to be there again.

Not only that, but the solution to the Sarah problem suddenly appeared in my mind. I knew exactly what to do.

I poked Dad until he woke up.

"Urgh?" he said.

I grinned. "Come on, Dad," I said. "We have a lot to do today."

# Fixing the Sarah Problem

The first part of the plan involved getting Sarah and Tom out of the house. I'll admit, I might have gone a *little* too far.

Tom was still asleep when I came back inside after heading out to get what I needed. The morning air had been cool and fresh when I walked around to the generator, a glass jar in my hand. I had moved quickly because it was *super gross* and I didn't want to think too hard about it. When I opened the living room door as quietly as possible, I saw that Tom was sprawled out on the sofa again, GameKid in one hand. I crept over to him, whispered: "Sorry, Tom, it's for the greater good," and emptied the jar of little red spiders all over him.

I felt bad doing it.

I felt *terrible* doing it. I mean, this was my *best friend*.

Then I sneaked out of the room and back into my bedroom.

Dad shook his head. "You're *sure* they aren't dangerous spiders?" he asked.

I nodded. "Positive. I checked on the internet like fifty times when we went to town the first time. They don't even bite."

## *"AAAAAARRRRRRGGGGHHHHHH!!!!!!"*

The scream echoed all over the cabin.

"He doesn't know that, though," I said with a grin.

Sarah rushed to the door and was about to open it when Tom burst out, running around in circles. "Spiders!" he shouted. "Spiders all over me!"

They were all over his face and arms. It made me shiver just to think about it, but then I got into character.

"Oh no! Tom, let me help you!" I picked up my towel and began to hit the spiders off him. Sarah joined in too. We managed to get most of them off.

"How did that happen?" Sarah asked.

"I... I don't know!" Tom said. "I was just sleeping and they were crawling all over me when I woke up!"

"Did any of them bite you?" I said.

"What?" asked Tom.

I grabbed him by the shoulders. "Did any of them bite you, Tom? I have a cream if they did, and you need to apply it soon or you'll get a *horrible* rash."

"A rash?" Tom's eyes widened.

"A *horrible* rash. Itchy boils which leak pus. Really gross. Luckily I had the cream last time and applied before it got bad." I nodded knowingly.

"What kind of spiders were they?" Sarah said.

"A bad kind. Not too poisonous, but annoying. I think the scientific name is the *Itchysupernastyaria spider*."

"Oh dear," Sarah said.

Dad called to me as he rushed into the room. "Dad! Bad news!"

"What is it, son?" I asked.

"We've run out of that cream you were using!"

"What?" I said, my eyes opening wide. "Oh no! You'll have to go down town to get some!" I said to Tom and Sarah. "Maybe even to a doctor, pronto!"

"Pronto," Dad added, as if that would help at all.

Sarah frowned and, for a second, I thought it wasn't going to work, but Tom stood up and began to gather his clothes. "I don't want a rash!" he said. "I need to get to a doctor!"

"Pronto," I said again. I *like* that word.

Sarah grabbed the car keys. "Alright, we'll go down to the town and see if we can find a doctor. You are both OK up here by yourselves?"

"Perfect!" I said.

"Pronto... I mean, great!" Dad said.

Sarah took Tom in her arm. "Come on, Tommy, let's

270

sort you out."

And like that, they were gone. We were alone in the cabin.

## Fixing the Sarah Problem – Part 2

As we watched the car drive away, Dad sniffed and said: "How long do you think we have before they figure out the spider... What was it called?"

"The *Itchysupernastyaria spider,*" I grinned.

"Yeah, *that,* doesn't exist?"

I shrugged. "Long enough, I hope." Now we just had to put into motion the *second* part of the plan. We went back inside the cabin, pressed our ears gently against the bathroom door and listened. For a while, all I could hear was the quiet sound of us breathing. Then:

*Scuttle scuttle scuttle.*

"Maybe it's just a tap dripping?" Dad asked hopefully.

*Scuttle, scuttle.*

"Maybe?" I replied, even though I was completely sure it was the sound of tiny feet scampering around the wooden floor of the bathroom.

*Scuttle, crunch, crunch, scuttle.*

"How do you think we can get it out of there?" I asked.

"I've been thinking about that and..." Dad walked into the nearby kitchen and came back out with a bucket. "Ta daaa!" he said. "The latest in rat catching technology."

I looked at it. "A bucket?"

Dad nodded.

"To catch a rat."

"It will be simple, right?" Dad grinned.

Wrong. He was so wrong.

Less than a minute later, I was crouched down by the edge of the door with the bucket in my hands.

"Why do *I* have to catch it?" I asked.

"Because you are the responsible adult," Dad said with a serious face.

I growled at him. "I think you are enjoying this too

much."

Dad put his hand on the door handle and gave me a thumbs up. "So much!" he grinned. "Ready?"

I took a deep breath. "Alright let's..."

Dad didn't wait for me to finish. He opened the door and revealed the small bathroom to the world.

The gross stink drifted out of the room. I wiggled my nose and held my breath.

We waited. Everything was silent.

It was still silent.

"Maybe-" I began.

*scuttle Scuttle SCUTTLE!*

A small brown flash zoomed towards me! I slammed the bucket on the ground with a triumphant roar. We had caught it!

"I got it!" I yelled. "I can't believe that worked!"

"Er... Jack..." Dad said.

"I mean, a *bucket*? It seems a bit crazy if you think about it."

"Jaaaaack..."

"But here we are, with a rat in a bucket."

"Jack, it's not in the bucket," Dad said with a panicked voice.

"What do you mean?" I said, suddenly very aware of a warm, heavy feeling on my back.

"Don't move," Dad whispered.

Slowly I turned my head. A brown face with a long twitchy nose and two black beady eyes stared back at me from my shoulder.

Rats, it turns out, are a *lot* scarier and bigger in real life than you would think they are.

I kept completely calm and focused on the plan. I just needed to get the rat into the bucket.

"ARGH!" I screamed, jumping up, feeling the little rodent dig its claws into my back. I spun around and around and the rat squeaked in shock trying to hang on, its pink tail flying through the air behind me.

"Stop Jack, stop!" Dad shouted, but I wasn't listening. I ran to the open front door and leaped out onto the ground outside, colliding hard with the muddy floor. The rat, finally releasing my back, flew off into the nearest bushes with a triumphant squeak. It paused to look back at me, as if to say *I win,* and then disappeared.

I lay on the ground, panting, trying to stop my throat from closing up in terror. Dad, being as helpful as ever, stood in the doorway and laughed.

"Well, that way works too!" he said, spinning the bucket on his finger.

"Yeah," I said. "Great."

I spent the next few hours on my hands and knees, with a peg on my nose, scrubbing brush in the other hand, trying to get rid of the thick layer of grime that had built up all over the bathroom. After about half an hour, I stopped thinking about what the grime could be and just got to work. *It's for Sarah,* I told myself. *Just do it for Sarah.*

I didn't throw up, but it was very, *very* close sometimes.

Meanwhile, Greg, with the help of Dad, replaced some of the moldy wooden beams outside the front of the cabin with brand new ones. When I told him it was a present for Sarah, Greg was more than happy to help out. Stacy even joined in: she brought us a cake with Sarah's name spelled across the top in strawberries.

When the car finally pulled up again outside the cabin at the end of the day, it almost looked like an entirely different place.

Sarah, confused, was directed to the clean and fresh smelling bathroom, where she was allowed to finally have the shower she had been waiting for all week.

Then, once she was clean, we all sat down for a meal in the kitchen, the cake with her name on it in the middle of the table. Before we began to eat, I stood up, holding a glass of water in front of me. "To Sarah," I said. "I'm sorry I got caught up in the holiday and forgot what was *really* important which is, of course, you. You're great," I grinned. They were the *right* words this time.

Everyone cheered, even Tom, who later admitted that Sarah was really upset all day and it was a relief not to have her complain about me anymore.

Sarah stood up, smiling, threw her arms around my neck, kissing me on the cheek. "You are terrible, you know that?" she said.

I nodded. "You choose to hang out with me. What does that say about *you?*"

"You're walking a fine line, Mister," she said and hugged me again.

I think the plan might have just worked.

I glanced at Dad. He was smiling too.

# Into the River

When I woke up the next day, Dad seemed a completely different person. I was drawn to the kitchen, following a smell of bacon which made my mouth water, and found him already awake and preparing breakfast for everyone. As I entered the room, he grinned at me, placing bacon and eggs onto a plate in front of Sarah, who eyed it hungrily.

"Hello!" he said cheerfully, turning back to the next serving that was still sizzling on the frying pan behind him. I sat down next to Sarah and a plate was placed in front of me as well. She only paused for a second from chewing on her mouthful of food to say:

"I didn't realize you enjoyed cooking so much, Jack!" she said. "This tastes amazing!"

Dad walked over to me, patting me on the back as I forked a salty cube of bacon into my mouth. "I was inspired by my dad and his *amazing* cooking skills."

The bacon lodged itself in my throat and I choked on it. Dad smacked me hard on the back, dislodging it straight away. "I am an inspiration to all!" I said, once I could finally breathe again, but then wondered if I was complimenting *myself* or Dad. Dad didn't give me time to think about it.

"So great," he agreed.

"Mmm," Sarah said sarcastically. "You look very inspirational with ketchup around your mouth."

I grinned, spreading more ketchup around my mouth like it was a gross lipstick, and then I blew a kiss at Sarah.

"Eww," she grimaced and we all laughed.

When Tom finally arose from his sleep and joined us in the kitchen, the rest of the morning was spent joking and having fun. It was like a weight had been lifted, and we were finally starting to relax into the whole situation. Dad even suggested, once we had all finished, that we go for a walk in the nearby mountains and see what we could find.

Tom, who believed this was a sign that we were the closest ever to finding 'Fun Dad,' agreed with the idea with such enthusiasm that he nearly pushed us all out the door.

The journey to the mountain was longer than expected, but it didn't do anything to dampen our spirits. We all joked and sang along to songs on the radio in terrible voices. As she drove, Sarah kept looking at me and smiling. It was a relief to know that I had fixed the problem. She was now behaving in a completely different way to the previous few days and had even offered to drive. I couldn't help but smile back. This vacation was finally starting to feel like a vacation.

When we reached the mountain, the sun was high in the sky and the weather was hot. The trees around us were a lush green that you only find when you are far from cities, and the air smelled fresh and clean. We all put on backpacks filled with snacks and drinks, ready for the walk ahead, and set off along a dusty path through the forest, the mountain rising up ahead of us.

As we walked among the trees, the only sounds to be heard were the singing of the birds, the whoosh of the wind through the trees, and Tom laughing loudly as he messed around with Dad. They raced each other up the hills, hid behind rocks and trees, and constantly challenged each other to bigger and bigger tasks. *Maybe we have found Fun Dad,* I thought to myself as I watched them. *Maybe it has all worked out.*

"This is great," Sarah said suddenly, breaking my train of thought. "I'm glad we are all here."

I nodded. "Yeah, it did turn out alright, didn't it?" A little smile broke out on my face. For the first time in weeks, I felt relaxed. I thought back to home and to Holly. Maybe I could bring *her* here some time. *Would Dad allow it?* I watched him run past me again.

"Yeah, I feel like we are..." Sarah paused as Tom ran past us. I looked at her and saw that her cheeks had flushed red.  When she next spoke, it was quiet, almost like the meaning of the words would run away if she spoke them too loudly. "... a family."

I didn't respond straight away. I just watched Tom and Dad hanging out, how we all seemed to fit together as a unit, all playing our own role, but willing to let the others in as well. I smiled. "Yeah, I suppose so."

Sarah smiled at me and pushed on forward, chasing after Tom when he got too close.

As the path continued to wind its way through the trees, we found ourselves following a river, the sound of running water in the distance slowly getting louder and louder. It almost sounded like it was raining in a torrent when we turned the next corner, but we quickly found out why.

"Awesome!" Tom said.

The clearing was something out of a fantasy novel. A waterfall tumbled off high rocks into a small lake. It then branched out through the trees towards the path we had been walking along.

"Last one there's a rotten egg!" Dad shouted, charging past him.

"Hey!" Tom said. "No fair!" They set off in a race towards the waterfall and Sarah moved close to me again. I could feel the warmth of her body near my left arm.

"David," she said.

"Yes?" I turned and found her staring at me intensely. She leaned towards me. Alarm bells went off in my head. *DANGER DANGER! KISS ALERT!! KISS ALERT!* She was trying to kiss me! Instinctively, I took a step back and slipped up on a rock. Sarah grabbed out for me, only to fall as well.

SPLOOSH!

The water from the stream began to seep into my pants. It was c...c...cold.

Sarah, lying on top of me, burst out laughing. "Oh

David, only *you* could do that!" She tried to roll off me, but managed to get our backpack straps tangled, causing her to fall closer to me. Suddenly, her face was very close to mine, her brown eyes taking up most of my vision.

"This water is very cold!" I squeaked.

The tip of Sarah's nose poked mine.

"Hey!" I heard Tom's voice from nearby, angry, breathless. "Get off my mom!"

He charged down the bank of the river as Sarah managed to undo the straps of our bags and helped me up. As I got to my feet, Tom positioned himself between us, forcing me to take a step backwards, further into the river. I felt my shoes fill with stream water.

"Leave her alone!" Tom said, his face twisted. "You promised!"

Sarah tried to calm him down. She knelt in front of him. "Calm down, Tom. It's OK, we just fell into the stream."

"He was trying to *kiss* you, I *saw* it!" Tom snapped.

"I wasn't!" I began. "Honest! We just fell over."

Dad was standing on the bank now, watching the scene with a concerned face. I began to walk towards dry land again, but Tom stood in front of me and scowled.

"Listen, Tom," Dad said. "I think..."

"I don't care!" shouted Tom, not even turning to look at him. He placed a hand on my chest and shoved me backwards a step. "Stay away from my mom!"

Sarah stood up now, her face furious. "Tom!" she shouted. "That's enough! You have gone too far!"

"But, Mom..." Tom said, turning to her.

"No," she said. "David can kiss me and I can kiss him if I want to! You aren't in charge here, Thomas!"

Tom mumbled and fumbled, his face flushing red. "But he *can't* kiss you," Tom said, my secret on the tip of his tongue. "Because..." I flinched. I could already feel my world crashing down around me.

"Enough!" said Sarah. "I know you want to control

this, but you *can't.*" she said.

"But you *can't* be with him," Tom said quietly.

"I can be with him, Tom," she said softly. "I'm in love with him."

"You're *what?*" Dad said, his eyes widening.

"You *what?*" Tom shouted.

The water was flowing freely through my shoes and socks now, but I couldn't feel it. *Oh no,* I thought. *This is bad.*

# Back at the cabin

The best way to describe the journey home would be a word that I have just made up right now. That word is: *SuperreallyOMGawkwardnotawesomeatallwowhowdidwegethere.*

It's a pretty long word, but I think it describes with great accuracy everything that was rushing through my mind as everyone tried desperately not to make eye contact with each other.

Just don't ask me to spell it, OK?

To really put the icing on the cake, as we drove back along the winding roads, where we had laughed and joked on the way towards the mountain, we now sat in silence and watched dark, angry clouds roll over the landscape ahead of us. As we got closer to the cabin, the same clouds began to spit out lightning and rain.

As the car came to a stop, Tom got out and stormed off towards the cabin, slamming the door angrily behind him.

"Tom!" Sarah shouted, chasing after him.

I sat with Dad in the car and we listened to the sound of the rain rattling against the metallic roof. I closed my eyes and sighed. How had we got *here*? Everything had been completely fine this morning.

"Well," Dad said after a moment's silence. "That could have gone better."

I nodded, staring at Sarah who was trying to calm Tom down underneath the porch. Tom looked back at the car, shook his head and disappeared inside. Sarah followed him.

"*You* know I wasn't trying to kiss her, right?" I said, looking anxiously in Dad's direction.

Dad smiled at me. "Don't worry, son, I believe you."

I breathed a sigh of relief.

"She was definitely trying to kiss *you* though," he said with a smirk. "Perhaps you should stop pretending to be me so *well*."

I turned towards him. Somehow, in a strange way, he was *enjoying* this.

"She keeps trying to do that. I don't know how to avoid it, but at the same time I don't want to do anything stupid to ruin it," I groaned. "It's like trying to juggle chainsaws."

Dad chuckled at that. "Welcome to adulthood, Jack. It's non-stop excitement. Let's get inside."

As he opened the door, cold air rushed into the car. Even though the distance was nothing, it was raining so hard now that we were completely drenched by the time we reached the cabin. Thunder crashed as we closed the door behind us, and Dad reached for the light switch. *Click.*

Nothing happened.

*Click click click.* He pushed it a few more times, just to be sure. There was no denying it. The power was out.

"Great," Dad mumbled.

*BOOM.*

Thunder shook the windows of the cabin.

Sarah's scream echoed from the living room.

We charged inside and found her standing by the far wall, rubbing her head sheepishly.

"Is everything alright?" I said.

Sarah grimaced. "Sorry, the thunder made me jump. I head butted this cupboard." She pointed at the cupboard at the side of the room.

"Is the cupboard OK?" I asked.

A small smile played on Sarah's face, even though she tried to stop it.

"What's that?" Dad said, pointing at a piece of paper on the floor.

"It fell off when Mom hit it," Tom said quietly from the sofa. He had his phone raised up in front of his face. It was his way of trying to ignore everyone when he was grumpy, but I knew he would be watching me and his mom closely.

Dad knelt down and picked up the piece of paper, blowing off a layer of dust that had accumulated over it. I realized that the paper must have been on top of the cupboard for years. I leaned over to see what it was.

*Uh oh.*

It was an old hand-made card. It had been made years ago, from blue paper. On the front was a rainbow, scribbled onto it in crayon with the words 'Happy Father's Day' written under it in a black pen. It looked like something that would be made in a kindergarten project. Slowly, Dad opened the card and looked inside.

I tensed up. It was another relic of the time long passed, of a time when Dad and Mom were together and we were a family unit. The last thing I needed at this moment was Dad storming off again, I thought to myself, but there was nothing I could do.

What actually happened, however, was completely different. Dad smiled and began to chuckle, and then slowly, it grew and grew until he was laughing his head off!
For a second, I thought Dad had completely lost it.

He stood in the center of the living room and he laughed and he cried, and his whole body shook as he did so. Everyone looked at him in confusion.

"Are you OK?" I asked him.

Dad finally began to calm down. He handed me the card, still chuckling, and I looked inside.

This is what it said:

*To Daddy,*
        *After every storm there is a rainbow. I'm sorry I broke your laptop. Also*
        *HAPPY FATHER'S DAY!*
        *Love from Mommy and Jack*

Mom had written my name neatly alongside hers. I

don't think I was even old enough to hold a pencil when this card was made.

Dad looked out the window. "After every storm, there is a rainbow. Lana's favorite quote," he said quietly and then: "*Mom's* favorite quote," a bit louder, for Sarah and Tom. "Seems pretty fitting right now."

We all looked at the dark storm that raged outside. It was getting worse with every passing second. I hugged myself subconsciously.

"What does it mean?" Tom said, standing up.

"It means," Dad said, "that life is crazy. Life can be tough. Sometimes everything goes wrong and it seems like there is no hope." He grinned. "...But you have to *smile*. You have to know in your heart that it will get better. That's how you get through the stormy times."

I smiled a little. I guess Mom was always filled with useful advice for everyone.

Sarah laughed. "That's beautiful." She moved over to Dad and put her hands on his shoulder. "Your mom was a real smart lady."

"She was," Dad nodded.

*Squeak.*

The sound made us all turn in unison towards the doorway. The rat had somehow made its way back in!

"Ugh!" Sarah said, leaping away from the door.

It was Tom's turn to burst out laughing. He stood up on the sofa where the rat couldn't reach him and laughed out loud. "That's *horrible*," he choked.

I laughed too. I couldn't help it, it was contagious.

"The storm," Tom laughed. "No electricity, a rat in the house...." he wiped a tear from his eye. "It's the worst!"

"The whole vacation has been awful!" I agreed through body-shaking belly laughs.

Soon everyone was laughing. It was like all the frustration and the stress of the last few days was being forced out of our bodies. The rat looked at us like we had all gone insane. Maybe we had.

Dad grabbed Sarah by the hand. "This way!"

"What?" she said. "No, I..."

But Dad wouldn't let up. He pulled her out the door, passing the rat, who watched with interest, and then right outside! He danced around with her in the rain and they laughed as they spun around in circles.

I glanced at Tom. He shrugged. "I guess it's too late to say no?"

"That's right," I grinned and soon we were dancing outside in the cold rain with them. We laughed and we danced, the water washing away the pain from earlier. As Dad, Sarah and Tom formed a conga line to go around the cabin, I stopped for a second and, through the rain, I thought I could see a figure standing on the porch. She leaned on the wall and watched us all with a smile.

*Mom.* I thought to myself. *We did it.*

Another crack of lightning shook the world around us, and we danced like it was a hot summer's day.

# Going Home

On the final night of the holiday, I slept like a log. When I woke up, Dad had already packed all of his clothes and was halfway through packing mine. He glanced at me as I sat up in bed and yawned loudly and shook his head. "Next time we come here," he said. "Try to pack *more* than four t-shirts. I think I smell like old cheese," he sniffed his armpit and grimaced.

"No change to usual then," I joked.

Dad threw a t-shirt at me as I laughed. I narrowly avoided it but it was true, it did leave a smell of old cheese in the air.

By the time I was up and dressed, the cabin was looking more and more bare. I was surprised by how much we had managed to fill it up in the short time we had been here.

"Leaving today then?" Greg stood in the doorway, holding a pie in his hands, as I dragged my suitcase from the bedroom.

I nodded. "I'm afraid so."

"Stacy made you another pie," he smiled sadly. "I hope you enjoyed your stay."

I awkwardly accepted the pie from him and balanced it on the end of my suitcase. The plastic plate it sat on was still warm.

"Always," I grinned. "We'll try to come more often from now on. We'll see you next year?"

Greg's grin grew wider at that. "Absolutely, buddy. I can't wait."

"Well I..." Greg moved forward and crushed me with a hug before I could finish what I was saying.

When he finally released me, I tried not to cry out as my bones returned to their normal positions.

"I'll miss you," he said. His eyes got a little misty. "I've... gotta go..." he stumbled out of the house.

What a weird guy.

Sarah was already standing by the car when I reached it. Even though we had plenty of room in the trunk, she was still trying to find the optimal place to put each bag so that it would take up the least amount of room. A small pile of suitcases, neatly stacked, took up one side. There was still enough room for a fully grown adult and a bike on the other side.

"Do you need any help?" I asked.

Sarah smiled, forcing her bag into the trunk with a final push and turning to pick up mine.

"No, I'm good," she smiled. "I think Tom might need a hand packing inside though."

"Alright," I nodded walking away.

"David?"

I turned back to her. She lifted her hand up to her lips and blew a kiss at me.

I grinned and caught it in midair.

When I knew she had turned back to the car, I wiped the kiss on my top. I didn't need any more trouble right now.

I found Tom dragging his bag down the steps in front of the cabin. He stopped as I reached him and looked at me with narrowed eyes.

"Jack," he said quietly. "I know you're my friend and have been for years." He leaned in closer. "But if you don't find a way to swap your body back with your dad soon, I swear I am going to tell her everything."

I was speechless. He didn't wait for an answer; he just took his bag and carried on towards the car. I felt a shudder go through my body. He was serious. Deadly serious. For the first time, I looked at Tom in a way I never thought I would. I *didn't trust him anymore.*

It didn't feel good.

Dad came out of the cabin shortly after.

"I think we are almost ready to go," he said. "It's been a bit of a crazy vacation, eh?"

I nodded, pushing down my feelings about Tom into a small box inside me. I would think about them later. "Crazy. Not very relaxing, now that I think about it."

Dad laughed. "Yeah, I don't think Dr. Turner is going to like that."

We both stared at the cabin fondly, letting the fresh air and the smell of the forest fill our lungs one last time.

An electronic piano started playing.

"Oh, that's my voicemail," he said. "I'll just get that."

I continued to stare at the cabin as Dad walked away. "Bye, Mom," I whispered quietly, a warmth filling my heart. "I'll see you next year."

I turned towards the car, but paused when I saw a deep frown on Dad's face as he listened to his voicemail. He raised his hand to his mouth as if he had just heard something horrifying and looked up at me with something in his eyes that I didn't like: fear. He listened a bit more, then walked over to me as he hung up the phone.

"What's the problem?" I asked, the peace from earlier dripping away, replaced by a cold, nervous feeling in my gut.

"It's.... it's about my job," he said. He took a deep breath. "Something about the fact that Dr. Turner got in touch with the school. Mr. Thomas has found out and is lobbying the governors of the school against me."

I blinked. There were a lot of words there that I didn't understand. But I could just imagine Mr. Thomas causing trouble in any way that he could.

"But what does that all mean?" I asked, frowning as I stood there waiting for him to explain.

"You coming?" Sarah's voice cut across the field. I turned and grinned, but it felt like a mask.

Dad put his phone back into his pocket and turned towards Sarah with a smile. "We'll be there in a second." He turned away again and took a breath. "I'm going to be fired, Jack. I won't be allowed to teach anymore."

As soon as he had spoken those words, he took a deep breath and erased the look of fear from his eyes, replacing it with a smile. He ran towards the car like any child would do and shouted: "I want to sit in the front."

"Too late!" Tom shouted back and they play fought to try and get in the front seat.

I was left behind, and as I slowly walked towards the car, I tried to consider the implications of what he had just said. What would happen if he lost his job? How would we be able to keep living where we were?

"Are you alright?" Sarah asked as I got closer. "You look like you've seen a ghost."

I smiled at her, and lied again. "It's nothing. I'm fine. Let's go home."

But one dark thought kept hovering in my head as I

closed the car door behind me. *What will be waiting for us when we get back?*

\*\*\*

# Book 4

# The Switch

# The Wait

I don't understand how adults can drink coffee. Coffee is *disgusting*. There must be something wrong with adult brains. I think it's like when you leave cheese out of the fridge for too long, and it starts to get a strange blue mold growing on it. Adult brains have a strange blue mold on them too.

It makes them forget what it's like to eat *tasty* things.

They start to go weird and drink coffee (which is basically hot mud in a mug) and they start eating *salads*. Who would want to eat a plate full of leaves?

I miss the good old days of candy and soda.

Unfortunately, while I was sitting in the small waiting room at my school, on a very uncomfortable chair, I had to *drink* coffee.

It was the worst.

I forced every little sip down, the hot liquid scraping down my throat. It tried to come back up but I swallowed harder. When it finally settled in my stomach, I smiled as if I was enjoying it. Mrs. Jade, the school receptionist, smiled back from her desk on the other side of the room. Her round face flushed red and she pushed thick glasses up onto the bridge of her nose.

She had handed me the coffee cup a few seconds earlier, saying, "I know it's your favorite. I made it especially for you."

She was wrong. So very, very wrong.

Well… *kind of* wrong. It's my dad's favorite drink. As I am stuck in his body at the moment, I have to pretend it is my favorite drink, too.

I forced another sip down and rubbed my stomach. "Mmm, tasty," I said.

Mrs. Jade's nose crinkled as her smile deepened. My mouth tasted like rotten mud.

When I was in my own body, Mrs. Jade only ever scowled at me and spoke to me in short, sharp instructions.

"Jack! Don't run in the halls!"

"Jack Stevenson, what are you doing? Stop it."

"Jack! You're late! Get to class!"

But now she thought I was my dad, she was all smiles and blushes and giggles.

I missed being a kid. This was weird.

But the universe didn't *want* me to be a kid. It wanted me to sit here in this room, drinking horrible coffee, and trying to think of a way to stop Dad from being fired from his job.

You see, Dad was in trouble. We had been coming back from vacation when Dad got a phone call from the school. He had been summoned to a meeting with the 'school board of governors.'

That's why I was in the waiting room. The school board members were in the next room. Soon – too soon – they would call me in.

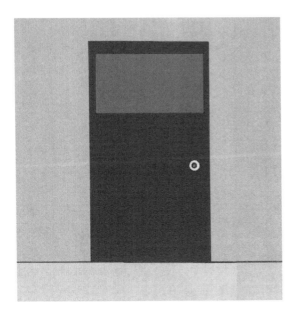

On the other side of the room, directly in front of me, was a blue door. I didn't want to look at it. Occasionally, a sound would get through the closed door, like a scraping of a chair or a loud cough. It sent a jolt of fear through my body, but, for the moment, the door remained closed.

When I first asked Dad about the school board, he seemed to think talking to them was a *bad* thing. At least, I *think* that is what he was saying. What he actually said was, "Oh no, I'm going to lose my job!" and "Why me? What have I done to deserve this?" and *Thump. Thump. Thump,* which was the sound his head made as he banged it against the bedroom wall.

So now I'm here, and I have to try and save his job. We do have a **plan,** though. It was all written down on a piece of paper shoved into the pocket of my jeans.

But who *are* the school board?

I think they are some kind of secret organization that runs the school. A secret *evil* organization.

Dad says they aren't evil, but come *on*. How can you run a school and *not* be evil? It's their fault I have so many Math lessons.

There were three people I had to look out for, according to Dad.

First off was Mr. Tubbs, the head of the board. Dad described him as 'the grumpiest man on the planet,' and one of his favorite activities is apparently making the music teacher, Mr. Gibbins, cry. Sounds pretty *evil* to me.

Second was Ms. Kenyon. She had been the mother to a student who came to the school, and was 'so horrified by what they did to her child' that she just *had* to join the board and make things 'right'. According to her, 'right' is more homework, longer lessons and basically everything made as boring as possible. So much *evilness!*

The third was, as Dad put it, the wild card. Owen Turner could go either way. Among the teachers, he had earned the nickname of 'Turncoat Turner' because he swapped sides and changed his mind so much. Even if I managed to persuade him to let Dad keep his job, there was no guarantee that he would not go back on his decision the next day.

THE EEEEVIL!

I was *terrified*.

I had to stand in front of these people, prove that I was a perfect teacher, and that I knew everything about everything when it came to teaching.

Even though I didn't know anything except that teaching was boring, hard, and I would much rather be playing games while eating pizza.

My hands were sweating as I heard another movement behind the blue door. My eyes flicked to it and then back down to the coffee mug in my hand.

"It'll be fine, I'm sure," Mrs. Jade said comfortingly, although her eyes seemed to scream '*You're so doomed. Run! Run while you can!*'

I smiled and nodded, but in my head I was running around in circles and trying to find the nearest exit.

*Buzz buzz.*

My phone vibrated in my pocket.

As Mrs. Jade turned away, I threw the remains of the horror coffee into a nearby plant pot. I realized too late that the plant was made of plastic. Hot, brown coffee seeped into the yellow carpet next to me. I pretended not to notice it and pulled out my phone.

#HOWISITGOINGJACKAREYOUINTHEMEETINGY ET?

I sighed. Dad had recently discovered social media. When I had caught him trying to log in, he had told me he was trying to be 'a super cool dude who knew about all the stuff'. That would *never* happen.

Thts not hw hashtags work Dad, I replied.

#Sorry. #How #is #this? he replied a few seconds later.

I was beginning to regret leaving him outside. He was getting bored.

Fine, I replied, and put the phone back into my pocket. I looked up to find Mrs. Jade standing right in front of me.

"AGH!" I jumped, nearly falling off my chair.

"Sorry," she grimaced. "They're ready for you now, David."

I peered around her. The blue door was open. Darkness lurked on the other side. A chill ran through my body. I suddenly wished I hadn't thrown away the coffee.

Mrs. Jade placed a hand on my shoulder.

"You always were my favorite," she said. "Mr.

Thomas is wrong."

I didn't know what that meant, but I knew it couldn't be good. I swallowed the fear that caught in my throat and stood up. Mrs. Jade shot me one final apologetic smile as I walked into the next room and tried not to collapse in fear.

This was *not* going to be fun.

# Board Stiff

Have you ever had that feeling in your stomach, right before you have to give a presentation in class, or before a dentist's appointment? It feels like everything is twisting and turning inside you, like there's a snake in there trying to get out. Everything in your body feels like jello, all wobbly and hard to control. That's how I felt as I entered the room, except times fifty trillion zillion.

Somehow, I managed to stumble my way to the center of the room and lean on the long wooden table that took up most of the space. At the far end of the table were the big three. Mr. Tubbs was in the center, a fat man in a suit with a scowl that put every other scowl in the world to shame.

To his right was Ms. Kenyon, a thin lady with short, bright blonde hair and a permanent, fake smile fixed to her face. As I looked at her, she flicked her long, fake lashes at me and tried to smile even wider. Then, to Mr. Tubbs's left, was Oliver Turner. Dressed in a casual t-shirt and jeans, and playing with his phone, he glanced up at me when I entered and shot me a smirk. Nothing about it was very comforting.

Standing at the far end of the table, I felt like everyone was one thousand miles away from me.

There was a silence. We looked at each other for a while. I felt like a gazelle stumbling into a cave filled with lions.

Mr. Tubbs cleared his throat and adjusted his tie.

"Mr. Stevenson," he said.

"Please," I smiled, turning the charm up to one thousand. "Call me David."

It was the first point on the **plan**: be as friendly as possible.

"Mr. Stevenson," Tubbs said again, slightly more forcefully. "Please take a seat."

As I sat down, my eyes flicked to Ms. Kenyon. The

smile hadn't moved from her face. I briefly wondered if she was some kind of robot. No one could hold a smile for this long, surely?

Mr. Tubbs cleared his throat again. "I'm sure you are wondering why you are here, Mr. Stevenson."

I was about to reply when Oliver spoke for me.

"Come on, Alfred," he said, putting his feet up on the table in front of him. "Of *course* he knows. He's white as a sheet. Stop teasing him."

Ms. Kenyon, not breaking her smile, stood up and pushed Oliver's feet off the table. Oliver shot her a look and, although I wasn't completely sure, I thought I saw the smile flicker slightly.

"Of course," Mr. Tubbs said, looking back at Oliver. "Let's get right to business. *Ahem.*" He adjusted his shirt again. "Mr. Stevenson, some information has come to our attention which the board finds very… worrying. We would like to discuss it with you."

"So, this *isn't* about my promotion?" I joked.

No one laughed, but Oliver smiled widely.

"I like him," Oliver said. "He's funny."

"Thanks?" I said, my voice squeaking slightly.

"This isn't a joking matter," snapped Mr. Tubbs, adjusting his belt. "You are *not doing your job*, Mr. Stevenson. We have reports of *fruit* being drawn on Math worksheets, loud noises erupting from the classroom, no evidence of any *education* taking place in your lessons! What do you have to say for yourself?

This was it. This was the time that I had been waiting for. I pulled the crumpled-up piece of paper from my pocket, unfolded it carefully and cleared my throat. This was the speech that Dad and I had spent all night preparing.

Well, we'd spent *half* the night preparing. I spent the other half *improving* it. I had given it an injection of awesome.

This is what it said:

~~Dear Members of the Board,~~ To my besties, my buddies of the board,

I speak to you today about a matter ~~very~~ **really super** important to me. The future of my **really super important** job. I understand that there have been **dumb** issues raised about my teaching style **which are totally wrong,** and I would like to inform you that there is no need to worry. **I am an awesome teacher who is really super good at teaching.** ~~In my twelve years of teaching,~~ **I've been teaching for like forever** and I am constantly trying to ~~improve myself as a teacher~~ **push my teaching skills to the MAX** and this does not always work out in an expected way. I see now that I need to work ~~harder~~ **to the MAX,** for the best of the students **(who are really super important to me)** and will put one hundred percent into ~~making sure they get the education they deserve.~~ **being the awesomest teacher in the world, and also the UNIVERSE. They will love me because I am so great. (Pause for applause and cheering)**

As I got to the end of the speech, I waited for the inevitable applause (I mean, I spent longer on that speech than I spend on most of my homework). But the applause never came.

Mr. Tubbs' face seemed to have gone a strange red color, Ms. Kenyon's smile was beginning to crack and Oliver was desperately trying not to laugh out loud.

Something in the back of my mind suggested that maybe the speech hadn't gone as well as I thought it would.

They could have at least cheered a *little* bit. I secretly wished Dad had let me bring balloons. I would have had them fall from the ceiling. The president does that all the time and everyone seems to love it.

But there were no balloons. Instead, Mr.Tubbs said:

"Mr. Stevenson, I don't think you grasp the *seriousness* of your situation. We have had complaints from your fellow teachers that-"

"Was it Mr. Thomas?" I groaned. "That guy hates me." I could already imagine the cruel Math teacher's mocking smile in my head. This is *exactly* what he wanted.

Oliver snorted. "No idea why," he said. "You're great!"

Mr. Tubbs stood up, slamming his hands down on the table. "Never mind who it was!" he snapped. "You are *suspended,* Mr. Stevenson, until we can sort this mess *out.*"

Suspended. The word rattled around the room, slamming on the walls around me like a hammer. This wasn't part of our **plan**. I decided to improvise like they did in the movies.

"You can't fire me!" I shouted. "I quit!"

The board members glanced at each other.

"We aren't firing you, dear," Mr. Kenyon smiled. "You just need to take a few weeks off while we work out what to do."

I blinked. I realized I was completely out of my depth.

"You can quit if you want," Oliver added.

"No, no, no, no!" I said quickly. "You can't *fire* me, but *suspending* me is totally fine. No quitting here, everything is good."

The board members all stood up. "It has been decided," Mr. Tubbs said. "Please leave the school grounds and do not return until we summon you again."

I blinked and stared down at the speech in my hands. Why could things never turn out the way I wanted them to?

Dad was *not* going to be happy.

# Suspended

"I'm suspended. Suspended. I'm suspended."

Dad paced around the kitchen. He had been doing that for about an hour now. I had tried to break it gently to him, but it didn't seem to make a difference. He wasn't taking the news very well.

"Suspended," he muttered again, pausing to look out the window at the gray clouds in the sky.

I stood in the doorway, unsure what to do.

"Suspended," he said again. He poured himself a glass of water.

"Well, I think what's important here is to focus on the *good* things," I said.

Dad turned to me. "What good things?" he asked.

I opened my mouth and then closed it again. I frowned. "You know, I was sure I had something," I said.

Dad flopped down onto the floor and stared at the wall.

"My job," he said. "I'm going to lose my job."

I felt bad. I was, after all, a *little* responsible for all of this. Not as much as the evil, manipulative and cruel Mr. Thomas, but a tiny, weenie, itsy bitsy bit.

"You're *sure* you used the speech? Exactly as I wrote it?" he said with narrowed eyes.

"*Exactly* as you wrote it," I lied. What? I wasn't going to *admit* to him that I was a tiny, microscopic amount responsible for what had happened! With Mr. Thomas out to get him, I decided that Dad was probably doomed anyway.

We sat on the floor of the kitchen for a while and didn't say anything. Neither of us really had any idea what to do next.

Well, I had an idea, but it involved building a robot and training it to fight crime. Dad wasn't going shopping until Saturday, so I didn't have the parts I needed yet.

When Dad finally spoke, it was quiet. "It's getting late. We need to get ready."

I sighed. We had agreed to hang out with Tom and his mom, Sarah, but I didn't exactly feel like company right now.

As I slowly stood up, Dad placed a hand on my shoulder and looked me in the eye. "Don't tell Sarah about what happened," he said. "She'll be worried, and there's no point in putting that stress on her. This is *our* problem and we'll sort it out. OK?"

I shrugged. "Sure. That makes sense. It shouldn't be too hard."

That was my life now. Lie after lie after lie. I wondered when – and if – it would end.

Tom and Sarah turned up at our front door an hour later. They were an odd-looking pair. Sarah was a short woman with brown hair tied into a ponytail. Tom, however, was tall, and lanky. At first glance, you wouldn't have thought they were related, until they smiled. Then they looked almost identical.

Sarah smiled when I opened the door, and gave me a big hug. Over her shoulder, I could see Tom wince. My best friend was *not* comfortable seeing his mom hug me. To be completely fair, neither was I.

"How did it go?" Sarah asked, finally freeing me.

"They're still thinking about stuff. I'll know in a few days," I lied. "I'm definitely not suspended or anything."

Dad kicked me in the back of the leg. I coughed to hide the pain and tried not to break my smile.

Sarah nodded. "I'll make my special pasta dish. It will make us all feel better!"

My stomach rumbled at the thought of food. It wasn't a terrible idea.

Sarah turned to Dad. "You probably need cheering up too, with this whole Holly thing." She rubbed a hand in his hair. "Don't worry, you'll be fine."

"Mom!" Tom hissed. "He *doesn't know.*"

A sharp pain twisted in the pit of my stomach.

"Doesn't know *what*?" I asked. Sarah's eyes widened as she looked between Tom and Dad.

"Oh, shoot…" she said. "Sorry. I thought everyone knew Holly has a new boyfriend."

It felt like someone had punched me in the gut. Holly, my ex-girlfriend *who I was sure was going to be my girlfriend again sometime soon*, was with someone else.

"W-w-who?" I managed to splutter out. Tom looked away. So much for being a *best* friend.

"Does it *really* matter?" Sarah said. "We don't need to hurt Jack any more, he is clearly struggling."

Dad glanced at me and then quickly said, "Oh yes, I'm very sad. Very, *very* sad."

"Who. Is. It?" I said more forcefully. Sarah frowned and Tom sighed.

"It's Chad. Chad Vanderhauser." Tom shrugged. "I saw them together at the skate park."

Chad Vanderhauser. The biggest, baddest guy at school. He made great white sharks look like puppies. Holly was dating him? They met at *our* skate park?

I didn't know what to do.

"Are you OK, David?" Sarah asked. "You look a bit pale."

"I-I-I think I ate something bad at lunch," I said quickly. "I just need a glass of water."

I stumbled away from the front door and into the kitchen. Dad followed me, leaving Sarah and Tom at the door.

"You need to get it together," he hissed. "You aren't meant to react like this. I am."

I poured some water into a glass. "Chad?" I whispered. "What does she see in him?"

"It doesn't matter!" Dad said.

"How can it not matter?" I said back. "It's my life!"

"Are you OK?" Sarah came into the room.

"Dad thinks he is going to be sick," Dad said quickly. "He probably needs to go to bed."

"I see," said Sarah. "I'm sorry, David."

"I think I will be fine actually," I said, quickly straightening up. Dad shot a look at me, but I ignored him. "Let's have some pasta and I'll feel better!"

Sarah smiled at me. "Fantastic!" she said.

"We'll be in the living room, playing games," I said. "Won't we, Jack and Tom?" I gave them a look that showed they didn't really have a choice. They both nodded.

"I guess I'll cook this pasta myself then…" Sarah mumbled as we left the room.

I couldn't help her though, because I had something much more important to do. I was going to get to the bottom of this, and I knew exactly how to do it.

# Personal Space

There were two things I was *really* good at, and neither of them were Math. The first was sleeping. If my dad didn't wake me up in the morning, I'm pretty sure I could sleep forever. The second thing was *flying space ships*.

That's why, when my engines roared to life on my X-50 Tactical Spacecraft, a grin spread across my face. The ship rose from the docking bay on the mothership, and prepared to exit into the darkness of space. The evil robot race of Sector Seven, the Robosapiens, were attacking again, and it was up to us to stop them.

Beside me, Tom gave a thumbs up from the cockpit of his X-50. It was similar to mine except for its color, a sleek blue instead of a deep red. On my other side, a large, bright yellow X-48 bumbled into view. The ship looked a bit like a hippo, and flew like one. There was a metallic *Thump* as it bumped against the deck.

"How do you get this thing to go *up*?" Dad snarled through the comms. "I don't understand!"

"Pull the stick down," I said. "Down is up and up is down." My ship's engines ignited again, pushing me forward towards the exit. Tom kept pace beside me. Dad hissed as his ship hit the *ceiling* of the docking bay.

"That's going to scratch the paintwork..." Dad mumbled as he fought to gain control again.

When I emerged from the ship, I immediately twisted my commands to the left, dodging a green laser that almost hit my hull.

"Robosapiens," I rolled my eyes. "When will they ever learn?"

Tom joined me in a familiar formation, flying just behind my left wing. Any ships that I missed, I was sure he would hit them. We had done this thousands of times before.

*Pew pew pew!* I squeezed on the trigger. My ship

began to fire back red lasers, each hitting the enemy ships with pinpoint accuracy. White, metallic ships turned into explosions before my eyes. Then, once one was destroyed, I adjusted my sensors and locked onto the next ship. None would escape me.

"Ah ha!" Dad grinned. "I managed to get out of the mothership! What do I do now?" His comms crackled slightly. "People are *shooting* at me!" he gasped.

"Shoot back, shoot back!" Tom said, barrel-rolling over an asteroid to catch a ship that almost got away.

"Quickly!" he yelled in a panicked voice.

I decided it was time to put my plan into motion. Hitting the breaks on my ship, Tom went flying past me. I could see the fiery light of his engines in front of me.

"How could you not tell me about Holly?" I said. "I thought we were friends!"

Tom pulled up, shooting another robot that got too close. It exploded into sparkles.

"What?" Tom asked. "You are asking me now? How-" *Pew pew* "-would-" *Whooosh. Pew. BOOM.* "-it have helped you?"

*Pew Pew. BOOM.*

"I don't know," I said, as I aimed my crosshairs at him. "But you should have told me!" I pulled the trigger. *Pew pew pew!*

Tom's ship spun like it was on ice, his left engine catching fire.

"Hey!" he shouted. "We're on the same team!"

"Are we, Tom?" I snarled, lining him up for another shot. "Are we?"

Tom fired his thrusters, trying to pull away from me, but he never could handle a spaceship like I could. I kept on his tail.

"Tell me everything, or I'll blast you out of the sky!" I said, my finger hovering over the trigger.

Tom tried to drop down behind an asteroid, but I

fired a warning shot over his hull. It skimmed across his nose, leaving a black singe in its wake. He knew I wasn't bluffing.

"How long have you known?" I asked.

Tom sighed. "It's been a week. I saw them hanging out in the park and went over to ask them what was up. Apparently, he wanted to take her to the movies. He wanted to take her to see…" he paused, shaking his head, "…the next Metal Dude."

Metal Dude. It made sense why Tom was so reluctant to tell me.

Metal Dude was a superhero movie that Holly and me *loved*. I had all the old ones on DVD and a poster of it stuck on my bedroom wall.

Holly had bought me the poster.

I had been so caught up in my own problems, I didn't even know the next one was coming out.

"But that's *our* thing," I said quietly. A laser scored a direct hit on my wing. I ignored it.

"Not anymore," Tom said.

My ship had caught fire. Red alarms flashed across my screen.

A Robosapien ship was coming right at me. Tom put a hand on my shoulder. "Sorry, dude," he said. "I didn't want you to feel bad."

BOOM. The ship coming towards me exploded. A bright yellow X-48 bobbled into view. Dad grinned at me.

"I think I'm getting the hang of this!" he said, igniting his engines and pushing off again.

"Woah, Jack," Tom said. "Your dad is… he's about to get the high score!"

I frowned. "What?!"

I looked up at the top of the screen, suddenly finding myself back on the couch in the living room, squeezed next to Dad and Tom. Dad's eyes were fixed on the screen. He handled the X-48 like a seasoned pro.

It had taken me *years* of playing SpaceFlightAwesome™ to get that score, and somehow, Dad was about to beat it.

Tom looked at me. "Ejector seat?" he said.

"Ejector seat," I nodded.

Tom grinned and raised his hand into the air. He brought it down, slamming the controller out of Dad's hand.

"Hey!" Dad said, his ship spinning into a nearby asteroid and exploding.

"EJECTOR SEAT!" Tom and I both shouted, laughing at the joke.

Dad was not impressed but Tom thought it was hilarious.

It was a joke we used to play on Holly whenever she was here and gaming with us. It suddenly hit me how long it had been since I last saw Holly. We used to be so close, and now it was like we barely knew each other anymore.

Then an idea crept into my head.

Everything was about to change.

A grin spread onto my face.

"I have an idea," I said.

BOOM. My ship exploded. Tom's ship exploded. Dad reached into the air and whooped in excitement.

"I win!" he shouted.

"WE'RE ON THE SAME TEAM!" Tom and I shouted back. He would *never* understand games.

# Spy Games

The iron gates of the skate park loomed in front of me. It was another gloomy day, but that didn't stop me from studying the park through my sunglasses. It was empty. We were early.

Tom stood next to me and yawned. "Why did we have to come so early? And why are you wearing sunglasses?"

I peered at him over the top of the glasses. "I'm *incognito*," I replied. "Also we needed to make sure we got here before Holly, so we could study her actions all day."

Tom frowned. "What does incognito mean?" he asked.

I shrugged. "It means I get to wear cool sunglasses."

Dad finally appeared. "Why are we here, Jack?" he sighed. "What crazy scheme have you cooked up this time?"

"Ah ah!" I waved a finger in his face. "We are *incognito*. That means we have to use our codenames."

"Really?" Dad rolled his eyes.

"Yes. Now get into position," I said.

We all walked through the iron gates and ducked behind a low wall nearby. It gave us full access to the whole skate park. All we had to do was wait.

## 9:00 hours – Skate Park – Thursday

For a long time, everything seemed normal. Nothing was out of place. It was *too* normal.

Something wasn't right.

I could smell it in the air.

I lifted my phone to my mouth.

"Seagull, this is Red Eagle, do you read me?"

Seagull looked at me with a raised eyebrow. "Seagull? I thought we agreed my name was Blue Eagle? And why are we hiding behind this wall? My legs are cramping."

I shook my head. Rookies. They always asked too many questions.

"Seagull, your code name was never fully confirmed so I assigned you a new one. How about you, Sleeping Badger, do you read me?"

Sleeping Badger, who was standing on the other side of me, rolled his eyes. "This is ridiculous," he said. "Can't we just go back home? I need to look for a new job, remember?"

I pulled Sleeping Badger down behind the wall before he compromised our position.

"This isn't the time for complaining, Sleeping Badger!" I said. "Sometimes you've just got to grit your teeth and get the job done. Then we can all go home happy as clams."

Both Seagull and Sleeping Badger gave me odd looks.

"What have clams got to do with it?" Sleeping Badger asked.

I sighed, lowering my sunglasses. "Could you focus, please? Just for a little while?" I looked at them both pleadingly.

They looked at each other and shook their heads, finally giving in and hiding behind the wall next to me. Seagull pulled out another pair of sunglasses and put them on. After a second of adjusting his coat, he looked up at me.

"Red Eagle, this is Flaming Seagull, I read you loud and clear. We have a negative on any movement in the park yet."

"Thank you, Flaming Seagull," I said, pulling my glasses back down. "How about you, Sleeping Badger?"

He sighed again. "I don't see anything."

We turned to him.

"...Red Eagle," he added.

I nodded. "Thank you, Sleeping Badger. For our next move, I suggest-"

"Red Eagle, we have movement, I repeat we have movement. Sunflower has entered the Zone with the Beast." Seagull was peeking out over the wall. I peeked over it next to him. He wasn't lying.

On the far side of the skate park, Holly and Chad were standing by some benches. They were talking to each other, laughing. Holly was joking around and she looked so happy.

Chad touched Holly's shoulder with his hand.

Some might have thought it was a friendly gesture, but it meant so much more and I knew it. I had to stop myself from charging out there straight away and demanding he leave her alone.

I took a breath. "So it's true."

Dad sat next to me. "I'm sorry, Red Eagle. This must be tough for you."

I nodded. "I don't know what to do."

Flaming Seagull stood up. "I think we should return to base," he said. "Make a new plan. Maybe have ice cream."

I thought about it. Ice cream *did* sound good.

But no. I knew I couldn't leave now. I needed Red Eagle to soar. I stood up and stepped over the wall. *Let's see how beastly this Beast really is,* I thought to myself.


Something grabbed my arm and stopped me. I turned around to see Tom holding onto my coat.

"Jack," he said. "You're going over there, aren't you?"

I nodded. "I have to."

"So, what exactly is your plan? Think about this," Dad said. "You could end up hurting her."

It was a good question. I hadn't really thought it through. What *could* I do?

Charge over there and demand Chad let her go? That would just look creepy. Chad would probably find it hilarious.

I briefly considered challenging him to duel like they did in those old-timey movies that Dad liked to watch sometimes. Were duels still a thing? I wasn't sure.

All I knew was that Chad wasn't allowed to be with Holly. It was wrong on so many levels. He was at least two years older than her. That was just *too weird.*

"Perhaps you should wait until she is alone and then talk to her," said Dad. "Well, I'll talk to her. I mean, you'll talk to her but through me. You know? We've done it before."

I sighed. It hadn't gone so well last time, but it wasn't a terrible idea. I stepped back over the wall and slumped against it.

"I guess it was a little bit dramatic leaping over the wall," I admitted. My knees were stinging where I had accidentally scraped them against the bricks. I suddenly just wanted to go home.

"Let's go play video games," Tom said. "We still have a few weeks left of the summer vacation, and it looks like it's going to rain soon anyway."

I looked up at the gray sky. Tom was right. It looked like the summer sun was going to be swallowed up at any moment. I nodded.

"Let's go home," I agreed. We all stood up to leave the park.

"Jack?"

I froze. Tom and I looked at each other. Dad let out a little squeak. We all turned slowly, praying that it was just a trick of the wind. Holly and Chad weren't *really* standing right behind us, right?

Holly and Chad were standing behind us.

A big, fake smile forced itself onto everyone's faces.

"What are you doing here?" Holly asked Dad. "This is such a surprise!" The way she looked at us made it clear that it wasn't a *pleasant* surprise.

A thick, shark-like grin was plastered onto Chad's face.

He barked out a laugh. "I was *right!*" he said. "It *is* David Stevenson!"

"That's *Mr. Stevenson* to you!" Dad snapped, forgetting again that he wasn't himself.

"Not what I heard," Chad shrugged. "Word is that your dad is out of a job big tiiiiime." Chad looked at me as he said that. I resisted the urge to challenge him to a duel right there and then. Instead, I swallowed my anger and counted to ten in my head.

*One.*

"Ahh Holly, fancy meeting you here," I said. "And with my favorite student! Who let you out of detention, Chad?" I asked.

Chad's grin grew wider and nastier. He smelled blood in the water.

"H-hi Mr. Stevenson," Holly said quickly. "We were just leaving."

*Two.*

"So were we!" I said, my eyes not leaving Chad's. "What a fun coincidence."

"Er...yes," Holly said quietly.

"Fun. Lots of fun!" Tom said loudly. "This is the most fun I've ever had ever. So much fun is being had right now."

*Three.*

We were all standing in silence for a moment, staring at each other. No one seemed to want to move.

"Well," I said.

"I-" Holly said at the same time. She flushed red with embarrassment.

*Four.*

"We should go," Chad said. "Before the awkwardness gets even worse."

"Yes," I agreed. "Let's all leave the skate park."

Chad and I stared at each other as we turned towards the iron gates. Everyone else seemed to focus their eyes on the exit and try to get there as soon as possible, but I wasn't done yet.

*Five.*

"Holly," I said. "You and Jack should hang out some more. I haven't seen you at band practice in ages."

Holly blinked. She seemed surprised by my sudden interest in her and the band.

But my plan to get her alone so Dad could talk to her

crumbled at my feet when Chad spoke.

"A BAND?" he said. "You never told me you were in a band," he said to Holly. "I should be in it too. We could all rock out together."

Holly's eyes flicked to Chad, who seemed to be enjoying this whole encounter far too much.

*Six.*

"We're all friends, right, Jack?" Chad continued. "Maybe we should all start a band together."

"Do you play an instrument?" Tom asked as Dad's face went pale.

"Yeah," Chad shrugged. "Probably."

"Uh… huh…" Tom said.

"This will be fun, won't it, David?" Chad grinned even wider.

*Seven.*

I narrowed my eyes at him. He was playing with me, I could tell. But little did he know, I was a *master* at playing games. He'd just started a fight he *could not win.*

"Yeah, it will be *amazing*, I'm sure," I said. "You will have so much fun."

"Um…" Holly said.

*Eight.*

"I'm not sure-" Dad began, but I silenced them both with a raised finger.

"How about tomorrow?" said Chad.

"Great!" I replied through gritted teeth. "See you both then!"

When we reached the gate, Chad and Holly turned a sharp left and I turned a sharp right and began to walk. After a few moments, Tom caught up with me.

*Nine.*

"Jack," he said, "you're walking in the wrong direction. We also need to go left."

"I don't care," I snapped. The thought of being near Chad a moment longer sickened me. I just needed to get as far away as I could from him. I needed a moment alone to think. To think about how I was going to defeat Chad and win Holly back.

*Ten.*

I didn't feel any better.

# Preparations

*WHAM.*

I slammed a piece of paper onto the refrigerator and pinned it into place with a magnet shaped like a cheese wedge.

"OK," I said, spinning around. "Here's the mission briefing."

Dad and Tom sat uncomfortably on small stools in front of me. They exchanged a worried glance, but I ignored it. I was too super awesome to be affected by things like that.

"Things have gotten *slightly* out of control, but I've figured out how to solve all our problems," I grinned.

"Great," Dad said, rolling his eyes. "For a minute there I was getting worried."

Tom laughed. "Is your plan to run away to Mexico? That worked out *really* well when we tried it in second grade."

I frowned. "Well, that's because I thought Mexico was the shop down the road. You can't blame me for that one."

Dad shook his head. "Why stop at Mexico? I hear Antarctica is nice this time of year. At least there is no one there to mess things up!"

Tom cut in again. "Lots of penguins, though."

I narrowed my eyes and coughed loudly. *AHEM.* When they had finally settled down, I picked up a long piece of raw spaghetti and pointed it at the piece of paper on the bridge.

"This," I said, "is our ENEMY."

On the piece of paper was a perfect representation of Chad. I had drawn in blue felt tip, a fat guy with really bad teeth, stink lines coming from his head, and flies all around him. To really push the point home, I had written down words that I felt described him perfectly: words like smelly, ugly, really-not-cool, and evil. Underneath the masterpiece the name CHAD was scrawled in big letters.

I pointed my spaghetti at the C in CHAD. "Luckily, our enemy is well named. C stands for *cruel*." I moved to the next letter. "H stands for *horrible*." I looked at Dad and Tom. They nodded in agreement. "A stands for *awful* and D stands for… It stands for…" I paused.

"Disgusting?" Tom suggested.

"Yes!" I agreed. "*Disgusting*! Well done, Tom!"

Tom grinned triumphantly at Dad, who sighed.

"Really?" Dad said. "This is what you called me in here for? I have work to do, you know."

"Shhh," I said. "This is important."

I marched around the kitchen waving around the piece of spaghetti. "It is VITAL that we defeat this enemy!" I said. "Because if we don't…" I paused to let the importance sink in. "…then the world will end."

"I don't think-" Dad began.

"THE WORLD WILL END, DAD, STOP INTERRUPTING," I said louder. I cleared my throat. "So, because of this IMMENSE threat –" I looked at Dad through narrowed eyes, but he stayed quiet "– I have got tasks for each of you to perform."

"Ew, like homework?" Tom groaned. "That sounds nasty."

I pointed the spaghetti at Tom. "No, not like homework, because this is actually important."

"Hey!" said Dad. "Homework is important!"

We both looked at him, unimpressed.

Dad sank down slightly. "It's *sometimes* important…"

I continued. "TOM!" Tom almost fell off his stool. "Your job will be *distraction*. I need someone to talk to Holly, keep her away from Chad as much as possible. You need to remind her how *great* the old times were, how much fun we had. How awesome our band was. How awesome *we* were."

"Sir, yes sir!" Tom said, saluting enthusiastically.

"My job," I said, "will be to take on Chad. I'm going to show him that he isn't right for Holly, how he would be so much *better* without her. Possibly out of the country. Maybe persuade him to go out of the *solar system*, if possible."

Tom nodded in agreement. Dad shifted

uncomfortably on his chair.

"What about me?" he asked. "What am I going to do?"

I scratched my chin. "Your job, Dad, is the most important one of all. If you don't do this job *absolutely right*, the entire mission could be a failure." I placed a hand on his shoulder and looked into his eyes. I put my serious face on.

"Yes?" said Dad, leaning forward. "Well, naturally, I mean, I am the oldest and most responsible one here. I have years of experience behind me. I'm very capable. You ask me to do anything and it will get done, absolutely."

I nodded in agreement. "Exactly. I can count on you. So, here is *your* job..."

Dad's eyes widened.

"I need you..." I paused for effect. "...to sit quietly in the corner and try to speak as little as possible."

Dad nodded slowly, and then realization crossed his face. "Hey! That's not fair! How come I don't get to do anything interesting? I mean, Tom has a job, you have a job, but I get to 'sit in the corner'?"

I shrugged. "You're always telling me to be quiet. I thought it would be a good idea for you to have a go at it and see if you enjoy it so much."

Dad opened his mouth to say something, but then decided against it. He mumbled to himself, folded his arms and looked out of the window. I grinned. I was sure he would get over it.

"Alright, team," I said. "Mission briefing is over. We can *do* this, I know it."

"Yeah!" said Tom, leaping off his chair. "Now let's go and play games!" He bounced out of the room. I went to follow, but Dad placed a hand on my shoulder.

"Jack," he said. He also had his serious face on. It was obviously something important. "Why did you do that?"

I frowned. "What do you mean?"

"This whole performance, why did you do it?" he

322

asked again with a frown.

I blinked at him. If he was trying to make a point, it was completely lost on me.

"You were acting like..." he paused. "... a *teacher*, Jack. You were acting like... well... *me*."

I thought about it. I looked back at the drawing. It was a lot like work on a whiteboard at the front of a classroom. I had assigned them both jobs, I had even congratulated Tom when he answered a question correctly. I shivered.

I *was* acting like a teacher.

"Why would I do that?" I said.

"Have you been feeling less like yourself recently?" Dad asked. "Maybe more like..." he paused as if he didn't want to say it. "More like *me?*"

I didn't say anything. It seemed too terrifying to comprehend.

"Jack," he said. "When we were gaming yesterday, I *really* enjoyed playing, and I was *good* at it too. Like, really good. Almost as good as-"

"Me," I finished.

"And I'm terrible at games. It's probably nothing," Dad mumbled. "But I just wondered if you think something is *happening* to us."

I thought about it. "I'm sure we're fine. It's nothing to worry about."

Dad nodded. "Yeah, you're probably right," he smiled. "Thanks, Jack."

As he turned away to go into the living room, I wondered if I should have lied. Something was wrong. But I didn't want to think about it.

# Nothing is under control

Despite everything that was going on, I felt surprisingly refreshed the next day. Dad was back to his crazy adult self, and I was on my way to a new high score in SpaceFlightAwesome™. I yawned as robots exploded in front of me, and put my feet up on the sofa. It was another lazy day. I could get used to this. Dad's job was so *boring* anyway.

Dad scurried past, carrying the vacuum cleaner. "What are you doing?" he snapped. "We have to get ready!"

He had got it into his head that the place needed to be clean before anyone new came around. I don't know why he was so obsessed, but it was just Dad being my dad, so I let it happen. I would *never* clean up for the likes of Chad.

Chad. His name sent a bubble of nerves through my body. It occurred to me how stupid the idea to invite Holly and Chad around for band practice had been. How did it help *anything*?

Answer: it didn't. I had just been trying to look awesome in front of Holly, and it had backfired completely.

I had signed myself up for a few hours of watching Holly and Chad have a great time together, and there was nothing I could do about it.

I guessed I could maybe close my eyes, stick my fingers in my ears and pretend nothing was happening. That didn't seem like a good plan either, though, since I was meant to be the *responsible adult*. Dad liked to repeat that time and time again.

Being an adult is lame.

Dad passed in the opposite direction, this time with a pile of dirty clothes in his hands. I sighed and picked up the TV remote, hoping that something on TV would distract me from my mistake.

*Click.*

A newswoman appeared on the screen. Her face was

serious. "A storm is gathering over the Pacific. Scientists predict it could contain record breaking levels of rain. Flooding is predicted in-"

Click. The news was boring. This time a colorful dog bounced around on the screen. "Where's the bone?" asked a cheerful voice. "Bobby the dog doesn't know!" The bone was clearly behind him. Someone really needed to train that dog better.

Click. Next up was a giant purple monster tearing through a city. It bared its sharp white fangs and claws as it attacked the buildings around it.

A small smile appeared on my face as it began to breathe fire and I imagined myself as the monster, and the buildings as Chad. Yeah. That would show him.

I doubted I could learn how to breathe fire within the

next two hours. Then again, Dad did have quite the range of spices in the kitchen...

My thought was brought to an end by the doorbell ringing. Dad looked at me. I looked at him. We both looked at the clock. We still had an hour before they were supposed to be here.

"Who could it be?" Dad asked, a panicked look in his eye. He was on tiptoe, trying to dust a nearby cupboard with a pink feather duster.

"I don't know," I replied.

"But who would ring the doorbell now?" he asked.

"Usually, you open the door and find out," I said, standing up. Dad put a hand on my arm.

"Wait!" he said.

I looked at him. He was *really* freaking out about this Chad thing.

"What if it's Chad and Holly?" he said.

I frowned. "They aren't coming for another hour. It'll be fine."

He paused. "OK, that makes sense. Open the door."

We opened the door. It wasn't Chad and Holly. It was Tom, breathing heavily, damp from the rain.

"I'm... sorry..." he panted. "I...tried...to...stop her..."

"Stop who?" I asked. I quickly had my answer. Behind Tom, protected by a colorful umbrella, Sarah stood grinning. She skipped down the path to our front door and stopped.

"Guess who got the day off work today?" she said in a sing-song voice. "I get to spend it with my three favorite people."

"Brad Pitt is here?" I asked, looking around.

Sarah rolled her eyes and hit me playfully on the shoulder. "Ha, ha," she said. "Now let me in." I stepped out of the way and shot a look at Tom. He mouthed the words 'I'm sorry' again, and shrugged. This day was about to get a whole lot more complicated.

I turned and smiled at Sarah. "What are you doing here?" I said. "I'd have thought you might want to do something else than hanging around this boring old house doing boring old things on your day off."

Sarah shrugged. "Doing boring things with the people I love is not boring." She skipped into the house.

*Love.* The word bounced around the walls and made me grit my teeth. On the vacation, Sarah had told everyone she loved me. Dad had *not* been happy. Tom had *really* not been happy. I had really *really* really *really* not been happy. I mean, why would she say something like that? It was really not cool.

Now she seemed to want to spend as much time with me as possible. She didn't seem to realize that *maybe* I had super awesome plans to destroy Chad underway, and I did not want to be disturbed. Girls are so weird and strange. I will never understand them.

"Jack!" Sarah said happily as Dad emerged from the living room with his feather duster. "You're *cleaning!*"

Dad looked between her and the pink feather duster in his hand. "Sarah!" he said, his face flushing red. "I mean, yes, I...er... Well. You're here! That's completely unexpected." He glanced at me and I shrugged. "That's great!" He opened his arms and hugged her. Sarah seemed to love it. Tom did *not* love it.

Sarah smiled again, and turned to me. Before I could do anything, she had kissed me on the cheek. "This is great!" she said. "All of us together again!" She wandered into the living room, leaving me, Tom and Dad by the door.

We stood in silence until Tom broke it.

"Dude," Tom said. "We need to tell her about everything. This is getting out of hand."

"No!" I said. "We can't!"

"Absolutely not," Dad agreed. "She would think we are insane."

Tom shrugged. "Better than all this hugging and kissing. That's my *mom*. It isn't cool."

"I know, Tom but..."

*Ding dong.* The doorbell rang again.

I rolled my eyes. This was getting worse by the second.

I opened the door. It got a *whole* lot worse.

Holly smiled sheepishly. Chad stood next to her, a manic grin on his face, and a metallic triangle in his hand.

"Did we come too early?" Chad asked innocently. "I hope you aren't *completely unprepared for us.*"

"Chad," I hissed through my teeth, silently cursing him in my mind. "Welcome to my house."

# Balancing Act

Chad's teeth shone at me from the other side of the door.

I felt my grip tightening around the door frame. Dad and Tom glanced between us, as if we were two lions about to fight over territory.

"Oh hello, Holly," Sarah said cheerfully, completely unaware that anything was going on. "I didn't realize you were coming around with..." she paused.

Chad suddenly transformed: his challenging grin turned into a pleasant smile, he stroked a stray hair out of his face, and straightened up his coat. In a flash, he went from vicious bully to charming gentleman. For the briefest of moments, I saw the lie that Holly probably believed in. "Hi," he said, extending a hand. "I'm Chad Vanderhausen. A pleasure to meet you."

Sarah shook his hand. "Hello, Chad. You're very polite." She looked at me. "Isn't he polite?"

I forced a smile onto my face. "Yep, Chad is great."

Chad turned to me, wickedness flashing in his eyes. "I am great, aren't I?" He looked back at Sarah. "And who do I have the pleasure of speaking to today?"

Sarah blushed and smiled. "Well, I'm Sarah, David's partner." Dad's eye twitched, but he didn't say anything. "Are you one of his students?"

Chad's eyebrows rose. "One of his students? Oh, no." Chad's eyes flicked to me. I felt a sinking feeling, like the floor was going to swallow me up. "David doesn't have *any students* anymore, do you?" He turned and flashed a set of white teeth at me.

Sarah laughed quietly, not really understanding the joke. She looked at me for a brief second, as if suspecting all my deepest, darkest secrets, but as soon as it appeared, the look was gone again.

She turned back to Holly. "How are you, Holly?"

"I'm fine, thanks, Sarah," Holly smiled. "Do you mind if we come in out of the rain?" I felt my heart melt slightly at seeing Holly again. We all stepped back, giving Holly and Chad enough room to enter. Tom, being as awesome as ever, still persisted with our plan.

"Isn't Jack awesome for letting us all have a band practice?" he said loudly. "Jack is *really awesome*. We haven't had band practice in *ages*. Go Jack!" He punched the air.

Alright, it was incredibly forced and embarrassing, but at least he was fighting in my corner, right?

I glanced at Tom and he winked at me. So smooth.

"Go me," Dad said glumly. "Shall we go to the garage?"

"Oh, absolutely." Chad grinned as we all began to walk through the living room to the garage door. Sarah put a hand on my shoulder and stopped me.

"Where do you think *you're* going?" she asked.

"Er…" I looked at her, and then at the door everyone was heading to. "The garage? I just want to check that they have everything they need." *And also make sure Chad doesn't do anything stupid,* I added mentally, but she didn't need to know that.

"OK, but come straight back," Sarah said. "We need to talk."

*We need to talk.* Why is it that those words always make me feel super uncomfortable? I didn't know, but as she said them, I felt a cold rush pass through my body.

"OK!" I squeaked, pulling out of her grasp and following the rest of my friends towards the garage. Chad had made a joke and Holly was laughing. Dad and Tom were glaring at him.

"Jack is really funny too!" I heard Tom say. "Tell them a funny joke, Jack!"

I knew that Tom was just trying to make me look great. I *knew* he was trying to help, but if there is one thing you *never* ask my dad to be, it's funny. Asking Dad to make a joke was like asking an elephant to do a backflip. I broke into a jog as Dad mumbled and spluttered, trying to think of something hilarious to say.

"HOW ARE WE ALL DOING?" I said loudly, bursting into the garage behind my dad. He was starting a story about how he had put on odd socks this morning. It was *so* interesting how he had only noticed *after* he had left the room and *almost* walked downstairs.

He had told me the story in the morning, and laughed so much that milk came out of his nose.

"Yep, we're all good," said Tom. He leaned a bit closer. "You need to get my mom *out* of here. ASAP."

He was right, of course. It would be very difficult to destroy Chad and everything he stood for with Sarah in the house, asking us if we wanted a drink every five minutes. I nodded, closing the garage door behind me. I had to trust that Dad and Tom would be able to keep things going without me for a while as I went back into the living room. They weren't *that* bad. Right?

Inside, Sarah was sitting on the sofa, waiting for me. She tapped it with her hand, indicating for me to sit down next to her. Somehow I could already feel everything collapsing around me.

"Hello, David," she said.

"Hi," I said, sitting down next to her, but leaving as much space as I could between us. She scooted up, closing the gap. Our legs touched. My eyes widened and I shifted a bit more, but the arm of the sofa blocked my escape. "How are you?" I asked.

Sarah brushed a strand of hair out of her eyes. She took a breath and then looked me in the eye. "I think we need to talk about *you*, David. About why you've been *lying* to me."

*Oh no.* My eyes widened. "W-w-w-what?" I spluttered, my heart hammering in my chest. "What do you m-m-mean?" The nearest window was only a few steps away. I decided I could jump out of it if I needed to, and run away down the street. Dad's long legs could get me pretty far in a few minutes.

Sarah shook her head. "I know *everything*, David."

I placed my hand on the arm of the sofa. How much *did* it hurt to jump through a window? It couldn't be *too* much, right? Action heroes did it all the time in the movies.

"I found out from Mrs. Stacey. Do you know her? She works at the shop on the corner," Sarah continued.

I frowned. What was she talking about?

"She's also friends with Ms. Kenyon on the board. Apparently, you haven't told me everything that happened." Sarah raised an eyebrow and looked at me.

I took a breath. Oh. *That.*

"Right, yes," I said. "The board. Look, I-"

I turned as Sarah placed a hand on my cheek. Electricity sparked across my face. "Why did you feel you had to lie to me, David?" Sarah said. "After all we've been through, I thought we *trusted* each other now."

I blinked, looking into her brown eyes. She was hurt that I hadn't told her everything. The lies were beginning to pile up and it was starting to hurt the people around me. I slowly raised my hand to hers.

"I'm sorry," I said quietly. "I wasn't thinking. Dad... er...I thought it would hurt you more if I told you. I didn't want to worry you."

Sarah laughed. "But that's the point, isn't it? Of family, I mean. We are *meant* to worry about each other, but we support each other as well. That's how it works."

My mind drifted to Dad in the other room, stuck with all my friends and enemies, trying to right something that was completely out of his comfort zone.

What had *I* done to try and fix his job issue? Nothing. Nothing at all.

Guilt welled up inside me. Lies upon lies.

"Listen, Sarah," I said. "There's something else."

"WHAT IS GOING ON?"

We turned to see Tom staring angrily at us. He had just come through the garage door. I thought about how it looked, Sarah tenderly stroking my cheek, us sitting very close on the couch. I stood up quickly.

"Listen Tom, it's not how it looks," I started.

"I think it's *exactly* how it looks," Tom snapped. "And it isn't cool!"

"I know, Tom, but listen-"

"No, *you* listen," Tom snapped. "I gave you your chance. I warned you, didn't I? I said back off, but you don't care! I thought we were friends!"

"We are friends!" I said.

"Obviously not!" he shouted.

Sarah stood up angrily. "Tom, what is your problem with David? Why won't you just let us be happy?"

"Because that ISN'T DAVID!" Tom yelled, his face red.

Everything went silent in the room.

Chad grinned behind Tom. "Oh," he said. "This *is* interesting."

"What?" Sarah said. "What do you mean?"

Tom stormed into the garage, shoving Chad out of the way, and grabbed Dad by the t-shirt to drag him out.

"Hey!" Dad snapped. "What are you doing?"

"That isn't David," he said. "Because *this* is! They swapped bodies!"

"They did *what?*" Holly asked.

*Uh oh.*

## Not Awesome

There was a strange silence around me, as if someone had put a bowl on my head. People were speaking. Loudly. In fact, they were arguing, but I couldn't really make out the words. Everyone seemed to want to speak at the same time, shouting at each other, but not listening. Tom was red in the face, shouting at Sarah. Holly and Dad were shouting at each other too, and occasionally they would point at me, which would only make them shout louder and more angrily.

The only silent one was Chad. He was standing in the corner, watching the scene unfold with a vague interest. He scratched his nose and leaned against the wall.
After a few seconds, he noticed me looking at him. With a dramatic shrug, he shook his head and left the room. It was too much, even for him. His eyes seemed to say, *You made this mess, you sort it out* as he shut himself in the garage.

It was just me alone in the chaos. I knew I needed to put a stop to it. I took in a long, deep breath.

"QUIET!!!!!"

Sometimes, having my dad's lungs was a real bonus.

The room was shocked into silence. Everyone looked at me with a mix of surprise and anger on their faces.

I hadn't really thought about what to say next, but I spoke anyway.

"Er... Hi, everyone," I began. It wasn't a strong start. Frowns deepened. Holly folded her arms. I had to recover quickly. "Listen, we aren't getting anywhere by yelling at each other. How about we all just sit down around the table and discuss this?"

"Like *adults*?" Holly said, spitting out the words.

I won't lie, it hurt, but she had every right to be angry.

"Like people who have something to say to each other," I corrected. I gestured towards the table. "Shall we?"

I won't say it was easy getting them moving. Everyone seemed reluctant. But slowly, as if they were walking through treacle, everyone moved towards the table and sat around it, staring at each other accusingly. There were only four seats at the small table in the corner of our living room, so I decided to stand. I felt a little bit like I was on trial, and they were the judges, jury and executioners.

Everything depended on what I said next.

"So," I said. "How are we all doing?

It was like I had opened the flood gates. Angry words and shouts poured out like a torrent of water, everyone speaking at once. I raised a hand and it quietened down again.

"Holly," I said. "Sarah. I know this must be confusing for both of you, but..."

"Confusing?" Sarah said. "It's *crazy*. Come on, David, you aren't saying it's true? A *body swap*?" She rolled her eyes. "This isn't the movies."

"It is true, Sarah. It has been for a while," Dad answered her. Sarah turned to Dad, surprised. "I'm sorry we lied to you, but we didn't think it would go on for so long."

"But..." she said looking between us. "This isn't *real*, it doesn't make *sense*."

"Is this what you were trying to tell me?" Holly said quietly. "At the school dance? When you chased me outside?"

"Yes!" I said, triumphantly. *Now we were getting somewhere.* "I just wanted you to know this *crazy* thing that had happened. I didn't want you to think I was ignoring you."

Sarah's mouth dropped open. "The *school dance?*" she said. She looked between Dad and me. A look of horror crossed her face. "Oh no," she whispered. "No, no, no, no." She stood up, pushing the chair back from the table and wobbling slightly.

"Mom?" asked Tom.

"I just…" She shook her head. "I need some air." She turned and walked quickly out of the room.

"Mom!" Tom said. He turned to me, his eyes angry and filled with hatred. "This is *your* fault," he snapped, and left the room as well.

It was just Holly left. She stared at the table, her blond hair loose. It had grown a lot since I had last seen her. She had changed so much, and yet she was still the same person I always knew. My Holly. Surely *she* would understand.

"Holly," I began.

"I'd like to go home, Mr. Stevenson," Holly said quickly. "I'd like to go home right now."

She wasn't looking at me. She was looking at Dad, in my body.

Dad nodded. "Of course. Feel free to leave whenever you want, Holly."

"Thank you," she said. She gave me one final glance, and I could see her eyes were filled with tears. I stood up to follow her, but she exited through the garage, taking Chad with her.

"Bye!" I heard Chad yell from the garage. "Nice place!"

And that was that.

Everyone gone.

Dad rested a hand on my shoulder. "Jack, I know-"

Anger burned inside me. I shook his hand off my arm and pointed at him accusingly. "You don't know *anything*!" I snapped. "If you had just *listened* to me right back at the beginning, we wouldn't be *in* this mess!"

"You're angry, I get it-" Dad tried again.

"Oh no," I continued. "I'm beyond angry. The *train* has come to *angry* station, picked up passengers and left. *Angry is a tiny speck in the distance!*" I started towards the door. "I blame you for *everything*," I said. "I can't even *look* at

336

you right now."

On that, I slammed the door behind me, went upstairs to my room and slammed the door there as well.

Dad didn't try to stop me.

I buried my head in my pillow. Dad was downstairs, Holly had left, and so had Tom and Sarah. No one was dealing with anything. We were all angry and apart, and the bad feelings just had time to thrive and grow.

I pulled my bed cover over my head and closed my eyes. I shut out the world around me and pretended it was not there. Everything was fine. I was Jack again, and none of this had really happened. *It is all a bad dream,* I told myself. *I'm going to wake up tomorrow and it will be school and life will be back to normal.*

I closed my eyes tightly and wished and wished. But, as usual, the only thing that happened was that I fell into a deep, restless sleep.

# The Oncoming Storm

The next morning, the world was dark and smelled like pancakes. More accurately, it smelled like my dad's *apology* pancakes. Rain was rattling against my bedroom window. Dad obviously felt bad about what had happened yesterday. I couldn't lie and say that I didn't also feel bad. I had lost my temper and tried to blame it all on him, where in fact everyone finding out our secret was – at least partly – my fault.

Also Tom's fault. Let's not forget about Tom.

I pulled the bed cover from over my head and squinted in the dull, gray morning light. The rain pounded against the window so hard that it felt as if my window was crying a river of tears. Yawning, I pulled myself out of bed and slowly made my way down the stairs, taking it one step at a time. My head thumped with tiredness, and by the time I reached the bottom of the steps, I had to stop and yawn again. The effort of moving so far was too much.

I peered into the kitchen.

"Morning!" Dad said, his voice far too loud and chirpy. "You're awake. I made pancakes!"

I suppressed a smile as I realized Dad had managed to get pancake mix into his hair, and all over his face. Obviously making his pancakes with my smaller hands had been a little tougher than usual.

"I can see that," I replied. "They smell great."

Dad placed two onto a plate. He put a bottle of maple syrup next to it. "I've just got to finish off the bacon," he said. "You can start if you want."

Arming myself with a knife and fork, I cut off a chunk and placed it into my mouth. It tasted *fantastic*. The fluffy pancake mix topped with the sweet and salty combination of maple syrup and bacon was my favorite treat. I continued to stuff them into my mouth and chewed contently, letting the taste blossom before swallowing them in a long gulp of satisfaction.

Dad put two more pancakes on my plate. "Listen," he said.

I raised a hand. "We have nothing to talk about," I replied. Shock and hurt flashed through Dad's eyes, but I finished my sentence. "We both said a lot of things yesterday, but we didn't really mean them. I think we should just move on and work together."

Dad took a breath and smiled. "Yes," he said. "I'd like that." He paused. "You know, you're actually pretty good at this adult thing. You're acting very responsibly."

I shrugged. "What can I say? I'm awesome at everything." I grinned. "You are *terrible* at being a kid."

Dad laughed. "I know. I am looking forward to getting my body back!"

We laughed together, but something small and bitter twisted inside me as I was reminded myself, once again, that we had no idea what to do to change back. I forced another pancake into my mouth just to distract myself, but I didn't enjoy it as much. Such thoughts were hard to process this early in the morning.

*Knock. Knock. Knock.*

Someone thumped their fist against the front door. I frowned.

Who might it be? Sarah and the police, coming to take me away? Holly, wanting to make up? The school board coming to fire me? Tom and… Nah, it wouldn't be Tom.

*Knock. Knock. Knock.*

The knock was more insistent this time. I glanced at Dad and walked to the front door.

Cold air rushed in as I opened it. A small man stood in front of me in a high visibility jacket, wet from the rain. He smiled grimly at me.

"Good morning, sir," he said. A rush of fear went through me. Was he the police? He didn't *look* like the police. He looked like a guy from an office.

339

"Morning," I squeaked, suddenly very aware that I was in my pajamas. "How can I help you?" I wiggled my bare toes on the floor.

"I'm a member of the Environmental Control Committee on the city council, or the ECC. I'm here to discuss an important matter with you. Have you been watching the news recently?"

I blinked. "Not really." Watching the news was the *last* thing on my mind.

The man sighed. "No one watches the news anymore." He looked at the clipboard in his hands. "I have been sent to inform you and your family that there's a large storm coming in this direction. A hurricane, to be more precise."

A *hurricane?* My eyebrows rose up my forehead.

"We think it will hit tomorrow evening," the man continued. "Large scale flooding is expected in this area. Flash flooding, falling power lines, a lot of *dangerous* activity."

"I...see," I replied. It sounded kind of awesome, like something from a disaster movie, but I kept the grin off my face.

"The city council, in their infinite wisdom, have decided to evacuate this area for the safety of its citizens, for the duration of the hurricane. We would like you to gather up some belongings and head towards your nearest rescue center within the next twenty four hours."

I blinked at him. We were being *evacuated?* I didn't even know how to spell that word.

"You don't have to leave, of course, but this would be in your best interest." The man took a piece of paper from his clip board and handed it to me. "Here is all the information you'll need, and the items you should take with you. Have a nice day."

And with that, he was gone. I glanced up at the sky. It was the color of old metal. Up and down the street, people in similar high visibility jackets went from door to door. A strange uncomfortable feeling settled in my stomach. How big *was* this storm?

Dad appeared next to me, a streak of pancake batter on his forehead. "What's up?" I handed him the piece of paper.

He frowned as he read it.

Then he grinned. "Cool."

I looked down at him, shocked. Dad didn't say *cool*. He glanced up at me. "What?" he said.

"Nothing," I lied.

"Oh, no," he said, reading further down.

"What?" I asked.

"Have you seen where the nearest rescue center is?" he asked.

He pointed with a pancake-y finger at the bottom of the page. The address of the rescue center was printed in big, red letters. A lump formed in my throat.

It was the address of my school.

"Huh," I said.

# Don't Forget Your Pets

"*Oof.*" I dropped the final sandbag by the front door of our house and wiped the sweat from my forehead. Flopping to the ground, I groaned. "Why is *sand* so *heavy*? It's *sand.*"

Dad, who was 'supervising' from a nearby beach chair, took a sip from his glass of orange juice. "You'll be glad it's so heavy when our living room doesn't get flooded."

"But it's *sand*," I said again, as if that would make it better. "Why couldn't it be soft and light like clouds *and* protect our house from the rising waters of doom?" I tried to wave my hand in the air, but my upper arms still burned from the effort, so I lay on the ground and stared up at the rapidly darkening sky above me. Dad chuckled.

"What's next on the list?" he asked.

I sighed. The information leaflets that the man had given us a had a looooong list of what we needed to prepare for the *possible* flooding of our house. It was boring and long and, most importantly, it didn't give any advice on how to solve the *more important* crisis in my life right now. I didn't think sandbags would help me persuade Holly and Tom to talk to me again.

Neither of them would answer any texts or calls. Sarah wouldn't open the door when we went around to her house. It was like we no longer existed in their eyes. I felt my heart being crushed inside my chest every time I thought about it.

Dad, however, always said the same thing.

"Don't worry, they'll come around."

He said it a lot. Between five and ten times a day, depending on how low I felt. I had a sneaking suspicion that *Don't worry, they'll come around* was yet another example of something I have come to know as an 'Adult truth.'

What is an adult truth? Here is my totally legitimate

and really smart definition:

**Adult truth** (noun): A lie told by an adult over and over again in exactly the same manner until they believe that it is, in fact, the truth. **Example:** "Of course spinach tastes nice!" or "Participation is just as important as winning!"

In other words, I didn't believe him. If this thing with everyone was going to be solved, it required me to think harder than I had *ever thought before*. Then I could figure out a way to persuade everyone that this body swap was not as disastrously bad as they thought it was.

Maybe I just needed to repeat some adult truths to them until they *believed* everything was alright.

I just wished that *I* believed everything was going to be alright. But deep down, I knew it wasn't.

I pulled the flooding list out of the pocket of my jeans. In big letters across the top it said:

IMPORTANT INFORMATION

- Make sure all electronic equipment is moved upstairs.
- Move vehicles to higher ground if possible.
- Fill any spaces around house with sandbags.

- Prepare a bag of equipment including food and electronics to help you in an emergency.

Then, underneath, was a list of things not to do:
- Do <u>not</u> forget your pets.
- Do <u>not</u> swim in the flood water.
- Do <u>not</u> drink the flood water.
- Do <u>not</u> assume your goldfish will survive in a flood.
- <u>DO NOT FORGET YOUR PETS.</u>

I wondered to myself how many people had forgotten their pets in a flood. It must happen a lot if they needed to put that on the list twice.

"Well?" asked Dad, standing up from his chair.

I looked inside the front door, where our backpacks of emergency equipment were waiting for us. Dad had made me take the candy out of mine (even though I was *sure* it would be important in an emergency). I had had to replace it with *clothes*.

Flooding, I decided, was the most boring emergency ever.

"I think we are ready to go," I said. But it was a lie; I would never feel ready to go. The last place I wanted to be right now was *school*.

"Alright," Dad nodded, giving the house one final pat. "Let's get moving."

\*　　\*　　\*

When we reached the school, the sky above us was so dark it seemed night time had arrived a few hours early. Fat drops of rain had already started to fall, hitting the floor around us with a loud SMACK. They littered the concrete with dark circles, each landing with more intensity than the last. I pulled up the hood of my dad's black raincoat and grimaced at the sky.

No matter how much I didn't want to go into the school, the weather was clearly not going to give us any other options. A storm was coming and it was going to be a beast.

"Oh, David!" a familiar voice squeaked.

I took a deep breath and turned. Mrs. Jade, the receptionist, stood smiling behind me. "I've missed you," she said, before flushing a deep shade of red. "I mean, *the school* has missed you."

I smiled and forced out the words: "I've missed it too."

I noticed she was dragging a small, yellow suitcase behind her, which rattled with every short step she took.

"Are you here for the rescue center?" I asked. She nodded quickly, clearly happy for the change of subject. "I hope you haven't forgotten your pets!" I joked, nudging her with an elbow.

She froze, her eyes widening. "SCRATCHYPANTS!" she shouted, before turning and bouncing off back the way she came.

Dad watched her go. "Wow," he said. "Just… wow."

"I was joking…" I said, but it was too late. She was out of earshot.

We continued up the path together. Someone had placed a large paper sign on the door to the school which said RESCUE CENTER in black writing. To make it more welcoming, someone else had gone around the words and drawn colorful flowers and smiling faces.

It didn't make *me* feel any better.

Dad and I stopped and looked at the sign.

"Well," he sighed. "I guess this is home for the next few days."

*Home*. It would never be home. The thought of school being home made me feel sick.

"You ready to go in?" he asked.

"No," I said.

We went inside anyway.

# Home sweet School

As we followed the signs through the school, I quickly realized they were pointing us towards the school gym. We walked down dark corridors filled with row after row of empty lockers. For the briefest of moments, I felt like I was in a zombie apocalypse. Living in a world where everything had been abandoned and left to rot.

Something about being at school during the vacation felt eerie and not right.

"Ah," Dad said as we turned the final corner. "This must be the welcoming committee."

Just outside the door to the gym, a few tables had been dragged from nearby classrooms. Across them, pieces of paper were stacked into untidy piles, and in the center of it all was a big map of the gym, covered in little gray squares. Each had a number associated to it. I didn't spend long examining them – the people standing *behind* the desk were far too distracting.

Mr. Thomas scowled at me as I approached. "David," he hissed. "You aren't allowed on the school premises! You should be fired on the spot!"

I almost said something very rude back to him, but Dad placed a hand on my arm and shook his head. It wasn't worth it.

"Now, now," said Mr. Tubbs, who was wearing *exactly* the same suit I had seen him in a few days earlier. "It's not as if Mr. Stevenson caused the storm, Bruce." Mr. Thomas's face twisted slightly. "He's allowed to stay here as long as it is a rescue center and he *promises to be on his best behavior.*"

Mr. Tubbs adjusted his tie and stared at me through narrowed eyes. Mr. Thomas shook his head disbelievingly. I glanced at Dad, who shrugged.

"Sure!" I said. "I promise to be the best-behaved adult here."

Mr. Tubbs nodded. "That's what I like to hear," he said. "Now, Bruce, assign them their beds."

A slow grin spread across Mr. Thomas's face. It sent a chill down my spine. He was planning something, and there was nothing I could do about it.

Mr. Thomas scratched his goblin-like chin in a comically overdone way. "Hmm," he said. "*Hmmm.* Which beds shall I give you?"

"Well," I began. "You could..."

"I know!" Mr. Thomas interrupted me. "I'll give you beds ninety-seven and ninety-eight! The best beds in the house." He took two red pieces of paper from one of the piles in front of him and handed them to us. The numbers were written on them in black pen. "Enjoy," he hissed. "I'll be watching."

I smiled at him in a way that said *I don't like you,* and tried not think too hard about Mr. Thomas watching me sleep. They were just beds, right? How bad could it be?

Answer: One *gazillion* times worse than the worst thing you can think of.

As we entered the gym, I had to blink a few times. It no longer looked like the gym. Gone were the climbing apparatus, the weird blue mats that smelled like sweat, the barrel of balls for playing dodge ball that I was *sure* had bloodstains on them. Now, in their place, were line after line of metallic camping beds, all in rows, each with a little number stuck to the end of them.

Around those beds were people. *Lots* of people. All chatting, or drinking out of plastic cups. I could see at least ten of my classmates scattered around the room with their families and friends, and a few unfamiliar faces as well. It was like the biggest (and worst) sleep-over in history. I could also see Ms. Kenyon carrying a tray of cups for people to drink from and-

"Oh no," I swallowed.

Holly stared at me from the end of the nearest row of beds. She was standing right next to Chad, who was getting something out of his bag. As soon as she saw me looking, she turned away, blushing.

I began to walk towards her, but an arm stopped me.

"Heyyyyy!" Oliver Turner said with a big grin. "Welcome to the party, Mr. S!"

He spun me around until I was facing him.

I sighed. "Hi, Oliver."

"Not planning on making trouble, are you?" he laughed.

As usual, his eyes were squinted shut at his own joke. He seemed to have a habit of doing that. Rolling my eyes, I wondered for a moment if he'd had plastic surgery or something. His skin was so shiny.

I glanced back at Holly. She was very focused on whatever Chad was doing now.

"No, Oliver," I sighed again.

"Good!" he said with a grin. "Your beds are this way."

Oliver led us on a winding path through the beds, occasionally apologizing to people as he stepped over their bags and squeezed past them. All the while he chatted to us, even though the last thing I wanted to do was talk.

"So," he said. "Whose wrong side have *you* got on?"

I raised an eyebrow. "Huh?"

He pointed at the tickets in our hands. "Ninety-seven and ninety-eight. Nasty beds. Worst ones in the room I think."

I frowned. "Why so?"

He didn't need to tell me: we had just reached them.

It wasn't that the beds themselves were bad. They were identical to the rest of the beds in the room (although they did look about as comfortable as the floor). No, the worst part was their location. They were right next to the fire exit.

This wouldn't have been a problem if the school had changed the doors to the gym more than once over the course of the last century. It wouldn't have been a problem if they had changed the doors within the last MILLENNIUM. But no, this school didn't like *new* things. Instead, the rickety wooden doors barely held onto their hinges, rattling and shaking every time there was a slight breeze.

And in a storm, there is usually *more* than a slight breeze.

WOOOOOOOOOOO RATTLE CRUNCH went the doors. I put my backpack down on my bed and took a deep breath.

"Great," Dad groaned.

"Have fun sleeping here, guys," Oliver grinned. "I'm going to struggle to beat the excitement you'll have here from my spot in bed one!"

I narrowed my eyes and quickly decided that I *didn't* like Oliver Turner.

With a groan, I flopped down onto my new bed.

*CREEEEEAK*, the metal strained beneath me.

I decided to try and stay positive. "How long can this storm last, anyway? I bet we'll be out of here by tomorrow afternoon."

"Four days," Dad said, his bed creaking as he sat down.

"Excuse me?"

"Four days is how long the news said it would last," Dad said unhappily.

I stared into oblivion. Four days. Four days of creaking beds and windy doors. How could it get any worse?

KABOOM. Thunder crashed loudly around us. Almost as if in response, the lights in the gym went out and the world was plunged into darkness.

Someone in the room screamed, and then said, *sorry*.

# Back to Kindergarten

WOOOOOOOOOO.
RATTLE RATTLE.
CRUNCH.
CREEEEEEAK.
CREEEEEEAK.
RATTLE RATTLE.
CRUNCH.
WOOOOOOOOOOOOOOOOOO.

Most of my night was spent staring at the ceiling of my school gym, shivering, listening to the sounds of the storm outside, with one hundred other people doing exactly the same thing as me. Occasionally, someone would sniff. Someone else would cough. A baby would whimper. Mrs. Jade's dog, Scratchypants, a tiny schnauzer-poodle (which she happily informed me was called a Schnoodle) would scratch. I soon became certain that I would *never* get to sleep in this horror show.

And yet somehow, in the early hours of dawn, I did.

It was when I woke up that things got *very* interesting.

When I opened my eyes, a very, *very* large man was standing at the end of my bed. He had a thick moustache under his nose, his t-shirt was pulled tight against monstrous muscles, and he scowled at me like I had stepped on his pet cat. I pulled my thin blanket up to my chin. He didn't look like someone I wanted to be on the wrong side of.

"Er… hi," I said. "What can I do for you?"

"Come wiv' me," he growled.

"But what about breakfast?" I asked.

"**Come wiv' me**," he growled a bit louder.

I flopped out of bed. "Yes, with you, excellent idea." I tried to blink the sleep out of my eyes as he almost dragged me through the beds in the hall.

Scratchypants the Schnoodle watched me leave, his pink tongue lolling out the side of his mouth.

Minutes later, I was escorted by the big man down the corridor to the other side of the school. The walls went from displaying essays and pictures of complex-looking Math work to colorful pictures of dogs and cats, and signs that said things like HAVE YOU WASHED YOUR HANDS? and FRIENDSHIP IS A TREASURE!

This could only mean one thing: we were heading towards the kindergarten classrooms.

I crinkled my nose as the smell of little kid and glitter entered it. It wasn't pleasant. "Ahh, kindergarten," I said with a roll of my eyes. "I can't say I've missed it."

The big man grunted and opened the door to one of the classrooms. "In 'ere," he said with a snarl.

He did *not* want to be my friend.

I squeezed past him and through the doorway. I found myself standing in a room filled with tiny chairs and tables. The walls were a bright green and yellow, and at the far end, Mr. Tubbs and Ms. Kenyon were trying to not look too uncomfortable (and failing).

Ms. Kenyon smiled painfully as I walked towards them.

"I thought I told you to keep your head down, Mr. Stevenson," Mr. Tubbs said, his face red. "We've been here one night, and I already have to talk to you."

I frowned. "What have I done?" I said.

"We've had complaints, dear. People are not happy." Ms. Kenyon shook her head. "If this keeps up, we'll have to separate you from the main room."

"But I haven't done anything except freeze and not sleep!" I said. "What can people possibly be annoyed about?"

Mr. Tubbs shook his head and produced lots of small, square pieces of paper from his pockets. He placed them on

353

the table in front of him.

"Did you think this was *funny?*" he asked. "I don't understand what you thought this would achieve!"

I bent down and picked one up. Someone had printed on a computer the following message:

Your son, William, is the *worst* student I have ever had to teach. I am glad they are firing me, just so I never have to listen to his whining ever again.

-Mr. David Stevenson

Mr. Tubbs shook his head. "This is not a time for *jokes,* Mr. Stevenson. Consider this an official warning. One more step out of line and your job is *gone.* Do you understand?"

A cold feeling gripped my gut. This wasn't me. I couldn't have done this. I was in bed the whole time, and…

*Mr. Thomas.*

I took a deep breath. He was stirring up trouble to try

and get me fired. "I shall return to my bed and lie there and I swear you won't hear a peep from me until this storm is over," I said. "Please, just give me one more chance."

Mr. Tubbs glanced at Ms Kenyon. She nodded slightly.

"Alright," he said. "But *one tiny peep* from you and you are being *removed,* do you understand?" The way he hissed the word *removed* through his teeth sent a shiver down my spine.

"Bert? Can you take him back, please?"

I turned and the big guy, Bert, was right behind me, nodding.

"Ahh!" I jumped. Bert shook his head slowly, grabbed me by the arm and pulled me out of the room.

The gym felt like a completely different place when I got back. I suddenly realized that everyone was watching me, and they *weren't* happy. One parent deliberately put her foot out as I walked by, making me trip. Another said, "Worst teacher ever," loud enough for me to hear as I got close. It didn't feel good.

I kept my head down and headed straight for my bed. Dad was waiting for me when I got there, playing with his phone. He looked up at me and frowned.

"Wow," he said. "What did you *do?*"

I sighed, showing him the piece of paper from Mr. Tubbs. "Someone has been spreading these around."

"*Pshhh,*" Dad sniggered, trying to contain the laugh with his hand. He looked up apologetically, but giggled a little bit more.

"This isn't *funny,*" I hissed, sitting next to him. "You could get fired!"

Dad shrugged. "Well, that would probably solve a lot of issues at this point."

We both looked at the door next to us. WOOOOOOOOOO, it said.

355

"I don't think it would," I said.

Dad leaned back on the bed and picked something off the floor. It was a paper plate with toast, and a polystyrene cup full of dark liquid. "I got you some breakfast," Dad grinned. "While you were being interrogated."

My stomach rumbled when I saw the toast. I realized that I had been so busy worrying about everything else that the thought of food hadn't even crossed my mind. Now, however, it was *definitely* on my mind. I snatched the food off the plate gratefully and bit into the toast. It was cold and hard as a rock, but I was grateful for it anyway.

I took a sip from the drink. It went down smoothly, energizing my entire body, and I broke out into a smile.

"Aaaaaah," I sighed in relief. "What is this? It's great!"

Dad blinked at me. "That's coffee, Jack. I thought you *hated* coffee."

I looked down at the drink in front of me. The hot mud. The *tasty* hot mud.

I took another sip. "Apparently not," I said.

# Follow me

BOOM.

Tom and Sarah entered the gym while a crash of thunder shook the walls. A few of the girls from my class screamed and pretended to hide under their blankets. A handful of adults chuckled nervously. Everyone was glancing at the windows. The sky was black with twisting clouds and sharp rain. Although it was getting close to lunch time, it might as well have been midnight.

They were soaked from head to toe, dripping wet. Tom shivered as Sarah guided him over to the two free beds at the other end of our row. If they noticed me, they didn't acknowledge it. In fact, they seemed to go out of their way *not* to look at me or Dad.

*Thump. Rattle. Thump,* the fire door said. I ignored it.

I tried not to think about Tom and Sarah. I turned away to find myself looking right at Holly and her parents, who were on beds nineteen, twenty and twenty one, in the first row of beds. Chad was with her, too. He had managed to get bed twenty two. I squinted at them.

"Do you think he bribed Mr. Thomas to get that bed?" I whispered to Dad. "I mean, how else could he be so close to her?"

Dad sighed. He was already lying in bed with the cover pulled up to his chin. "Does it matter?" he said. "I mean, you know it's just going to end in disaster if you follow that strand of thought. Let's just give up now."

I looked at Dad. He turned away and faced the wall, curling up on his bed like a little ball. I had never heard Dad be so negative before. It was like he had just given up completely. I couldn't say that I didn't understand how he felt. It was like everything in the world was against us and we could do nothing about it except wait for the storm to pass by, shut up in this room. The only problem was that everyone in here hated us.

I glanced at Sarah and Tom again. She was sitting on her bed and drying Tom's hair with a towel. I looked back at Dad. He hadn't moved. A little idea popped into my head.

*She* would know how to make Dad feel better. I just needed to persuade her that we weren't as bad as Tom had made us out to be. I made my decision. I was going to make her make Dad feel better, if it was the last thing I did. I stood up –

"Hey...er... Jack?"

"AGH!" I almost fell back over my bed, but a soft hand managed to catch me and pull me back up. It was Holly. She was standing next to me. I righted myself and blinked. "H...H...Holly?" I said. "W...what are you doing here?" It was a silly question and I knew it, but it was too late to take it back.

She tucked her blond hair behind her ear and looked up at me. "This is all weird and wrong and difficult and strange."

"I..."

She lifted a finger. I stopped talking.

"It's horrible and disgusting and just... messed up."

I nodded, feeling a sudden sadness swell up inside me. It seemed Holly had just come over here to insult me.

"But..." she finally said. "It's not your fault."

I blinked. I did *not* expect that.

She held her hand out in front of her and opened it. Inside was a small yellow piece of paper. "This was on the end of my bed this morning," she said.

I took it and opened it.

*Holly is the ugliest girl in school. I hope she fails at every dream she has.*

*- Mr. David Stevenson.*

I gasped, crumpling up the paper into a small ball. "This... this wasn't me!" I spluttered out. "Someone is..."

"I know," Holly said, shrugging. "This is clearly a lie. I mean, I'm *gorgeous*." She grinned at me.

For a second, it almost felt like we were back to normal. I smiled back and we both laughed. But then the storm rumbled outside and I was brought back to reality. "Which is *why* Chad and I are going to help you."

I blinked. "You and... Chad...?"

Holly smiled. "We know it's Mr. Thomas doing this. He has it out for you, so we came up with a **plan**."

"A... **plan**?" I realized I was just repeating everything she said to me. I wondered if I was in some kind of strange dream.

"Oh, yes." Holly rubbed her hands together. "We are going to stop Mr. Thomas before he has a chance to do anything else to you."

Holly spun around and began to walk towards the front of the gym.

"Follow me!" she said.

# Bye Bye, Mr Thomas

"Who wants some soooooooooup? It's beaaaautiful!" sang Mr. Gibbins, the music teacher, as he bounced around in the school cafeteria. He wore a large white chef's hat on his head and a white apron, but his sparkling pink tie poked out from the top of it. He was dancing behind a big metallic pot and serving out soup in little plastic bowls to anyone who dared to get close enough. I could smell the soup from where I was in the queue.

It smelled like someone had burned some cheese and had tried to cover it up by burning some milk as well.

Holly was standing right behind me. "There he is!" she whispered. "In the corner!"

Mr. Thomas sat in the corner of the room with Mr. Tubbs and Ms. Kenyon, laughing about something. I frowned at them. Why did *they* have that made them so happy? Then I noticed something else: none of them were eating the soup. They all had sandwiches.

"OK," I whispered through the corner of my mouth, "what do you want to do now?" Holly had dragged me to the canteen as soon as lunch was announced, but she hadn't given me much of a clue as to *why* we were here.

"Now we do *this*." Holly winked at Chad who was holding his bowl of soup at the other end of the queue and pretending to examine the salt and pepper. He looked up at us and the shark-like grin appeared on his face. He began to walk towards Mr. Thomas's table.

"What is the **plan**?" I asked. "What are we doing here?"

Holly turned to me. "Have you seen Mr. Thomas sleeping in the gym?"

At first, I didn't know how to answer. The thought of Mr. Thomas asleep was too creepy to even consider. I tried to picture a bed, a blanket, covers, and on top... Ew. No.

"No, why would..." I paused as Mr. Gibbins served

me some soup. It was a very unhealthy looking shade of yellow. I tried to smile and look positive, but also not to breathe too deeply.

"I made it myseeeeelf!" the music teacher sang. "Enjoooooooy!"

I walked away and dropped the bowl of soup into a nearby trashcan in a most ninja-esque manner. A quick glance into the trashcan revealed I wasn't the first person to do that. Holly quickly caught up with me.

"Anyway," she continued. "You haven't seen him sleeping because he *isn't* sleeping in there. He has his own little nest somewhere."

"Where?" I asked.

Holly grinned. It was a similar grin to Chad's. I felt a little uncomfortable seeing it on her face. "We are about to find out," she said.

"ARGH! WHAT IS WRONG WITH YOU, YOU LITTLE MONSTER?!"

The shout made me turn. Mr. Thomas had stood up. His jacket and pants were covered in gross, burned cheese soup.

Chad was trying to look apologetic, and failing completely. "Oops," he grinned. "Sorry about that."

"You... you..." Mr. Thomas went red. It looked like he was about to explode.

He turned to me and his eyes widened. "Yooooooooou!" He stormed across the cafeteria. Everyone was looking. "You did this!"

I made a big gesture of looking around the room. "Me? I was getting soup. I don't know what you're talking about."

"I *know* you're up to something!" he hissed. "I know it!"

I shrugged innocently and looked him up and down before whispering: "You've got something on your jacket. Might want to get it cleaned up before it stains or..." I pretended to look disgusted. "...melts your skin."

Mr. Thomas was about to yell something, but took a deep breath and stormed off. Holly patted me on the shoulder. "Come on!" she said. "We've got to follow him!"

\*　　\*　　\*

Following Mr. Thomas wasn't that difficult. The sounds of angry ranting and curses against my family name allowed us to keep track of him, whilst at the same time staying far enough away that we could duck behind a corner or a trash can if he decided to turn around. He never did, though, because he was busy trying to scrub the soup out of his pants. As we headed towards the gym, I glanced at Holly, but she pointed at him. Just as it looked like he was about to go in, he went in the opposite direction, cutting through the school on a route that seemed particularly familiar to me.

We were almost there when I stopped Holly and dragged her to the side. "I know where he is going," I whispered. "He's staying in the teachers' lounge!"

Holly nodded. "Of *course*! He would have an almost endless supply of coffee in there, and who knows what else. He would set himself up in there."

"Plus, comfy chairs!" I said.

Holly raised an eyebrow at me.

"What?" I asked. "I've been in there a few times in this body."

Holly rolled her eyes. "Of course." She turned back to the door of the teachers' lounge. "Now we just need to sneak in there while he gets changed, and..."

My eyes widened in horror. "You want us to *what*?"

Holly sighed. "Look, he's going to have to shower to get the soup cleaned up, right? It went all over him!"

"I guess..."

"Well, *that's* when we strike." Holly grinned again. "It's a perfect opportunity!"

The thought of Mr. Thomas in the shower was suddenly imprinted on my mind. I grimaced, trying to think of anything else.

*Pink elephants*. I thought to myself. *Pink elephants*.

Holly, however, had already carried on wordlessly after Mr. Thomas. All I could do was follow her, and hope nothing went wrong.

*     *     *

I could hear Mr. Thomas singing in the teacher's lounge shower room before I even opened the door.

"RAINDROPS ARE FALLING ON MY HEAD," he screeched like a baby owl. "AND SOON THEY WILL HAVE TO FIRE MR. STEVENSON, HA HA HA HA HA!"

"Those aren't the lyrics," I grumbled.

"Focus!" hissed Holly.

CREEEEEAAAAAAK. The teacher's lounge door was a bit louder than I expected. I grimaced and waited for Mr. Thomas to charge out of the shower, but he just kept on singing to himself.

I let out a breath and continued.

The teachers' lounge wasn't as big as you would've thought. Cushioned red chairs took up most of the room. They were positioned in a square around a white table in the center. On the edge was a small kitchen section, and walls of boring looking educational books which no one would *ever* want to read.

Mr. Thomas had turned the red chairs into a bed for himself. In the far corner was a suitcase filled with his clothes, spilling out of it untidily.

"There!" Holly said, pointing at it. "Grab them all!"

"His clothes?" I said, but it was too late. Holly was stuffing shirts and pants inside of the suitcase, preparing to steal it.

SSSSSSSSSSSssssssss. The sound of the shower slowly turned off.

Holly looked at me wide eyed.

We had to hide and we had to do it quickly.

I dropped to the ground and squeezed underneath the nearest set of chairs. The floor underneath me smelled like dust and old coffee, and something soft lay next to my face. It was socks. Mr. Thomas's socks. I tried not to gag.

I heard Holly move. I didn't see where. The door to the shower room clicked open and I closed my eyes (the *last* thing I needed was nightmares after seeing Mr. Thomas naked!).

I heard his wet footsteps *splat splat splat* across the carpeted floor and could smell the flowery scented body wash that he had used. He paused. I could hear him breathing.

Could he see me?

What about Holly?

What was going on?

Everything seemed to freeze as a thousand thoughts went through my head at once. I didn't know what to do. I couldn't even breathe.

"Hmm," Mr. Thomas said. "Where did I put my socks?" I squeezed my eyes closed tighter, praying for invisibility.

He turned and walked back into the shower room.

Everything happened in a flash. I rolled out from under the chair. Holly squeezed out from behind a cupboard.

"Go!" she hissed, grabbing his bag of clothes. "Go! Go!"

I scraped Mr. Thomas's socks off my face, and we left the room as quickly as we could.

When we were back out in the corridor, we paused to breathe.

"Phew, that was close!" I said.

"Pretty close," another voice said. We turned. Oliver Turner was standing in the corridor, looking at us. My heart dropped.

"This isn't what it looks like!" Holly said quickly.

"Really?" Oliver Turner said. "Because it looks like you're stealing Mr. Thomas's clothes in response to that cruel trick he played on you this morning, Mr. Stevenson."

I blinked. "Then it's exactly what it looks like," I admitted.

Oliver Turner laughed out load. Instead of being annoyed, he was obviously very amused. "Have fun!" he chuckled.

Then he turned and walked away.

Holly and I glanced at each other. I decided that I *did* like Oliver Turner after all!

# In Trouble

"I'm pretty sure that *isn't* my suitcase," Dad said as Holly and I tucked Mr.Thomas's bag underneath his bed. "What have you been up to, Jack?"

I stood up and looked around. "Suitcase?" I asked. "What suitcase? Do you see a suitcase, Holly?"

Holly stood up too. "Nope. I don't even know what a suitcase looks like."

Dad narrowed his eyes. "I see," he said. "Well, I've got an announcement of my own. You see, I've been..."

Dad didn't manage to finish his sentence. Tom charged over from his side of the gym, anger flaring in his eyes. He pointed accusingly at me and Dad.

"What are you doing?" he said to Holly. "Hanging around with *them*?"

Dad and I glanced at each other. We had both known that this was going to happen, but I was hoping it could wait until the storm had died down a little.

Rain pounded on the nearby fire escape. RATTLE RATTLE, it said. I ignored it.

"Tom, I just want us all to be friends again," Holly said. "Sure, Jack is stuck in his dad's body, but he can't *control* that. We shouldn't push him away just because he is in trouble, we should be *helping* him."

For a minute, I saw Tom relax slightly, but then the rage came back, stronger than ever. A cold feeling crept up from my stomach.

"No," said Tom. "It isn't *fair*. He's using his position as an adult to have fun *no matter what it does to everyone else*."

I didn't know what Tom was talking about, but I knew this had to end soon. "Listen, Tom," I said, putting a hand on his shoulder. "I get that-"

"No, you don't get *anything*," he snapped, batting my hand away. "Mom hasn't been the same since she found out about you."

People were beginning to take an interest in what was happening. Dad glanced at me uncomfortably. "She has been really quiet and I'm pretty sure at one point I heard her *crying* in her room. That's on *you*." He poked me in the chest, but he didn't need to. It hurt enough there already.

"Could we just be a bit quieter?" Dad suggested.

"No!" Tom shouted, making us all flinch. "I've had *enough* of keeping your secrets!"

"Let me talk to Sarah. I just..." I began.

But Tom had already turned and stormed off. He pushed through the crowd that had gathered around us, wiping tears from his eyes. I was about to go after him, but Holly put a hand on my arm. She was thinking exactly what I was thinking. There was no way I was going to get through to him now.

When they realized the excitement was over, everyone else in the room began to move away, murmuring to each other and talking about us.

I sat down on the bed and put my head in my hands. "I don't know what to do," I groaned. "What should I do?"

Dad sat down next to me. "I... I'm not sure," Dad said. "I really think that-"

He didn't get to the end of his sentence. As if on cue, Mr. Thomas barged into the gym in his underwear. "YOU!" he boomed, his finger pointing at me accusingly across the hall. "WHERE ARE THEY?"

Everyone in the hall turned to look at me again. I was suddenly back in the spotlight. "Er... hi?" I said, nudging his bag of clothes deeper under my dad's bed. "What's going on?"

Mr. Thomas barged through the hall, shoving anyone out of the way who dared not to move fast enough. Mr. Tubbs followed closely behind him. People complained and shouted, but Mr. Thomas was in a blind rage, so their complaints fell on deaf ears. Bert hopped behind them with surprising nimbleness, apologizing and helping pick up anyone who fell over in Mr. Thomas's mad rush.

I tried not to laugh as I saw his bright pink underwear with yellow flowers on.

"Where are my clothes?" he snapped. I didn't reply apart from a half-hearted shrug. "TELL ME NOW!" Mr. Thomas snapped.

Rage boiled inside my stomach now. I'd had *enough* of people yelling at me. "Why don't you tell me why you've been spreading notes all over the gym, with *my* name on them?!" I shouted back.

Mr. Thomas glanced around as everyone in the gym suddenly became a lot more interested. He shook it off. "It wasn't me," he said. "That was all you, David Stevenson. Failed teacher."

Mr. Tubbs sighed and stepped forward. "I told you to *behave*. Mr. Stevenson, but it's clear that isn't going to happen. I have no choice but to have you *removed* from the gym, for being such a disruption. Bert, could you?"

A hand with fingers like tree trunks wrapped around my arm. Bert pulled me to my feet.

"You can't do this!" shouted Holly. "You don't have any proof!"

"I don't *need* any," Mr. Tubbs snapped. "I have the full support of the school board behind me. Take him away, Bert!"

I tried to resist, but Bert's strength was insane. He lifted me up like I was nothing and began to pull me across the hall. I heard Holly and Dad following after me, shouting angrily. Soon other people in the hall began to shout as well, all wanting to know what was going on and questioning why I was being removed from the hall. The gym doors opened and slammed closed behind us, leaving the angry crowd to shout at nothing.

I was left standing on the other side with Bert. Then I spotted Sarah, who suddenly appeared out of nowhere.

"What did you say?" she snapped at me.

Bert paused. Sarah was standing with her arms folded, right in front of him.

"Please, move," he grunted, but she refused.

"What did you say to Tom?" she asked me again. "He's run off and I can't find him!"

"What?" I said. "I didn't say anything! Please, Sarah, you have to understand-" I didn't get to finish what I was saying, as Bert began to drag me away again.

"Where's Tom?!" Sarah shouted as I was pulled away.

"A child is *missing*," I snapped at Bert. "We've got to go look for him!"

"Not you," grunted Bert. "You've gotta be locked away."

"Locked away?"

I soon found out what he meant by 'locked away'. I was thrown into the very same Kindergarten classroom that we met Mr. Tubbs in earlier.

"Huh," I said to myself. "This is bad."

I heard the door lock shut behind me.

# The Great Escape

It wasn't long until Dad was thrown into the room with me. He smiled uncomfortably and said, "They found the suitcase."

At first I was excited. With Dad in the room, we had *twice* the brainpower to figure out a way to escape! (Well… one and a half. Dad was an adult, after all.)

However, we quickly came to the realization that Kindergarten classrooms were the school equivalent of Fort Knox. Having thirty or so toddlers in the same room, climbing, chewing and puking on everything obviously meant that security had to be pushed to the max. Unfortunately, that doesn't help when the room is being used as your prison cell.

"Come *on!*" I snarled at the final window which refused to budge open. I flopped down onto a tiny chair. "This is super lame. How are we supposed to go out and help find Tom?"

Dad kicked the door of a nearby cupboard. "I can't even open these to see what's inside!" he snapped. "What do they use to seal them? Superglue?" He slumped down next to me and we sulked in silence together.

I could make out the black silhouette of Bert the Security Beast standing cross-armed by the door. There was no way we were going to get past him, even if we managed to figure out the complex sequence of childproof locks that seemed to decorate the door handle. Nothing short of the key was going to crack that baby open, and the key was on a rope around Bert's thick slab of a neck.

It's usually at this point in the action movie that the hero, locked away in the dungeon by the villain, figures out some crazy-but-amazing escape method. Unfortunately, this wasn't an action movie, and in Dad's crumpled blue shirt, I couldn't have felt further from an action hero. Instead, we sat in the tiny chairs and Dad calmly played with a red toy truck he found on the floor, making engine noises out of the side of his mouth.

"*Screeeeech*" he said, making the red truck swing on its side and crash into my arm. "*Oh no! The horror!*" He pretended that the truck had burst into flames, and made little action figures run around the wreckage in an attempt to put it out.

I sighed. The torch light that had been left in the room with us (as our only light source) flickered. It was running out of battery.

Dad groaned and picked it up, hitting it with his hand. "Come on, really?"

The yellow beam of light flashed up against the ceiling and our escape plan was revealed to us. A grin spread across my face.

"Hey, Dad," I said. "How do you feel about being an action hero?"

Dad blinked at me and then turned to see what I was looking at.

"Oh no," he groaned. "Can't we just stay in here?"

*    *    *

Five minutes later, Dad fell onto the floor.

"No!" I snapped. "You have to step *on* my hands or we will never get up there!"

"Stop wobbling your hands so much then!" he hissed back. It was the fourth time he had fallen on the floor. He was going to have some big bruises when this was all over, but I wasn't going to take the blame for it.

There was a vent. I don't know why it didn't occur to me right away. Action heroes ALWAYS escape through the vents. There was a small one up on the ceiling, and because it was out of reach of tiny hands, it didn't have any super protection over it. I *knew* it was our means of escape. The only problem was, in Dad's body, I couldn't fit in there.

There was only one of us who could squeeze into such a small space, and he would need to climb onto my hands.

"I know we need to find Tom, but couldn't we try something different?" he said, rubbing his head. "Maybe we could bribe the guard or something?"

"With what?" I asked. "Glitter glue and bad drawings of dogs? No, this is the only way. Come on."

I bent down, linking my fingers together again. Dad placed his foot on my hands and I lifted him up.

My back ached. Whatever Dad had been doing with my body in the time he had been occupying it had *clearly* made it triple in weight. I let out a slow breath.

Dad pulled on the vent. It didn't budge. He pulled again harder. Something in my back went *click*. I winced against the pain, but kept holding him up.

"Any... time... today..." I hissed.

"Hang on," Dad replied. "Nearly..." He tugged again and again until...

*Crunch. Eeeeee.* The vent door swung open. "Ah HA!" he said triumphantly. "Oh, no..."

We were falling backwards and there didn't seem to be any way to stop it. Dad's back, or rather, the spine that I was using, had given up and my arms dropped away. In one final flail of effort, Dad leapt towards the vent, catching the bottom of it with his fingers. He pulled himself up as...

*CRASH.* I collided with a bookshelf full of books about colourful animals. One about a goat hit me square in the head.

"Ow..." I groaned.

When I managed to look up, I saw Dad squeezing into the vent, his sneakers the only part of him sticking out. With a swift slide, they disappeared.

I grinned. It had *worked*! Now all he had to do was get Bert to...

*Click.* The door of the classroom swung open. In the doorway, a torch light shone on me, collapsed in the bookshelf.

There was a pause as I picked myself up. This was going to take some serious explaining.

"Er…" I said.

"I don't really want to know," Chad replied, lowering the torch. "I managed to persuade Bert to take a break. Come on, I'm breaking you out of here so we can find Tom."

"Er…" I said again.

Chad frowned. "What's the matter?" He looked around the room. "Hey, where's your dad?"

I glanced up at the vent. I could still hear Dad scurrying away on the mission I had sent him on.

"Er…" I said for a third time. "We might have to find *him* first."

"Oh, no…" Chad groaned.

# Escaped

Dad stared daggers at us from the other side of a vent, like an angry cat. The vent was on the lower part of the wall near the floor, just outside the door of the kindergarten room. I had no idea how he'd managed to get to that spot but at least we knew where he was.

Chad scratched his head, staring at the vent. "Wow," he said. "You're really wedged in there, huh?"

Dad looked at me and his eyes narrowed. "Seems so. Just me, a decade's worth of dust and..." he took a breath. "Spiders. Lots and lots and *lots* of spiders. Please get me out of here."

"Hey," Holly came from around the corner. "I think that we still have some time to-" She stopped talking and looked at Dad in the vent. Covering her mouth with her hand, she made a small squeaking sound as she tried not to laugh. "Is... your dad stuck in a vent?" she asked quickly, between giggles.

"With spiders!" I grinned evilly. "Many, many spiders."

"Ha. Ha." Dad rolled his eyes. "Can we..." Dad started wriggling. "Oh no, oh no, I think I can feel a spider in my hair, oh no GET ME OUT OF HERE!"

He slammed his hands against the metallic grating which separated him from the corridor and shook and wriggled. Something black, fat and hairy crawled over his forehead.

"OK, wow, that is the biggest spider I have ever seen," Chad chuckled.

Dad began to whimper.

"That really isn't helping..." I said, desperately looking around and hoping that I'd somehow gained the power to materialize a screwdriver out of thin air.

But Holly had a better idea.

Fire extinguishers are heavy, but when Holly picked

it up, she wielded it as though she had done it a hundred times before. Chad glanced between me and the grate and took a step back. Holly raised the extinguisher above her head. "Hold on, Mr. Stevenson, I'll save you!" she shouted. We all ignored the fact that the hairy blob now had two other hairy blobs next to it.

BANG! She slammed the fire extinguisher on the edge of the grate. The metal vibrated but it didn't budge. BANG! She hit it again. It wouldn't move. BANG! BANG! BANG!

The grate stood triumphant against all attack.

"Huh," I said. "I was sure that was going to work."

Dad cried out. Chad leaned forward.

"Oh," he said. "There's a little clip right here." There was a small click as he unlatched the grate from the wall and it swung open. Dad tumbled out onto the floor and began to roll around like he was on fire.

"Get them off me! GET THEM OFF ME!" he screeched. A few black blobs scurried away into the dark corridor. Chad and I patted him down and pulled him whimpering to his feet.

Holly shrugged. "That works too, I guess."

"Right," said Chad. "Now that's all done, shall we stop climbing around in vents and go and find Tom?"

I shrugged. Dad nodded very enthusiastically. "Let's get out of here," he groaned.

*       *       *

Once we had left the building, I bet Dad wished he was back in the warmth of the vent. Every drop of rain felt like a spear of ice against exposed skin, and the wind spun around us like a tumble dryer gone berserk. Chad shouted something at me, but it was lost in the chaos that surrounded us. He pointed towards the bike shelter at the end of the parking lot and we all headed in that direction.

Every step was a fight. The wind didn't want us to get

there, the rain didn't want us to get there, but we stepped forward slowly until finally we fell into the shelter and the wind lightened slightly.

"Phew," I said, wiping the rain from my face. "Weather is a bit bad today, isn't it?" I looked at Chad, Holly and Dad. They didn't seem to find my joke very amusing.

"OK," Chad said. "When Tom left, he said he was going home, but Sarah has already checked there and there is no sign of him." He turned to me. "Jack, you know him best. Where do you think he has gone?"

My mind swirled. Tom had disappeared and there were a thousand places he could have gone. I couldn't stop thinking that the storm had swept him up and carried him away, never to be seen again.

"Jack!" Chad shouted again. "Quickly! This storm is going to get worse before it gets better."

I nodded, desperately trying to think. Then, in another flash of lightning, it came to me. "The skate park!" I shouted. "It's our place. I know it!"

Chad nodded. "Alright, you and David head there. I'll go with Holly to check around the rest of the school. Sarah is going to check the house again."

Part of me was jealous that Chad seemed to know exactly what to do and had organized everything so quickly, but I pushed it away. Now wasn't the time to be jealous.

"But how are we going to get there?" Dad asked. "This storm is much, *much* worse than it was when Tom left."

Chad pulled a set of keys out of his pocket and then pointed at the parking lot behind me.

"I stole these off Mr. Thomas when he wasn't looking."

In the car park behind us was a small, yellow car that looked like it had seen better days – and those days probably still had dinosaurs roaming the earth. It was Mr. Thomas's car. Chad placed the keys in my hand.

"You can do it, Jack," he said. "I know we don't like each other, but that doesn't mean I don't respect you."

I didn't know what to say. Chad *respected* me? Why? At the end of the day, I realized, it didn't really matter. All I needed to do was focus on the here and now, get Tom back safely, and then I could figure out the rest.

I looked at the keys in my hand. A slow grin spread across my face.

"No," said Dad. "No, no, no, no."

I turned to go, but Holly stopped me.

"Jack," she said. "Be careful."

She looked up at me, her blue eyes wide with worry. I moved a wet strand of hair away from her face and smiled. "I'm *always* careful."

I turned to Chad. "You look after her. That is a boyfriend's job after all."

"Boyfriend's…" Chad looked at me, confused. He then looked at Holly and burst out laughing.

I frowned. "Am I missing something here?"

Holly smiled too, and stood on her tiptoes. She kissed me on the cheek. Her lips were warm compared to the cold of the rain.

"I'll tell you later," she said. "Now go!"

As I ran through the storm towards the car on the other side of the parking lot, I could still feel the warm patch of skin on my cheek where Holly had kissed it. I promised myself that I wouldn't let *anything* happen to Tom. Not on my watch.

# Into the Storm

"ARRRRRRGHGHGHGHHHGHGHGHGHGHGHGHGHGHGHG HGHGHGGGGGHHHHHHHGGGGGHHHGGGHG!" Dad screamed as I turned on the engine and it rattled to life. I shot him an angry glare.

"If you're going to keep making noises like that, I'll make you get out and walk," I snapped. Then I shook my head, realizing that was *exactly* something that Dad would say. "No, no, no, I'm *not* you. Everything's fine."

I floored the acceleration pedal and the car screeched to life. It shuddered forward, coughed loudly and then bumped into a brick wall on the far side of the parking lot with a soft *crunch*.

I smiled weakly at Dad. "Oops… That'll probably be easy to fix, right?"

Dad sighed, rubbing his eyes. "OK, new plan," he said. "I'M DRIVING."

I laughed. Surely he didn't think that – before I could finish my sentence, Dad was climbing across the car, his elbows and knees hitting everything until he was sat on my lap. "Sorry, sorry, sorry," he said as he tried to get comfy and elbowed me in the ribs three times. I twisted and grumbled until we were both sitting on the same car seat, Dad with control of the wheel and me with control of the pedals.

Dad put the car into reverse. "Right," he said. "Push down on the pedal a *little* bit."

"Really, Dad?" I asked. "We're going to do this?"

Dad folded his arms. "Who is the adult with years of driving experience, and who is the child who needs to do as his father says?"

I rolled my eyes and pushed down on the pedal. Slowly the car began to trundle backwards. Dad turned on the windscreen wipers to knock away at least *some* of the water that was pouring down on us. It didn't do much, but it was better than nothing. He flicked the stick back into drive and the car seemed to groan with effort.

"Alright, this is going to be tough. The rain is going to make the road slippery and hard to navigate, and on top of that, we don't know what damage the storm has done in the meantime. Are you ready, Jack?" he asked.

"We've got this," I said. "Let's go find Tom."

Dad nodded. "OK, forward."

We began to drive.

About five minutes later, we had managed to make it onto the road. It took this long not because Dad shouted "BREAK!" every few seconds (although he did), but because the storm was in full flow.

We finally began to see the full effect of it when I was inching down the road. Parts of trees and tiles from roofs littered the road. Dad was twisting and turning to avoid the car hitting anything, but still the occasional THUMP BUMP CRUNCH could be heard as we drove over branches.

Dad would always mumble something along the lines of "I meant to do that," or "That's probably nothing," but I could hear the strain in his voice. He did *not* want to be out here, and the more destruction I saw on the roads and the houses around us, the more I realized that I didn't want to be here, either.

So what was it like for *Tom?*

I put my foot down a bit more on the accelerator.

"What are you doing?" Dad squeaked.

"Well, we will never get..." THUMP BUMP CRUNCH "-there at the rate we-" BUMP BUMP BUMP RATTLE "-were going, so I think we need to go a bit-" CLINK CRUNCK KERCHUNK "-faster."

The car engine took on a weird wheezing sound as we reached the end of the road and turned the corner. Before either of us had a chance to react, there was suddenly a cold feeling around my feet.

We had driven right into a flood.

"Oh no, oh no…" Dad said as the car engine let out a final pathetic cough and died. I pushed on the pedal again and again, but it was too late. The car was dead.

We sat in silence for a second.

"Well…" said Dad. "I guess that's that then."

My eyes widened. "We can't give up now!" I said. "We need to keep going and find Tom, he could be in danger and…" Dad was grinning. I stopped talking. Why was Dad grinning?

"Of course, Jack," he said. "I meant that is the end of the car. The engine is flooded. It isn't going anywhere. Honestly, I'm surprised it got this far. Are you ready to get wet?"

Without giving me time to answer, he pushed open the door and the water flowed in, not only from the sky but also in a brown swirling pool around our feet.

"Try to keep out of deep water!" Dad shouted over the wind. "You don't know what could be floating around in there."

"OK!" I shouted back, although I could barely hear my own voice over the crackling of thunder.

As I stepped out of the car, it felt like I was underwater. I wished I had more than the little waterproof coat that Chad had found for each of us. It was as if I had jumped into a swimming pool, but the pool was filled with dirty, ice cold water.

Dad grabbed hold of my arm as the wind almost carried him away. I realized this was going to be mainly on me. I got him to climb onto my back and began to wade through water toward the sidewalk. It was slightly higher than the road. I could see the swinging iron gates of the skate park in the distance. We were so close to our goal.

"Nice day for a walk," Dad shouted in my ear.

I laughed loudly, so did Dad. It was insane what we were doing, walking through a flood, in a storm, and still making jokes.

"I'm *loving* this," I said back. "We should do this more often."

"Next Sunday good for you?" he asked.

"Ah, no, I'm too busy tanning in a tornado," I joked.

"Well, I'm..." Dad paused. "Jack, Jack, quickly climb up that tree. Jack, you need to do this right now."

Dad's voice suddenly sounded terrified. I could feel him shivering on my back. What did he mean, climb that tree? Next to the sidewalk was an old oak. A few of the branches hung lower and I could probably reach them, but why did he want me to climb up there?

Looking up the road, I could see why. A large brown wave of water was rushing towards us, carrying cars, trees and houses with it. If we didn't climb the tree, we'd be swept away.

# In a Flash

One way to describe the flash flood would have been a wall of water rushing down the street towards us. It was a frothing mass of brown and white, and anything that got in its way was either swallowed into the mass of the wall, or dragged along with it to its unknown destination. It didn't *look* that strong, but it picked up cars like they were empty crisp packets and carried them down the street towards us.

You could also describe it as *I* did when I saw it, which was something like: "Nonononononononononononononononononononononononono!" Fear and adrenaline fought for control inside my body as Dad climbed off my back and into the lower branches of the tree. As he climbed higher, I couldn't help but stare at the flood rushing towards me. It was like a monster out for my blood.

I snapped back to reality when I heard Dad screaming at me to climb up. I wrapped my hands around the lowest branch of the tree and pulled.

*Snap.* It came off in my hands.

I wasn't as light or as small as Dad, and the tree seemed to want to punish me for it. I made a silent promise to whoever was listening that I would go on a strict salad-and-water-only diet after this if I could only get up into this tree.

I reached up into the tree again. The rain from the storm had made my arms cold. My limbs were sluggish to respond. The next branches slipped out of my grip.

I looked up at Dad in my body. His eyes were wide with horror as he looked down at me, standing in ankle deep water with a raging torrent coming towards me. He seemed to be moving in slow motion. The *world* seemed to be moving in slow motion. My fingers fumbled for another branch and I looked up at Dad again.

"This is *so* uncool," I mumbled.

"Jack." I heard his voice, a whisper over the crashing of the storm around me. "Please," he begged. "Please, climb up. Please."

Dads can be *so* demanding.

I clenched my fists and gritted my teeth. There was no way I was going to be defeated by some stupid tree. Taking a step back, I bellowed out a roar and jumped as high as I could.

SMACK.

My face hit the trunk of the tree. I could taste something metallic in my mouth.

But... my fingers had wrapped around something sturdy. A thick branch higher up in the tree. With a groan and all my effort, I pulled myself up, slowly.

As I lifted myself up into the branches, rubbing my painful nose, the water hit the tree. There was a soft *thump*. The whole tree shook, but managed to withstand the flood as I settled myself onto the thick branch with Dad opposite me. I glanced up at him and grinned.

"Well, *that* was exciting."

Dad shook his head. "Don't you *EVER* scare me like that again, Jack Stevenson!" he snapped, in his telling off voice.

I laughed. I leaned against the trunk of the tree and I laughed. Not because it was funny, but because I didn't want Dad to see that I was shaking in fear. It was a strange reaction, but my body couldn't stop shaking with chuckles, bubbling up from my stomach as I watched the water rush past beneath us.

Dad shook his head and patted me on the knee. "You're a strange one, Jack."

I looked at him. "Well, it could have gone a *lot* worse."

Dad nodded.

*Creeeeeeeeak*. The trunk of the tree seemed to shake slightly. We both stared at it. The tree, which had seemed so strong and powerful just moments earlier, was suddenly showing its true colors. The roots weren't as deep and as strong as we had hoped.

Dad mumbled a very rude word under his breath.

"Language!" I said, before covering my mouth with my hands. "Ignore me. Ignore that."

*Creeeeeeeeeak.* The tree strained once more against the push of the water.

I looked at Dad. "Dad, I think… I think I need to say something."

Dad frowned. "What is it, Jack?"

"If…" I swallowed and tried to focus on the words. "If the tree falls, I want you to focus on saving yourself."

Dad's eyes widened. "What?" he said. "I'm not going to…"

"No, *listen,* Dad," I said more forcefully. "I'm older than you. I'm stronger than you. I don't want you to get yourself into more trouble by worrying about me. I need you to get *yourself to safety.* Do you understand?"

Dad didn't say anything at first. He just stared at me with a strange, distant look in his eyes. He took a deep breath and then shook his head.

Finally, after a long pause, he said: "I'm sorry, Jack, but no."

I was about to respond when he continued.

"Jack, you are the most important thing in my life." He leaned against the trunk of the tree. "I think I lose sight of that occasionally. I get too focused on my job or I get distracted by something else, and I'm sorry." He sighed. "I'm sorry for everything, Jack. You are everything and nothing else matters. I don't care about my job; I don't care about grades or anyone else. *You* are my biggest success. *You* are the reason I can get up every morning with a smile on my face. *You* are my world. So, if we fall, Jack, I'm coming for you and there is nothing you can do about it."

I looked at the boy sitting across from me. My dad.

The man who had raised me and made me who I was. I smiled. "I've spent the last few months trying to fix my life, but I guess it wasn't really that broken, was it?"

Dad reached out and grabbed my hand. "I love you, Jack."

I grabbed his hand too, and found myself smiling, despite the storm, despite everything that was going on around us. "I love you too, Dad."

BOOM.

The sky shook above us with a roar of thunder. Dad laughed at it.

"Well, this is *great*," he said. "Stuck in a *tree* in a thunderstorm. This is the *worst* place to be."

I shrugged. "Still beats Mr. Thomas's Math class."

Dad laughed. "Yeah, I bet..."

KABOOM.

Lightning flashed off a nearby roof. We both flinched, holding onto the branches of the tree.

"Huh," Dad said. "That was pretty close."

KABOOM.

Another strike. This one hit the iron gate of the skate park, barely a few meters away.

"You don't think that-" I said.

KABOOM.

The tree shook. We didn't even see where that one hit, it was so close.

"Jack," Dad said. "Hold on to the tree. Don't let go, Jack, I mean this. Don't fall in the water."

I looked up at the darkening clouds above us, a spark of lightning crept across it, preparing for another strike.

"Oh, no," I groaned
.

The world went black.

## After Math

The news reporter's serious face stared at me from the television screen, high up in the corner of the room. "The two victims, a man and his son, were found clinging to a tree during the devastating flash flood last night. Apart from a minor back injury, neither of them were seriously hurt, and thanks to the local fire department, they were rescued when-"

"Clinging to a tree?" Dad grumbled as he came back from the doctor's reception desk. "That's a bit extreme. We were holding onto it for a bit of support." He looked at me, sat down in the waiting room chair next to mine, and smiled. "Coffee?" He held out the cup in his hand.

I crinkled my nose and turned away from the vile liquid. "I think I'll need a few more years before I want to drink *that* again." I couldn't help but smile as I looked at Dad in *his own* body. The tall, unshaven body that I hadn't looked after very well for the last few months.

"So true," he agreed, then frowned. "Huh," he said. "Was I always this tall?" He wiggled his foot in front of him.

"Weird, right?" I grinned.

"David?" Sarah's voice came from the doorway of the office. She was standing at the door with Holly and Tom. She ran over to me and threw her arms around me in a huge hug. I winced as I felt my newly returned bones being crushed.

"They've just let us out of the rescue center. We came here as soon as we heard." Sarah squeezed me tighter. I fought to get enough air in my lungs to reply, but could only squeak out a response.

"I'm right here," Dad said with a laugh. "And still in one piece too."

Sarah released me with a frown.

"Thanks, Dad," I managed to choke out.

Sarah stepped back. "Wait… Dad?" she said. "Does that mean-?"

Dad didn't let her finish. He swept her up in his arms in a grand, dramatic gesture, wrapped himself around her and kissed her on the lips. Her eyes widened briefly before she smiled and seemed to flop into him.

"Ew," I said. "Get a room. Am I right?" I turned to Tom.

Tom looked at them and shook his head. "Yeah, gross." He glanced at me. "Hey, I'm sorry for everything. I guess I should have told Mom where I was going."

I raised an eyebrow at him.

"I went to the changing rooms. No one was in there and it was right on the other side of the school by the football field, so it took a while for Holly and Chad to find me."

"Ahhh," I said, trying not to think about how stupid

my idea of the skate park was. I shook my head. "Don't worry," I said. "We're best friends, right? We can forgive each other."

Tom grinned. "Yeah, we can."

Holly, however, wasn't in the mood to forgive. She poked me in the chest with her finger. *"Don't scare me like that again!"* she snapped angrily, poking me twice more for effect.

"Ow, ow, ow!" I said. Holly then leaned forward, grabbing me by the front of my t-shirt and *kissed me as well.* As she pulled away, I blinked, too shocked to say anything. She smiled a little, her cheeks flushing red.

"Ew, not you guys too," Tom groaned.

"What about Chad?" I managed to squeak out. "Isn't he your boyfriend?"

It was Tom's turn to look embarrassed now. He shook his head. Holly laughed at me. "No, silly," she said. "He's my *cousin.* I was just hanging out with him for a little while. I didn't expect you to get all jealous and weird about it."

Her *cousin.* Not her *boyfriend.* I suddenly felt incredibly stupid for not *asking* her in the first place. I glanced at Tom. He shrugged helplessly.

As she wrapped her warm hand around mine, I stopped feeling anything bad at all. I realized I was the luckiest guy in the world.

Tom sighed. "Can we go home now?" he asked.

"I think that's a great idea," Dad replied.

# Epilogue...

## Back to School

It had been two weeks, but everyone was still chatting about Mr. Thomas getting fired. They had found him writing horrible things about the students and teachers at the school, and trying to hide them in the lockers. Considering what was written on the notes, Mr. Tubbs had no choice but to fire him on the spot.

Tom, however, was still going on about the flood.

"You didn't think to look for me in the changing rooms?" he said. "Why wasn't that the *first* place you looked? We used to go there *every week!*"

I shrugged. "We go to the skate park a lot too."

"Yeah, but it was the *worst storm in forever*," he replied. "Why would I want to go outside?"

I opened my mouth and closed it again. I didn't have a good answer for that one.

He had been bugging me about it all day. I was beginning to suspect it was his way of avoiding the topic of Sarah and Dad getting married. That was going to take a *long* time to get used to. Still, I could see a small smile on his face whenever the topic was brought up. I think the word 'brothers' seemed a lot better to him than 'best friends'. I definitely felt the same way.

When we reached my locker, I opened it and a pink note fell out. Frowning, I picked it up.

You are invited to go to the
Winter dance with the most
beautiful girl in school:
HOLLY!

Say yes or suffer the
consequences!! ☺

I laughed and closed the door to my locker. Holly was standing on the other side of it.

"Well?" she asked. "Did you like my note? It's all part of my **plan**."

"A **plan**, eh?" I grinned. "I guess I have to say yes then, don't I?"

Holly kissed me on the cheek. "You do," she said.

"JACK STEVENSON, WHY AREN'T YOU AT FOOTBALL PRACTICE?" Dad's voice boomed down the corridor.

Tom looked at his watch. "Oh yeah, gotta go." He sprinted off down the corridor, before Dad could stop him.

Holly closed my locker. "Good luck," she whispered before disappearing in the opposite direction. I turned and looked at Dad through narrowed eyes.

"Well?" he said.

"Shouldn't *you* be marking the Math papers you gave

out today?" I countered.

Dad's face broke into a grin, and he let out a laugh. "You make a convincing point," he said. "Maybe football practice and marking can wait. What do you say we go and get ice cream instead?"

I thought about it and nodded.

"Sure, Dad. Let's do that."

So we did.

***

*Thanks so much for reading Book 4 of the Body Swap series.*
*I hope you really enjoyed it!*
*If you could leave a review, that would be awesome!!*
*I can't wait to hear what you think!*
*Katrina* ☺

Like us on Facebook
@ Diary of an Almost Cool Girl

And follow us on Instagram
**@freebooksforkids**
**@juliajonesdiary**

Here's some more funny books that you're sure to enjoy…

And here's some more great books that we also hope you love!

51276566R00223

Made in the USA
San Bernardino, CA
18 July 2017